OTHER BOOKS OF FICTION BY JOE LYON

Kilmer's Ghost (Book Two of Astar's Blade)
Temple of Valor (Book Three of Astar's Blade)

Poetry is Cool (another book from Joe Lyon)

CHECK OUT MORE STUFF AT THE WEBSITE:
www.astarsblade.com

MUSIC BY PURPLE TOAD:
available on iTunes and streaming services.

Music to Swim By (1984)
Legacy (2013)
Self-Inflicted Wounds (2016)
Anything You Want (2017)

ASTAR'S BLADE

THE PROVENANCE

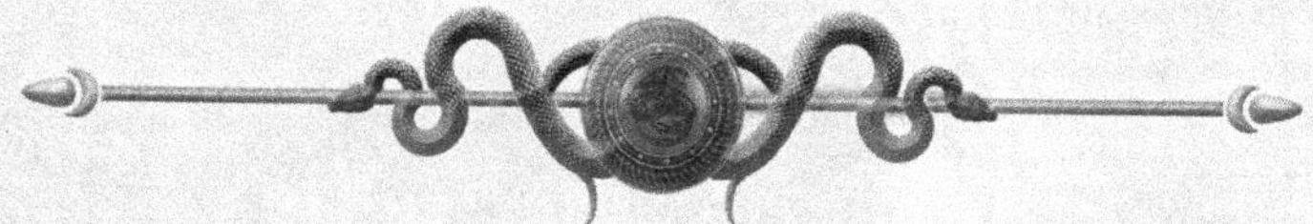

AN EPIC FANTASY

JOE LYON

First Edition

Printed in the United States of America.

ISBN: 978-1-956189-01-8

My sincerest thanks to the following contributors, without whom this book would not be possible:

Edited by Clem Flanagan
Developmental Edit by Rebecca Brewer
Developmental Consulting by Sophie Lyon
Chapter 5: *The Forerunner*, co-written by Seth Lyon
Proofreading by Alana Joli Abbott
Cover Design by Story Wrappers, Artist K.D. Ritchie
Audiobook Performance by Lisa Negron
Songs by Purple Toad

Typesetting by Colleen Sheehan at Ampersand Bookery

THE WORLD SETTING

ONLINE VIEW OF MAP:

Map of Odessa—Astar's Blade

(astarsblade.com)

THE WILDS
HUSBAND
ST. EHLONAS
THE BLUE MOUNTAINS
CASTLE
ODESSA
MAUVEGUARD PASS
CAVE
SANGUINE FOREST
CASTLE
ORLO
NOMAD
CAMP
DARBY
BLAISE

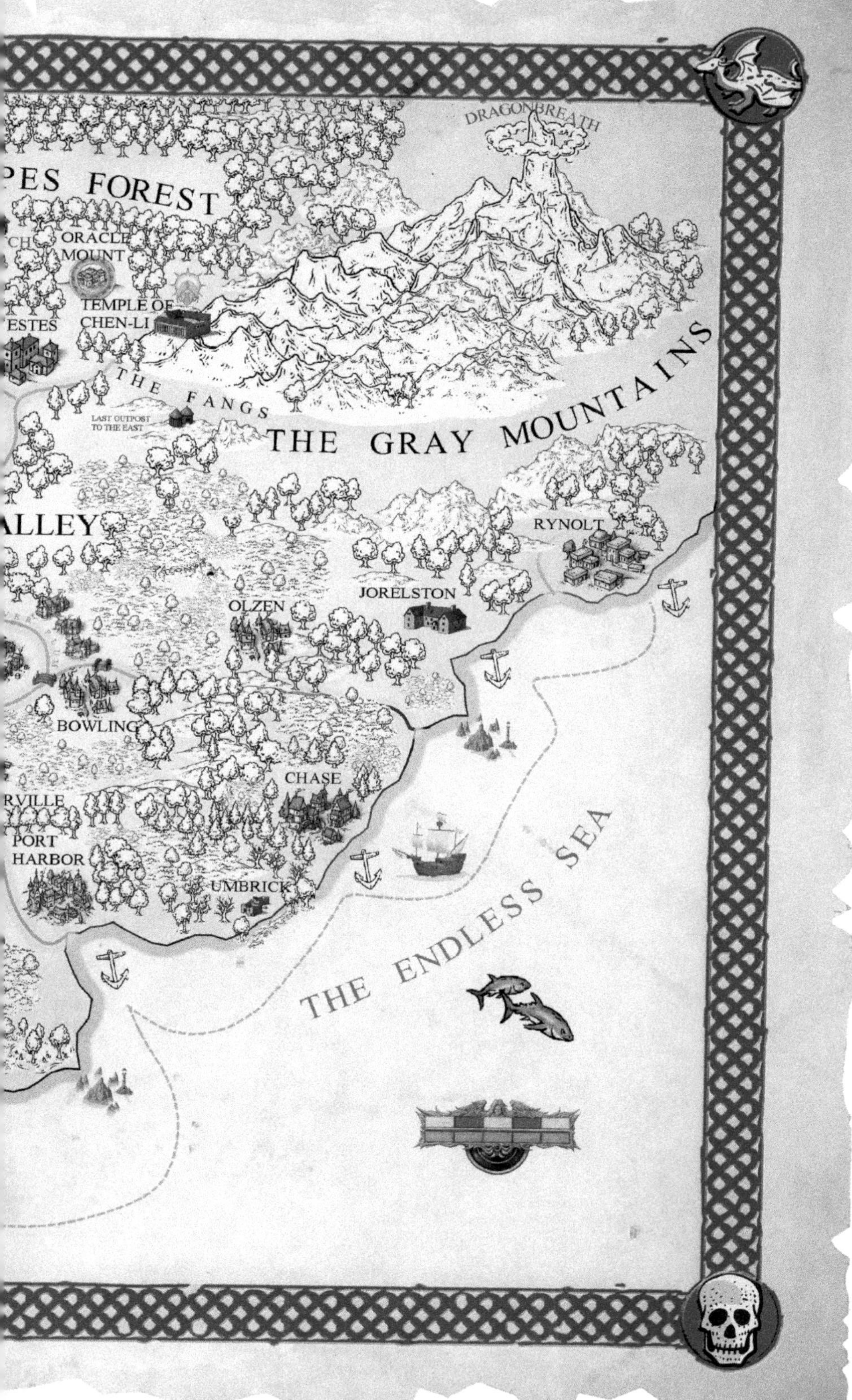
PES FOREST
DRAGONBREATH
ORACLE
MOUNT
TEMPLE OF
CHEN-LI
ESTES
THE FANGS
LAST OUTPOST
TO THE EAST
THE GRAY MOUNTAINS
ALLEY
RYNOLT
JORELSTON
OLZEN
BOWLING
CHASE
RVILLE
PORT
HARBOR
UMBRICK
THE ENDLESS SEA

FOREWORD

One more final push and Johanna heard the baby cry, signifying the birth was over. Three midwives attended her and received the newborn child. Johanna released the wooden handles of the birthing bed and covered her eyes with a wet elbow.

"It's a boy," one of them said. "An heir for the House of Erland."

A boy? The midwife's voice echoed in Johanna's mind. *A male child born to the House of Erland?*

The baby was cleaned and wrapped in swaddling linens. Then, carefully laid upon her breast. Johanna uncovered her eyes to look upon the face of her son for the first time. The baby had tufts of curly red hair. She could see the resemblance.

Just then, her husband, Erland, walked into the room after receiving the news of the birth of his only son. Together, unable to contain their joy, the father and mother beamed at their baby.

"Such a blessing," one of the women said. "We are truly blessed this day."

"Look at that curly red hair, just like his father's," another midwife spoke up. Erland and Johanna shared a look of concern. They could see the mark upon him, which meant this child had stumbled into this world, born into the curse passed on to yet another generation.

"What shall we name your son, Erland?" One of the midwives asked, prepared to write a name down.

Johanna nodded at him, and despite herself could only smile.

"His name will be Almon."

Almon Plum-Kilmer

INTRODUCTION

Thank you for your interest in *The Provenance*. This is the first book in an epic fantasy series, intended to be the definitive guide to the places, sources, origins, records, and events that fuel the world of *Astar's Blade*. This book consists of a re-telling of history that weave together the fabric of legends. Taking a bit of a creative license, they do not always get told in chronological order. So, to clarify things, you will find signposts referencing the general time and place before each chapter. So, for example, you will see something like this:

Mid-Run Valley in the Year 840 of
Human Recorded Time (HRT)

In the world of *Astar's Blade*, there was a time before human development. The world consisted of molten rock and lava, and the climate could not sustain human life. However, once the world cooled, in an event known as the Great Cooling, human beings were sprinkled in the world and started multiplying, as humans tend to do. Eventually, to mark the cycles for planting and hunting, they started looking at the stars and keeping track of time. This is the basis for Human Recorded Time or HRT, as it is referred to in later chapters. One note to remember about HRT is that it is not the age of the world but a running calendar only significant to humans.

Additionally, HRT does not imply a time that the gods respect or feel applies in any way to them, for it was the gods that sprinkled humankind in the world before their time keeping. The gods are mysterious and make no attempt to explain any precise time of their comings and goings. So, please keep that in mind considering their actions, and hold them in special reverence, with an open mind and without regard to HRT.

This book is written in four acts. The first act contains stories told in parallel, at two different times in alternating chapter intervals; the first (even chapters) is told in the distant future, and the second (odd chapters) is told in the distant past. But do not fret dear reader; they will converge together by Act II. After that, most (but not all) of the storylines from there are more-or-less in chronological order. Yet, along the way, as you explore the paths of this book, you may have to check the signposts firmly marked at the beginning of each chapter, as some events are played out in different places or times. Also, a Glossary is contained at the end for your convenience that outlines character names, relationships, places of interest, and timelines. Everything you will need not to get lost. We would not want to lose anyone as we make our way through the wilderness of *The Provenance*.

Well, that is all I have to say for now. Oh! I almost forgot. One more thing. In the following few pages, you might observe some things that dislike being observed. I think it is fair to warn you. If you choose to continue, you might want to carefully consider how to handle some of the information provided in these pages for your own good. But if curiosity gets the better of you, do not say I did not warn you.

– Joe Lyon

ACT I

Gods,

Ghosts,

Mountains,

&

A Growler of Red Curl

"Maybe it's better off this way,
To turn my back but want to stay.
I'm better off to just walk away.
Oh, my heart!
It should have known better."

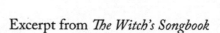

Excerpt from *The Witch's Songbook*

THE HOUSE OF ERLAND

THE MID-RUN VALLEY IN THE YEAR 1040 OF HUMAN RECORDED TIME (HRT)

Almon looked back at just the right moment to see his father fall off his horse. He saw Erland tumbling hard in a billowing cloud of dust. With rising panic in his chest, Almon leaped off his horse and ran back to help him. Fearing the worst for taking too long, he finally slid on his knees, reaching his father.

Erland sat in the field, dazed and dusty, repeatedly mumbling, "I am ready to die."

He patted the dust from his father's body, searching him for broken bones. "Did you break anything?"

"Leave me alone. Let me die here."

"Listen to me, listen. You are not going to die." Almon reached his arms under Erland's and dragged him out of the sun, and into the shade of a nearby white oak.

Being pulled away, he exclaimed, "What are you doing?"

"You fell off your horse."

"Did I?" Erland asked matter-of-factly. "I don't remember that."

"You're delirious. I think you hit your head."

Erland hacked uncontrollably, coughing up blood. It pooled in his hand. Both men saw it, and they shared a look of concern. Almon dragged him the rest of the way into the shade and propped his father up against the trunk of the large tree. He pulled out his canteen and gave him a drink of warm metallic water. Erland could only drink a small amount before bursting out coughing again.

"Are your ribs broken?"

"They're sore," Erland said, feeling his sides. "No, I don't think so."

"You gave me quite the scare." Almon continued to inspect him, trying to catch his breath.

"What happened to my horse?" Erland asked, starting to regain his senses. All three of them were nearby, grazing on tall grass as if nothing had happened. They were not Almon's primary concern at the moment.

"Let's just rest here a while," Almon said as a cool breeze passed through the shade. He turned on his back and slid down the trunk, coming to rest beside his father. Beads of sweat formed on his face. He wiped his forehead with the back of his hand, then looked their situation over.

"Well, it's getting hotter, and yet, here we are."

"How far are we from home?" Erland said, coughing.

"Haverhill is over eighty miles away."

"You're upset with me, aren't you?"

"I just don't understand you," Almon said, rubbing his face. "If you were sick, you should have called off this trip."

"I wanted things to be normal."

"That's not true, and you know it. Why don't you admit it? You knew you were dying before we left Haverhill. You got me out here with you so that you could die in the Mid-Run Valley knowing I would take care of you."

Erland did not object. He did not say it, but there was no other place for him to die than in the Mid-Run Valley and no other person he would want to be with more than Almon. He looked at his son and considered him.

All the Plum-Kilmer men were tall and athletically built, and Almon was no exception. He possessed the same dark reddish hair like his father, although Erland's hair was shorter, grayer with age, and his beard was more tightly cropped than his son's.

"It was this time last year Mother died." Almon looked at Erland resting beside him. He noticed how frail his father had become. It darkened his face and took the edge out of his voice. "Is she here with us?"

"Johanna," he said fondly. Erland laid his head back and rested, remembering her. "No, not in that way. Only in memory."

But that was not entirely true.

He had visited her crypt below the House of Erland the day before they left. He could still remember the acidic, corrosive smell of being underground. The flame from his candle bathed the tomb in a warm glow. There, flush to the stone floor, lay the crypt of Johnna Plum-Kilmer.

He could feel her energy there, more so than anywhere else in the House of Erland. Although the dusty chamber did not immediately reveal any sign of her lingering spirit, that was about to change. He could feel a growing apprehension, the oppressive heaviness in the air, that made him aware that he was not alone. The feeling made his spine tingle in a chill.

Then, appearing from the shadow, within the darkened corner, Johanna's brown eyes, her pale face, slowly emerged into his soft candlelight.

"Johanna, my darling," Erland whispered to the spirit. He extended his hand and took a step closer to her.

Johanna's pale hand moved to take his; yet, she stopped short.

Someone is near, she said in a hollow voice. *Almon is coming.*

Suddenly, Erland's candle flame flickered, causing shadows to dance eerily across his face. He looked at it, then glanced upward, across the ceiling. Now sensing the disruption for himself, he withdrew his hand and delicately closed it, the space between them growing ever apart.

"We were so close," he whispered.

Movement stirred the flow of air in the crypt, followed by a loud bang from above; it was the metal door at the top of the stairs leading to the tombs. Erland's eyes turned briefly to the side, then back at Johanna as he heard heavy steps coming down toward them.

He worries about you, Johanna said. *He suspects the truth.*

"Then we will wait, but soon, and we will be reunited again," Erland promised her, extending his palm in a motionless wave. Without a further word, Johanna's spirit slowly retreated into the shadows. Then her spirit was gone.

Erland wondered silently to himself. *Where does she go?*

All will be revealed, the fading voice of Johanna answered, reading his thoughts.

Just then, Almon appeared at the bottom of the stairs and opened the crypt portcullis with the slight creak of metal against metal.

"I thought I would find you here," he said, entering the tomb.

Erland walked into the darkened corner, where Johanna had previously emerged, longing to absorb any of the lingering energy that remained of her. Slowly, he turned and acknowledged his son.

"Hello, Almon."

Almon approached, seeing his mother's face, or at least the likeness of it, chiseled in stone on top of her tomb, embedded flush to the floor. He looked at Erland. "Am I disturbing you?"

"No, come join us." It was no strange occurrence for Erland to spend quiet time in Johanna's crypt. In the year since her death, he had grown ever more melancholy. His health was failing, too. He had developed a raspy cough that had long been getting worse. The two stood quietly together, sharing a solemn moment to look upon her chiseled face in the stone.

Whispering to keep the reverence, Almon broke the silence. "I'm getting our supplies ready."

Erland did not seem to hear.

"For our hunt tomorrow?" Almon added.

Erland looked up slowly, a blank expression on his face.

"Are you all right?" Almon asked him.

"Yes, of course. The hunt tomorrow."

The hunt will be our time, he heard Johanna's voice say, speaking to his mind again, where only he could hear.

"What's wrong?" Almon said, Erland's disengagement made him wonder. "Are you still wanting to go? Are you feeling up to it?"

"We go every year." Erland looked at him through his lashes.

"Yes, but you've been under the weather, haven't you? We can postpone it. Just until you feel better."

"I canceled last year; I can't cancel again."

"Why, when it's just you and I?"

Their annual trip had always been a favorite time to the senior Plum-Kilmer. His life revolved around it, the planning, the preparations, but because this hunt would be the first one since Johanna's death, this time it was extra special.

"Because," he answered Almon, "the hunt will be our time."

What a strange reply, Almon thought. But before he could say anything more, Erland blew out the candle, leaving the two of them in utter darkness in the crypt, with only the single torch in the stairwell as the solitary light, and led the way out.

The next day their trip got underway, but it did not start well. Conversation between them seemed forced; it had never been before.

Erland had taken up talking to himself and appeared cold and depressed, more so than usual. They rode out on horseback from the House of Erland, an enormous stone mansion, the largest in all of Haverhill. Their packhorse accompanied them with the supplies they would need and paced alongside Almon. Erland took up the rear and did not speak, deep in his own thoughts; if not for the occasional cough, Almon would have thought he was alone.

"If that cough doesn't get any better," Almon warned, "we will need to head back in."

"Sorry, but no chance," Erland said between coughs. "I'll be fine."

"But what's the point if you scare away the deer? You know they can hear you a mile away. If you keep it under control, this hunt might not be pointless. Isn't there anything you can do?"

"I'll try, Almon." But he could not keep silent. His cough continued as the miles rolled away.

"Stop it!" Almon grumbled.

After his outburst, he shifted in his saddle, annoyed. He knew his father would continue the hunt, even if it killed him. "You're so loud."

"I'm sorry, Almon."

Around the mid-day heat of the second day, they stopped for lunch. Erland did not eat, he did not even try. Instead, he wrapped himself in a blanket, even though the sun was brutally hot. Almon tried to convince him again they should return home. But like before, Erland insisted they continue, telling him he just needed help to mount his horse, and that he would feel better once riding on the trail. Almon suspected he would say as much. Shaking his head, he kept silent, and helped Erland up in the saddle.

But the pair only made it a couple of miles before Erland fell off his horse and could not get back on. Almon saw the riderless horse and his father sitting in a daze in a cloud of dust.

Now here, under the cool shade of the tree, Erland opened his eyes again. He had not realized he had fallen asleep.

"I was dreaming about Johanna," Erland said, "and that day in the tomb, the day before we left Haverhill for the hunt." He looked again at his son. Almon returned with a grim look of his own. They held each other's gaze steady.

"I need to ask you something," Almon said softly. "Even though we've never talked about it before. Is it true? That you speak with the spirits of the dead?"

Even now, Erland seemed reluctant to talk about those specific aspects of his life.

"What does it matter? You understand more than you think. Even more than you want to believe."

"No, this is not about believing. I just want to understand it."

Erland furrowed his brow. "Be careful what you say out loud, Almon. Your words betray your emotions, and there are some that will feed upon them; look how it has grayed my hair."

"Do these spirits feed on depression?'

"Depression is merely a side effect," Erland said, struggling for breath. "Our family has long suffered from what has come before us. But we bore it in silence. Yet you know every generation has had its ghosts."

"I am twenty-five years old. Why has no spirit ever appeared to me?"

"You will have to find these things out for yourself, Almon," Erland said, getting out his words between coughs. "Nothing I say will help you understand it any better, I'm afraid. I am sorry."

Erland tugged at his ring. "But this, I must pass to you while there is still time."

He worked the ring off his finger. Almon had never seen it leave his father's hand before. But here, in the shade of the big oak, Erland handed the ring over to him. "I carried this legacy as far as I can. Now my time is over. You will be our strength. It is your turn to bear it."

Almon looked at the ring in the palm of his hand and knew what it meant. Erland Plum-Kilmer had access to a large family inheritance passed down for generations on his father's side. It had long been the tradition of the rich to adopt a surname to keep their wealth in their own blood lineage. What the surname Plum-Kilmer meant to the rest of the world was that his family belonged to the original aristocracy, the ruling class, meaning that they were to be handled with respect and privilege. The ring came from the first and original Kilmer, a well-known knight to the realm who served under the first Leopold kingdom two hundred years ago. Crafted in thick, solid gold on its face, rubies and diamonds formed their family crest. Etched along the sides of it were scenes of the hunt, with deer leaping among rivers, trees, and oak leaves. The ring possessed immense value on its own, for the raw materials of gold and precious stones, but as the Plum-Kilmer family crest, it was a priceless heirloom as a piece of history.

"I cannot bear putting this on," Almon said. "This is your ring."

"It is your inheritance now; do with it as you will. Where I am going, it will not help me. Death is the great equalizer; it makes paupers of us all."

Dismayed, Almon put the ring in his shirt pocket for safekeeping.

"I am going to die soon," Erland said without opening his eyes.

"I know," Almon said in acknowledgment, reaching to loosen Erland's collar. "You knew that before we left."

Suddenly Erland's eyes widened and fixed in space. His lips trembled but made no sound. Then he arched his back in a spasm.

"No, don't do this! Please don't leave me!" Almon said, crying. His voice rose in panic. He lifted his father by the shoulders, embracing him. "Please. Don't go."

"It is passing," he whispered in Almon's ear.

Then, Erland Plum-Kilmer breathed his last as death finally overwhelmed him.

A long howl of anguish rose in Almon's throat, knocking the wind out of him. Gently, he rocked his father in his arms, holding him close, struggling against the gravity pulling his lifeless body down.

Eventually, Almon released him to rest on his side in the soft grass. He cried looking at his father, imagining him reviving, expecting to see him move.

Erland remained still.

His thoughts were racing. Daylight would be running out soon, and he was days from home. Whatever he decided, it would not be easy. The sun was too hot to take his father's body back to the House of Erland, and that would be a two-day journey. But here, the vultures were already circling, and soon other predators would catch wind. At any rate, he knew being taken back to the House of Erland was not what his father genuinely wanted.

Reluctantly, Almon forced himself to make the preparations.

At last, as the sun was going down, Almon stood over a fresh mound of dirt. Underneath it, resting in a shallow grave, lay the remains of Erland Plum-Kilmer.

He reached into his shirt pocket and pulled out the ring: The Plum-Kilmer family crest. It felt heavy when he slipped it onto his finger. He admired it for a moment, considering what it represented, then looked over at his father's final resting place. He wondered if a host of spirits might rush in on him after the death of the senior Plum-Kilmer. But he stood there alone, unmolested.

He ran the events of the last two days over in his mind. He immediately had regrets about the things he said, and the way he'd acted. Looking back down at the grave, Almon leaned against his shovel and thought he should say some appropriate words.

"I am now the last Plum-Kilmer that remains, and I am terrified about the future without your strength. I knew we shouldn't have come out this far. Why wouldn't you listen?"

That was a bad start, and his words stuck in his throat. Almon reminded himself that staying in Haverhill would not have changed a thing. Erland would be just as dead.

He looked at his dirty boots and tried to start over.

"I'm sorry. This is where you belong," Almon said, fighting back emotion. He looked up at the remaining daylight and squinted. "You loved the Mid-Run Valley. You always have. You loved our trips. In your heart, you were always the hunter. I want you to know that I always admired you. You were always my hero. You faced death the same way you faced life: You did it on your terms. I really wish I could be more like you. There was nowhere else you would rather be than here, and so now, you will rest here in this valley forever, just as you wanted. Now you can reunite with your darling Johanna in the next life. Today marks the end of your hunt in this world. Now, you can begin your hunt in the next one. Good hunting, Erland Plum-Kilmer. Until we meet again."

It was late in the evening, and Almon made camp beside where he buried his father, just to stay nearer to him once more. After a fitful, restless night, in the morning, he gathered as many stones as he could find and laid them on Erland's grave. He took great care to mark the exact location on his map; this place was sacred ground to him.

He rode out with the morning sun, riding home alone with Erland's riderless horse. Returning to Haverhill was a colorless journey for Almon. He rode the miles away, numb to a sense of time or direction. Luckily the horses knew their way back, and after what seemed like a blur, he was back at the House of Erland.

The next few days, he walked along the familiar pathways and empty halls of the House of Erland. The stone mansion felt more like a tomb to him now, a monument to his despair. Everywhere he looked, he saw stained glass memories of his mother, his father, and generations of the Plum-Kilmers before him. Memories lingered in every keepsake and they all made him heartsick. Everything was left in their familiar places; Almon did not have the heart to change anything, yet he resolved to spend less time there, in the House of Erland.

It took him some time to realize he was free. He had played the role of the dutiful son for so long he did not realize how much it defined him; now, having that role removed, he did not know what to do. It all happened so quickly. Unprepared for his newfound freedom, he spent his days in mourning over the loss of his normality.

That is precisely when the ghost, at last, made its entrance.

"Sometimes, I get so frightened.
When the sky starts turning blue,
Then I see a light on the horizon
A light so gently shining—from you."

Excerpt from *The Witch's Songbook*

THE FIRSTBORN HEIRONOMUS, GOD OF LIGHT

WORLD-AT-LARGE IN THE YEAR 511 HRT
AFTER THE GREAT COOLING

These were the days of the beginning of life in the world. The sun rose as it had for five hundred years since the Great Cooling of the land. Birds sang in the trees, the wind blew through the leaves, and water bubbled over the stream's bed. An eagle cried overhead; it called out with a single cry as if to say good morning to the God of Light. Then, with a single push from its wings, it soared far away over the hills and out of sight.

Heironomus awoke, the sunlight energizing him. Immediately, his body illuminated with an inner radiance that shined outward in a glowing light. He sat up, rubbing large fingers through his curly red hair and grizzled red beard. He rose from the thick ferns and soft moss that made his bed, stretching naked. A golden radiance encircled him, banishing shadows, and a brilliant yellow glow followed him wherever he went.

He felt a fly land on him, and he smacked it dead. *Hexor's damn flies!* he thought. *My brother makes too many of them.*

A short walk through the forest led him to the Spring of Silent Rising, a pleasantly warm spring that was at its highest in the morning, providing warm bathwater. He splashed in.

His red hair, now weighed down with water, flattened and darkened. He swam on the surface for a few moments. Then, holding his breath, he dove far underneath, into the very depths of the spring. His massive hands searched the sand until he found what he was looking for. Coming back up to the surface, he exhaled mightily and swiped the hair from his eyes. He splashed out of the spring, feeling refreshed, holding a clam. He carefully worked it open with broad and powerful fingers, yet with a delicate precision. There it was, under the clam's tongue: a pearl. He wriggled it out before throwing the clam back intact to the depths of the spring.

Examining it for any imperfections, he lay back on the rocks, drying himself naturally in the sun's warmth. He held up the pearl and admired it.

Once dried, he walked to a tree with forked branches extending from a crooked trunk. Reaching in, he pulled out a little wooden box and placed the pearl inside, on top of the many others he already had.

A gift for Ehlona, he thought.

He turned away from the forked tree and put on his clothes. He draped a thick wooly fur of ram skin over his right shoulder, then trussed it around his waist with a cord of golden vines. On his feet, he wore large fur boots.

"Now, it is time I work!" he shouted.

With a mighty push, he leaped into the air, sailing over the treetops into a white sky. Along his arc, several geese flying in a V-formation joined and flew with him. Heironomus laughed heartily to be in their company and blessed one with a kindly pat on the head.

The geese honked their approval to have him flying in their formation. But Heironomus was not flying; he was leaping, and as he came down from the sky, the geese continued their own way.

Heironomus landed with a crash that rocked the ground with a loud rumble, shaking houses to their foundations, causing fruit to fall off trees, water to slosh from washbasins, and birds to take flight from miles away. Inside their homes, the villagers cautiously peeked through their curtains to get a glimpse of the great God Heironomus who had come back.

Heironomus strained against himself, flexing his muscles with a loud grunt, and his entire body grew larger. With each incremental flex of his muscles, his body grew bigger and bigger; until he was as tall as a forty-foot tree and stood as wide as a house. He watched the villagers cower in fear as he became a giant; his laughter came out as a thunderous boom. But he was not here just to scare villagers. He had another purpose entirely.

He took his massive fist and punched down into the ground. With his mighty hand, he scooped up a wide channel of dirt and rock. The broken layers of limestone weighed tons. Yet he hoisted them over his head with a minimal effort. Spinning the heavy load back with a twist of his giant body, he swung forward and released them, sending the mammoth slabs of stone sailing like a discus. They flew overhead for miles, over the faraway hills in the west, landing with other piles of slab he had been throwing there. They hit the ground with a boom like distant thunder. He admired his throw for a moment, grinning, and then he punched into the ground again to take up another load. Heironomus had been hard at work like this for months, building up the foothills of the Blue Mountains to the west. It was to be his new mountain range.

It took over ten years of work like this to create the Gray Mountains to the east; he considered them his crowning jewel, his masterpiece, with their dramatically sharp Fangs leading up to the magnificent Dragonbreath as its centerpiece. They would be difficult to top. So, he did not try. Instead, his design for the Blue Mountains would not be as lofty, but still glorious in pure scenic beauty. At least they would be, once completed. But maybe most important, the Blue Mountains would serve Heironomus for a specific function. He built them with the idea in mind that when the sun kissed their summit, he would have an hour of sunshine left in the day. So it was that Heironomus built the Blue Mountains to be his timepiece.

After several hours of throwing the mountains into place, Heironomus stopped momentarily to catch his breath. With his hands on his hips, he admired the progress to the west. But to the east, behind him, some commotion caught his attention. He turned to see that some villagers were coming out of their shelters; four mortal men carrying large wicker baskets as an offering to their god. They approached him cautiously with their heads bowed. Slowly, they all dropped to their knees and offered the wicker baskets on the ground before them. Then, they backed away, singing:

"Hail Heironomus, God of Light!
Shine your glory upon us
You are Sovereign in our sight!
See your servants and favor us!"

Heironomus smiled as they approached, delighted with the gesture. He let out a series of long, mighty exhalations that reduced his body size. With alternating breaths, he shrank to a more comfortable level, a smaller form, back to villager size. He walked to the wicker baskets and examined them. They were full of grilled meats, cheeses, fruits, vegetables, and loaves of freshly baked bread, fresh cool water, wines, and more potent spirits. He gave a hearty laugh when he saw their offerings and how pleasing they looked.

"Thank you, good people," he said. "Such fine offerings you have prepared! It is a feast fit for a god! But it is too much for me, in my minor form. Won't you join me? Come, all of you, let us commune in fellowship together."

Cautiously, the four villagers approached him on their knees, bowing low in reverence. Heironomus lifted a bunch of purple grapes by the vine to his mouth.

"Stand! Stand, like men," he told them. "So I can get a better look at you."

There was a man there, short in stature and round in the middle; he wore an enormous hat that was narrow at the brim and widened dramatically at the top. The hat doubled his height, and despite its encumbrance, it made him just as tall as his other three comrades, although he was far shorter than the others.

Heironomus laughed at the hat. "What a hat, sir! Tell me, what is your name, and what is your clan?"

"Great Heironomus, I am from the clan of Botta. My name is Delbert Botta, your humble servant."

Heironomus tore off a large piece of fresh, crusty bread and put it in his mouth. As he chewed, he asked with his mouth full, "What is your profession, Delbert Botta?"

"I am a fisherman, oh great one, as are all the Bottas. It is our family trade."

"I see. Then, you know ships?"

"Oh yes, Great Heironomus."

"Have you ever sailed the Endless Sea?"

"I have. We Bottas are proficient with ships and sails, ties and knots."

"Ships and sails! Ties and knots! Very good! Delbert Botta! I wish to give you something, for your offerings here today, for your ships, sails, ties, and knots, but mostly for such a wonderful hat." Heironomus burst out in a hearty laugh. "I bless you and your clan, the Botta clan, with the prosperity of the Endless Sea. May you take my blessing with you always."

"Thank you, Great Heironomus! Oh, thank you!" He bowed and extended his hands.

In the future, Delbert Botta, the man in the enormous hat, would establish the city of Port Harbor. That sleepy village turned into the bustling shipping town it is today as the Mid-Run Valley's primary port and would be the center of commerce and trade from the shipping lanes that sailed the Endless Sea, turning Delbert Botta into a very wealthy man. But that would still be years in the future.

For now, Heironomus reached for a piece of blueberry pie while turning to look at the rest of the men before him. He ate the pie with his fingers. Looking at a sturdy, round man covered in black soot, he asked, "Why are you so dirty, man? Who are you, and what do you do?"

"My Gracious Lord, I am Hobrick, of the clan of Jeter." Hobrick smiled, revealing an ample space between his two front teeth. His hair and scruffy beard were as dark as his skin, blackened from dirt. Hobrick was a muscular, round man with a round head and round body. His blacksmith duties demanded him to be such. "Our family mines the mountain ore with the picks and axes we make, producing metal works, smelting metals into swords, shields, hinges, hammers, buckets, plows, and all manner of tools. The instruments of our labors are strong and never break, as are our hearts, for your divinity."

"Hobrick Jeter, you are a hard man after my own heart. For your iron will and steel heart, I wish to bless your family, the Jeter clan, with the prosperity of the Mountain Smelter. May you always pull ore up from the roots of these mountains."

"Thank you for your blessing, Great Heironomus," Hobrick said, bowing low with his face to the ground.

The Jeter family, led by Hobrick, would in the years to follow establish the village of Hammerville, the most industrious of all the villages, mining the hills for ore and producing metal implements of all kinds. The success that Hobrick would generate from his mining business would produce generations of wealth for the Jeter clan. But for today, he accepted Heironomus' blessing with a humble and contrite heart.

"And what about you?" Heironomus said to another villager, licking the blueberry pie off his fingers.

"My liege, my name is Nat Whitney, your faithful servant from the Whitney clan; we are builders and building designers. We fashion building materials from wood and cement bricks and blocks." Nat Whitney was only thirty years old, but his hair was completely white—not gray, but pure chalky white, unkempt and long. His lanky height could not be fully appreciated, not while on his knees in front of Heironomus, but when he stood, his knobby knees and knobby elbows gave it away that he was the tallest of the four—by far. "We build homes, wells, fences, and businesses. But most importantly, a church to your sovereign. The Church of the Illuminated, named after your shining magnificence."

Heironomus walked up to Nat Whitney, laying an enormous hand on him earnestly. "For your faithful service to me, I grant you my sincerest blessing. You shall always be prosperous in construction, especially constructing my Church of the Illuminated and establishing many villages across the Mid-Run Valley in the future. My blessings will be upon you and the clan of Whitney."

"I praise you. Oh, Heironomus!"

Nat Whitney's family clan established the village of Haverhill, one of the largest in later years. Located in the center of the Mid-Run Valley, Haverhill was the heart of the village evolution to modern dwellings, and the Whitney's were the foremost family of builders, for which they were handsomely compensated.

Heironomus sat back down and pulled a rack of grilled ribs out of the basket, and he tore away at it. While he chewed, he studied the fourth and last villager. Heironomus did not say so, but to him he motioned with his chin, pointing a rib to the man. The man displayed a large black mustache that extended at least one foot on each side of his cheeks. Through the man's bushy black eyebrows, he could see Heironomus continued eating while eyeing him, so he acted boldly and introduced himself.

"Most wonderful Heironomus, I represent the family of the clan of Plum. My name is Fortis Plum. We are traders, trackers, explorers, and adventurers. We raise cattle, pigs, chickens, and livestock. We take to the hills and forests to track and hunt game in the Wilds. We brew beer and make wine and stronger distilled spirits to make life worth living. We trade our wares with others and establish commerce with all. In this, we praise you, all-powerful Heironomus."

"Your wares are certainly delicious, Fortis Plum. Your labors bring joy and celebration to those around you. Accept my blessing for you and your family clan, Plum. Through your trade and commerce, the Plum family will remain forever blessed in the hunt and profitable in trade."

His name was Fortis Plum, and he would later go on to establish the village of Plum, the center of trade and commerce. The village turned out to be the wealthiest of all the villages. Fortis Plum would also name the river that snaked its way around the village, calling it the Plum River. Through the years, his family would be the wealthiest of all the original four families.

With Heironomus' blessing, these four families would create the ruling aristocracy for generations to come. They would be blessed with long life, wealth, and prosperity. They would develop the land of the Mid-Run Valley and make it a home for mortal men.

In the meantime, Heironomus lifted a jug of red wine. Tipping it back to satisfy his voracious thirst, he spilled on his face as much wine as he consumed. Wiping the excess from his beard with the back of his hand, he moved on to eat a head of cabbage like an apple.

Eventually, Heironomus had his fill. He rubbed his muscular belly under the wooly ram's skin and gave a short burp.

"Delbert, Hobrick, Nat, and Fortis, please, join with me in this feast. It is not right for all this food to go to waste. Please! Eat with me! Tell your clans to come as well and join us!"

By now, the other villagers, family members of the clans present, from the Bottas, the Jeters, the Whitneys, and the Plums, were watching and slowly came out of their homes. Initially too scared, they crept toward Heironomus, intending to join the fellowship. Eventually, they joined in on the feast with their god. In Heironomus, they found strength, and in his blessings, hope for the future.

In those days, the villages had no names. The people inhabiting the world were primarily nomadic. Having entered fellowship with him, Heironomus blessed the boldness of the original four villagers that brought him the first feast. But soon the villages of Port Harbor, Hammerville, Haverhill, and Plum would spring into existence.

Heironomus enjoyed the people of the world. He realized the more he traveled, the more he appreciated the mortals. Not all of them, mind you. But he enjoyed his people, those who loved the light, loved to work outdoors with their hands, enjoying the bounty of their labors, and those who built churches to honor and worship him.

That day, the villagers spoke freely with Heironomus. They laughed, ate, and drank wine together with him, until at last, Heironomus noticed the sun about to kiss the western peak of the Blue Mountains. He had to be off.

"I thank you all, and wish you well," Heironomus said. "Bless you all."

"We praise and worship you, Oh Great Heironomus," all the clans said, falling to their knees.

He bid them farewell and leaped once more into the sky. The villagers watched him go with a bittersweet look on their faces. They hated to see him go, but they appreciated having been so close in fellowship with the big, gregarious god.

In the skies overhead, Heironomus smiled. Being an all-powerful being was a lonely business. He had no one to talk to, no one to trust, no one to laugh with or express himself to. Indeed, not his brother, the treacherous Hexor, the God of Darkness. He was glad for the good folks in the village—the Bottas, Jeters, Whitneys, and Plums. He might not have got as much work done on the Blue Mountains as he had planned, but to him, it was worth it.

In the years to follow, the people created churches to Heironomus, and they called them the Church of the Illuminated. Soon, the call to worship sounded. The horn they used was a ram's horn, the Horn of the Faithful, and the ram's horn became the symbol of the God Heironomus. In return for his blessings, they worshipped the God of Light. Hearing the call to prayer, streams of worshippers walked to the Church of the Illuminated dressed in animal skins to ask Heironomus's continued blessings upon their families and their wares. They would congregate together to pay homage to their red-haired, gregarious god. Their creed was hard work. Early to bed and early to rise, to wake with the sun, making the most of the day.

They built the Churches of Illumination on hilltops and as open structures, welcoming the sunlight inside. The parishioners nurtured vegetable gardens, tended fruit trees that bore delicious fruit and vegetables inside the church's confines. Animals grazed freely in the church while herders sat resting under scenic views of distant mountains and lush forests.

Heironomus landed with a crash near the Spring of Silent Rising, glad to be back home again. He was covered in dirt from heaving limestone into the Blue Mountains. Off came the ram skins and his big, oversized fur boots. He cleaned himself in a great waterfall, as the Spring of Silent Rising had now rescinded twenty feet down into its crater.

Once clean, he picked out another set of skins. Donning his boots again, he walked back to the forked tree and pulled out his box of pearls. He knew Ehlona liked to walk along the babbling brook downstream from the waterfall. He relaxed and watched the western sky as the last hours of the day ended. As the sun dipped behind the peak of his beautiful Blue Mountains to the west, the sky glowed. Changing now, it slipped gradually from white to purple, to orange, and finally, to red. The sunset had finally arrived!

That meant Ehlona was nearby.

"I see all those little children
And all those old men turning gray
And now I can't let life slip by me.
I can't seem to fade—fade away."

Excerpt from *The Witch's Songbook*

THE GHOST ARRIVES

THE VILLAGE OF HAVERHILL IN THE YEAR 1040 (HRT)

The night had reached its darkest hour. Almon tried to sleep through another restless nightmare, not immediately noticing that the room had chilled; his warm breath came out as vapor. Finally, around midnight, startling from the bad dream, he awoke to the stench of the grave.

From outside his second story window, he heard a light tapping on the glass, like a faint bumping, not unlike a winged insect trying to get out. He rose from his bed and walked over to the window to investigate what could be making the noise. Looking out through the glass, he expected to see his own reflection; instead, a face not his own looked back at him. The reflection revealed the shrouded body of a dead man, wrapped in moldy linens, its face obscured in dirty loose wrappings, and a blood stain smeared across the bandages covering its open mouth. The bloody corpse slowly, deliberately, tapped on the glass with a long, broken fingernail. Once observed, the dead man withdrew, disappearing into the darkness, replaced by a sudden knock on the front door.

A knock on the door at this late hour would have startled him in ordinary times, but after seeing the corpse's reflection, it froze Almon's blood. As he cautiously proceeded down the stairs in the dark, the pounding continued, even more frantic now, the closer he got. Reaching the door, he opened it quickly, but no one was there, just the night air rushed in. A ghastly feeling lingered on him, as if he had just walked through a spider's web with his face. He closed and bolted the door tight, then returned upstairs.

When he entered his bedchamber and climbed back into his bed, he looked on in shock, for as much as he wanted not to believe, he could only stare at what he knew was really there.

Glowing like the candlelight, standing by the window, a ghostly figure slowly turned to face him. Floating with no connection to the floor, it resembled a spirit of energy tossed on waves of invisible water. If this was the same spirit he saw in the reflection, it was now different. The ghost wore a gray robe, a deep hood obscuring its face, a gray beard protruding from under its hood. Most certainly, Almon could tell, it was not the ghost of his dead father, Erland.

The ghost hovered above the floor by the window. Almon pulled the covers up to his neck and stared in wide-eyed horror. At length, pulling the blanket from his mouth, he addressed the ghost.

"Who are you?" he nervously asked. "What do you want in the House of Erland?"

The spirit struggled to speak but could only make muffled sounds.

"Erland is no longer living. Are you the ghost passed to me from him?"

The ghost mumbled, trying to say something, but again, it could not speak.

"Spirit, if there is a face, unseen under your hood, is speaking to me forbidden? Why do you not answer?" Almon whispered.

Abruptly the ghost stopped making any noise. It now stood in silence, staring at Almon. And then the ghost answered him, but not in the way he expected. Almon's ears started ringing; his head began humming. He put his hands to his ears, hoping it would stop, but the room kept spinning. A vision penetrated his mind.

Although he never left his bed, the vision found him flying in his mind, across the Mid-Run Valley, traveling faster than the wind. He rapidly accelerated over the increasingly higher mountains, until he approached the base of the largest one with a distinctive cloud covering its top. There, he came abruptly to a halt at its base. No sooner did he stop than up in a flash, he felt himself rising to its summit on the very top. But he never reached the top; instead, as he entered the cloud surrounding it, his vision turned to pure white, leaving the view of the summit still a mystery.

He recognized that mountain in the vision. It was not just any mountain. Distinctive for the dense cloud perpetually obscuring its summit, it could only be the Dragonbreath Mountain. Located in the Gray Mountains to the east, it was the tallest one in all the world.

The image vanished and his head cleared, returning him to the House of Erland, where he sat in his bed. After sweeping across the Mid-Run Valley in the vision, he had gone nowhere. His room in the House of Erland was now warm and quiet again.

The ghost had departed with the vision, along with the freezing cold and the sulfuric smell. It was hardly a relief that these things were gone. Sleep was impossible after that, as he found himself now wide awake and still in shock, his heart pounding.

But the ghost would appear to him again. The next night, and for three nights in a row, the ghost appeared to him in the same manner. Each time the ghost appeared it communicated only in visions. Night after night, the ghost took him on the same spiritual journey across the miles of the Mid-Run Valley, up to the Dragonbreath Mountain. Afterward, both the vision and the ghost would fade away.

Almon had sleepless nights after that. His waking hours were just as dreadful. Any noise startled him; his heart leaped at any sound. He remained excessively alert and watchful, wondering if, and when, the spirit would return. If this was the ghost passed down to him from his father, it was not what he expected, and he wanted no part of it.

After three nights of terror, the nightly visits thankfully stopped as abruptly as they had started. By then, the thought of returning to an ordinary life was impossible. He felt himself changing; the House of Erland became his prison, and the ghost his tormentor.

He went to a local tavern, a short walk from his home, simply named the Haverhill Inn. The Haverhill Inn, a popular establishment, did a brisk business, especially on special occasions, such as after the harvest, births, wedding celebrations, and even funeral wakes. At such times, it provided a familiar distraction for whatever ailed a person. Maybe Almon could find distraction there from his ghost and visions of the mountains.

In less interesting times, Almon managed a brewery located on the grounds of the House of Erland. It had long been in his family, as far back as the time of his ancestor, Fortis Plum, and each generation of Plum-Kilmers continued their family's brewing traditions. Almon was no exception; it was in his blood. He named his homebrew the Red Curl, as a parody of his red hair, and he would sell and transport large oak barrels of it to the Haverhill Inn.

Mose and Jacko owned the Haverhill Inn and made for an excellent pair of business partners because of the way their personalities complimented Almon's. Outside of their business relationship, Almon also considered them his friends.

He walked into the Haverhill Inn. A moderate crowd filled the place, allowing Almon to walk in with no one immediately noticing him. He sat on a stool at the bar, threw down a coin, and uncorked a growler of Red Curl, pouring the ale into an empty mug. He took a deep swallow that left foam in his mustache. Licking at the foam, he scanned the tavern for familiar faces.

As usual, a dark-haired man with a handle-bar mustache tended the bar. Mose was a hefty man of about forty years, significantly older than Almon. He had been married a few times in the past but was too gregarious in personality and fun-loving in habit to remain that way. He wore the same brown beer-stained smock over his street clothes; he was always spilling something on himself. Mose provided the voice of the partnership that owned the Haverhill Inn.

Jacko, the silent partner, was cleaning a table. While Mose had extra personality to spare, Jacko was the quiet, awkward one. Tall and skinny, he stayed out from behind the bar and mostly waited on tables, wiping them off and serving customers' drinks.

This was a familiar place for Almon, but tonight, it was not the same. Too many things had happened. He did not feel like talking much and was more content to watch the bubbles rise in his beer. Memories haunted him now; perhaps being in public would not only reduce his melancholy, but his chances of seeing the ghost again.

"I knew the brewer," said Mose from behind the bar, finally turning to recognize Almon. "He used to make the best brew. The Red Curl, I think he called it. But he died of old age, sitting right there in that chair." Mose pointed to the barstool where Almon sat.

Brewing the Red Curl seemed like a distant memory to Almond. If he heard Mose or not, he made no reaction.

"You all right? I've seen better mugs on a pig's snout!"

Mose considered Almon. Looking at the ring on his finger, the Plum-Kilmer family crest, concern crept across his face.

"Hey, I heard about Erland. I'm sorry for your loss. Your father was a good man. I'll miss him. He was like a father to me, too, since mine died years ago. It takes a while to—well, it just takes a while."

Almon looked up. "What's the best way to get to the Dragonbreath Mountain?"

Mose wrinkled his face. "The Dragonbreath Mountain? Where did that come from?"

"Lately, I can't get it off my mind."

"Why? Thinking of climbing it, Almon?"

"You never know; maybe I'll give it a go," Almon said, taking a sip of Red Curl. He wrinkled his brow while Mose started laughing at him.

"You want to climb the highest, most unclimbable mountain in the world?" Mose's laughing trailed off. "Hey, Jacko! Almon wants to be the first to climb the Dragonbreath Mountain."

Jacko shouted across the inn. "Only a fool tempts the dragon."

"Don't even think about," Mose told Almon. "That mountain will kill you."

"But what is the best way to get there?" Almon asked again patiently, trying not to get perturbed.

Mose thought to himself, cleared his throat, then leaned forward. "Well, first off, you would want to leave Haverhill, go to Port Harbor, and book passage to Jorleston. That will cost you, but you can afford it. That will cut hundreds of miles off your overland distance and get you there quicker, cut about a week off, as opposed to just walking there. Then, once you hit Jorleston, you head due north. There is a place there, the Last Outpost to the East. Go north until you hit that landmark, then turn sharp to the east."

By now, Jacko stood nearby, listening. "Yeah, the Last Outpost to the East is when you turn east to go up to the Chen-Li temple. Right?" Jacko asked.

"Right. Past the ruins of Chen-Li," said Mose. "And then into the Gray Mountains."

"What next?" asked Almon.

"After that, it's anybody's guess, as it's never been done before. You're on your own from there. By then, that big ol' mountain will loom large right in front of you. I suppose you have to follow your instincts and climb through the Fangs."

"The Fangs? I've heard of them; never seen them, though. What do you know about them?"

"They are brutal. Steep and treacherous," Jacko said.

Mose continued, "The Fangs are this nasty series of jagged teeth before you get to the base of the Dragonbreath. But even if you can make it past them, and that is a really big if, from there you'll need a lot of luck. If anything happens, no one will be coming along to help you. Make just one tiny mistake, one slip, one false step, and it's bye-bye, Almon."

"You're not seriously going to try it, are you, Almon?" Jacko asked.

"Only a fool tempts the dragon," Almon repeated, tipping his glass back. "Another Red Curl, Mose?"

"Yeah, best to stay here and drink with us, Almon," said Jacko.

Mose and Jacko smiled at him. But at length, they looked at each other, their smiles giving way to worry. They both knew some people went into the Gray Mountains to commit suicide-by-mountain. After all these years they hoped they knew him better than that and he was not one of those. But one can never tell, and he had been through a lot lately. With losing both his father and mother within a year, he was not himself. No one knew the depths of his grief.

Later that night, Almon left the Haverhill Inn for home. On his way, he got a strange feeling he was being watched. Looking behind him, he saw the ghost standing in moonlight and shadows. It was the first time the ghost appeared to him anywhere outside the House of Erland. Almon's heart raced. He froze. The ghost moved toward him, floating in the air, coming up to him close enough to touch. Almon quickly turned his back on the ghost. He waited for its icy touch but felt nothing more than the cold night air breathing on his neck. He was afraid to turn around to see if it was still there, knowing it still was. He could not breathe. His heart was in his throat. He was paralyzed with fear.

Finding the courage to step away, then stepping more quickly, he raced for the House of Erland. By the time he reached the outer gates, he was at a full sprint. He made his way to the door, then quickly spun to see if it had followed him. It had: the ghost stayed within arm's reach of him the entire way and maintained the same distance behind him as it did outside the Haverhill Inn. The vision hit him again, more intense than it had been the three times before. Once again, it was the image of the Dragonbreath Mountain forcing its way into his mind, lingering there, making him see and experience it. Then, like before, the ghost and the vision were gone.

He found himself on the steps of his front door, quivering from shock. He frantically scanned the landscape, searching for any remains of the ghost. There were none, but in his conscious reality, everything turned into what could be the ghost. He saw it in every shape and shadow. This time, the fear would not go away. He knew it would never go away.

Unless maybe there was a way, he thought.

It was still late at night. The dawn would not come for several hours. Yet he could not sleep. Instead, Almon packed his bags and collected rations and gear. As if guided by a force not his own, he went through the motions, as though looking down on another person, not himself.

Well before the sun came up, the House of Erland rolled away in the distance behind him. He had no desire to look back as he left Haverhill in the darkness, walking toward the distant lights of Port Harbor.

Reaching the docks of Port Harbor early in the morning, he could smell the salty, rotten sea foam of the shore and searched the notice boards for a ship heading to Jorleston. Leaving in about an hour, he found one in a ship called the *Forerunner* under the command of Captain Fortosa. He paid the harbor master, a dark man more interested in his pipe smoke than Almon, for the fare and booked his passage on the *Forerunner* to Jorelston Harbor.

With his ticket, he proceeded to walk along the numerous ships tied off to the long rows of docks. A perpetual splash of waves rocked against their wooden sides and jangled a distant buoy bell. He found the ship named the *Forerunner* and walked up the outstretched wooden gangplank, slippery and wet. The sounds of corded ropes being stretched, straining against the ships mast, mixed with the occasional flap of the tall sails in the wind. His footfalls creaked the ramp under the heavy strain of the rattling gear on his back.

He saw the captain of the *Forerunner* leaning against the railing smoking a pipe. The captain certainly looked every bit the part: he wore a faded but distinctive blue uniform, a gold braid around his shoulders, a flat black hat, with his bushy white hair bursting out from under it, and a long white beard. No one could mistake him for anything but the captain of the ship.

"Captain Fortosa?"

"One and the same," the captain said, puffing out a blue cloud of smoke from his pipe.

"Permission to come aboard, sir," Almon said, presenting his ticket, stamped PAID.

"Now, let's see. What do we have here? Where ya be going?" Captain Fortosa said, flashing a grin, revealing a gold front tooth. "The *Forerunner* hasn't got first class I'm afraid. You'll have to man-handle your own gear onto her."

"It's all right here," Almon said, pointing to his pack and equipment on his back.

"A one-way ticket to Jorleston, eh?" Captain Fortosa gave Almon a scrutinizing eye. "Well, at any rate, it is not my habit to ask about another man's business. That is between you and the gods. Welcome aboard. We should have a good sailing, at least halfway to Jorleston."

Almon looked puzzled. "Halfway to Jorleston?"

The captain pointed with his chin to the sky. "There's a bad storm brewing out there. It's going to get a little dicey. Hope you packed your sea legs. Come, welcome aboard the *Forerunner*."

It did not escape Almon when his trailing foot left the gangplank, that for the next few hours, he belonged to the mercy of Captain Fortosa, and the Endless Sea.

"I pay the price they're asking,
Then I take my seat.
But it's not what I was expecting.
So in the dark, I trip all over my feet."

Excerpt from *The Witch's Songbook*

THE SECOND-BORN
HEXOR, GOD OF DARKNESS

WORLD-AT-LARGE IN THE YEAR 511 (HRT)
AFTER THE GREAT COOLING

There is a strange comfort in the dark. It can be like a protective blanket, woven in fabric of black, cloaking movements as well as intentions. At night, the darkness opens another world, expanding the world as a vast emptiness. When darkness falls upon the Mid-Run Valley, the mountains become indistinguishable from the shadows, and windows brighten up like tiny stars upon the dark land while thousands of real ones shine up in the firmament.

The night is quiet, but it is a world of movement and motion. The nocturnal creatures come out in the darkness with glowing eyes of neon colors. Predators are in their element; they prowl the night hunting for the weak while scavengers busy themselves cleaning the world of the rotten and the dead. For some, they will not survive the night.

It is a ruthless world. This the realm of Hexor with his hateful eye, the God of Darkness. His red hair is dark, combed back, short, and neatly trimmed. Draped in long sleeves, his black uniform buttoned to his chin, and with his pants tucked neatly into his leather boots, he stood with his hands behind his back overlooking the Mid-Run Valley.

Hexor kept himself clean; clean from the weak, clean from decay, clean from the dead and the dying. In Hexor's world, only the powerful survived. He cared nothing for the politics of the world, especially the indecision of humans. He cared only for what creeped and crawled in blind obedience to their given purpose: insects, rodents, disease, molds. There were no compromises with them; there was no debate. You could not reason with them or change their intended purpose. They were clean, like him.

He thought of the two other gods, Heironomus, his twin brother, and Ehlona, an unwanted distraction. They spent too much time pandering to humans and not enough time fulfilling their intended purpose. They complicated matters by interacting with humans.

They are weak and unclean, he thought.

He stood on a hill and considered his brother's progress with the Blue Mountains. He laughed to himself. *What purpose do these serve? What was wrong with a flat Mid-Run Valley? What a colossal waste of time.*

Hexor's hateful eye, his right eye, remained his most distinguishing feature. It was white where the other was black, and black where the other was white, a perfect negative of the other.

Switching to look out of his hateful eye, he saw the world in a different way. Nothing living could hide from the hateful eye. It lifted the darkness, turning all the creeping, crawling things into red orbs of heat, like balls of fire in his sight, revealing outlines in reds, orange, and yellows. With his hateful eye, he watched the creatures crawl, move, and fly. He could detect everything until death made their fiery colors of heat cool and dull, eventually turning them to a dark blue, the color that symbolized the stillness of death.

Hexor kneeled on one knee. Reaching down, he took a pinch of dust from the ground and sprinkled it between his thumb and first finger. He released the dust back to the ground, and instead of landing as dust, it dropped to the ground as insects. Over and over, he picked through the dirty soil, sprinkling the ground with newly created beetles, spiders, cockroaches, scorpions, snakes, centipedes, locusts. All of them fell as dust from his hand, but landed as living insects, clicking away on tiny, armored legs to fulfill their purpose: to devour whatever they could find.

Then he threw pebbles into the air, and crows, bats, moths, flies, and wasps took flight, replacing the stones. Some circled Hexor for a moment, content to follow him, as if in gratitude for creating them. But not for long, as they would soon fly off, obeying their instinct to clean the world. They had no time for politics.

They are strong. They are clean.

Hexor turned to go down the hill, to a place where sulfuric steam hissed from the ground. The sickly bluish cloud obscured the mouth of an entrance to a deep cave. He passed through the steam of hot noxious vapors and entered the cave. Continuing downward into the bowels of the world, he walked down a long zigzagging stone path. A high stone wall protected his right, and on his left, the ledge dropped into the endless molten depths of the world. The clouds of steam reflected the fiery red from the lava caverns below.

The path led him down into a sprawling expanse until it opened into a large, featureless chamber. Here, dead human bodies hung on hooks from the walls. They were dropped in from caskets sinking out of their graves above and down through the roof of the cavern. Many coffins hung partway lodged into the roof of the cave. Hexor used them as propaganda, reminding the underworld of death, decay, and the depravity that the surface dwellers represented.

He passed the cavern and walked further down into the subterranean levels, where breathing became difficult for men with its sulfuric heat, but Hexor had no problem. Along the way, he encountered a group of slaves, weary emaciated humans, shackled and toiling away, chipping at the hard stone wall with pickaxes. These poor souls were derelicts from the village who made deals with Hexor for debts they could not repay, debts for worldly riches: for gold or diamonds, things of value to humans, but only common trinkets to Hexor. They'd forfeited their freedom and were pressed into hard service, working to the death as repayment. Hexor found human slaves to be much needier, requiring constant attention, more so than his nocturnal creations. Humans needed to be given food and water constantly to live. Even the lowliest of his cockroaches could at least feed and water themselves. Hexor had no sympathy for them and passed them with no interest.

Deeper down into the hot caverns he descended, following a steady sound of crunching stones resonating from the dark tunnels below. Dropping to the lowest part of the cave, he came to the end of the tunnel. Blocking him from going any farther was an enormous mass of fatty meat, grayish-blue flesh, its chubby folds pulsating with each crunch. The massive bulbous creature pressed against the tunnel's circular walls, conforming to the creature's circumference, big enough for Hexor to stand in comfortably, even providing space above his head.

Hexor reached out and touched the massive purple blob on its hindquarters. The crunching abruptly stopped, and the thing quickly turned to protect its rear. In a furious roar, it spit out acidic saliva and gravel shot out of its enormous mouth. Hexor could see past seven rows of sharp teeth, down into the creature's throat, through a hole so big that it could easily swallow a grown man. Unfazed, Hexor pleasantly scratched the monster's side, and it twitched its fatty layers in silent satisfaction at its master's touch. The thing lived in the depths, in the dark, having no need of eyes.

The rock larvae were one of Hexor's most favorite and loyal creations. Unleashed to feast, they fed non-stop on the subterranean stone, creating a magnificent maze of labyrinths and tunnels.

The underworld tunnels were home to many things. Hexor let them obey their instincts, mostly because he knew nothing could run or hide from the inevitable purpose of life or the ultimate destruction of death. He knew this included humans, and more of them that were not slaves lived in these tunnels: these humans were outlaws, murderers, and thieves, men who obeyed their basest instincts. They were renegades, most of them hiding, fugitives from the mortal race. These men co-existed with the slaves, rock larvae, and a host of other dangers that could take their lives at any moment.

Naturally, Hexor thought, the fundamental weakness of humans was that they had a hard time avoiding their need for politics. This was no surprise to Hexor, and as expected, a human sub-culture formed from those who were wicked, those who worshipped strength and power. In this realm of darkness, no one had more power than Hexor, the God of Darkness. The underworld worshipped him. They made red banners and hung them in the caverns in his honor. Blood sacrifices were made to his name, some animal, some human. They formed a dark religion with Hexor at its center; the humans called it the Cult of Horrors.

Hexor wore all black. And so, the Cult of Horrors would not allow any human to dress all in black. To do so was sacrilegious, blasphemous; the penalty was death. Only Hexor could be pure enough, worthy of solid black. Instead, they dressed in red robes adorned with black stripes on their sleeves, showing rank. The High Priest of the Cult of Horrors was the only exception, and there could only be one. To be distinguished from the others, the High Priest wore a black robe with red stripes on the sleeves, showing his ascendency to the highest human position in the Cult of Horrors. Hexor sometimes amused himself in the cult, mostly for his own purposes, but communicating with none other than the High Priest alone.

When Hexor did speak to the High Priest, he did so only in private. No one knew what was said except the High Priest, and so the message was often molested for the dark purposes of the High Priest himself. The mystery of these conversations was the primary source of the High Priest's power. It was completely a human political theater. Hexor had to laugh, knowing precisely that the High Priest would deviate from his order to serve his politics. It was the exact political manipulation that Hexor expected and hated from these humans: their pathetic indecision and inability to perform their simple intended purpose.

When it was not amusing him so much, it readily disgusted him. Sometimes he gave the High Priest impossible quests or hard-to-understand instructions, then punished the High Priest with death for failure. This allowed for a constant turnover of the High Priest, creating a power vacuum within the Cult of Horrors and the struggle to keep it filled. He kept the Cult of Horrors a blood-thirsty movement who fought amongst themselves just to have a chance to play their politics as the High Priest emerged. But no matter what, the High Priest had to be the strongest of them.

They had to be strong. They had to be clean. But they were always only temporary.

Otherwise, the God of Darkness strolled the world and the caverns alone. The sad fact was that Hexor had been so efficient in the works he had put in motion. He had an abundance of time on his hands. In his world of darkness, he had precious little to do. He did not work nearly as hard, or as much, as his brother worked.

The humans did that to him, he thought. *But I will not let them do it to me.*

Through the High Priests, word got to him that Heironomus had blessed four families of the village, and they were fellowshipping with him. This was a problem. It had the potential to offset the balance.

Am I the only one of the gods who cares about the balance? Hexor thought.

"So, my twin is having a little picnic with the commoners, eh?" he told the High Priest. "We'll see about that. Who are these villagers and what were they blessed with?"

The High Priest spoke. "To the clan of the Bottas, Heironomus blessed them with prosperity on the Endless Sea."

"Hear my words, High Priest. They will find such a blessing that I cannot undo. So, while I cannot curse this clan of Botta on the sea, they will find a curse on the land. They will prosper on the Endless Sea but will find no peace on solid land. Their clan will be liars and cheats, hated amongst all the other humans. Tell me more, High Priest."

"There were some dirty miners there, the round-faced clan of the Jeters. Heironomus has blessed them with riches and wealth from the mountain. The blessing of the Mountain Smelter," the High Priest told him.

"The Mountain Smelter? I see. I curse this clan of the Jeters to be slaves to their mountain. Their duty to it will never be satisfied. They will eat and breathe their dirty ore. They will languish in the black dust of the underground, and never see the daylight again. They will never be able to wash the dirt from their bodies, and the dust will stick to them forever. Who's next, High Priest?"

"To the clan of Whitney, all gangly men, tall, with white hair, he promised success in building construction."

"I curse the Whitneys that their construction turns to destruction. Let wars tear down all they build up. And now, tell me the final clan, High Priest."

"To the clan of the Plums, Heironomus has blessed them to provide celebration."

"The Plum clan will provide celebration to others but will only know melancholy for themselves. They will make the world happy, but they will be inconsolable in insurmountable grief."

"Your will shall be done, Great Hexor," the High Priest said with a bow.

"Now leave me. Go play your games."

"As you wish, Oh Mighty One," the High Priest said, and left the cavern to spread whatever lies would benefit him. But Hexor had other things to concentrate on than the Cult of Horrors, the family clans, or what his brother was doing. He had designs for a magnificent castle.

Hexor called dark clouds to him, and he molded the clouds like clay, forming his plans for his castle. Waving his hand, if he no longer liked a certain piece, it would turn to vapor and blow away. He could never settle on a final design, but so far he designed the castle with seven tall towers, twisting in spirals, high over a main stronghold, topped with a golden dome. He continued to add to the design for years, changing it aesthetically and functionally depending on his desires. One day, when he had the design perfect, he planned to call down this castle, not in the cloud formation, but in real stone in the world itself. Until then, the clouds held his grand design for his castle.

Yet he would never see his masterpiece completed.

The night was almost over now. The sunrise drew near. Dismissing the dark clouds, he wanted now to relax and rest and think. He seldom gave a thought about the third god in their midst, Ehlona, the Goddess of Beauty, but this night he did. His final thoughts for the night turned to her. Although he found her to be haughty, stuffy, and full of herself, Hextor knew she would be a great addition for him to possess as a trophy, and as a treasure.

She would be a pearl, he said to himself with a chuckle.

Hexor knew his twin brother had a sweet tooth for Ehlona, or more simply put, a weakness for her. It interested Hexor that Ehlona had an important part to play in this game. Her usefulness was inevitable, but it had not yet revealed itself.

In the meantime, Hexor did not concern himself with her, the humans, or his conflict with his brother. Instead, he fully believed that in the end, victory would be his. But only if he stayed true to his intended purpose:

To keep himself strong.

Keep himself clean.

"It was a deep-sea diver's dream.
Rolling on the tide
In tales of lives the sailors lost
And bells that ring on high."

Excerpt from *The Witch's Songbook*

THE FORERUNNER

On the Endless Sea in the Year 1040 of HRT

"Only fools climb the Dragonbreath Mountain. Everyone knows that. Even if someone were to get up those first cliffs—blast!" Captain Fortosa rubbed a wet hand across his forehead. "Now I forgot. What's the name of them?"

He nudged his boot into Almon's side, who was kneeling just in front. He stopped rummaging through his backpack and squinted up at the question.

"The big sharp ones," the captain shouted over the crashing waves. He snorted and spat upon the deck. "It's the one in front with the bones scattered along the bottom."

"You mean the Fangs?" Almon shouted over the storm. "The Fangs are the mountains that lead to the Dragonbreath." Almon grabbed onto one rope of the masthead, grimacing. Lightning struck the water some distance from the *Forerunner* and sent jagged light into the distant fog.

"Yes, that's it!" the captain said to Almon. "Even if you were to get past the Fangs, there's still a lot a mountain to go." A wave splashed onto the deck and pushed Captain Fortosa over a little, but he hardly noticed. "And consider this: even if you were an excellent climber, the Timmutes would get you. Nasty little things. My youngest son used to hunt with a man who tried to climb the Dragonbreath once. Rest his soul. By thunder, they are dead now."

The captain lamented and stared at the waves ahead. "Both of them. Dead now."

"That's a tragic loss. I'm sorry," Almon said. He had heard something about the Timmutes but thought they were rumors.

"Captain Fortosa," he asked, swaying with the boat as it bucked to both sides. "The Timmutes? Are they real?"

The captain was thoughtful. "Well, let's just say, sailors aren't the only ones who like to tell stories." Then he pointed to a glow in the distance. "That's our port, and just in time! Something wicked is brewing in those clouds!"

Almon could hear a bell from the dock, but the lighthouse had become just a faint glow in the rain. "Are you sure this storm won't pass? Somebody told me the weather in the valley of the Gray Mountain is unpredictable."

A tackle box sitting just behind the mast scraped across the deck, unsecured in a gust of wind that tossed it overboard, into the water, lost upon the next wave.

"Secure that tackle!" the captain shouted too late. "Damn it all to hell!"

"I was expecting less rain."

The captain laughed and adjusted his shirt as it flapped in his face. "Never is," he said. The boat pitched to one side, and half of the crew veered along with it. "If I didn't know any better, I'd say you brought the rain with you!"

Almon wiped the rain from his face with his gloves and breathed in the cold mist. A woman sitting next to some crates comforted a small boy who was having trouble balancing. She looked to the captain and asked, "And you'll be off first thing for Port Harbor tomorrow morning?"

"First thing tomorrow morning, yes, ma'am. With or without you," the captain said and turned back to Almon. "Jorleston has a tavern just up the front here with an excellent brew. A couple of mugs and the storm will pass before you know it."

Men with lanterns shouted they could see the harbor as they drifted closer to the shoals' barnacled rocks, jutting up in the fog. The captain reached behind him and fastened a buckle, securing some rigging.

"Don't look so grim!" Captain Fortosa slapped Almon on the back. "You look like you've seen a ghost!"

Almon's eyes widened, lost in the irony of the words. The ghost was here on the ship with him. It made its way from Haverhill to appear in spirit to Almon. Yet again. The pale ghost stood staring at Almon, almost standing on the masthead, adorned in luminescent gray, his hood shading his face, his beard ruffling in the gale. The ghost stood fixed on the bow, effortlessly indifferent against the motion of the wild sea. Wave after wave crashed across the bow and right through the spirit, impervious to the perpetual motion of the raging sea.

"Do you see him?" Almon turned to the captain and lifted a finger. "There, on the bow, almost on the masthead. Is that a real man or a ghost?"

The captain laughed. "That's a funny one. I told you, you'll make a fine sailor yet." The captain turned, and it was apparent he saw no one as he continued to lean with the waves of the pitching ship. The ghost did not have to lean against the rolling seas; it stayed fastened securely to the bow without holding onto the rigging or anything else on-board.

Almon turned again toward the bow, hoping the ghost had gone, but the spirit was still there. The ghost made no threat, and no words passed between them. His purpose was to fill Almon's mind with visions of the Dragonbreath Mountain. Almon was sure it would not be the last time.

The *Forerunner* rode an enormous wave upward. High into the air, the ship and the ghost rose until only the dark space of swirling clouds framed them. The boat came down hard on the opposite side of the wave until nothing but foamy saltwater filled Almon's eyes. The ship slammed into the sea; a giant wave splashed across the ghost, obscuring it from view. When the wave drained away, the spirit vanished. The vision of the Dragonbreath Mountain remained in Almon's mind.

Almon rubbed his forehead. It did not go unnoticed by Captain Fortosa.

"If you're going to puke, send it over the railing. Don't puke on my deck unless you're going to stay behind to clean it up."

Almon searched the ship for any remaining signs of the ghost, but there were none. He ran to the rail to peer over the side and see if the apparition had been real and not a man washed overboard. There were no signs of a man, nothing. Almon convinced himself that the ghost either departed or must have been a figment of his imagination.

"We are going the right way," Almon felt compelled to shout out loud to Captain Fortosa. He knew the ghost was leading him onward.

The captain gave Almon a sarcastic look. "So glad you think so."

For the rest of the trip, the *Forerunner* navigated through the storm's rocking until it reached shallower water. The captain used the lighthouse as a reference to guide the ship around the rocky trolls. Eventually, the *Forerunner* glided through the harbor to the docks, with only minimal damage from the gale. The crew stepped ashore with the heavy ropes and tied off the *Forerunner* to the pier. Soon after, the gangplank was extended out.

"ALL ASHORE!" Captain Fortosa announced. "Watch your step."

The sailors were ready for a meal and a potent drink to get the taste of saltwater out of their mouths. Almon took a moment, collected his gear, and walked down the gangplank in the rain.

He walked down the dock and away from the *Forerunner.* As he put down his gear, he turned to look at the sturdy ship one last time. Captain Fortosa was watching him with great interest. Standing high on the vessel's railing, the captain gave him a long smile; his gold front tooth glittered in the distance, even in the darkness.

"It's bad luck to dwell on the dead," the captain shouted. He tapped his temple. "Remember that."

Without a gesture, Almon picked up his gear and continued the short walk toward the Jorleston Inn. When he looked back, the captain was gone. *It is bad luck to dwell on the dead*, he thought to himself.

He needed a drink to calm himself. He kept seeing the ghost standing on the bow of the ship. The mystery of this spirit and the way it only appeared to Almon was frightening. He never knew when that awful spirit would reveal himself. Almon believed that the ghost of the old man was always with him now. Was the ghost's appearance to send him away from danger or lead him to it? Almon felt more compelled than ever to continue toward the Gray Mountains, the Fangs, and then on to the Dragonbreath beyond.

He avoided the eyes and the surrounding talk from strangers in the Jorleston Inn. After a drink or two of rum in the crowded inn, he felt better. He paid the innkeeper for a single night. The room was economically plain. It would be the best he would see for a long time, his last night not spent under the stars and exposed to the weather. He took advantage of it and went to sleep early in the evening.

Almon drifted off and started dreaming, never knowing for sure if just a few feet away the old ghost stood in the corner and watched him in his sleep. Was this vision of the spirit real or only a part of his dream? Or just his memory playing tricks on him? Was it the musty smell of this old harbor room, or was it the smell of the ghost returning?

He laid his head on the pillow and tried to sleep, but questions with no answers plagued his dreams.

"He takes her in his arms when all the lights are on.
Together they lay down the rhythm of their song.
She's a little out of tune, but he don't really mind.
Her strings might be in doubt, because he plays her all the time."

Excerpt from *The Witch's Songbook*

THE THIRD GOD EHLONA, THE GODDESS OF BEAUTY

World-at-Large in the Year 511 HRT
After the Great Cooling

A golden glow appeared above the mountains. She appeared with vibrant colors surrounding her. In one hand, she held back the light of day, and with the other hand, she grasped the darkness and the night. She walked between them in a trail of fiery, smoky, red-orange light.

Behold, Ehlona, the Goddess of Beauty.

Beguiled by the last rays of a golden sun, and darkened by the approaching night, she came down from the mountain. Her face was fair and bright, cheeks blossoming like a flower in a rosy glow. She wore a circlet of gold inlay upon her head, her thick, auburn curls tumbling full and long over her shoulders. Her long white gown parted slightly to allow her slender legs to step unhindered. A golden oak leaf belt adorned her waist. With dainty shoes and interlacing gold straps, step by step, Ehlona traversed the path down into the valley.

She played a golden lyre, her fingers skillfully working the strings in a mystical blue light. As she played, she moved and sang. Her voice was like a sparrow with undertones of rushing waters. Colors spilled around her.

She sang:

I like the way you hold my hand
Your eyes tell me you understand
I like the way
You kiss my cheek when there's no one around
You give to me all I'll ever need.
I like the magic in your smile
Won't you come and sit with me awhile?
You are to me
The sunshine in every rainy cloud.
You give to me all I'll ever need.

She stopped singing; but continued humming the tune. Looking back, she could tell by her colors how much time she had. This was her time. She ruled over the sunsets and sunrises.

Heironomus waited for her. He sat on a rock by the waters. Seeing her, he rose to his feet.

"Beautiful Ehlona, grant me a minute in the presence of your splendor?"

"Heironomus, you have been waiting for me? We've been meeting like this for three hundred years now. Haven't I become old and boring to you?"

"Every day, my eyes look upon you for the first time."

"You flatter me, God of Light."

When she walked past, Heironomus caught the fragrance of sandalwood that followed her. Pleasantly, her essence stirred Heironomus and lingered with him.

"Your Blue Mountains are looking grand." She turned to face him. "The world will enjoy them for thousands of years. Well done, Heironomus."

"I have a gift for you."

"A gift for me?"

He opened the box, showing her the pearls. "Fifty pearls, from the mouths of clams living on the bottom of the Spring of Silent Rising."

"I thought the bottom of the spring too deep to reach?"

"Not for me." Heironomus took her hand and wrapped her fingers around the box. Then he released them and withdrew with a smile. They both radiated light; Heironomus with a golden glow and Ehlona with her red and orange.

The pearls were flawless, more elegant than any she had seen before. The luster of them glimmered in the dying light.

"They are beautiful, the most beautiful I have ever seen."

"You are the most beautiful I have ever seen."

The soft, red glow beyond the mountain was dazzling; the light glowed like amber torchlight. Ehlona looked into his blue eyes. Heironomus had a strong, muscular, rugged body, but his smile was warm and gentle. Lifting her hand to touch his face, she leaned forward and kissed him.

"How can I ever thank you?" she whispered. "Thank you."

"I will see you tomorrow morning?"

She gave him a grin and a sly look. They both knew he slept in the nude and spent most of his mornings that way.

Lifting an eyebrow with a tilt of her head, she answered. "In the morning?"

Leaning forward, they kissed again.

With that, Heironomus walked toward his mossy bed. The sky now had turned from a deep red to a modest purple.

Ehlona watched him go as she continued to walk down the path by the brook. She loved the sound of running water over the rocks; it soothed her. With the time she had left, she neared the place where the villagers had erected a structure in honor of Ehlona: The Temple of Valor.

The Temple of Valor, with its mirrored ponds full of large fish, where large palms grew among green leafy plants and twisting vines wrapped around fluted marble columns extending up to the ceiling, supporting a round opening in the middle, letting in the air, moon, and stars. Here, in the Temple of Valor, priests called Acolytes dressed in white robes and healed those in need. Empowered by the blessings of Ehlona, the Acolytes moved quietly between sweet-smelling plumes of sandalwood incense that permeated the air, attending to the sick. Flowers adorned stone pedestals, placed there by her Acolytes.

Healing was her magic, her power. Her purpose was to mend the rift between day and night. Through an abundance of empathy and love, she bridged the gap between the twin brother gods, and the sick and the healthy. Upon seeing her enter the Temple of Valor, the Acolytes began singing, and musical strings rang out. Ehlona placed her lyre on the stone pedestal and listened with her eyes closed. The music pleased her. When she opened her eyes again, she looked down at the box Heironomus gave her. The pearls gleamed in a dark brilliance now that the sun had gone down.

"May you all be blessed," Ehlona spoke to the Acolytes. "Bless you all."

The Acolytes served as the core group responsible for the temple. They were composed of both women and men. Between them, they supported and operated the Temple of Valor with lovely precision. To follow her, the Acolytes must pledge to love her and all living things. The Acolytes worshiped and loved Ehlona and gave over their lives to follow her.

She turned away, and something to the east caught her eye. Standing in the darkness was a figure of a man silhouetted in the dark. Misty streams of sandalwood incense flowed around him; the only feature visible to her was one bloodshot eye.

Ehlona closed the pearl container. She knew it was Hexor; she could tell by his hateful eye. He had been a distant observer of her for years. But now he was back, and he watched her intently.

"Who is that hiding in the shadow of the temple's archway?" one newer Acolyte whispered to another.

"That's Hexor, the God of Night. Don't look at him. He is the most dangerous of them all."

"He stares at the goddess strangely."

"Give him no attention at all." The Acolyte continued folding linens. "He is a mystery and rarely allows anyone to see him. It is best if you avert your eyes."

The young Acolyte did as she was told, although she could not help the occasional glance.

"Hexor?" Ehlona called to him. "Is that the God of Darkness standing in my archway?"

He did not answer her. Standing in the circling smoke of sandalwood, he kept his distance and did not say a word. Hesitating momentarily, he turned to go. Soon he disappeared in the distance, swallowed up by the darkness—a darkness which was his home.

Ehlona stepped to the temple's archway and looked out upon the dark night. Hexor was gone, but her foot bumped into something. Looking down, she noticed that Hexor had dropped it. There, on the floor, was a folded piece of paper. She unfolded it and saw that Hexor had made a drawing containing nudity and a collage of carnal behaviors. She folded the note back as she found it.

"My lady, the darkness has come," an Acolyte with long, flowing, fair curls interrupted her thoughts. "It is time for your rest."

Ehlona thanked her and walked through her Acolytes until they fell prostrate on the ground as she passed. Ehlona looked over her shoulder, expecting to see Hexor still standing through the archway where she saw him last. But he was not there and was long gone.

She entered her private chamber. Her glow had now diminished. The darkness of the evening rested upon the Temple of Valor. Inside her chambers were many paintings and poetry she had created, and that others had given her. She was the Goddess of Art, Music, Poetry, and the finer things that color the lives of gods and mortals alike.

She slipped out of her golden oak leaf belt, took off her circlet, and laid it on the table. She unstrapped her shoes before removing her long white robes. Female attendants of the Acolytes carefully, solemnly, took her garments away. Standing naked in the candle-light, she reached for an emerald robe to cover her.

She lay on a stuffed couch, long and soft. Before she could get comfortable, though, she realized she had left the pearl box Heironomus gave her by the lyre on the stone pedestal. She lifted herself from the couch when she realized she still held the drawing on the folded paper. *Strange,* she thought, that she would leave the pearls and keep the drawing. Alone in her chambers, she rested back into the soft pillows of her couch. She slowly unfolded the paper and looked at his drawing again. *Why don't I know him better?* she thought. As crude as the drawing was, it did not diminish the mystery to her. Hexor presented something sensual, something dangerous. Ehlona knew he had a large following of his own. Much like Heironomus and much like herself.

She wondered what Hexor was up to, because she knew nothing about him. Hexor was Ehlona's fellow god, but they knew him to be troublesome. He was one to be handled with an abundance of caution; he was dangerous. The meaning of the note was obvious.

Is that what he does out there in the darkness?

"I might fall to pieces tomorrow.
Would you still be around?
Or I might decide to climb that mountaintop tonight.
And if I do, I'm never planning on ever coming down."

Excerpt from *The Witch's Songbook*

THE DRAGONBREATH MOUNTAIN

THE GRAY MOUNTAINS IN THE YEAR 1040-1041 HRT

From the moment he left Jorleston, Almon felt eyes upon him, even though no one gave him a second glance; still, it was a feeling he could not shake.

The way to the Last Outpost of the East comprised a gentle rise from the Endless Sea. Almon walked north all day in the wilderness without incident. He found a little clearing in the trees beside a small creek; he made his camp there for the night. The time spent with his father on their hunting trips in the Mid-Run Valley prepared him well for sleeping out in the bush. Almon had never seen the Gray Mountains before. Their misty heights provided beautiful, breathtaking views. He had a growing sense of excitement that soon he would be up in those heights.

The ghost did not appear to him anymore after leaving the *Forerunner.* The oppressive feeling he had in Jorleston had faded and been replaced by a sense of adventure.

He reached the Last Outpost of the East, which was nothing but a barren old shed abandoned long ago. Almon heard it used to be a bustling center of trade. Now, it was just a rundown wooden structure, leaning severely and in need of repairs that would not be forthcoming.

It was a day trip from the Last Outpost of the East to the ruins of the Temple of Chen-Li. The structure was magnificent, with its marble columns long toppled over, and massively cracked walls. But as awe-inspiring as the temple was, this was not his goal. He took a long last look at the ruins, then continued toward the Dragonbreath Mountain that towered in the background.

Upon reaching the top of the first of the Fangs, he put his hands on his knees and let out a loud groan. It was the first of several peaks, one of the smaller ones, and it was harder to climb than he thought it would be. Peering over the steep edge, he could see the drop already hundreds of feet below. He gave a long whistle.

"That's a long way down."

One thought kept running through his mind. *Am I good enough to be doing this?* He was having his doubts. But up here on top of the first summit, the view was incredible. He faced back to the west to reflect upon where he came from in equal portions of accomplishment and amazement. He could see the ruins of the Temple of Chen-Li, the Last Outpost to the East, and the foothills of the Mid-Run Valley. He turned back to look ahead of him; the Gray Mountains stretched out for miles. The Fangs rose like giant teeth slanting up from the limestone rock. At the edge of the eastern horizon lay his destination, the massive Dragonbreath Mountain, standing high above all the other peaks. Just like in the visions.

Almon had heard the legends. They said that a dragon slept on the summit. They said the ever-persistent cloud coverage was steam coming from a sleeping dragon's nostrils. Almon, of course, thought that was nonsense. There had never been any proof of real dragons. But one thing he believed for sure: The Dragonbreath Mountain was unforgiving and did not give away its secrets cheaply. It was the place to find death, dragon or not.

He continued climbing. This high on the mountain there was no vegetation; nothing grew here at all, nothing could survive for long. It was a gray world of rocks, wind, and ice, with vast empty spaces around him. Since he left the Temple of Chen-Li, he had been following the goat trails weaving broadly on the high broken ledges; now, not even those remained.

He climbed freestyle into evening. When it came time to sleep, he produced a hammock from his pack. Attaching the ropes to the sheer rock face by way of rock screws, then his safety harness to the ropes, he settled in.

"Only a fool tempts the dragon," he mocked and relaxed back into the hammock. Reaching into his jacket, he took an inventory of the scant food he had, consisting mostly of hard biscuits, called hardtack, and salted dried beef. He took out a piece of hardtack and gnawed on it. Afterward, he was still hungry, but he was too tired to think about it. Lying back in his hammock, he rested his eyes.

He was just fading off to sleep when the ghost appeared. It looked over the edge from the ledge above. For the first time, the ghost revealed its face, and it was a face Almon had never seen before. It was an old man with pale, blistered skin and a long gray beard. Its eyelids were stitched together with thick interlacing leather thongs pulled tightly together. Even with these terrible mutilations to his eyes, somehow, he still watched Almon.

The ghost tried to speak, wiggling in a struggle with his mouth under his beard. Finally, in a terrible motion, he ripped his mouth open. The leather thongs that had long secured his mouth from the inside now dangled free from his lips. His mouth now opened as wide as it could stretch, and the spirit released a silent scream. Black fluid gushed out of its mouth in the billowing winds. Agony disfigured its hideous face. He made no sound; nothing came out but blood. Then the old man took a long deep breath, and a single sound came out.

"KILMER!" the ghost screamed and pointed at Almon.

Almon froze in terror. There in the hammock he had no place to run. Unsure if this was a dream or reality, consumed with hopelessness, he was forced to look upon the agonized spirit.

The ghost's scream went on, echoing for a long time across the hills. The scream eventually trailed off, and silence returned to the canyon. The ghost took another deep breath, and Almon expected the worst. But then the ghost stood, turned, and walked out of Almon's view. This time, there were no visions.

Almon trembled, his eyes welling up. Although the ghost bore no resemblance to his father, memories of Erland and his sudden death in the Mid-Run Valley filled his mind. He remembered the details of that day, just before the sunset, like wrapping his father in linens and laying him low in the grave. He recalled shoveling the dirt over his father's shrouded body. But before doing any of this, he had sewn his father's eyes together with leather thongs; and likewise stitched his mouth shut as well. Only he knew about these preparations. But the ghost seemed to know as well, as if it were revealing his mind. This ghost was using the guilt of his father's death to torment him.

His grief became more than he could bear, and suddenly all he wanted to do was roll out of the hammock and plummet down the slope. He reached up and disconnected the safety clip. Pulling out his knife, he had the intent of cutting the bindings holding the hammock to the ledge. Placing his blade against the taunt rope, he took a deep breath, preparing to make the cut.

Yet he hesitated, for at that moment, another, more unexpected, event happened. A cloud of glowing orbs, like fireflies, burst over the ledge above. The glowing orbs came upon him like a swarm of wasps. Hundreds of them charged at him flying at incredible speeds. Like a cyclone, they encircled him, spiraling fast enough to create a vacuum, a cushion of air, that pinned him against the rock wall. In the whirlwind, he shielded his eyes from debris.

They are going to kill me! Almon thought. But they did not harm him.

They continued spinning around until he re-attached the safety clip back to the rope. Then, just as suddenly as they had pressed him, the pressure ceased. The glowing orbs decelerated, dispersing to float in the great expanse before him. Yet they did not leave. They remained with him throughout the rest of the climb. He watched them in fascination.

Are these the Timmutes? he wondered. If he was not mistaken, the glowing orbs demonstrated a collective intelligence and frightening abilities. He tried to catch one, but there were too many of them to focus on any individual one. Plus, they were very fast, too fast to capture.

Accompanied by the swarm of golden orbs, he finally reached the base of the highest peak: the Dragonbreath Mountain itself. He had made his way through the Fangs. Very few had ever made it this far. Here he found the bones of goats, rams, snakes, and other animals scattered about, but also a human skull. The more he looked for human remains, the more he saw.

He looked up at the heights of the Dragonbreath. Touching the cold stone with his bare hand, he took a long breath. His forehead rested for a moment on the smooth, unforgiving surface. The mountain ascended straight up until it penetrated the cloud obscuring its summit.

He found a good foothold, then started up the side. It was not long after he started that he abruptly halted again.

"Another skeleton," he said to himself, seeing more bones.

They were human bones crumpled facedown along the path. He imagined them as a living person, full of life, with hopes and dreams of their own, someone who was once loved in life, and now only remembered in death and memory. What might their fate have been? Had they reached the summit? Their secrets remained forever silent among the dead who had never returned alive to tell their tale.

It's bad luck to dwell over the dead. He suddenly remembered Captain Fortosa's words, and Almon was oddly thankful for them.

Keep moving, Almon. Don't stop here; keep moving, he encouraged himself.

He kept moving, kept climbing. Soon the bones were far below him, but it was not the last of them. He found his path littered with more remains, former brave souls, unknowns, those who died trying. He climbed past them all with no more thought.

Every step, every breath, was painful and labored. He was higher on the mountain now. Breathing became more difficult. The higher he climbed, the more he felt that he was about to pass out.

The golden orbs gathered to him once again, circling him, growing in number. They were swarming him again. He felt a cushion of air lifting him. He had the feeling of floating, no longer climbing under his own power. After a blur, he reached the bottom of the perpetual cloud that enveloped the summit. He floated up into it.

Inside the cloud, visibility reduced to just what was in front of his face. But just being in the cloud filled him with energy. As his mind cleared, he realized he could breathe more easily with an ample amount of oxygen the closer he got to the summit. Could it be that the cloud was actually suppling him with fresh oxygen?

This is impossible, Almon thought. Yet as impossible as it seemed, he was climbing on his own now. The glowing orbs released him and flashed through the cloud like lightning. As his head cleared, for a moment he wondered if the legends could be true; maybe this was magic, maybe the dragon was real.

But that's crazy! He felt a rising panic in his chest. *Isn't it?*

With the increase in oxygen, his summit fever peaked. He knew he had to be close to the summit now. Even with the increase of air, every effort was exhausting. Tears welled in his eyes from the intense effort. Soon, the memories of his mother, father, the ghost, the pile of bones, the golden orbs, everything flashed through his mind, attempting to distract him. Still, he climbed.

Then his hand grasped a tree root, running snake-like up the mountain. But he had to have been mistaken; nothing grew this high. Yet there it was, twisting up the rocky heights like a vein. He touched the root to make sure he was not hallucinating. It emitted a strange vibration, a dull movement just under the surface, like an infant's kick inside an expectant mother. The higher he went, the more tree roots he discovered. They converged to become a single tree trunk. Thick, solid bark provided better handholds than the slick limestone, so he traversed laterally from the crumbling rock to the tree. Ignoring the dull thumps of movement underneath, he continued to climb. The tiny orbs of golden light circled him like angry wasps but caused him no harm.

As he climbed higher, he could see the tree had grown into the form of a woman, resembling a praying lady, arms outstretched, reaching up to the heavens, frozen, locked in eternal prayer. The more he looked at it, the more he marveled at its lifelike details.

It is the most beautiful thing I have ever seen, he thought.

The tree distracted him, so that when he reached the top, it surprised him. There was nothing left to climb. Carefully he stepped off the tree and onto the top of the smooth rock surface. He had made it to the top! He had reached the forbidden summit of the Dragonbreath Mountain. He was the first man to ever do it.

Taking a moment to catch his breath, he took his first steps at the top. He was breathing easier now. The summit was unexpectedly still and quiet. He perceived no movement other than the circling orbs. Taking advantage of the Praying Lady tree in his presence, he looked in its leaves for wind, but no wind blew here.

How strange, he thought. *Something is not right.*

He walked away from the edge of the abyss and away from the tree. Walking up a gentle rocky slope, he took his gloves off, letting them fall to the ground. He dropped his backpack, his ropes, and all the hardware hanging from him; they all crashed to the ground in a rolling metallic sound. He left it all where it fell. The golden orbs circled each item as they hit the ground.

He dropped his gear, feeling lighter and stronger all at once, and focused on the tiny orbs floating in golden light around him. He reached out again to catch one, but the fast little orbs avoided his grasp. He had the same feeling of being watched as he had back in Jorleston. He had not felt this in a long time, but now he expected the ghost to appear at any moment.

He walked through the mist, and much to his surprise, a dark blur started to take shape ahead. A square building came into his focus. The closer he got, he could determine that it was a little wooden cottage, a one-story structure with four corners and a slanted roof. It had no seams, no boards, no buckles, no nails or knots or fasteners. It seemed to be carved from a single piece of wood. Something like this would be difficult to do at sea level, but to attempt building it at this elevation was *impossible.* Or if it was not constructed on top of the mountain, then that meant it had been built below and carried up. But that was just as impossible.

Is this the magic of a dragon? he thought. *But why would a dragon need a little wooden cottage?*

The human-shaped tree, the miraculous cabin, the golden orbs, mysterious air supply—it all defied any reason, any logic, and all explanation. All but one. This was a place of the gods. The concept was beyond what Almon could imagine. But it made him tremble all the same.

He approached the little house, reminding himself to be careful. He was still on the tallest mountain in the world; he would not want to slip off now. When he turned to look behind him, the Praying Lady tree faded away in the distant gloom. He approached the cabin. It had a single door and a tiny window on the right side of it. Pressing his face to the dirty window, he peered inside. The view was dark and obscure. He could not make out a thing inside. He could only see his reflection and that of the orbs flying behind him in the glass.

Almon cleared his throat.

"Hello?" he called out, listening for any reply.

He thought he heard something, a noise coming from inside the cabin, but he could not tell what it was.

Cautiously, Almon opened the door and stepped in.

"Sometimes at night, when all the world is quiet,
I open my eyes to watch you sleep.
Somewhere in deep, familiar places.
You're everything I want you to be."

Excerpt from *The Witch's Songbook*

THE GRAND WEDDING

World-at-Large in the Year 800 HRT

The villagers decorated their homes with garlands, flying banners of gold and white flapped in the breeze. There were wreaths on doors, and flowers adorned their fence posts and wells. Bells rang out in the wind, and music filled the air. The farmers and villagers woke early with the sun, donning their best clothes and coming out in hordes to join in the carnival-like atmosphere. They came out to see a once-in-a-lifetime sight. For as long as they would live, no one would ever see an event like this: two gods joined in marriage.

"How splendid, look, Heironomus," Ehlona said, pointing to the houses in her view.

"Yes," Heironomus said, "the villagers have decorated their homes in celebration of us, Ehlona. They celebrate with us, on this special day of our Grand Wedding."

When Heironomus and Ehlona appeared together, the villagers dropped what they were doing to fall to their knees in worship of their gods as they passed. Just seeing Heironomus, just saying his name, would invoke his blessings upon the people. When the large, barrel-chested god gave his blessing of a long life, the recipients would live until a ripe old age.

"A healthy and long life for you!" Heironomus would greet them. These were Heironomus's people; he enjoyed being around them. He laughed when they fell to their knees. "Get up! Stand up! For you are all blessed; today is my wedding day!"

Heironomus made for a striking figure, with his hair combed back with scented oils and his dark red beard meticulously trimmed and straight. Gone were his usual garments of ram skin. For his wedding, he came adorned in a cape of thick white bearskin, a vest made from intertwined eagle feathers, and a golden crown made from jeweled elk horns decorated with berries and flowers. His shirt and pants, made of golden threads of silk, contrasted with his fiery red hair and beard. He walked confidently, full of light and infectious laughter, his personality shining with his legendary spark and enthusiasm.

The fair Goddess Ehlona smiled so vibrantly, beaming with natural beauty, her auburn hair as soft as silk and crystal-blue eyes sparkling bright. She appeared with white robes stretched across a perfectly feminine form. The pearls that Heironomus gave her draped around her neck. A crown of interwoven golden bands adorned her head, and a sheer veil of white lace cascaded down the crown of her head and over her face. With lace gloves gracing her hands, she held a bouquet of long-stemmed golden roses. When she passed, the fragrance of honeysuckle followed.

Horns blasted from the Church of the Illuminated. In the distance, far and wide, bells rang out from the hilltops, announcing that the ceremony was about to begin. Praises rose from the villagers to Heironomus and Ehlona, and the people cheered and rejoiced in their gods.

The bells and the horns eventually gave way to a symphony of stringed instruments. The two gods followed a trail of flowers, garlands, and banners, and arm in arm, they walked until the path narrowed, eventually ending in an archway of simple white lattice and flowers.

Two priests, a man from the Church of the Illuminated and a woman from the Temple of Valor, joined them under the arch. The two priests received the gods and presented them with gifts of gold, incense, wine, and flowers.

Heironomus and Ehlona took each other's hands to begin their wedding ceremony.

The priest representing the Church of the Illuminated lifted a torch over his head. Then he spoke these words:

"Heironomus, God of Light.
Heironomus, who rules over the day.
He who roams the bright and natural realm of the outdoors.
He who holds power over the forces of nature.
He who created all fruitful things.
He is the god of birth.
The god of creation.
From his mighty hands come the giant trees that shade the gentle running brooks, the mossy steps in the Great Mapes Forest, the lush grasslands of the Mid-Run Valley, and the spectacular stone risers of the Blue Mountains in the west that frame the setting sun. Heironomus who created the trees, the cool shade, and the gentle blowing wind.
He who created the cool moving waters, suitable for a drink and refreshing in its life-sustaining flow.

He made for us the oats that grow to harvest, the fruits, and the animals that bear milk, eggs, skins, and substance.
He provides the grains that make bread, baked in our stone hearths by human hands.
All the work of our God Heironomus, who created all that still exists today.
Just as he started them from the beginning.
All peaceful living creatures in this world are thankful to him for his being and his creations."

When the priest of the Church of the Illuminated finished, he stepped back and lit a golden candle. Then he passed the torch to the Acolyte of the Temple of Valor. She accepted the torch, smiled, and lifted it over her head. She then addressed them next.

"Oh, Great Ehlona,
Goddess of Beauty.
Who rules the sunsets and the sunrises.
She enlightens our mortal lives with the power of vivid colors, the arts, the painters, the writers, the musicians, and the sculptors.
You give us, and show us, the power of love.
Through love, you heal our afflictions.
Your beauty and appearance provide purpose in the birth of living things and understanding of death as renewal.
Ehlona, you represent the balance of all things.
She loves the music of the rolling river.
You who give us the sounds of the babbling brook, the

sound of water rolling over rocks.
You, who play the lyre and sing with a voice so sweet.
Then, there came the day when Heironomus, the God of Light, glowing bright with love for you,
Courting the Goddess of Beauty, asking her to marry him.
And Ehlona gave this reply.
She said yes.
May this glorious union bless this world equal to the heavens."

The Acolyte of the Temple of Valor lit a white candle. Then, together, both priests put the torch back in its holder. The priest of the Church of the Illuminated produced a horn, while the Temple of Valor's Acolyte pulled out a lyre. They played a beautiful tune together.

With the music playing from their priests, Ehlona smiled and sang directly to Heironomus:

"Ripples on the lake like time that slowly passes.
Sweet lips that taste like wine. Love finds my heart and crashes.
And your skin's so soft, lying next to mine.
You know that you warm my heart time after time.
A thousand debts,
A thousand lies,
A thousand words turn into
A thousand rhymes,
A thousand dreams."

Then it was Heironomus's turn, and joyfully he sang in a low baritone.

"So now, let us stop and ask.
Is it such a bad thing?
Look on your finger my love,
You wear my golden ring.
The candle's burning low,
All the wine is nearly gone.
The dress of white you wore,
The beauty of your song."

Then, they both sang in perfect harmony:

"A thousand debts, A thousand lies,
A thousand words turn into
A thousand rhymes.
A thousand dreams,
We're dreaming a thousand,
A thousand dreams."

The music faded away and a general cheer went up throughout the land.

"Oh, Ehlona, I love you even more than I love the world," Heironomus said, and they kissed longingly.

Heironomus turned and shouted, "It is done; we are married!"

The villagers, numbering in the thousands, applauded. Flowers exploded into the air. Bells rang and horns blew from miles around. From the Blue Mountains to the village of Rynholt, from the Great Mapes Forest to the Port Harbor, they celebrated the marriage of Ehlona and Heironomus.

In the years to follow, they spent their time celebrating their happiness together. They walked along waterfalls and relaxed in the cool shade, enjoying the company of each other. Heironomus showered Ehlona in gifts of silver and gold, brightly colored flowers, and sweet-smelling incense. The two lay together during the bright light of day. In the morning, they would wash clean with the fresh rain, warm and gentle upon their skin. They walked past the streams and trees and boulders, enjoying each other's companionship.

In those days, the sky was white. But, as Ehlona's gift to her husband, she colored it blue for him, and for the rest of time the world would see it as such.

To Ehlona, Heironomus gave the Blue Mountains, whose high summit peaks were now hers to paint at every twilight in vivid colors. The Blue Mountains were all but complete except for a small narrow pass the mortals called the Mauveguard Pass. Heironomus pledged to get back to finishing them after the wedding.

But he never got that chance.

"Shine a light into a darkened place.
Illuminate the colors of your face.
Walk me down the steps of the staircase
Into my room of long-forgotten waste."

Excerpt from *The Witch's Songbook*

THE SUPREME HISTORIAN

THE DRAGONBREATH SUMMIT IN THE YEAR 1041 HRT

Almon opened the door and the golden orbs funneled in. The dust shifted inside, producing streaming light from the opposite window. The room had papers stacked in corners, leaning in high piles, lying in crumpled rolls, and littering the floor. But the most immediate concern was a dead body propped in a wooden rocking chair by the large window. The corpse had its head wrapped in linen bandages. Almon nervously scanned the rest of the space. A table sat on the right, and a wooden bench on the left, but the dead body was his first concern for the moment.

He stepped lightly; still the floorboards creaked under his feet. The glowing orbs darted in the distance between him and the body in the chair. He left the door open behind him as he walked deeper inside. Keeping a steady gaze upon the body sitting in the chair, he got closer. A thin layer of dust covered it. He detected no foul smell, no smell of death, yet the air possessed an overbearing heaviness. Then a soft voice spoke out.

"Oh, there you are." The arm of the body dropped to the wooden chair, resulting in a cloud of dust. "I've been waiting for you."

Almon fell to the floor, crawling backward, kicking over piles of papers, anything to get away from the reanimated dead man.

The body in the chair started moving. It lifted its arms, unwrapping the linens around its head. With each turn, the linens loosened, falling into his lap, and Almon could tell it was an old man. Now free of the bandages around his head, he turned in Almon's direction with an audible crackle of long stiff bones. His eyes met Almon's. They were the most brilliant blue, radiating with alertness. His skin had stained beyond gray, blackened from dirt, dust, and grime. Yet there was something reassuring about his impossibly blue eyes.

Almon had seen his face before.

He was the ghost from his visions.

"You! I thought you were dead, but you're not dead. You're not dead, are you?"

"No, I am not dead. I never have been," the old man said. "And any rumors of my demise were ill-founded."

"Who are you?" Almon asked.

"Well, I'll be. You mean you've come all this way up here, and—" The old man seemed flustered. "I've waited all this time, and you don't even know who I am? Well, I'm Aberfell!"

"Aberfell?" Almon looked in shock at the old man. "You mean the *real* Aberfell?"

"One in the same. Who were you looking for?"

"I-I wasn't looking for anyone," Almon stuttered. "Ghosts, dragons maybe?"

"Dragons?" Aberfell rolled his eyes. "Yes, of course. No dragons here, sorry."

Almon had heard of Aberfell, but that was a long time ago. Aberfell's legend started when he was just a baby, born under the sign of a blue comet, the arrival of which was foretold by the Star Prophets in a book called *The Constellation Volume.* They predicted that he would become the Supreme Historian, the boy who could never forget. Put simply, he would be able to remember everything. But the history books said he lived a long time ago. So long ago, in fact, that Almon had no idea how old the man must be. Certainly he could not be the real Aberfell, not the Aberfell from the old legends.

But still, here he was at the top of the world. Almon needed to exercise caution until he could figure out what was happening here. He watched the man get to his feet.

Aberfell slowly stood up with a series of snaps from old bones. "I suppose congratulations are in order on your summit of the Dragonbreath Mountain. Quite an accomplishment. You are now the second person to get to the top of this mountain, second of course to me, and about ten million Timmutes. But don't worry, I won't tell anyone. No, you can claim the title of being first. I am famous enough already, and the Timmutes don't care about such things."

Almon looked confused. "The Timmutes?"

"Yes, the Timmutes," Aberfell said, holding out his hands, motioning to the tiny golden orbs. "They have been taking care of me for a long time now. But be careful around them; they are a dangerous sort. They can be rather possessive. So, if you are here to end me, they might have something to say about that."

"I'm not here to end anyone," Almon said. "I mean you no harm."

"They never would have let you get this far if you did not have the right intentions. Somehow, they know; they always know."

Almon, absent-minded, looked around. "I didn't expect to find anybody living on top of the tallest mountain in the world."

"I have been on top of this mountain for, well, two hundred years, by now. I should be the oldest man in the world. I am 255 years old. Have you ever heard of anyone older?"

"No, not even close."

"Well, I have." Aberfell laughed. "There are much older. But I am, perhaps, the oldest person in the world. Some are older, but they are not persons; they are gods. I think they are still around somewhere."

Aberfell considered Almon for a moment. "And who did you say you were?"

"Almon. Almon Plum-Kilmer."

"Almon Plum-Kilmer. A Kilmer, eh? Remarkable." Aberfell stared at Almon for a long minute, then said, "Yes, I can see the resemblance. You can get off the floor now."

"I can't believe you are the real Aberfell," he said, standing up.

"Tell me, Almon, do they still talk about me down there, down below?"

Almon cleared his throat. "You were a legend, with a—a pretty public life. I can't believe it, the real Aberfell?"

Aberfell nodded. "I was the only human being in the world who was ever born, who would ever be born, to never forget. I remember everything. Did you know, I lack the capacity of the fading memory?"

"It's legendary."

"Legendary, bah! It is nothing of the sort. It is not a talent; it was just a defect I was born with. Do you have any idea what it is like not to be able to forget? Of course, you don't, but it is a horrible ability to have. The world is so full of bad people doing bad things. It is all so unfortunate and depressing. You don't know how fortunate you are to be able to forget. I wish I could. I stay here in this little cottage, removed from the world. I wrap these linens around my head, around my eyes, my ears, and nose, so I experience nothing new as to add to my backlogged memory. Can you understand?"

Almon stood staring at him.

Aberfell straightened. "Forgive my manners! You must be hungry and thirsty, after all that exertion of climbing. For heaven's sake, are you injured?"

Aberfell motioned with a sweep of his hand, and a bowl of fresh fruit glided to Almon from a cabinet, floating in the air, as if carried by invisible hands. A glass of milk floated to him in the same way. Then, a loaf of bread followed, gently touching down on a floating cutting board in mid-flight, on its way to Almon. A knife and butter soon sailed to him, along with towels, some fresh linens, and an alabaster jar of ointment used to care for any cuts or bruises.

As the trays and items neared closer to him, he scaled up the little wooden bench in reverse until the wall of the cabin prevented him from retreating any further. Then he backpedaled, scuffing the floor with the heels of his boots. Loose papers went flying around the room as he tried to get away. All the floating items, the bowl of fruit, the glass of milk, the cutting board and bread, the towels, the linens, and the ointment came to rest beside him on the bench. Then they were still and moved no more.

"What is happening?" Almon stared wide-eyed. "There are spirits here."

Aberfell saw the worry in Almon's face. "No, not spirits, Timmutes. Those are the Timmutes. Eat. The fruit is fresh."

"What are these Timmutes?"

"I will be glad to tell you, but first, eat." Aberfell watched as Almon slowly turned his attention from the Timmutes to the food. He cautiously poked at some of the fruit in the bowl. Then he poked the bowl itself.

"How can this be?" Almon asked.

Aberfell continued without looking at Almon.

"I might be old, but not even age can dull my memory. The gods made me the way I am. They gave me a memory that writes in indelible ink. It's my destiny, and now it is yours too."

Almon gave him a sideways glance. "I am a part of your destiny?"

"I have waited so long for somebody to find me here so I could impart what I have stored up here in my memory. I thought it would be sooner. Didn't know it would take so long. But I do not decide those things. So, I sat here waiting for you, and now here you are. The strawberries are fresh, try one."

"You have been waiting to impart your memories?" Almon bit into a fresh strawberry. "Why?"

"Why? Because I knew your forefather, the original Kilmer. But more than just knew him, he and I were friends. Tell me, do ghosts haunt you too?"

Almon quit chewing. "It was a ghost that led me here."

Aberfell smiled. "Kilmer spoke with ghosts too. What is it like for you?"

Almon swallowed hard and paused for a moment. "I have seen your face before, Aberfell. It was you that came to me on the mountain. You were the one that led me here. You, are my ghost."

"Remarkable. The gift manifests differently in each of you Kilmer's. A past ghost haunted the first Kilmer, and a future one haunts you. I say future ghost, considering how I am not dead yet. How else would this ghost appear to you in my form? I'm sorry but your ghost is most interesting and makes me wonder what it could mean. But first things first. What do you know about the Provenance?"

"The Provenance?" Almon asked. "I never heard of it."

"It's the beginning of things, their origin. You must know the Provenance to have confidence that what I tell you is true, and for the other things to make sense to you."

Almon nodded, then shook his head in confusion.

"You know," Aberfell noticed his confusion, "the Provenance!"

"Yes of course," Almon acknowledged. "The Provenance."

"Now, you asked me about the Timmutes. Exceptional question! It's a great place to start, but I cannot just tell you about the Timmutes, because you would not understand it yet. To understand them, I must start at the beginning of the story. And then when you understand that you will understand the nature of all, including the Timmutes. Everything!

"Now, are you ready?"

"I turned my head, and my halo slipped.
And the wings I bought, well, they didn't really fit.
The bones I broke, and the blood I spit,
Never meant a thing. Just walk on water."

Excerpt from *The Witch's Songbook*

THE GREAT NEGATION

World-at-Large in the Year 800 HRT

As long as Hexor was lord of darkness, and Heironomus the lord of light, it was inevitable that all the things the brothers created, all whom they blessed, were despised by the other. Hexor had heard about the Grand Wedding between Heironomus and Ehlona; he would deal with them later. For now, he was more interested in achieving the balance for what had been done at the grassroots level. Hexor knew Heironomus had blessed a few of the peasant farmers with long life. Here, he would begin to set the balance straight. This would be the first place Hexor would apply his scorn. He wanted to stick a dagger into the hearts of the people, to give them what they deserved.

Deploying the Cult of Horrors to locate each one of the peasant farmers, Hexor began to orchestrate his vengeance. He waited until night, when he was at his strongest. Then, he paid a visit to each one of them. Approaching their houses in the darkness, he watched them through their windows with a fiery eye. They took comfort in the place where they thought they were the safest, the confines of their warm little homes.

"There are no safe places from the icy breath of the lord of darkness," he said, breathing heavily, fogging the glass.

The farmers and their families had lived such trouble-free lives to this point. Every minute he watched them, he seethed in anger for the ways of his twin. They were happy and carefree, blessed by their gods, but that was about to change. They were about to see another side of the divine.

"Kneel to my brother, will you? A curse upon your family."

He invoked his curse with a simple flourish of his hands, producing a dim yellow light that flashed against all people he could see, except for the blessed peasant farmer himself. At that precise moment, the farmer's wife and child broke out in fevers that would worsen before morning.

"They will not live out the month," Hexor said grimly. He watched them a bit longer, then turned to go.

After the curse, the condition of the man's wife and child worsened, becoming deathly sick. Just as Hexor predicted, they died before the month was out. With his spirit crushed, the farmer would keep the blessing of long life, but would have to bury his wife and child. And thus Heironomus's blessing of a long-extended life would become a curse of loneliness and remorse would mark the rest of his long days.

It did not amuse Hexor, but the balance had to be restored. He was the only one who understood and respected the process. Granting extended life denied a life force from returning to the Cosmic Creation, which would receive its fabric back as scheduled through fate. Cursing the family righted the balance, returning a couple of smaller souls early for the one taken away by his brother for extending it. He was providing a service, adhering to the true purpose of the Cosmic Creation, to which the gods were bound. For that, Hexor considered himself the best of all the gods.

As far as the Cosmic Creation mattered—and *that was all that mattered,* Hexor thought—he considered himself good, and Heironomus the willfully evil one.

Mounds of fresh dirt sprung up in increasing numbers as fresh graves were dug. In the cemeteries, new tombstones went up almost daily at an alarming rate. Just a few years ago the farmers had been so happy to receive Heironomus's blessings of long life; now they somberly walked away from new graves, bitter and saddened. They found no solace in the blessing of long life, nor did they worship the day anymore. Darkness obscured them. Tears of grief rained over their lives.

Satisfied with the results of his curse, it was now time for Hexor to turn his attention to the real issue at hand. *What to do with the God Heironomus and the Goddess Ehlona*? It was the only thing left on Hexor's mind. He walked away from the villages and the farmers and descended into his underground labyrinth to think.

Standing looking over the bubbling hole steaming below him, he searched deeply under its surface. He channeled the events of late, concentrating on what he might have missed. Soon his hateful eye revealed visions to him.

They have blinded themselves with each other. They no longer see me as a threat.

The marriage of Heironomus and Ehlona went on blissfully for years. Eventually it came to pass that Heironomus and Ehlona were to have a child. Heironomus was delighted that she was pregnant, and Ehlona thought optimistically that their best days were still before them.

But one day soon after their pregnancy was revealed, as Heironomus and Ehlona were walking together on a forest trail, they passed Hexor sitting on a rock, and he mocked them as they walked by.

"A curse upon your children," Hexor said with a hiss.

"Today is a beautiful day, brother," Heironomus said. "Too beautiful to have you to spoil with your wagging, lying tongue."

"You watch the day, Great Heironomus? When you have the Goddess of Beauty by your side? Why, I would rather damn the morning to frogs and rats, and even curse the night to maggots and lice, just to hold Ehlona's hand. I would consider all the treasures of this world as nothing more than mere perishable waste, just to look upon her beauty for a single hour."

Ehlona was flattered by Hexor's words. She had not seen him in years, and the more she heard his voice, the more she remembered a strange feeling. It was a calling of purpose for her. After all, she was created to provide beauty for both the day and night. But lately she had been focusing solely on her husband. She had forgotten about the God of Darkness and how much more she wanted to learn about him at one time in the past.

"Leave us. You are wasting your breath, Hexor. The Goddess Ehlona has no interest in you."

"I do not need you to remind me of that, Heironomus. The Goddess Ehlona knows no pleasures except for the soft mossy dungeon you have imprisoned her in. Ehlona, where has your freedom gone? Is it that your beauty became so dull to your husband that he has doused your beautiful light to brighten his own? You appear not a goddess, but a possession. But what about your desires, Ehlona? Have you forgotten?"

Hexor was spinning his words as skillfully as if he were casting a spell. Ehlona was immune to spells, blessings, and curses of the other gods, but she listened with interest to his words. The look in his eyes, those mysterious, strange eyes, reached deep within her.

Heironomus looked at both of them, trying hard not to lose his temper. Hexor refused to acknowledge his brother. Instead, he continued to speak directly to Ehlona.

"It doesn't bother you to be separated from your world of pretty colors, music, and art? Freedom is your weakness. Are you too weak, afraid to be free? You have been imprisoned, trapped for all time to listen for your master's call. Do you wait for a voice to possess you? Are you satisfied in your new purpose? To have someone to crawl to. Any one of my base vipers can do that."

Heironomus moved toward Hexor, but Ehlona touched his arm to stop him. "Don't. He's not worth it."

"You, Ehlona, are a goddess," Hexor said. "You need to act like one, but instead of a goddess, you are merely a wife."

Ehlona recoiled from his hurtful words. There was no more powerful spell than the truth; and the truth was that while her life had changed drastically after the wedding, Heironomus continued with his life as before. All the changes, all the sacrifice, had been hers to endure. Hexor was right to point out that Ehlona regretted giving up her independence. After all, her true purpose was to distinguish the day from the night. Maybe she had made a mistake, taking a husband of one god.

Before he took his leave, Hexor turned and added, "I think it is unfair that the world calls me the God of Destruction."

He finally made eye contact with his brother, and as he walked away, the day gave way to darkness.

Hexor's words continued to haunt her after that. Ehlona could not sleep. Her mind was worried, and her thoughts were restless. She had doubts, knowing a child would trap her even more.

With a worried mind, she slipped out of her soft, mossy bed. The sky darkened in the east, but to the west it was still light. It was during this dusky time when Ehlona's power was at its prime. As she walked along her way, she heard someone calling her name. The voice that called her traveled on the wind, and she followed. A double row of thick candles lined the way in soft golden lights along the rocks of the brook. She followed the melting candles to an outcropping of sharp rocks.

There she saw Hexor standing silhouetted in darkness. Behind him hundreds of black crows looked on perfectly still, and his hateful eye glowed red, following her, watching her. Something inside of her heart simmered as she approached him. After all these years, she had never been this close to him before. Hexor extended his hand to her. She started to reach for his, but then hesitated.

"Be the goddess you were meant to be," Hexor told her. Touching his hand, she found it set a fire ablaze inside her. He took her in his arms, and they embraced in a kiss, falling upon the rocks.

Soon, the fire that boiled inside her burst forth, manifesting all around them in a raging inferno, under the blood-red moon, they touched, surrounded by rolling, licking flames.

Not far away to the west, it was still light, and Heironomus startled to see deer running past him. He turned to see where the deer came from and saw flames. Soon, other animals were rushing past him. Alarmed by the fire, he rushed to extinguish it.

Initially confused when he came into the clearing and saw them, they continued to please each other despite his presence. The stone's sharp edges pierced Ehlona's skin, causing her blood to flow into the ground. In her satisfaction, she turned and saw her husband. All she could do was smile, as if unaware of what they were doing would have any effect upon him.

"Look, here comes my brother," Hexor said, now focusing his hateful eye upon his twin brother. Still in her arms, he clenched his teeth in a wide smile, and whispered in her ear. "He only desires to extinguish your fire."

Heironomus stood in the flames of Ehlona's passion. The fire reflected red-hot in his pupils. His face turned to a fiery scarlet. He let out a scream that bent the trees, throwing himself upon Hexor's neck, scattering the hundreds of crows. Heironomus wrapped his massive hands around Hexor's throat. Hexor reached up, sticking his thumbs in Heironomus's eyes to gouge them out.

The collision was violent, and Ehlona was knocked backward, tumbling through the trees. The two brothers viciously attacked each other. Their combat flashed in a bright crackle of lightning. As they struggled to kill the other, they toppled over and levitated off the ground. They tumbled and rolled in conflict, lifting higher and higher into the sky. They rose higher, towering over the mountains, and sparkled brighter until they shined like the sun. Unaware they were leaving the world, they continued to slash at each other in vain, one unable to defeat the other. They continued to rise to a height far above, deep into blue sky—until, at last, the battle flashed a final burst of lightning.

And then the gods disappeared.

ACT II

The Witch, Timmutes, & Castles in the Sky

"Lately, I've been careful what I do

You see, I've been around a time or two

You never would've believed all the things that I've been through

Maybe I've been lucky, maybe I've been a fool.

Remember, gods are watching over both of you."

Excerpt from *The Witch's Songbook*

THE COSMIC CREATION

THE DRAGONBREATH MOUNTAIN—THE FIRST 800 YEARS AFTER THE GREAT COOLING (AGC)

Aberfell paused for a moment. He sat in a chair by the big bay window, whittling at a small piece of wood with a little knife. As the wood chips fell, the Timmutes promptly whisked them away. Almon watched him for a moment, expecting the old man to continue, but he had stopped talking. Finally, Almon broke the silence.

"Where did they go?"

"When you must go, use the leaves outside the door. Just kick them over the edge, when finished. The Timmutes will replace them."

Almon grimaced. It was good information to know, but not what he was asking. The golden orbs of the Timmutes carried on with their duties inside the cottage. Almon considered them for a moment before returning his gaze to the old man.

"The stories you've been telling me, the beginning of the world, the Twin Gods, Heironomus, Hexor, the Goddess Ehlona, all of it. You told me about the Grand Wedding. Then, the Twin Gods began fighting, in the Great Negation. You said they disappeared. Where did they go?"

Aberfell laughed. “Oh! Where did they go? I thought you asked about something else. I’ve become a little hard of hearing over two hundred years.”

Aberfell chuckled and continued to carve.

“But seriously, kick it over the edge,” he added without looking at Almon.

“I will be sure to,” Almon responded.

“Now, you asked me about Heironomus and Hexor, the Twin Gods. Yes, I said they disappeared, and disappear they did. You asked, where did they go? Now, that is the question, isn’t it? Well, their attack disrupted the powers that be. Their direct battle invoked a recalling of their powers, back to where they came from, the Cosmic Creation.”

Almon stared at Aberfell for a while. “I don’t know what that means.”

Aberfell stopped whittling and put his hands in his lap, looking solemn. “This is perhaps the most sensitive information I know. Information passed on from the unlikeliest of sources.”

“You’re hesitating. Why?”

“I’ve never told anyone this information before. I’m not even sure what will happen if I do.”

“What is the problem?” Almon asked him.

“They were stories told to others that made their way to me. Stories from the other world.”

“Your unlikely sources.” Almon got a chill. “Ghosts?”

“Yes, ghosts of course, and demons too. Unseen forces, the bridges between our worlds.”

Aberfell thought for a moment, then whistled. “Maybe it is best if you leave now. You already have quite a few stories of the Provenance and the gods. Maybe we should be satisfied with that and stop here.”

“You said you would tell me about the Timmutes.”

"Um, them?" Aberfell looked around at the golden orbs impatiently. "Oh, a witch created them. There, now you know."

Aberfell's old bones crackled as he rose, extending his arm in hospitality. "I'll walk you out, and the Timmutes will help you down."

"Wait, now," Almon said, objecting. "What are you afraid of?"

Aberfell sighed. "I have volumes of information saved in my mind, and I don't mind passing it on. But this type of information, derived from ghosts and demons, well, that's getting into a nasty sort of business. Almon, it could have unintended consequences. It's dangerous—too dangerous."

"How can that be?"

"Some information is not even supposed to be known, let alone passed on to others. Especially for us mortals. We are dealing with knowledge about a subject, that… Well, they know when they are being observed, and if you get a good enough look, they might take offense to you being the observer. They do not like being observed or talked about very much. They can see us and hear us. That's the problem."

Almon looked at Aberfell seriously for a moment, then burst out laughing. "You want me to believe that if we talk about ghosts, they will hear us and take offense?"

Aberfell dropped his arms and cocked his head. "You, all of people, should know better as a Plum-Kilmer. The ghosts of your fathers are all around you."

Almon stopped laughing. Looking at his feet, he shook his head. "No, I can't do it."

Aberfell squinted at him. "What do you mean, you can't do it?"

"I can't leave," Almon said, looking at Aberfell. "Not when I know I am so close. There are so many things yet to learn, especially about this subject: The spirits of the dead. So, please. I want to know. I need to know. Tell me."

But Aberfell remained unconvinced.

Almon lifted his ring. "This is the ring of the House of Erland; it is the Plum-Kilmer family crest. Over two hundred years of history living with ghosts in the family line. You said it yourself, they have haunted us for generations. No one ever spoke of it because no one ever understood it. Or they were just too afraid to talk about it, like you are. So, instead of learning, they just experienced it. I could be the first in the Plum-Kilmer family to actually understand it."

"Understanding may cost you dearly, Almon."

"I don't care what it costs."

Aberfell sighed heavily once again. Sitting back down in his chair, he placed his hand over his mouth. At last, he nodded and picked up his whittling knife once again.

"Very well, young Plum-Kilmer. I will relay the information that I, myself, received secondhand. Information that was never intended for mortal man to pass on. Information that was told to others, then told to me, by entities not of this world."

Aberfell began sculpting again. "Just don't say I didn't warn you."

"Go on," Almon encouraged him.

"Since the beginning of time, the fabric of all things between this world and the next exists to serve what is known as the Cosmic Creation. Like the stars themselves, the Cosmic Creation has no emotion, no personality, no morality. We cannot consider it to be good or evil but wholly balanced on the neutrality of its own survival.

"When we are born, the Cosmic Creation is self-evident to us at the time of our birth. It molds us, designs us, determines whether we are male or female, healthy or unhealthy, if our eyes are blue or green, if our hair is red or blonde. On the pure mechanics of randomness, the gears spin like a giant gambling wheel in the sky, and they decide what we are with all the chance of inherent arbitrariness. Before we are born, our lives are blessed or cursed. We come into this world regardless, with no say in the matter. In return, we carry ourselves as the primary observers to the design. With all the things we learn, the memory of the Cosmic Creation gets pushed out of the minds of men. Most minds except mine.

"At the time of our deaths, the Cosmic Creation is equally self-evident. When we die, we return to where we came. Our bodies stay and decay, but the energy of our souls returns for recycling. Occasionally, this energy gets lost; it gets blessed or cursed and cannot, or will not, stay crossed over; these are your ghosts, Almon. But for most, the Cosmic Creation serves as the place our spirits go once our time in this world ends. To us mortals, it is a terrible thing to lose somebody we love, but to the Cosmic Creation it is a good thing, a reuniting of one part with the whole.

"In short, it is from the Cosmic Creation we come, and it is to the Cosmic Creation we go. In between our comings and goings are life and death. The Cosmic Creation can only influence the lives of human beings in sporadic cases, times when the gulf between the two worlds can be bridged or breached. A great expanse exists dividing life and death, renewal and recycle, and it is a great expanse that divides the Cosmic Creation from this world. An expanse that cannot be spanned by ordinary men, aside from two specific times, by birth and death.

"However, there are some unique ways that the Cosmic Creation can be breached.

"One way is through interdimensional beings, such as gods or demons, sent from the Cosmic Creation. These beings have immense power and can traverse the gap between the Cosmic Creation and this world.

"Man can breach this gap too, but only in spiritual forms: ghosts or spirits. These are the unhappy souls of humanity that are lost, existing dimly in both worlds but entirely in neither.

"All the gods, demons, spirits, and ghosts work in ways that are unpredictable and sometimes incomprehensible to mortal man. Occasionally, a man like me comes along who is none of these things. Leopold was like this for his extraordinary willpower. Valen for her healing. And your forefather, Kilmer himself, for your family's sensitivity to spirits. That is why it is so dangerous."

"Do you have a connection to the Cosmic Creation? Do you know what it looks like?"

Aberfell shrugged. "I do not. A vast chasm exists between our two worlds. But I can tell you this: I was born the boy who cannot forget. I did not make myself that way. The Cosmic Creation made me like I am. The purpose of having an unfailing memory was neither for good nor bad, but to serve humanity, as I have served as the Supreme Historian. It was the reason for which it purposed me."

"Purposed to remember our stories," Almon said. "And pass them on?"

"I suppose there is no purpose in the creation if there is no one to observe it," Aberfell said. "My purpose is to make sure humanity remembers. That is why I came along. That is why I had this power never to forget. Our observations of the Provenance are what our current generation has long forgotten. It was my destiny, but I cannot do it any longer."

Almon thought for a moment. "Do you think that is why the ghost appeared to me and led me here to you?"

"I imagine so," Aberfell said with a nod. "In the beginning, the Cosmic Creation existed alone, and there was no one to observe it.

So, it duplicated itself, bringing this world into being perfectly balanced. But there was a problem: it was empty. The Cosmic Creation needed an observer. It needed a god. But not just one, for to have only one god might tip the scales of balance between the two worlds. One all-powerful god could seek to destroy the world or the Cosmic Creation it came from. There needed to be a check to the balance.

"When both Heironomus and Hexor came together with murderous intent to kill the other, they triggered a pre-set vector unknowingly. They were recalled back to the Cosmic Creation.

"They empowered the gods in this world, establishing life and death. Not as a moral imperative but as a functional one. They took new fabric from the cosmic design for birth and returned older fabric in death for recycling. Through this round-and-round process, the gods created the cycle of life.

"The three gods, Heironomus, Hexor, and Ehlona, lived in the world and called it their home from the very beginning, right after the cooling of the land. They created all the things in the world. Heironomus shaped the Gray Mountains to the east and the Blue Mountains to the west. The Mid-Run Valley sat between the mountain ranges in an immense flat grassland.

"Soon, the villages of men formed in the Mid-Run Valley. They established the laws of men based on the worship of their gods and their way of life. There was a time when the gods and humans coexisted together. Those were the happier days: the Era of the Gods.

"After hundreds of years, the Twin Gods soon realized that one world was not large enough for them both. They tried to tip the scales of their balance, and they used Ehlona to do it. Heironomus wanted to possess her; Hexor wanted to seduce her. But it had severe consequences.

"Direct violence between the gods was violence directed at the Cosmic Creation. The balance had to be maintained. Once joined in this battle, it locked them in it. Hexor and Heironomus negated each other. Neither one could win the struggle; neither one could stop it. To this day, the cosmic battle that negates their power will rage forever.

"Because of their decisions, the Twin Gods set an incomplete world in motion.

"Having no hope of future divine intervention, the people of this world lost interest in their churches and temples. No one wanted to worship a god that abandoned them in the world. The Church of the Illuminated decayed, grew over with weeds, and broke down. Hardly a stone remains of them now. Their worshippers faded away. Yet even today, when thunder rumbles overhead, people say it is Heironomus and Hexor tumbling in their endless war. It has become a superstition. A very few people, I last heard, still wear Heironomus's sign of the ram.

"The Cult of Horror piqued. Then it existed for a while longer after the departure of Hexor. But after years of corrupt High Priests, cutthroat politics, and persecution by the surface dwellers, these thieves and murderers faded away as an organization, mostly, though that did not put an end to liars, killers, or thieves.

"The Goddess Ehlona was thrown from the force of the Great Negation. Her white gown was now stained, undone by Hexor's hands. She watched the two gods tumble higher into the air, clashing in the lightning. Then, to her shock, they disappeared, and they were gone. The Great Negation was over. Now, Ehlona was bearing two children, one belonging to the God Heironomus, the other to the God Hexor.

"In tears, she ran away."

"I'm running out of time.
I think I'm losing my mind,
I've run as far as my two feet
Can carry me away from all this madness."

Excerpt from *The Witch's Songbook*

BEAUTIFUL BLESSINGS

THE VILLAGE OF HUSBAND / SAINT EHLONA'S
IN THE YEAR 800—801 HRT

Inconsolable in her grief, Ehlona ran as far as she could. She continued west through the Blue Mountains and into the land of the Wilds. She did not know what happened to the gods, where they were now, and what would happen next. In her fear, she panicked, running westwards until the coast prevented her from running any farther. Searching for a place to stay, she went to an orphanage in a village named Husband.

There, she found comfort with a kind woman, Sister Catosa, the headmistress. The orphanage took in children whose parents either abandoned them or died. Sister Catosa was expecting a child, like Ehlona, though she was farther along in her pregnancy than the goddess. Sister Catosa was no stranger to Ehlona: She had once been an Acolyte of the Temple of Valor. She had recently left to establish the orphanage. Ehlona found her to be a familiar face, and a woman she could trust.

But Sister Catosa was not the only one in the orphanage to support Ehlona. When she left the Mid-Run Valley, three Acolytes left the Temple of Valor looking for her. The three Sisters were named Dunhi, Chavise, and Jule, and they found the goddess in the village of Husband. Sister Catosa and Ehlona welcomed them, though it made for a crowded house. At times, Ehlona found comfort with them, but mostly she only found grief.

"The gods are gone," Ehlona confided in them, lamenting through her tears. "And it's all my fault."

It is all my fault, she repeated.

None of them could be sure what would happen without the gods, or what the future would hold. They all knew something had changed, and whatever it was, Ehlona blamed herself.

"Mother Ehlona, I am humbled to have you in my home," Sister Catosa said to the goddess. "Are you comfortable here with us, Mother?"

"I feel so much love. I am grateful for your hospitality."

Sister Catosa took her hand. "You are mourning the loss of your life with the gods. Over time, their spells will fade, and the influence of Heironomus and Hexor will get easier to live without."

"I hope you're right," Ehlona said. "I feel so isolated in this world."

Sister Chavise appeared from the kitchen, bearing a tea service on a silver tray complete with dainty ceramic teacups painted in ivory with blue flowers.

"Let us help you reclaim your independence," Sister Chavise said, setting the tray down next to Ehlona and Sister Catosa. Pouring steaming water into a cup, she offered tea to the Goddess of Beauty. Ehlona smiled and considered Sister Chavise, with her long dark hair streaked with gray tied in a bun behind her head.

"Oh, Sister, your heart is pure. But I don't think things will ever be the same. Without the gods, I have lost my purpose. I cannot return to the heavens. I am forced to live here in the realm of mortals."

The other two Acolytes, Sisters Jule and Dunhi, joined them.

"Is it so bad, to be in our world?" Sister Jule asked. The youngest of the four Acolytes, she resembled Ehlona with her golden hair and youthful appearance.

"Ehlona may not appreciate your boldness, Sister Jule." Dunhi gave her a stern look while adjusting her dress.

"Ehlona knows the love between us," Sister Jule said.

"None of us should be afraid of our feelings," Ehlona told them. "I gratefully admire all of you."

Ehlona stood and walked to the window. The others gave Sister Jule an angry look behind Ehlona's back. The young Acolyte ignored them and held her gaze steady at the Mother Goddess.

"You must understand, I have been in this world for hundreds of years. Heironomus and Hexor were my life. I don't know what to do without them." Ehlona closed the curtain and looked away. "I will be in the world for hundreds more. Whom can I love who will not grow old? Who will stand with me over the centuries? Without being in the company of the other gods, I will watch generation after generation perish as I stay the same. I am scared, more than you could ever know. That is what the realm of mortals means to me: Even as beautiful as it can be, it is my prison."

"Mother Ehlona." Sister Jule rose, to the chagrin of the others, and spoke. "In our mortal lives, we learn to love the creatures of this world even though their lives are shorter than ours. We can still find joy, even though it will be brief. Can the gods not love mortals so? The pain is unbearable to lose them, yet we live on. Over time, you will find new companions too."

"You have a beautiful mind, Sister Jule. I appreciate your words more than you will ever know. Your world consists of other humans for lasting companionship, and you have such good and faithful friends. But imagine if you were the only human being left in the world. Would being surrounded by the other world's creatures give you solace? I am the only one of my kind, the only god that remains in the world."

Sister Chavise rose, gently putting her hands on Sister Jule's shoulders, prompting her to sit down. Slowly, they sat together. Sister Dunhi put her hands in Sister Jule's to comfort her. The women continued their best to understand Ehlona, but nothing could ease the goddess's melancholy.

"I don't know why I did that." Ehlona turned her back again, looking out the window. "I don't know why I did what I did."

Raindrops hit the windowpane, streaming down like her tears. "I never should have married Heironomus. I never should have lain with Hexor. Yet I did both. Things I would find abhorrent later." She heaved a deep sigh. "It is all my fault."

The days and months passed in Ehlona's grief. But soon, she found a cause for joy. Sister Catosa's time came, and with the help of her house, she delivered a healthy baby girl that she named Luna. The Goddess Ehlona thought baby Luna was the most beautiful thing she had ever seen. An outpouring of love diminished her grief as she held her in her arms. Luna fascinated her.

"I have never held a baby before," she admitted. "Do you believe that? I have lived hundreds of years in this world, and this is the first baby I have ever held in my arms. It's so wonderful!"

Ehlona confided in the Sisters, trusting them as good friends, speaking openly about her origin as the Goddess of Beauty with the Twin Gods. She shared her thoughts and feelings with them, and they shared many things with her about their lives. All the while, Ehlona's pregnancy was advancing closer to full term.

One day, Jule, always the boldest of them, asked the Goddess Ehlona a question. "Mother Ehlona, will you grant a blessing upon us?" The other three women reigned her in before she could ask any more questions.

Ehlona felt grateful for their companionship. "I will bestow beautiful blessings upon all of you, but after my babies are born."

The four Sisters did not know what she meant, but it excited them.

With the Sisters attending to her, soon Ehlona's day came. Privately, they whispered like schoolgirls, eager to speculate what kind of blessing Ehlona would bestow upon them. It could be anything. It would not be long now. They had birthed many children before, but never from a god. It was somewhat of a surprise, then, to learn it was no different.

Soon, the first child was born, and Sister Catosa received the infant, wrapping the baby in linens. Catosa took the child to Ehlona, laying the baby across her bosom. The large child smiled at her with a tuft of red hair—it could only be Heironomus's child. Her elation turned to tears of love.

"His name shall be Marus; may my blessings be upon him; may his spirit soar as the wind."

The Sisters smiled at each other. But Ehlona had more work to do, and soon her pains started again. Catosa took the baby Marus to another room, while the other three Sisters stayed with Ehlona for the second birth.

After several more hours, the second birth was much worse than the first, yet a smaller child was born. Ehlona finally birthed her second child through tears, not because of the pain but from grief and regrets. The second boy resembled Hexor, with locks of black hair and pale skin, but his eyes were swirling luminescent and yellow, a most disturbing feature for those who saw it.

Sister Dunhi wrapped the baby in linens and placed him on Ehlona's bosom, as Sister Catosa had done with Marus.

"Oh, please, get him off of me!" Ehlona said, not wanting to look upon him. Filled with tears of despair, she looked away in disgust and never looked back at the child. This was Hexor's child, a product of the God of Darkness.

"This child will be a curse to the world," Ehlona said through tears. "Blood will flow in rivers waist-deep because of this child."

The Sisters shared a look of concern. Finally, Sister Chavise spoke. "Mother, peace is what we desire the most. You know my heart is full of love for every child both born and unborn. This vision of yours, the future you shared with us about this child, frightens me. Waist-deep blood? A river of blood? If these things come to pass as you say they will, the blood that this child will spill upon the world—oh! I cannot bear to say what is in my heart." Chavise could not finish.

"What Sister Chavise is trying to say," Sister Jule continued, "is what shall we do with this second child? The one you cannot bear to look upon. This child you foresee inflicting so much pain and violence upon the world?"

Her meaning was as well-intentioned as all understood it.

"You are asking if the boy should live?" Ehlona said, raising her hands to cover her eyes.

"If it will avoid future bloodshed, would it not be better if we took him to the woods? Wouldn't that be putting his fate into the hands of the gods?"

"There is no eternal reward," Ehlona said. "You would be cursed, beyond my power to save you. No, I cannot allow you to do that."

The Sisters shared a look of concern. At length, Sister Chavise asked, "What then shall be his name?"

Ehlona guffawed. The baby continued to cry. "Who can name such a thing?"

Sister Catosa, attending Marus in the other room, out of earshot, missed the entire conversation. She now came back into the room, holding the baby Marus.

"I was thinking Hazor would be a good name for the son of Hexor," Sister Catosa said. All the women turned at once to glare at her. "What? Did I say something wrong?"

"You have named my horror," Ehlona said softly, laying her head down. "Hazor shall be the name the world will scorn."

Hearing its name spoken for the first time, the child finally stopped crying. Sister Dunhi, who was still holding the baby Hazor, looked down at him. The baby's yellow eyes flashed at her. It was an ominous sign.

In the days that followed, excitement filled the orphanage. They took turns caring for Ehlona, her newborns, as well as all the other orphans living in Catosa's home. Ehlona slowly regained her strength, recuperating after her labor.

On the fourth day, she rose from her bed. The Sisters soothed her with a cup of tea, bathed her in warm water, and refreshed her. She dressed in clean linen, but common to the orphans, not the usual luxurious white clothing she had grown accustomed to. Instead, she wore tones of gray and black, as the Sisters often wore.

"It is unfitting for the Goddess of Beauty," Sister Dunhi said. "These clothes are clean but they are too drab, torn, and faded for you."

"Please, all of you, come to me. Join me," Ehlona said, ignoring the judgments of Sister Dunhi. Walking to the largest room in the orphanage, she called all the Sisters to her. They came and sat around her. She removed her gold bracelets and all her jewelry, placing them all on the floor.

"Today, I will give my beautiful blessings to all of you."

It excited the four Sisters to be receiving something special. They all thanked her, not knowing what they would get through her blessing. The goddess prepared to give them something extraordinary. They sat in a semi-circle on the floor as Ehlona spread open her arms and approached them. A hush fell throughout the room.

Ehlona placed her hands on the back of Sister Jule's head. Then, she began the first blessing.

"Sister Jule, I bless you with the Orphanage of the North. Go to the village of Estes; there you will find blessings. Gather to you the young, the vulnerable, and the hungry. Feed them, teach them, protect them, and establish your own order. I bless you with one quarter of my beauty as a shield to wield and a sword to rule. Place your trust in no man, but give your love to all. From this moment on, nothing can separate you from my blessing."

A strange emerald energy crackled between them in a blinding light. When the light faded, Sister Jule looked more beautiful than before, vibrant and without blemish, and glowing with inner beauty.

But after giving Sister Jule her blessing, Ehlona changed. With a quarter of her beauty now gone, she developed lines in her face and a streak of gray in her hair. Jule could not see the change in Ehlona, but the other Sisters did. Not wanting to embarrass her, they said nothing, keeping their observations to themselves. They only sat smiling at her.

Next, she moved behind Sister Chavise. Putting her hands on the back of her head, Ehlona began the second blessing.

"Sister Chavise, I bless you with the Orphanage of the South. Go to the village of Plum; gather to you the children, the refugees, the widows. Give shelter to all who come to you, protect them, honor them, and establish your order. I bless you with a quarter of my beauty; it will be a shield to wield and a sword to rule. My spirit will forever comfort you. From this moment on, nothing can separate you from my blessing."

Blue sparks of energy crackled from Ehlona's hands to Sister Chavise. The sparks subsided and Sister Chavise, the eldest of the Sisters, now looked as vibrant as Sister Jule, the youngest. Her eyes sparkled, her skin smoothed to a flawless complexion, without spots, blemishes, or creases.

But Ehlona's skin changed to gray, deep lines creased her face, sagging, losing its form.

This time, all but Sister Chavise saw the change in Ehlona, and they gasped.

"Mother, are you not feeling well?" they asked.

"I am weakened," Ehlona said, shifting to stand behind Sister Dunhi to give her the next blessing. With a weakened voice, she continued with the third.

"Sister Dunhi, I bless you with the Orphanage of the East. Go to the village of Rynolt; gather to you the poor, the disenfranchised, the oppressed. Nurture those weaker than you, shower them with your blessings, and establish your order. I bless you with a quarter of my beauty as a shield to wield and a sword to rule. From this moment on, nothing can separate you from my blessing."

Upon uttering these words, a bright light flashed red. It crackled between them. With her blessing, it changed Sister Dunhi's appearance. She became illuminated, more beautiful than ever before, in the vitality of youth.

But Ehlona changed for the worse yet again. Patches of her hair fell out, and what was left of it was white and straggly. Wrinkles deeply lined the corners of her mouth, her voice deepened and cracked. Her eyelids became puffy and swollen.

All the Sisters gasped at her new appearance.

After she blessed Sister Dunhi, the Goddess Ehlona approached Sister Catosa to give the last blessing. But Sister Catosa objected.

"Mother Ehlona, I thank you for your blessings of beauty to my Sisters. But at what cost? Look what it has done to you, Mother. Your skin, your hair, you are changing in front of our eyes. You are aging an entire lifetime in front of us. Is this a result of the magic of your blessing? Will these changes pass? Will you recover from it?"

"No, my child," Ehlona cackled in a voice lower than it had been before. "My beauty was desired by the gods. It was that quality they fought to possess; it was their temptation, and vanity was mine. I no longer desire it; I no longer need it. It is mine to give, and I desire to give it to you."

"No, I can't let you do it," Catosa resisted, clutching Ehlona's hands. "As much as I may want it, as much as I am thankful, I just can't watch you destroy yourself. Not for me."

"Please, Sister Catosa," Ehlona pleaded with her.

But Catosa interrupted her crying. "No. I don't deserve it! Remember, I named the second-born. I am not worthy of your blessing!"

Ehlona laughed. "Listen to me. All of you. Through the four of you, I will establish a sisterhood that will have a profound effect on this world. Through you four, I will establish my order. Sister Catosa, I need to do this. Please, let me finish what I started. Help me bring some good to this world to balance the horror that is to be. Be the instrument of my righteousness."

Sister Jule spoke up. "But what of you, Mother Ehlona?"

"I will live forever." Ehlona smiled at all of them. "I have work I must do. I am going to make my home far from the human race. I must leave you, and you must let me go. I must turn my back on you to save you. I do not expect you to understand, but this is the way of the gods. If you genuinely love me, you will let me finish this blessing.

"Sister Catosa?" Cracks formed along the edges of Ehlona's lips.

The Sisters sobbed each of them in turn as she put her hands on Sister Catosa. Then Ehlona began the last blessing. Catosa bowed her head, allowing it to happen, accepting Ehlona's fourth blessing.

"Sister Catosa, I bless you with the Orphanage of the West. Stay here in your home to establish your order. Honor me, Sister Catosa; change the name of the village of Husband in my memory. You will be blessed for doing so. Heal the sick, feed the hungry, and love all who come to you. Take care of the stranger, the lost traveler, all that seek help, and all those in need. I bless you with a quarter of my beauty as a shield to wield and a sword to rule. From this moment on, nothing can separate you from my blessing."

A blast of yellow energy crackled between them. The magic of Ehlona's blessing flowed from her hands in a blinding light. When the energy faded, Sister Catosa was glowing and vibrant and as beautiful as Ehlona had ever been.

But with the four blessings complete, Ehlona's beauty had gone from her completely. Her spine twisted into a large hump. All the sparkle drained from her eyes, and darkness obscured her once brilliantly blue eyes, turning them bloodshot. Her hands wrinkled into gray, pockmarked flesh.

"And now, my Sisters," Ehlona concluded with a low cackle. "It is finished. I leave you now to face my destiny. My sons, Marus and Hazor, take care of them, as you will with all the children of this world."

They embraced Ehlona, crying, saying their goodbyes. Each goodbye lasted longer than the previous one. They spent several moments together.

"I love you all," the Goddess Ehlona said with a smile before she left.

Hazor let out a loud cry. Ehlona paused and listened. A queer look darkened her face.

"I must go." She suddenly turned and walked out of the door. The Sisters embraced each other, sobbing together, as they watched Ehlona stumble farther away.

Shortly after, the other three women left Sister Catosa's. Empowered by Ehlona's blessing, they became the Sisters of the Orphans. They went in their own directions to establish their orders, in what would later become a series of orphanages dedicated to the memory of Saint Ehlona, just as she instructed them.

They each looked young and beautiful. Even well past their age, years in the future, when death would finally catch up to them, the Sisters were never separated from Ehlona's gift. Beauty stayed with them until the very end. One by one, after serving a long and charitable life, they would leave this life with their beauty intact and a sweet smile on their face. A reward for a life well-lived. Even Sister Jule, who would be the very last of the remaining Sisters to go. When she reached the ripe old age of 104, even the grave could not separate her from Ehlona's blessing.

But that would be many, many years in the future. For now, Ehlona had two boys, Marus and Hazor, who needed to be tended to. They were raised by Sister Catosa.

As Marus grew, he kept close to Sister Catosa. He called her his mother and helped with the safety and upkeep of the orphanage. He came to realize he had powers of his own: He possessed a heightened sense of self-focus, which gave him the ability to control his physical dexterity as well as his spiritual energy. By practicing these skills, he kept himself in excellent physical condition. He stayed lean and trim, in contrast to his father, who was large and muscular. He also favored a cleanly shaven head, except for a single tuft of hair that he grew as a topknot. Over the years, he stayed with Sister Catosa at the orphanage until his eighteenth birthday.

Hazor, on the other hand, was disruptive from an early age. Because of his obstinance he needed discipline, and his punishments were swift and harsh. Yet they never worked: They only seemed to stoke his hatred for Sister Catosa and the other orphans, and for his brother most of all. Finally, when he turned ten years old, he ran away from the orphanage and never came back. No one knew where he went, but he would re-emerge in time. Soon, the entire world would know.

It would not be the last time they would hear from them.

"Surprised in how we get along.
You sing to me when the feeling's strong.
And I never would have believed,
That my life would last this long."

Excerpt from *The Witch's Songbook*

THE NATURAL ORDER OF THINGS

THE DRAGONBREATH SUMMIT IN THE YEAR 1041 HRT

Almon stopped writing and looked up at Aberfell. "How is it that Ehlona could be pregnant from two different men?"

Aberfell, chewing on an apple, considered Almon for a moment. "Because they were not two men; they were the Twin Gods, and that is how the gods willed it. The gods do not abide by the same rules of mortals."

"Sounds like my ghost," Almon said.

"Tell me more about your ghost. You said it looked like me?"

"It was a little more terrifying than you, Aberfell."

"You were scared of it?"

"I was terrified."

"You were right to be terrified, you know. This ghost was to be feared more than any other. It still is."

"You are not making me feel any better about it, Aberfell."

"I'm not trying to scare you, or make you feel better. But I can tell you this, Almon, your ghost is a harbinger of doom. My doom, most likely, not yours." Aberfell took his knife and started whittling on the wood again without a concern. "Your family had a long tradition of speaking with the dead. All of their ghosts were spirits of the past. But yours I'm afraid is much different. You saw a spirit from the future, a spirit who is not quite dead yet, considering how it reminded you of me, and I am still alive at present. Obviously, since my death has not happened yet, it is showing you something that will soon come to pass. Which can only mean one thing: After a very long life, mine is drawing to a close. Drawing nearer to its inevitable end every day. It seems, that you, your purpose anyway, has been to come find me with a summons of sorts, that my death is what is to come. So, I will be dead soon."

"What? Oh no! Aberfell? Are you sure?"

"Well, no, of course not. We are dealing with the Cosmic Creation, not a legend of make-believe dragons."

"If what you say is true, if this ghost really is a harbinger of doom like you say, and it might spell your death, doesn't that upset you?"

"Why? The gods do as they will. They don't give a spit about what old Aberfell thinks. Honestly, after all this time, at my age, I find it burdensome. I welcome the end. But there is something that still unsettles me. You told me that your ghost could not speak."

"Its eyes and mouth were sewn shut. It was just how I prepared my father for his burial."

"So, this ghost used memories meaningful to you, memories of the death of your father, and combined them with images of something in the future. You saw the future modulated in visions of the past."

"It filled my mind with visions; that is how it spoke to me," Almon said. "And it showed me visions of this mountain."

"Obviously, the ghost had other purposes than just scaring you or killing me. It was leading you here for some greater purpose. This ghostly entity wanted you to find me. It pushed you to me, although you did not know it at the time. You were being its instrument, a messenger, to fulfill some purpose that the Cosmic Creation wanted."

"As if the ghost wasn't scary enough, you are telling me the Cosmic Creation was involved, using me as a puppet?"

"Well, that's one way of looking at it, I suppose. Another way is to think that it had both of us in mind, combining our destinies, mine with yours. It is not for mortal men to know where that path is going or where it ends. But I promise you, if the Cosmic Creation is involved, it will end in a most amazing resolution."

"Maybe I should have stayed in Haverhill and attended to my brewery."

"I know your miss your friends, Almon, but I would have thought you wanted more for yourself than just a growler of the Red Curl. Even though I must admit it is a little sweet for my taste, I understand why it very popular with the Haverhill Inn crowd."

"You know about the Red Curl?"

"You Plums have been making brew since before my time. The Timmutes bring me things from all over the Mid-Run Valley. How and where they go is beyond my understanding, but I can only assume they are everywhere. Occasionally, a growler of Red Curl has found its way to me."

Almon dropped the quill and put his hands on his lap. "It must have been hard for you, living this long."

"It's the natural order of things," Aberfell said, looking back at him. "I admit, it has been longer than I expected. Yet, I have the Timmutes to keep me company, to take care of me. They carried me up this mountain, but you, you climbed it on your own; you possessed the skills to climb it. I did not."

"Not so. I faltered near the top, just below the cloud. I'm sure I would've passed out if the Timmutes hadn't been there to help me."

"Every man in your family has had an adventurous streak. But none of them can compare with you. Tell me, Almon, you are so young, why aren't you pursuing your business, or looking for love?"

"I always felt I would have time for that later," Almon said.

"None of us are getting any younger."

"My father knew ghosts all his life. All the Plum-Kilmer family did, all but me. I always wondered: What is wrong with me? Why was I so different that no ghost appeared to me? I was jealous of my father's ability to speak with the spirits, and I wanted it; I wanted my own ghost. At least I thought I did, until I received this harbinger of doom. It's funny, isn't it? You would think someone who saw ghosts would be crazy, yet I felt that I was crazy for not seeing one."

"I guess we are all a little crazy, Almon."

Almon nodded. "Everything changed when my father died. As he lay dying in the Mid-Run Valley, right before he died, he said, *it is passing*. Those were his last words. I've been thinking about that a lot lately, just what that meant."

"It could mean many things."

"But lately I can't stop thinking about it," Almon said.

"What do you think it meant?"

"I don't know what it meant to him, but I can tell you what it means to me. It means I would someday pass the curse to my children. It means that it never ends, but it has to end sometime. It has to."

"Maybe you are right. Then again, maybe you are looking at it all wrong. You see it as a curse. I am a little more inclined to believe that it has been a blessing. Your father, and all the other men in your family, amassed a great deal of wealth and lived long, successful lives. I think the ghost had something to do with that. In fact, it was these ghosts that looked over them and kept them safe. Consider this: Here you are at the top of the highest mountain in the world—what could be riskier than that? Yet the visions your ghost showed you were not driving you to your death. On the contrary, the ghost was leading you to something better: To meet me here upon this summit. It protected you. I don't think curses work that way, but blessings do."

Almon picked up the quill. "Well, in the end, I didn't feel like I had any choice. It was either come to these mountains or have the ghost drive me mad. Before the ghost came, I kept brewing Red Curl, curing skins from hunts, taking care of Erland. I was only passing time. Somewhere, I lost myself, as if I was a prisoner to the part I played. Then suddenly, I was free from it—I was free. The first thing I wanted to do was to get out of Haverhill, get away from the memories of the old life. At the crossroads of my life, I either remained haunted by the memories of Erland and Johanna or let this ghost guide me to discover something new. Hopefully, by discovering you, I could discover myself again."

"In your search for something new, it led you to something old—the Provenance," Aberfell said.

Almon looked down. "Yes, let us continue with that."

Aberfell felt sad for him. He told him, "I pray that you can discover a better, more meaningful, purpose for yourself, Almon. I truly do."

"Please, let's continue, Aberfell."

Aberfell stood up, walked behind Almon, and thoughtfully placed his hand upon his back. Then, he started telling the story of the gods once again.

"Ehlona represented overlap of the light and darkness. She always had a little bit of both of them in her nature already. That was something that Hexor understood, but Heironomus and Ehlona did not. It was how she was designed, how she was purposed. She was not only the Goddess of Beauty, but she was the Goddess of Love. Ehlona was meant to love both of the Twin Gods, favoring neither one over the other. Her balance kept the light and darkness in need of only a blending. She had been created in equal parts of the dark and light. But Heironomus needed to satisfy the light that was in him. Hexor wanted only to seduce her to the darkness. In the middle, Ehlona wanted nothing more than to please. She gave them both what appealed to their natures, which also satisfied her own needs. This is the true nature of the gods, as well as the problem with them. The world is imperfect because of their imperfections."

"It was by design, then?" Almon asked.

"Nothing the gods do is by design; it just seems so, to us mortals," Aberfell said, sitting in his chair once more and leaning back. "Personally, I think the world is better off for it. The world is a beautiful place because of its imperfections."

"Ehlona seemed fragile to me," Almon said.

"Ehlona was a powerful entity, but for whatever reason, she was strong where she should be weak, and weak where she should be strong, an unpleasant by-product of her design to please. This was clear in the way she dealt with her children."

"Leaving them with Sister Catosa?"

"Precisely. Now, if you are ready? Ehlona ran away and found herself suddenly alone. With all her legendary beauty gone, she hobbled into the forest. She had no idea how hideous she had become, but the deeper she went into the woods, the more she wanted to find out."

"You don't know where you're going
Frozen, stuck in time
It's coming down to this moment,
You leave the world behind
When your heart is empty, and your song refused to die
Catch your breath, breathe again,
Before you say goodbye."

Excerpt from *The Witch's Songbook*

THE WITCH OF THE GREAT MAPES FOREST

THE GREAT MAPES FOREST IN THE YEAR 801—810 HRT

Ehlona ran away from Sister's Catosa's house as fast and as far as her crooked back could carry her. She made her way through the forest until late evening.

Coming upon a grassy opening in a glen, she found a freshwater spring to drink from. Falling upon her knees, she saw her reflection in the still waters for the first time. After blessing away her beauty, she saw what she looked like. A slow and growing bitterness filled her eyes. Her lips trembled; then, like a wailing siren, she let out a long howl of despair. It gathered in intensity and carried through the woods. Making a shaking fist, she struck the water with a hateful splash and made a loud declaration.

"Let the name of the Goddess Ehlona be no longer spoken! Let the word go forth from this time forward that the Goddess of Beauty is dead! All that remains is the Witch of the Forest!"

She briefly fell asleep by the spring. When she awoke it was right before the dawn, and she continued shuffling through the dark trees.

Traveling deeper into the forest, she reached a point where no other human being would dare go. She found herself among the tall Great Mapes of the forest. These were ancient thick trees with wide trunks, over a thousand years old. They spread a dense canopy of branches and leaves overhead, barring the sunlight from entry. She moved through the dark underbrush in air that was damp and cold.

Here, I shall make my home, she thought. Yet her senses detected life all around her in the living things of the forest who were watching her with great interest.

She cast a simple spell, one that allowed her to communicate with all the beings of the forest. Blue energy crackled from her hands as she spread her arms. Suddenly the Witch's spell flashed upon the forest, empowering all the living things to have a voice. The trees, the bushes, the moss, everything received the means to communicate with her. But there was a problem: The forest excitedly spoke in hundreds of voices in their amazement. They all talked so fast, she could not understand a word of it. The trees bent in arches toward her; bushes rolled to her. All came close to running her over with their newfound ability to communicate.

The Witch held up her hands and addressed all the living things of the Great Mapes Forest.

"Long life to you, living things of the forest. I have come among you and have given you a voice so you and I may speak and reason together. I have come to ask you for your help!"

They spoke in a thunder of a hundred voices. The Witch listened and tried her best to understand their meaning. But try as she might, they all spoke out of turn with differing opinions.

Some pleasantly offered their help and said, *What would you have us do for you?*

We cannot wait to help you, a few of the voices declared.

Others were not so pleasant. *Why should we help you?*

Still others thought it an outright bad idea to get involved in the magic of a Witch. *It is far too risky. No, we will not help you!*

"It seems we are at an impasse," said the Witch finally. "Is there not one among you that may speak for all of you?"

From the forest's perspective, this was not going well. Embarrassed that they had so many differing opinions, a massive white oak tree finally took charge.

"This is a most uncommon occurrence, Madam," the white oak stated politely. "Never in our long lives have we been able to speak to anyone not a white oak, and so I am sorry to say, being unpracticed in these things, we cannot seem to speak in a single voice."

"Well, Master Tree, can you speak for the group?"

"Just a moment, Madam." The white oak turned its back. Hushed arguments ensued; the other trees, the vines, the moss, and the bushes all agreed to be represented by the Master Tree. He cleared his throat and turned back to the Witch.

"Excuse me, please. The forest would like to know, what is your desire?"

"I wish to make a home among you."

"A home? Is that all you require of us? We thought it might be more. Some of us heard your declaration by the spring. It sounded like it was vengeance you seek."

"My vengeance will come in my way, and in my own time, Master Tree. But right now, I only desire a place to call home, to live in peace with the living things of the Great Mapes, and to go about my work."

"And what work would that be, Madam?"

The Witch turned in a circle, speaking to the Master Tree but loud enough to address all the living things. "I will have to go about and collect some things from time to time. Nothing much, maybe just some toadstools, some healing herbs, tadpoles, and such. Things that you drop and have no need of anymore. But nothing I suspect you would miss. At least not that I think so."

Master Tree turned away again, and more hushed arguments ensued. Then Master Tree faced the Witch again.

"Excuse me again, Madam Witch, but, if I may be so bold, what is in it for us?"

"Fair question, Master Tree. Everything has a value. In exchange for shelter I can call home, you will have a Witch living among you. If I can make my home here among you, I will serve and protect you. If I am here, no harm will ever come to you. You will be impervious to the ways of man, such as the chopping of vines"—at this, the vines let out a howl—"the burning of the bushes"—the bushes gasped—"the overturning of rocks on their mossy side"—the moss screamed—"and the felling of trees by the woodsman's ax!" That last statement took back even the Master Tree, while all the other trees let out a scandalized cry.

The tree cleared his throat a second time, turning around to talk in private again. But he seemed different this time, more relentless, brimming with confidence. The hushed whispers were very few now. Finally, the tree turned back to the Witch to address her.

"We have reached a decision. We agree to help you, and welcome you to your new home, Madam Witch."

The Witch and the forest made their agreement and proceeded to work on making her a fair home in the Great Mapes Forest.

She easily pulled the vines as long as she wanted, stretching and tying them into twisting shapes and bindings. The bushes and branches bent, as pliable as she wished them to be, molding according to her building designs. Running her hand along the trees, she formed the living wood as if she were molding clay into whatever shape she wanted. Soon her home was coming along nicely, constructed from the roots, bindings, soft textures, and dense concentration of the living things of the forest. The walls, floors, and roof were formed from the trees and rocks. The moss and bushes formed chairs and comfortable furniture for the interior.

In no time at all, the Witch's home emerged in the Great Mapes Forest, and soon a thin plume of smoke rose out of the stone chimney. The forest could tell the Witch enjoyed her new home in the warm glow of the hearth inside.

Over time, the Witch found her way in the minds and tales of the folklore of men. As she went about her business, collecting herbs and roots for her magical recipes, legends started to circulate about the Witch that haunted the darkest part of the forest. Men considered the forest cursed, and only the bravest or most foolhardy went too deep into it. This corner of the woods was a place to be generally avoided and seldom visited by man.

The vines, bushes, moss, trees, and all the living things of the Great Mapes Forest felt a very silent satisfaction. For the first time in a thousand years, they felt safe with the Witch living among them.

Even more time passed, and what remained of her once legendary beauty decayed into horror. She became so terrifying that she produced fear among men without even casting a spell. Just seeing her from a distance, they would run for their lives.

Hazor still worried her, and she had plenty of time to think about him. She felt responsible for the violence he would cause in the coming age. She knew she would need a spell to cleanse the blood yet to come.

But what kind of magic would do?

She had to make it right. Compromising herself the way she did with Hexor diminished her power against him. She also had a reason to fear Heironomus for her betrayal; what fury might he bring against her in his vengeance if given a chance? To obtain the results she needed, she would be required to use all her remaining magic. She would have to concentrate on a single spell, a spell that neither one of them could undo. It would have to come from magic conjured from her blood to tie the balance back together.

Deep inside the Great Mapes Forest, her home emitted strange lights and weird smells as crackling magic flashed from her windows.

The Witch was an even better spell caster than she ever gave herself credit for. And one day, she was successful, though she never even realized it.

"I've been down in love.

I've been down in life.

I've been down so low that it don't feel right

Let the colors fade to black and white!

Through the tunnels of a brand-new life."

Excerpt from *The Witch's Songbook*

THE GOLDEN ORBS

THE GREAT MAPES FOREST IN THE YEAR 810—818 HRT

To bind her spell to her, the Witch pricked her finger and dripped blood into a small bowl. She added just the right amount to her magic recipe, then poured the entirety of the potion into her cauldron. She rotated the big iron pot over the flame, and the whole concoction simmered to a boil. She let the heat mingle the blood with the other ingredients, then waited and watched for the effect. With growing anticipation, she spun the hot cauldron out of the flame. She watched the bubbling brew congeal, finally seeing what it produced…

Nothing.

Another disappointing failure. She studied her recipe, carefully modifying it. With a piece of charcoal, she made some writing on the parchment.

"Maybe I need more bone marrow," she mumbled while writing, "and a touch less alfalfa."

Frustrated, she left the brew in the cauldron and walked out of the cottage. But as she walked away, some movement behind her stirred in the thick green soup in the big pot. She walked out of the cottage, pushing the door closed where it almost latched. But instead of closing, it slowly swung open again, letting in the cool forest breeze. As soon as the Witch walked out of view, the first orb bubbled up from the cauldron, then two more. Five more orbs closely followed with even more of them yet to come.

The Witch walked through the forest gathering feathers, bones, and toadstools for the next hour. She went about her business collecting ingredients and writing things in her book, like prophecies and star movements, and the occasional poem or song. Her days of moving as she had in the past were long gone. It took her twice as long to cover half the distance now, with her twisted spine and bad foot. Her left foot was not responding anymore, and she had to drag it along behind her as she walked.

As the sun set, she neared the house, but she did not go directly inside. The evening air was cool and comfortable. The fireflies were out, shining golden lights under the trees and in the bushes. Exhausted from her walk in the forest, she sat on a rock by a small creek, as she so enjoyed in her previous life. There, she invoked the spell allowing her to communicate with the living things of the forest again.

"Master Tree, are you well?"

"Madam, I am, thank you. The forest sleeps in peace tonight."

"Tell me, Master Tree, I've been wanting to ask you for some time now. I have wondered, do white oaks have proper names?"

"I do, Madam. From the time I was but a twig, I have been called Ulrig by the others."

"Ulrig. What an interesting name for a mighty white oak such as yourself. All this time I have been calling you Master Tree. Would you prefer I call you Ulrig?"

"You have been calling Master Tree for so long, I have grown quite fond of it."

"Then I will continue to call you that, Ulrig. I do not wish to be rude."

"Not at all, Madam. Would it be rude of me to ask you if a Witch like you has a proper name? I would think the Witch of the Great Mapes is your title?"

"I had a name once in my former life. I pledged never to repeat it."

"Permit my boldness, Madam, but I already knew your name before I asked," said Master Tree. "I remember hearing you speak it out loud for the last time down by the spring, and being a white oak, I have an exceptionally long memory. I already know who you are, or who you were. I do not understand your dilemma, but it shall not be me to press the issue. Without your objection, I will continue to call you the Madam Witch." If a white oak could smile, Master Tree would have.

"That is fair enough for me. Thank you, Ulrig. You are a good friend to me, Master Tree."

"The feeling is quite mutual, Madam Witch."

They said goodnight, and the Witch shuffled toward the light of her open door as fireflies floated past her face.

Strange, she thought, *a lot of fireflies out tonight.* But something was different about these fireflies: They never blinked. Ordinarily their natural state was dark, blinking on infrequently; these fireflies had a continuous glow.

Then she had a terrible thought.

Frantically shuffling into her house, she examined the cauldron only to discover that all the green brew was gone. Scanning the room, she noticed several orbs dancing inside the house. Moving to shut the door quickly, she then closed the windows as well. Before the last window closed, she saw more of the orbs floating outside in the darkness. Picking up a magnifying glass, she got a good look at the orbs and realized what she had done.

They were not a form of firefly, but something entirely new: Tiny humanoid creatures standing less than half an inch in height. The Witch laughed in delight. The tiny orbs could fly, or float, as if they were lighter than air. They came complete in male and female forms, communicating with each other in some unspoken language.

Perhaps telepathic? the Witch thought and jotted down the question in a book with the cover scratched in charcoal: TIMMUTES. She did not know how they could fly, or how they could do anything else for that matter. Captivated by their mystery, she continued to watch and take notes.

By the morning, it became apparent that the orbs were multiplying, and doing so with amazing alacrity, seemingly doubling in number every four hours or so.

By lunch, she was amazed to see they had evolved, developing industry, like producing textiles, fashioning hats, scarves, and fabrics made of beautiful colors, to clothe themselves with.

By that evening, they had moved on, evolving again to forge metals, such as armor and weapons to defend themselves with. This made the Witch nervous.

Most impressively, they possessed the ability to change their appearance and form, as golden orbs or tiny humanoids, and to camouflage themselves and blend in with any surface. When they would come to rest on the table, they became indistinguishable from it. When they came to rest on a rock, they became the rock.

They seem to be able to take any form, the Witch wrote in her notes.

The next morning, the Witch observed they could change color. They were turning red and swarming something in the forest in a dense intensity. The Witch discovered the first dead animal. It was a shock to see; the carcass was unidentifiable, it had been stripped down to just a greasy stain in the dirt. That was her first indication that the golden orbs were dangerous. Soon she found another dead animal, then another. Each carcass had been stripped of hide, bone, and meat, anything that was useful to the orbs.

What a horrible way to die, an agonizing death, the Witch thought.

The creatures had formed their own society, capable of either covering a wide area or coming together in a powerful show of force. These orbs went to great lengths to protect their privacy, not tolerating any animals nosing around their society.

The next day, the Witch found the body of man, a hunter that the orbs had swarmed and killed. What was left of the body lay face down, covered with thousands of small slices of removed flesh and bone. It became clear to her that this new creation would kill anything that encroached upon their territory. It had only been two days since the orbs first emerged from the cauldron.

Her discoveries were coming too late. They had grown beyond her ability to contain them, let alone control them. They lived and multiplied both inside and outside of her house, and the surrounding Great Mapes Forest. But her creation did not wish to harm her.

On the third day, a gift arrived outside her door. Then more gifts and objects floated to her, as if carried by invisible hands. The orbs presented the Witch with gifts of food, fruit, bread, textiles, and jewelry; all the gifts were in the proper proportion to fit the Witch. The creatures were recognizing and honoring her as their supreme creator, and as their god, they worshiped her.

But it did raise several problems. After more time, the Witch lived a life where she felt imprisoned by the faith of her creation. She feared what they might do if they ever lost faith in her; would they act to destroy her? This fear consumed her every day.

Then her concern turned to the forest itself. She had promised to protect them.

Would they destroy it?

A ceremony, the Witch thought, would appease them, and at the same time give her the opportunity to understand them better. The Witch walked out among the trees, calling out to the creatures, announcing her desire to conduct a ceremony in their honor.

"To all of you orbs, please hear my voice and come to me! Please, we can't have you going about the world without a name."

Soon the forest grew thick with thousands of the floating golden orbs. They came together, surrounding her in a dense swarm, but they caused her no harm. She nervously looked them over and began the ceremony.

"Welcome, golden orbs! My praise be upon you. Instrument of my making. For all your accomplishments, which are many, and in such a short amount of time, too. I see you are a noble, intelligent, and caring society. Thank you for your gifts, and your acknowledgment as your creator. To all of you I say this, it is essential to have a name in this world. As your creator, I wish to endow you with a name that you will be known by for all time. Beautiful orbs, from this moment on, you will be known as the Timmutes. To all of you, I give my blessing."

Immediately the Timmutes rejoiced for gaining their name. They showered the Witch with flowers, gifts of food, baskets, pots, and other things precious to them.

"Thank you for all these wonderful gifts," she said through the flowers.

Then, in tribute, the Witch experienced a once-in-a-lifetime event where the Timmutes displayed the full extent of their power. Several of the magnificent white oaks in her immediate view came tumbling down, collapsing into fragments, tumbling down into millions of tiny particles; they had all been comprised of colonies of Timmutes. An incredibly loud crashing sound echoed throughout the forest as more and more of the forest collapsed in Timmute colonies. This fragmentation of the forest went on for several minutes as the Timmutes expressed their joy for their name.

Then, after collapsing the forest, the celebration subsided. The Timmutes began reconstructing themselves from the ground up to form the multitude of white oak trees once again. Once assimilated, the Witch could not determine which were real and which trees were not. But most of what was in front of her were not trees but colonies of Timmutes, stacked up to the very treetops, out to the branches and forming the leaves. Soon the Timmutes removed any trace of being there at all, and the Great Mapes Forest returned.

All retuned to silence once again. The Witch gasped and stumbled backward into her home. Closing the door behind her, she turned and collapsed upon it, clutching her heart. Never had she seen such a display of power. A terrible thought came to her.

The Timmutes honored her, at least for the time being. But without her blessing and direction, the orbs might destroy the world out of blind vengeance for some future transgression. Certainly, they were capable enough, but if they decided to destroy the world, she knew she could not stop them.

Her mind raced. Unless of course she created some sort of disease that could overtake them, faster than they could reproduce. But she knew that was extremely dangerous. Before a disease could do the work, the Timmutes would revolt and do severe damage, maybe even kill her before they died out. Plus, those sorts of things had unintended consequences of the nasty sort, especially to other living things. They had a tendency to get out of hand, worse than the Timmutes. No, she could not risk it. So, an uneasy peace ensued.

As she continued to decide what she would do, one day the Witch noticed a spiderweb fresh on her doorway. Formed in the cobweb was a single word: *Liar.*

Ulrig. It must have been a message from the Master Tree. She went outside invoking the spell to communicate with the forest. Once cast, she heard many disjointed conversations. Over the din of a hundred angry voices, she called out for Master Tree. He provided no immediate answer. Then, at last, a faint and sickly reply came.

"Madam, you have been deceived," Master Tree said, speaking in a low tone.

"Master Tree? Are you well?"

"You are quite aware of our situation, Madam. Your creation, these Timmutes, are killing us. They kill the forest, killing us from the inside out, but they are killing us just the same."

The Witch listened. She heard a low constant mumbling in the background from the vines, moss, and bushes.

What are these horrible tiny creatures?

We cannot protect ourselves.

Why did you not prepare us?

You have gone against us, against your word!

What have we done to you, for you to betray us so?

You deceiver, liar.

"Oh no! Master Tree!" She did not know what to say to him. "I am so sorry. Please, what can I do?"

"What can you do? Command the Timmutes to stop. They are your creation. Honor your promise that you made to us. Hurry, Madam, do it quickly. Before it is too late!"

"Y-yes! I will, I must!" she promised.

Once again, the Witch went stumbling out into the forest, calling the Timmutes. A swarm of glowing orbs swirled thick around her. Looking nervous, she addressed them.

"My dear Timmutes! Your numbers are so many. I honor you and welcome you to the Great Mapes Forest. Look around and see the life here. These trees, vines, bushes, moss, they have all been living in this forest for a thousand years. They are a tolerant society and wish you no harm. You might not be able to see them as they are, you might not be able to sense them, but I can. The living things of the forest and I are in close contact with each other. They have pledged their loyalty to me, and in return, I have promised them safety. They have served me well, creating a place for me that I call home. Which just happens to be the very place of your origin. There, in the workshop of my cottage, you were created because of their pledge to me. They provided it to me. Can't you honor them, as you honor me? Can you respect them, and they will respect you? We can all live together. Timmutes! I call upon your honor, your birthplace, and your birthright. If you honor me as your creator, then uphold the promise I made to them years ago. My dear Timmutes, this is something I must insist of you as your creator. This is my commandment to you."

After the Witch completed speaking, a low rumble ensued. It started growing, increasing in strength, and turning into a constant hum. The Witch squinted her eyes as the sound pierced her ears. Then, at last, the Timmutes focused its hum into a single voice, a single tone comprised of a million voices merging and blending together.

And then they spoke.

At first, the voice was too loud, an overwhelming boom. The Witch winced as the voice shouted, "CREATOR, WE HONOR THEE!"

Seeing her expression, and knowing they needed to adjust, the Timmutes over-corrected. Now in an almost inaudible whisper, they said, "We join in a single voice to respond to our creator." The Witch now tilted her head to hear them better.

The Timmutes continued to adjust. Finding the right balance now, they spoke in a steady, normal tone. "Most gracious Mother Creator. Thank you for welcoming us to the forest. We do honor you and our birthplace. We are a respectful and honorable society.

We respect the living things of the Great Mapes Forest. As for the pledge you made to all the living things of the Great Mapes Forest, we honor in your name. Please forgive us, for we have transgressed upon these living things of the forest. We were not aware of the consequences of our actions. We want to live in peace. We will regulate our growth through the laws of our society that provide us with order. However, we need resources and must be able to continue to grow our boundaries. For this, some of us must go outside the Great Mapes and go into the world."

"Do you seek to consume the world?"

"We wish to be a part of this world, not destroy it. We will not provoke the hostilities of anyone against us. We do not want war. We only want to live in privacy. We will go out amongst the world, take what we need, and contain our growth in a lawful way. We will leave the world at peace, if the world leaves us in peace. But a warning: Any exploitation of our society, or any one Timmute, will mobilize all to protect any part of the whole. But that being said, please communicate our sincerest apologies to the established order of all the living things in the Great Mapes Forest and tell them that we will respect the pledge to protect the forest. With your permission, the Timmutes will even assist with the protection of the established order of the Great Mapes for a thousand years."

"I am so grateful to all of you. Thank you, Timmutes. Please take my blessing with you and find your way in this world, live in harmony with all things, and prosper in the way of your many numbers. I forgive you for your transgressions. You did not know what harm you were causing. And you did nothing with evil intent. You did not know my pledge to the Great Mapes. I can forgive you, but I cannot forgive myself. Hopefully, the Great Mapes Forest will not deal too harshly with me for my negligence. Now, please go in peace and accept my blessing."

In response, before they went, the Timmutes had one more surprise for their creator: They sang.

It began as a slow chant, then grew into intricate harmonies, filling the forest. Even the trees heard and basked in its splendor. Their voices carried through the Great Mapes Forest, and everything stopped before this event that would never again take place. A chorus of triumph and glory, a melody of mourning and melancholy, the harmonies carried together on the wind.

Finally, when the last notes faded, an echo of that miraculous event resonated in the Witch, who stood in awe for a long time.

Then, when the Timmutes had finished, the rustling of the wind returned to the forest. Now, she turned to face the Master Tree.

"Master Tree, I have reasoned with the Timmutes. They will do no more damage to the living things of the forest. They will even help us keep the safety of the forest in future years. I know there is no reason for you to do so, but I beg for your forgiveness, as the Timmutes begged for ours."

For several moments there was only silence from Master Tree. At last, he spoke.

"Did you forgive them?"

The Witch nodded. "I did."

"Then we, Madam, forgive you as well," Master Tree said.

"Thank you." The Witch breathed a sigh of relief.

"We forgive you. But compensation will be required, Madam. For as I speak with you now, I am incomplete, as many of my brothers are incomplete. The Timmutes have damaged and consumed many of my branches and leaves, my root barely survives. The Timmutes have replaced those parts of me they consumed and are now as much a part of me as was the bark of my trunk. If they were to leave me now, I would die. Therefore, our society demands recompense."

"What would you have me do?"

"You must carry the same burden we carry. A limb, Madam. One of your own choosing."

The Witch gave him a worried look. "And if I agree to your terms, will the Great Mapes extend their forgiveness?"

"You already have our forgiveness, Madam. What the terms of this agreement will fulfill is the continuance of our pledge. Without the terms of our pledge fulfilled, the forest will reclaim all that we have provided you. In short, you will no longer have a home here, as we will expand and grow over what we have given you."

"I understand," said the Witch. "I am willing. I agree to the terms."

The Master Tree slowly turned and spread his branches apart in a sweeping motion, revealing a light shining outwardly through a large open knothole in its trunk.

The Witch bowed her head, rolling up her left sleeve. She shuffled closer to Master Tree, rubbing the flesh of her left arm. "With this arm, I once embraced the gods. Now, I sacrifice it for compensation to the Great Mapes Forest in a continuance of our pledge. With this action, may we have peace for a thousand years."

The Witch slowly inserted her arm into the knothole. Gradually the hole squeezed until it tightened, compressing her flesh. A numbness spread in her arm. Master Tree waited for a moment, then the cut was swift. The Witch fell backward, dropping to the ground without her left arm.

She grasped her shoulder and scrambled away from Master Tree.

"I am so sorry for this necessity, Madam Witch. Now, you are like us. We are both deformed. Complete in our pain, yet we live on. Our pledge can live on as well."

"Master Tree," the Witch struggled to speak through clenched teeth. "Thank you for your mercy, forgiveness, and understanding. Now, I must leave you."

Master Tree did not have to answer her; he knew she had to take care of her wounds, as he must do.

Time was of the essence to stop the bleeding. She stumbled into her house and cauterized her wound upon the hot cauldron. Then she passed out.

The following morning, it surprised her that she still lived to see another day. Her wound seared with pain, but she had survived the cut. She applied an ointment to her stump and wrapped her wound in fresh linens.

Opening the door the next day, she found that the Great Mapes Forest and the Timmutes had worked together to come to her aid. There on the doorstep, a gift waited for her: A wooden arm. They gave her a perfectly formed replica of her own left arm, which was now a possession of the Master Tree. But another surprise waited for her. As she looked upon the wooden prosthetic arm, she noticed it moved on its own. The fingers worked as if they were alive, the elbow flexed, catching her attention as she considered it laying on her doorstep.

The Witch unwrapped the linen bandages and considered the fitting of the arm. Aligning it to her stump, she laid it upon the flesh of her shoulder. The Timmutes, working inside the arm, scrambled to mend a connection between the Witch and the arm. She felt a series of ticklish wriggles, a tingling in her shoulder, as the necessary Timmutes extended their reach inside her muscle structure. They squeezed and tightened against the sinews of her shoulder, pulling the wood of the prosthetic arm, sealing the gaps, and smoothing the surfaces to work all as one. After it finished binding to her, the motion from the arm became still, until it responded to her own muscular commands in much the same way as the original.

She worked the fingers of her new wooden arm, clenching and unclenching her hand, and seeing that it worked perfectly with her will. She bent the arm at the elbow, testing the flexibility, and that, too, worked just as she willed it.

As wonderful a device as the arm was, it still presented her with a slow process to trust it. It felt unnatural to use at first, so she relied less on her left hand, favoring her right, until she got more used to working it. But after a while, it became more natural.

In return for the prosthetic, the Witch spent her days talking casually with Ulrig and sitting outside in the shade. From that moment on, a stronger bond existed between them.

"And what of the Timmutes?" The Master Tree asked her.

"Many of them have moved on."

"Doesn't that worry you, Madam?"

"I feel they have a purpose," the Witch said, jotting down thoughts in one of her books. Then laying her head back, she closed her eyes.

The Timmutes gave no more problems to the Great Mapes Forest after that. They continued to expand, but to where was anybody's guess. The Witch knew better than to attempt to pry in Timmute business. They went to extreme lengths to make sure that no living thing, even the Witch herself, knew of their comings and goings.

So it was that the Timmutes were created and became a natural part of the World.

"See them coming from miles away.
See their courage and feel their pain!
Never-ending, no, life's the same
Come next year, I'm going to fly again."

Excerpt from *The Witch's Songbook*

THE RED SWARM

THE DRAGONBREATH SUMMIT IN THE YEAR 1041 HRT

Aberfell continued to tell the story of the Timmutes as they became agitated by his words. Regardless of their behavior, he continued.

"Some might say she sacrificed her arm needlessly," he said. "Why else would she put her left arm in that knothole?"

"She sacrificed it to keep the peace, between her, the Timmutes, and the Great Mapes."

Aberfell guffawed. "Don't you think, with the power she had, that she could have cast a spell destroying the Timmutes? Or left the Great Mapes, to make a home wherever she wanted? She could have abandoned them, and that vengeful forest, taking her real left arm with her elsewhere."

"Are you saying there was another reason?"

"If it were me, I would have called down some powerful spell, some terrible fire or lightning to destroy all of them in a single stroke. It would have been major magic, but certainly in her power. Then she could have started over again."

The Timmutes could hear Aberfell, and they started swirling in the cottage, faster, and changing in color from gold to red.

"Aberfell? I think you are angering them."

Aberfell looked surprised, slowly searching around the cottage. Almon was right. The Timmutes were small, often overlooked, but they heard everything Aberfell said about the possible destruction of their society, and they did not like that, not one bit. They turned a fiery red, racing around the room like angry hornets. They were circling, picking up speed, gathering in fury.

"I think you are right, Almon. That would be a huge mistake."

But he spoke too late; the Timmutes were already angered. A fearful swarm of red orbs swirled, multiplying rapidly into something resembling a hurricane inside the little room.

Suddenly, daylight poured into the room: a gaping four-foot hole opened in the upper corner of the ceiling. The roof and wall were crumbling apart in red particles. The orbs were breaking away from the structure, exposing the cloudy sky beyond and the heights of the Dragonbreath Mountain. Even the air became thinner, and Aberfell's papers and rolled manuscripts were tossed around the room, swirling in the sudden rush.

Aberfell stood; the heavy rocking chair flipped over, while cups and dishes went flying. Almon's hair was blowing wildly; he squinted to keep debris from blinding him. Aberfell's hood blew back, his beard now flowing behind him. Everything rolled or tossed, blown by strong winds, as the house was coming apart.

"Aberfell! Do something!" Almon screamed over the noise.

"Wait, I beg you Timmutes!" Aberfell lifted his hands, shouting in a plea, scanning the activity. "The Witch had the power! Of course, she did! But she loved the Timmutes dearly. She loved and respected her creation. She loved the whole Timmute society more than she loved herself. You Timmutes were everything to her! I was just telling a story. Please forgive me!"

The orbs circled more slowly but remained red in color. Aberfell continued to address them directly.

"Now, what I was saying before, I never had the Witch's power. So who am I to judge the Witch or her possible actions? I am just so grateful to the Timmutes for taking care of me all these years. Without you, I would have died long ago. I owe you my life. I owe you everything. I apologize that I offended you. I'm just an old fool who talks too much. Please forgive me!" Aberfell said, chuckling nervously.

The Timmutes eventually turned from scarlet to a milder, more familiar golden color. As the general calm returned, once again they assimilated the form of the sturdy structure and patched up the hole they'd created. Gradually, the blowing winds slowed, then stopped. Papers floated down, drifting in arcs to settle in piles on the floor. The light inside returned to a misty, dimmed level.

Then, just as if nothing happened, once again, the Timmutes dutifully went about their business, straightening up the papers, setting the cups and the chair upright, picking up the pieces tossed around in the fury.

"Almon?" Aberfell asked him quietly. "Are you hurt?"

"Yes. I mean no, I don't think so."

"That was a close call," Aberfell said breathlessly. "You had better watch that."

Almon protested. "Look, I don't mean to blame, but…"

"So, where was I?" Aberfell started to sit, and the chair magically lifted from the floor just in time to support him. "Oh, yes! After the Witch lost her arm, the Timmutes and the Great Mapes Forest cooperated for the first time in history to make the Witch a new prosthetic arm. After she got used to it, her new left arm worked so well that she hardly noticed that she was missing the appendage."

"Aberfell?" Almon said, still in shock. "Is this whole house made of Timmutes?"

"Oh, yes. Yes, it is. I thought you knew that?"

"By the gods!" Almon stood and walked to the wall. He put his hand against it. "Amazing. You mean, this wall is made from a colony of Timmutes?"

"Millions of them, maybe. Tens of millions, perhaps. I really don't know how many there are at any given time, and I don't want to. They pack themselves together seamlessly. They can be very dense."

"What do they eat? How do they sleep?"

"Oh, they come and go on their own. That is why you see so many of them floating around. They are coming and going."

"Incredible, incredible," Almon said. "I would not have believed it if I hadn't just seen it for myself."

"They disassemble, reassemble, all the time. Like bees in the hive, each one has a specific duty or role. Some are trained to serve, like the ones that attend us here. Some of them are trained for construction, like the ones that form the cottage, or the praying tree you saw outside. Then there are politicians; they legislate policy, laws, regulations, foreign and domestic policies, everything that effects the whole Timmute politic. Then you have the most fearsome, nastiest sort: The fighters."

In order not to anger them again, Aberfell put his hand to his mouth and whispered. "They are heartless, cold-blooded killers. But all of them, regardless of what position they fill or their official duties, are trained to defend *The Whole*. If you get one of them angered, they are all angered. That is why capturing a single Timmute is not only exceedingly hard, but also extremely dangerous. They are so fast and elusive and are nearly impossible to catch. But let's say you successfully captured one and put it in a jar. You will find that you have an enormous problem on your hands. For where there is one, there are many. I would recommend releasing it immediately. Because one Timmute represents the whole of their society. Capturing one little Timmute will arouse the anger the whole. If they attack, they show no mercy. They keep attacking until they are either satisfied or reunite the one with the whole."

Almon continued carefully rubbing the wall. It had no seam and felt as solid as you would expect a normal wall to feel, except for the slight vibration that he felt before on the cliff when he put his hand on the root. He could feel a barely perceptible movement under his hand: This was the colony shifting slightly to his touch, and the only thing giving it away that the wall was not simply an inanimate object, but a living thing.

"Have you ever heard them speak? Like they did during their naming ceremony?"

Aberfell laughed. "No, but I think we just saw them communicate. At least their meaning was clear enough to me. I told you, the Timmutes are a dangerous sort."

"And they have taken care of you all these years?"

"Of course, they have," Aberfell said. "But in all that time, I have never seen them turn red like that. That was a first."

"Would they have hurt us?"

"My dear boy, if they had swarmed, they would have stripped us to the bone in seconds. You may not realize how close you just came to death."

Almon nervously withdrew his hand from the wall and watched them dutifully go about their business in the room.

"They can hear us?" Almon whispered.

"They are always listening."

"Doesn't it concern you?"

"Almon, at my age, few things concern me anymore. Especially the thought of dying."

Almon returned to his seat. "What keeps you going?"

"Oh, purpose, I think. I believe I have one. But I do not fully understand it entirely. I am the only human created the way I am. Born with this infallible memory to be called the Supreme Historian. But I am not always sure why. In the end, I think it was all in vain."

"You think your life was all in vain?"

"Oh no, not me. I was talking about the Witch, losing her arm. I think that was all in vain. She had made a deal with the forest that was beyond her control to keep."

"Why was it out of her control?"

"Hazor, her son, was coming of age. Not good, according to her prophecy. Then, there was the demon. That was an unexpected problem."

"The demon?" Almon repeated.

"You know the one."

"She wears those pearls around her neck
But underneath, she's a total wreck
She's a dragon breathing fiery coals,
A scaly alligator in a sleepy hole."

Excerpt from *The Witch's Songbook*

THE BONFIRE

IN THE WILDS IN THE YEAR 810 HRT

The demon started as the wind, prowling at night through the trees. On this night, she stalked an unfortunate little boy, a child who chose the wrong night to be exploring the woods alone. She watched him through her silver eyes with intense interest, stalking him like a predator. She followed him through the woods slowly, deliberately, taking her time, anticipating the time she would strike. Prowling the night, she despised the world of the living, deriving power in the energy of fear. Her mouth watered for the tender young boy, wanting to rip him to pieces. Yet, she stayed hidden in the shadows, circling him, just out of his sight beyond the trees.

The little boy stopped in a clearing and dropped his backpack. The child had a youthful, thin frame, and was about ten years old, with thick black hair. He collected some sticks for kindling, and stacked firewood into a small triangular shape. After an initial spark from the flint box, the kindling simmered in smoke until shortly igniting into flames. Using that as a start, he added more substantial branches, fueling the little fire, eventually growing it into a more substantial one, until at last, it brightened the area all around him.

"Poor little fool," the demon said, amusing herself. "He thinks the bigger the fire, the safer he will be. He does not know what horror awaits him tonight."

The demon growled loudly enough to be heard over the rustle of the wind in the leaves.

The child heard, and sensing unseen forces, searched the night. Frantically scanning the darkened tree line, his anxiety grew. He fed more wood into the fire. The bonfire grew brighter and more intense.

Then the demon growled louder.

The boy took a glowing pointed stick from the fire. This only made the demon laugh. The boy prepared to protect himself from any kind of wild animal. But he was not being hunted by an animal.

The demon had denied herself long enough. The boy neared his end. Circling the bonfire faster in the darkness, she prepared to make her appearance known.

As the bonfire grew, the boy continued feeding it more wood. He went to his backpack and pulled out some bottles. He emptied one into the fire, causing flashes in the flames, sending crackling blue sparks into the air.

What is he doing now? The demon watched him curiously.

Emptying more bottles into the bonfire, he made orange sparks weave upward, burning out high above. Then, pulling out a larger clay container from his backpack, he circled the bonfire, pouring salt in a circle around it.

It had mesmerized the demon, but no longer. Her interest in the boy's actions diminished; she spun around the bonfire once more like a hurricane. She decided to strike, hoping he would run so she could pursue him.

Using the bonfire to make her appearance spectacular, she took shape inside the burning logs. The super-heated logs spit up a runny, molten sap; oozing in the hot bubbles, the demon's face formed in shape. Her face screamed emerging out of the fire logs, struggling to get out of the coals. She snarled, not in agony, for the fire was not unpleasant or unfamiliar to her, but in anger as her hunger for the boy's flesh could not wait any longer.

The boy saw the horned head emerging out of the coals. He stared with wide eyes, but he did not run. The demon continued to rise. After her horned head emerged, next came her shoulders, breasts, and torso. Her upper body squirmed from the logs, accompanied by more screaming, thrashing, and clawing as she tried to free the rest. Her snake-like body spilled out of the molten sap; her bottom half was a giant serpent tail. With her whole appearance now complete, her body towered in flames, menacing the boy. Half-woman, half-snake, the demon opened her mouth wide in an evil hiss. With a black forked tongue, she could smell the fear in the air.

She struck, as quick as a cobra, to bury her fangs into his throat. But suddenly, she slammed against an unseen barrier. As if hitting an invisible brick wall, the demon realized that she could not cross; something prohibited her from going out of the bonfire. The purity of the circle of salt! The boy lined the fire with it earlier.

"Clever little boy, but no matter," she said. "You come to me, child, and I will give you everything you ever wanted."

She delighted in the thought, but as much as she tried to mesmerize him, the boy would not come to her. He would not fall under her control, as if the boy possessed his own powerful magic.

"What is this? Who are you?" the demon asked circling around the fire in growing frustration.

"Stop it, Langula! You must obey me," the boy said. He held his palms toward her. "Do my bidding. Serve me, and the world will fear you."

Blinking at him through her silver viper eyes, she stopped circling in the bonfire that burned all around her.

"Where did you get such false confidence, boy?" the demon asked from the center of the bonfire. "I will enjoy this," she said, licking her fangs, laughing in delight.

"I propose a deal with you," the boy said.

"You want to make a deal with me?"

"You can destroy me, if you like, but only if you can answer one riddle. However, if you cannot, then you will serve me."

"Delightful," the demon said intrigued, unable to resist a riddle. "What is the riddle?"

"It is a very simple one, Langula. Merely tell me the name of one soul you took before you destroy mine."

"You are a doomed soul," she said. The demon burst out laughing. But when her laughter died down, she looked more puzzled than ever. Then her puzzlement turned to confusion.

"This is most strange," she said, then stopped short. "What kind of magic is this? I cannot remember a single soul I have taken before you."

"You remember nothing because there is nothing to remember," the boy said. "Have you not guessed it yet?"

The demon was silent.

"I am the one who has summoned you! I am the one who has created you! And I am the one you will obey, or I will send you back to the place I conjured you from. But if you chose to serve me, you will wet your fangs on human blood for a thousand years. It's your choice."

The demon cackled. "Not true. I will feast upon your flesh tonight!"

"What a strange proposition for a demon to sit in judgment of the truth, of what it is, and what it is not. I have called upon you for your service, your full demonic powers; I have no designs to limit you.

But you will make up your mind quickly. Shall you be my servant in this worldly realm, or shall I send you back to the destruction you came from?"

"Warlock!" The demon pointed and screamed. Incensed, she spun inside the fire and salt line. This amused the boy now, and he walked around the fire. "But I cannot deny that you are right. I can remember nothing. You have cast a spell upon me."

"I told you there is nothing for you to remember. It is no spell of mine. You have no past, you have no memory, you only have the future. Now what is it going to be? Langula!"

The demon stopped. It was the third time the boy used that name. Her agitation lessened.

"The name is as ancient as the mountains," the boy said. "As fearful as the night. It is the name you were born to be."

Langula now listened.

The boy continued, "Together, you and I will strike fear into the heart of this world."

"Who are you?" Langula asked.

"I am Hazor, the son of the God Hexor and the Goddess Ehlona. Call me the Zorn, for I am scorn, and I will call you the First Lady of my Zornastic Order."

"So, it is as I thought. You are an immortal after all. Yesss," Langula hissed with her forked tongue. "Very well, whatever you would have me do. I will obey you, Master Zorn."

The Zorn turned with a smile. He did not release her just yet though. He considered her further as he sat on a log and ate a strawberry. But upon further examination, it was not a strawberry he consumed; it was a small pig's heart. He ate the raw organ with a dainty precision, not wasting a drop of it, or dripping any blood upon him. Langula hungrily watched with desire in her silver eyes. The Zorn wiped his mouth with a napkin while considering Langula. Then he reached into his backpack, pulling out a second heart. He flipped the heart toward her. She caught it between her hands, funneling it into her mouth. She gobbled up the raw pig's heart, swallowing it down in one ravenous motion, leaving blood upon her chin. She smiled, licking the blood off her lips with a forked tongue.

"Now I will release you upon the world," the Zorn said to her.

"Look at me, Look at me.
I've walked a thousand miles.
I've been awake for days.
I cannot bear the weight.
Of all the friends I've made
Now all the feeling is gone."

Excerpt from *The Witch's Songbook*

A WANDERING PRIEST

THE GREAT MAPES FOREST IN THE YEAR 818 HRT

One day the Witch had a visitor. A man came walking through her part of the forest toward her house. She had seen no one in the Great Mapes for quite some time. He did not look like any ordinary hunter or woodsman. He looked like a priest, wearing a white robe wrapped over a thin muscular build. His head was shaven, except for a long braid of red hair banded and tied at the top of his head.

No matter, she thought. *The Timmutes will handle him.*

But she could not keep her eyes off him. There was something oddly familiar about the priest. She felt sorry for him as the Timmutes swarmed to surround him in scarlet orbs. She hoped they would run him off, let him go with just a warning, with only minor injuries, which was better than being dead. Yet he walked right through the middle of them, unharmed.

Why are the Timmutes letting the priest pass unmolested? She wondered.

After walking through a cyclone of Timmutes, the priest approached her house untouched. He surprised the Witch by knocking politely on her door. Ever since she had made her home in the Great Mapes, no man had ever gotten as far as this; the Timmutes never allowed it. Usually, they would have either driven them away or simply killed those stubborn enough to ignore the warning signs.

Why this priest? Why now? the Witch thought.

With one word, the mystery ended.

"Mother?" the priest asked.

The Witch stopped in her tracks.

"It is me, Marus."

Memories filled her mind, reflections of years long past. Her memory had become so dull that she could not remember her own son, and she looked for comparisons. He looked nothing like the burly, gregarious, red-headed Heironomus, God of Light. He had an athletic, lean body where Heironomus had a large, muscle-bound frame. Instead of thick red hair like Heironomus, the priest shaved his head except for the long-banded topknot. But more than that, the priest did not resemble anything she remembered of herself. Providing her mind could remember her former self at all.

"What was that name you said?"

"Marus, son of Heironomus. My father was the God of the Light. My Mother, Ehlona the Goddess of Beauty. I am Marus, your son." The Witch heard names she had not thought of in years. "Sister Catosa, your Acolyte from the Temple of Valor, raised me as my mother. She took great care of me. I have grown strong, as a man."

She trembled, a tear forming in her eye. She turned her back on Marus. If this was Marus, she did not know what to say to him after all these years. For the first time since leaving Sister Catosa's house, that fateful night of the Beautiful Blessings, she found herself self-conscious about losing her beauty.

Marus cautiously entered the house, carefully shutting the door behind him. He looked around at the clutter. Books and papers stacked loosely around the room. The wax of half-burned candles melted down in hardened streams upon the table. The deformed bodies of tadpoles floating in jars on shelves, along with roots, berries, and herbs. Returning his gaze to her, he addressed her again.

"Yesterday was my eighteenth birthday, and as a gift to myself, I wanted to find you. I wanted to many times over the years, but I wanted to respect your privacy."

"Until now," the Witch remarked. "Eighteen years? Has it been so long?"

"I wanted to let you… let you know that I have become a man, and that I am well. It was important to me to tell you that."

"You don't know how much those words—" She choked. "You don't know how much that means to me."

He stepped to her side to try to get a closer view of her. Yet, she turned away again.

"Do not look upon me," she said. "I was not always this way."

"I know, Mother. I know of your sacrifice, of what you lost, and what you gave away. I know what you did, what you did for me, and what you are doing for the entire world. Do you even know what you started? The Sisters of the Orphans have established their orders, just as you blessed them. They provide protection for children everywhere. You gave them the hope they needed. They call them Saint Ehlona's orphanages."

She gave him a quick glance over her shoulder, still shielding half her face.

"All named after you, Mother. You are called Saint Ehlona outside of these woods."

She shifted on her feet, then walked to a cabinet made of living white oak. Marus watched her open a door of the cabinet and pull something out. Then she sat on a little stool.

Soon, musical strings began filling the air. Facing away from him, she played her lyre and sang in an unsteady voice:

I love to fly under my own wings,
Consulting with the angels about heavenly things.
I like to hide where they can't find me,
Just to look at all the faces
Of those who said they would always love me.
But you can't see me since I have wished myself away
While the world keeps turning in its own way.
Now I find myself laughing until I cry.
But I am not laughing anymore.
I'm just a tear,
Just a tear away.
It may be dark, and I might lose my way.
So, float a soft light to me; I'll send my love into the flame.
Close your eyes! Close your eyes! And wash the sorrow from your eyes.
And make a wish on angels' wings before they fly too high.
But you cannot see me since I have wished myself away
While the world keeps turning in its own way.
Now I find myself laughing until I cry.
But I am not laughing anymore.
I'm just a tear,
A tear away.

The house fell silent.

"Thank you for returning to me," she said to him.

Marus said softly, "I could never forget you."

The Witch turned a milky eye to look upon her son. "Where will you go now?"

"I will still help the Saint Ehlona's orphanages, to protect them, assure that no harm befalls them. The word has gone out that Chen-Li protects your orphanages. Chen-Li is the name my followers have given me."

"Chen-Li? The magical symbols for body and soul? The Chen your body, and the Li your spirit?"

"You might not remember, but when I was born, you gave me a blessing that my spirit may be as the wind. That blessing granted me mastery over my body and soul. I have obtained control of my spirit, allowing it to separate from my body. I can travel anywhere in my Li form. No person, no place, no prison can hold my spirit down."

The Witch rotated on her humped back as best she could. She turned around to face him. This was the first time Marus saw her unimpeded. Her face was frightfully hideous.

Upon seeing her face in its entirety, he had to control his fear. Her appearance had become fearful for men, and being her son granted him no more immunity from that fear than anybody else. Her appearance took his breath away. He gripped against his fear, breathing deeply, making himself look directly into her eyes. Yet they had become milky and whitewashed to the point he had to fight the urge to run. Taking a deep breath, he deliberately paused, slowing his body down to control his fear. Then, he smiled and spoke kindly.

"I will make my home in the east, atop the Gray Mountains with my First Wives. They will meet me there, and I will establish the Temple of Chen-Li."

"You are already married?"

"Tyla and Myra are my First Wives."

"First Wives?" the Witch asked. She found it peculiar that her son had more than one wife, after she was punished for having both of the gods.

"My followers will include my children."

"Followers? You are forming an army? What will you do with this army, Chen-Li?" the Witch asked suspiciously, walking around the table, getting closer to him.

Marus could feel the very air thinning between them as she got nearer.

"I will train them in the art of Chen-Li fighting."

The Witch extended a boney finger to him as if she wanted to touch his face. But she stopped short. "What will you train them to fight for?"

"Hazor has disappeared."

The Witch dropped her finger and gazed to the floor. "Yes, of course, Hazor, the son of Hexor, the God of Darkness. May the gods protect you. Do you know anything about his whereabouts?"

"He ran away from the orphanage eight years ago."

"Eight years ago," she repeated.

"He goes by a new name."

"What is it?"

"He is brainwashing captives into following him mindlessly. He calls them priests of his Zornastic Order, and he himself, the Zorn."

"The Zorn," she said, turning in thought. "The magical word for scorn."

"There's more. He has summoned a demon to lead the Zornastic Order."

The Witch looked at Chen-Li, again with heightened interest. "A demon?"

"Together the two of them are bent on the destruction of humans. With his Zornastic Order he has created an empire of dark priests."

"Where is his empire?"

"We don't know, only feel the effects of it. I have not been able to locate it yet. Somehow it escapes my visions."

"I fear that his power protects its location. It will be strong. You may never locate it."

"Yes, that's what I suspect as well. So, I make my home in the Gray Mountains and train and prepare for the day my brother will emerge. When that happens, Chen-Li's might be the only force capable of stopping him"

"You will need help, Marus," she said.

"What about the Timmutes? I know they are a very formative power you have created. Will they help me?"

"No, that's impossible. They made a blood pledge with me. That explains why they allowed you to approach through the Great Mapes Forest unharmed. Because you are of my blood, and they believe that any one part is equal to the whole. So, as they see you, they see me, they see themselves, and they will not harm you. Unfortunately, they will see Hazor the same way. Because of their pledge, we are all related, and they cannot kill any part of the whole."

The Witch reached into a big bag and pulled out a white feather.

"But here, take this," she said, offering him the feather. He took it and considered it. "With this feather, your body will be lighter than the wind, even lighter than your Li. You will soar to the treetops and land as gentle as a breeze. Consider it a gift, for your birthday. Take it and be well, my son."

"I will treasure this forever, Mother. Thank you."

"Marus, my son—or Chen-Li if you prefer. I see the warrior in you. Do your best to recruit a following you can trust, one that will be loyal. Train them to be fearless. Teach them to fight with passion. Also, know this: When you see the signs in the sky, it will tell you that the Zorn is at his strongest point. Use all your skills to create a weapon that will defeat this demon of his. But do not use it, or seek it out, for it will be a curse for any that tries to wield it. Instead, send it out among the people. There, the weapon will gravitate to the one that it will give its blessing to, rather than curse them. It will find its own champion. I will send more help, as best as I can, when the time is right. At some time in the future, lead your Chen-Li warrior army on the field of battle. If the fates favor you, you will be victorious. If not, well…" the Witch trailed off. "Well, then Hazor will accomplish everything that he set out to do."

"That is a big gamble, isn't it, Mother?"

"It will exact a most extreme cost," she answered. "Blood must poison the waters before the balance will level."

"When will I know the sign?"

"There will be no mistaking it; the entire world will see it and know it."

Chen-Li nodded. He did not understand completely, but knew his mother had always been mysterious in her ways.

"There is no time to waste then," Marus said and stood up. "Will we see each other again, Mother?"

"Not for a long time."

"Then know that we will only be separated by space, but forever joined in blood. Be well, Mother. I will always keep you in my heart." With that, Marus turned for the door.

"Marus," the Witch called to him.

He stopped short and turned to face the Witch once again.

"Close your eyes," she said to him.

He did what she told him to do without question. As he closed his eyes, tiny lights danced behind his eyelids. He could feel a spell being cast on him, but he did not resist; he trusted her and let the magic happen.

A vision of Ehlona the Goddess of Beauty appeared in his mind's eye. She came to him wearing flowing white garments, golden bands on her arms and wrists. Her soft blonde hair braided in bright glowing bands. Her skin so smooth in youth. Her brilliant crystal-blue eyes sparkling, and sunlight reflecting off her ruby-red lips. She leaned closer and gave him a kiss. He felt an actual kiss upon his cheek. In the house in the Great Mapes Forest the Witch kissed him, but in his mind, it was the beautiful Ehlona, and as long as he kept his eyes closed, the vision was real.

When at last he opened them again, he was standing outside in the forest. Far away from the Witch's house that now sat far behind him. In the window, a shadow, the silhouette of the Witch, gave him a final wave goodbye. The vision of Ehlona was gone, and Marus smiled. With a tear in his eye, he waved back, lingering there, looking at the house and the shadow within for a moment. Then Marus turned and leaped in a mighty bound, sailing through the tops of the trees, carried by the Witch's feather. He rose higher and out of sight.

Inside the cottage, the Witch covered her eyes, and sobbed.

"Shame, shame, shame, but I don't feel a thing.
From the flames, there's a better day.
From the evil, there is great.
We're headed into the wild."

Excerpts from *The Witch's Songbook*

CASTLE IN THE CLOUDS

Castle Orlo in the Year 825 of HRT

In the darkness of the chamber, it reeked of mold and mildew. Four heavy iron grates covered as many sewer drains centered into its stone floor, one in each quadrant. Rotting corpses lined the walls, still manacled where they died, never released from their torments, even in death.

The demon Langula slithered within the chamber, hiding in the shadows as the Zornastic priests escorted the captives in. One by one, a steady cadre of hooded figures walked in, priests of the Zornastic Order. Each one of them brought an offering, a prisoner for the blood sacrifice, and led them to the center of the room.

These were the missing persons from nearby villages. Fathers, mothers, soldiers, children, nomads, all kidnapped from the surrounding area. They had either refused the initiation, or their physical limitations meant they were not worthy of becoming priests of the Zornastic Order.

Like obedient ravens, the black-hooded priests made them stand in the center, naked and shivering, as they took their places in a semi-circle around the walls of the chamber. Their robes bore the emblem of the black crescent moon sewn into a silver circle in the middle of their black robes. They came in chanting over and over:

"Your days are gone, never to return! Your days are gone, never to return!"

"Zornastic Order!" Langula said with a hiss. "What is this gift you have offered to the Zorn?"

The hooded figures all stood still in their black robes and spoke in one voice.

"A feast of blood!" they all said. Then, the chanting continued.

"Your days are gone, never to return! Your days are gone, never to return!"

The prisoners were strangers to each other, yet they huddled together, clinging to one another in wide-eyed terror in the center of the chamber. These men, women, and children in the middle had already suffered much cruelty at the hands of their captors; their bodies were slashed and bloodied, their faces bruised and dirty; they were covered in sores, sweat, and stink.

A dark-hooded priest came through the east-facing door and shut it with a loud bang. Then a door on the west side of the chamber opened to reveal the shadowy figure of a slender man standing alone in dim light. Suddenly the chanting ceased and quiet filled the room. After an uncomfortable silence, a single voice at last spoke out.

"I know what it is like to be hated," said the voice. His words resonated ominously throughout the room. He slowly stepped inside, and with each step, a hard footfall reverberated against the walls of the chamber. When he walked past the torches, the light revealed him to be an impeccably groomed man with a clean-shaven face and thick, black hair combed back, oiled into place to give it a reflective sheen. He wore a black uniform with gold buttons running up on his right side. Two dainty red buttons held in place a high collar buttoned all the way up to just under his chin. The most unusual feature, though, were his yellowish, glowing eyes; fog seemed to swirl in his irises. At a distance, the man would be able to pass for human, but up close, he looked unnatural.

He continued to address the prisoners.

"I, too, know what it feels like to be alone. To sleep on cold stone. To be hunted and humiliated. Beaten and coerced to make pledges of fealty that you have no intentions of honoring. Made to confess lies, and saying anything just to make the hurt stop, even things that you do not believe. Like you, I have had sleepless nights worrying about such things."

This was the Zorn, and they knew it. No longer the little boy Hazor summoning demons around the bonfire, he was a fully grown man now, if he could be considered a man at all. His powers, inherited from his father, the God Hexor, made him an immortal among the humans. He paced the room, tall and confident, in the prime of his power.

He approached one of the children.

"Please, have mercy," one prisoner pleaded with him. "You don't have to do this."

The Zorn put a finger to his lips, and the pleading stopped. He patted the boy on top of his head.

"Ever since I was just a small boy myself, I have been hated and despised by all men. Do you think they had to do that to me?"

He walked around the circle now. "And for what? What did I ever do to anyone? I was just a baby; I had hurt no one. My only desire was a mother's love, yet for that, I was hated. Not on my own merits, mind you. But on my situation, my station in life, the misunderstanding that I was born into. Like, for instance, being the second-born in a whore's womb. How was that my fault, I ask you?"

The Zorn contemplated while he continued to walk. "I spent so many years in that orphanage. Absorbing punishments, the whippings, the unjustified abuse. Impotent beatings from old crones as they tried to disguise love as oppression and discipline—that orphanage of my so-called saintly mother. What saint would abandon their own child on the first night of life? The first night alive in this world. She looked upon me in disgust while I had not yet shed the filth of my afterbirth."

He spun to face the group and shouted, "ABANDONED ME!" His voice echoed off the walls then trailed off. The prisoners trembled.

Noticing their reactions, he softened. "But have no fear. You will never abandon me. I know it. Our flesh will become as one flesh." He walked to a table on the far wall and picked up a sharp, oddly shaped instrument. After a consideration, he looked back at the prisoners and released it. It fell on the metal table with a loud bang.

"Let me welcome you to Castle Orlo," he announced cheerfully. "Welcome to my castle, my home. Isn't it wonderful?" He walked around the chamber with his arms outstretched. "There are many rooms here. This is but one chamber. There are so many more. It's almost too much!"

He motioned to a man to come to him. The man was a carpenter just days ago before his nightmare began. He approached slowly with hesitation toward the Zorn. "Come, come!" the Zorn encouraged him. As the man got closer, the Zorn pointed to a spot on the ground before him. The man kneeled before the Zorn as commanded.

"Do you like it here?" the Zorn asked him with a tilt of his head.

The man choked and begged. "Please, I want to see my daughters again."

The pleading only angered the Zorn, who shouted, "I asked, DO YOU LIKE IT HERE?"

The man bowed his head and nodded while he cried without any shame.

"Orlo is a magnificent castle, isn't it? You know it formed in the clouds? After leaving that forsaken orphanage, I followed the sky and instinctively arrived at this very location. The village of Orlo was just a little forgotten farmland when I found it. But once I came, the clouds parted, and a wondrous vision appeared to me. It was this castle in the sky, there, in the very clouds, bursting apart like a scroll to reveal itself to me. It was built in the vapor in its entirety. Majestically it formed on high with its towers of spiraled peaks, its marble central dome, thick impenetrable walls, foreboding iron gates." The Zorn laughed. "I knew it had to be mine. I had to have it. I knew I had to possess it. It called to me deep in my dreams. It welcomed me. It screamed with a mighty voice into my mind; it screamed: YOU HAVE COME INTO YOUR KINGDOM!"

The Zorn stood, throwing the man to the cold, damp floor, spreading his arms wide. "I called this glorious castle down to its rightful place, this mighty fortress, this Castle of Orlo. I commanded it down into these cornfields. It sanctified this place. It obeyed me, and I trembled. Then, it whispered to me in a very humble voice. It whispered: May we approach you, as your humble servant? Will you allow us to wash you in blood?"

With this, the Zorn simulated stabbing the man with an invisible sword. The prisoner flinched, even though he was in no pain. The Zorn turned and gave a slight shrug. "How could I resist?" Then he motioned for the man to return to the group in the center of the chamber, which he immediately did.

"Then, at that precise moment, my castle fell upon the ground with a loud crash, fixing itself deep into the rock of the world. Yet Castle Orlo held one more surprise for me. The castle is guarded by magic; it remains unseen to human eyes. Unless I allow it, the stones remain hidden from view.

"It was a gift, I believe it was, from my father. Locked in cosmic combat, forever fighting for survival with a hateful god, he too was hated for no reason. His want for a woman betrayed him, ruined when she took a red-headed buffoon as her bumbling husband. I get angry every time I think about that Witch!

"But now, a time has come for an accounting! It is a time for a reckoning. A blood payment must be! Just the latest in a long line of recompense!"

The priests and the Zorn loudly finished the chant together.

"Your days are gone, never to return!
In Zornastic fire, your soul will burn!"

The Zorn extended his hands, energy arced between his wrists. With a crackling fury, hundreds, if not thousands, of black oily rats erupted out of the metal drains in the floor under the prisoners' feet. They landed upon them with a wave of vicious teeth and ripping claws in ravenous hunger. The captives shouted, dropping where the rats attacked them, having no defense against the swarm. They fell, disappearing under a thick layer of crawling, bristle-haired, blood-thirsty rodents. They drowned in their screams, as the rats consumed them.

As they perished, energy swirled through the Zorn's body, his flesh invigorated with fresh vitality. Sticky blood streamed down the drains, one in each corner of the chamber. The sounds of screams were replaced with crunching from the rat feast, and laughter from the Zorn and Langula.

The Zorn waved his hand, and the rats dispersed back into the drains in a purple mist. The scene revealed that the swarm of rats cleaned the flesh of the prisoners down to their very bones. The hooded cult members of the Zornastic Order hailed the Zorn for the sacrificial blood feast. They collected the bones singing praises to the Zorn.

"Another blood payment," the Zorn said. "There will be many more."

Langula called out to the Zornastic Order. "All hail the Zorn!"

An enthusiastic cheer from the Zornastic Order rang through the chamber.

"Now leave us," Langula said, and the Zornastic Order turned to go.

The Zorn's mind switched rapidly to Langula.

"Langula, you are perfect," he told her. "These latest prisoners made excellent sacrifices."

"I am pleased that you approve," she said.

"It is an acknowledgment of your splendid wickedness," the Zorn said, circling his throne before he sat. "The beast inside you craves the best, my darling."

She maneuvered herself to slither upon his lap. "These mortals have flesh so young and sweet. There is nothing like the young to satisfy my bloodlust."

"Your desires are insatiable," he said looking at the demon with curiosity. "But you also thrive on corrupting the lives of men. You are the reason they are aroused in the middle of the night by sensual dreams."

"You know me well, Hazor."

"Seduction and manipulation are your most powerful spells. Men have no defense for you."

"They give no resistance. I can do whatever I please."

"Nevertheless, I worry about you," the Zorn said. "You are prone to taking too many chances when you are by yourself."

"I hunt alone," Langula told him.

"I think you need someone to watch over you."

"Would you like to come and watch, Zorn?"

"Come with you to watch? No." The Zorn had no interest in that kind of hunting. That was not the idea he had in mind. "I could have summoned any demon I wanted. You are my only desire. We have business enough here in the castle, growing our army of priests, the Zornastic Order."

Langula delighted having his attention. She laid her head on his chest, flashing her fangs, giving him a flick of her forked tongue. When they were together like this, it was the closest they came to love. But love was an emotion mostly foreign to them, and tonight, she could feel something different as she held him in her coils.

"What troubles you?" she asked, but she received no response. The Zorn ignored her. He stared blankly up in the chamber's space. "What is wrong?"

Suddenly, his body tensed. The Zorn immediately stood, throwing her to the floor.

"You dare!" Langula said hissing.

Holding up his hand, he silenced her. Staring now into the darkness of the empty chamber, the Zorn scanned the dark room. At last, he looked her in the eyes, saying quietly, "We are not alone."

She immediately searched the chamber for the threat but saw nothing.

The Zorn's yellow eyes swirled in a kaleidoscope of colors staring into dark nothingness.

"The bloodline is calling out to me," he said. "My brother is watching."

Why do we hurry,
When all we've got is time?
Come sit beside me and lay your weary head upon mine.
The fire's dying slow, the ember's glow,
and is all nearly gone."

Excerpts from *The Witch's Songbook*

THE TEMPLE OF CHEN-LI

The Fangs in the Year 819 HRT

It was a fine piece of marble, cut from the finest stone of the Gray Mountains, quarried over ten miles away. Inspected along with twelve other blocks that arrived that day, it was selected for its color and brilliance over all the others. As far as marble blocks went, the builders designated this one as the best. As a result, this piece of white-and-gray-veined marble served, with much fanfare and celebration, as the cornerstone and the first stone laid for foundation of the Temple of Chen-Li. Adorned with a ceremonious gold plaque, the inscription upon it read:

Dedicated in Honor of Heironomus, God of Light,
His wife Saint Ehlona, Goddess of Beauty,
This Priesthood of the Temple of Chen-Li
Established the warrior priests of the White Eminence
On this date, in 819 Human Recorded Time

The temple construction began five miles past the Last Outpost to the East. Chen-Li handpicked this location for his temple to sit atop the first of the Fangs. Farther east, the mighty Dragonbreath Mountain towered in the background; these were the days the summit could still be seen before the perpetual cloud obscured its top.

On a second, higher peak, Chen-Li made a simple home. A small waterfall separated the two peaks, streaming through the rocks burbling in a relaxing ambiance. Light breezes swayed the leaves on the high treetops. The Temple of Chen-Li was being constructed in slabs of marble stone, but the frame of his home was simple planks of wood. The interior had a series of doors that could be arranged to change the configuration depending on how many doors were slid open or shut. Chen-Li dedicated the temple to be a structure that would survive for a thousand years but chose a simple home for himself and the First Wives. Both constructions were grand, but never lost the focus of their purpose.

The Temple of Chen-Li would be the home and training grounds for a fighting force of warrior priests called the White Eminence, aptly called this for their white robes. The temple would be their rallying place for training an army that would one day have to face the Zorn and his demon in battle. The warrior priests of the White Eminence had no other option but victory. They believed that when the day of the battle came, they would be the only force standing between the kingdoms of men and destruction. They focused daily on concentrated meditation and trained for a fight to come. When the time came, the White Eminence would be ready.

"Look, there he is," a woman announced. She pointed to the treetops, and Chen-Li came gliding down from his home on the second peak. He skimmed the upper branches of the trees with his feet, landing on a large branch. He appeared dressed in white garments, with wrappings tight around his legs and wrists.

"Don't point," another woman said, smacking at her hand. "It's not polite."

"I know, but oh! I don't care. Maybe he will see me and make me wife number, oh! What number is he on now? Is it six or seven? I lost track! Chen-Li, pick me! pick me!"

"Can you imagine being one of his wives?" another woman said.

"I can. It would be like a dream," still another commented.

By now, he mesmerized all who saw him. The White Eminence totaled about fifty warrior priests. The work stopped as they cheered for Chen-Li.

He smiled his infectious grin, then vaulted from tree to tree, before finally somersaulting flawlessly to the tallest marble tower. From this vantage point, he could see the progress of the temple, and gave an approving nod.

"Well done everybody." He observed the surrounding faces. "It is a fine start. You have made significant progress. To every single one of you, for your hard work, I thank you. Stay strong!"

Loud applause erupted from the White Eminence. Chen-Li bounded off the marble tower high above to the tree branches again. As the applause faded below him, he floated up to the second peak. There, he entered his wooden home. Two of his wives, from his First Wives, waited for him there.

"My husband," Tyla, the first wife, said. "Come, take a moment to rest."

"I cannot rest right now, Tyla. I must see a man before the hour."

"As you wish," she answered.

"How is the temple coming?" asked Myra, another wife.

"Faster than expected," Chen-Li told Myra. "We are ahead of schedule. The White Eminence are enthusiastic. Our morale is high, but our numbers are too low. We do not yet have a hundred, but thousands will be needed. If I could just discover the Zorn's whereabouts."

Myra nodded and went to join the other First Wives of Chen-Li. She stopped in the doorway before leaving and turned. "All of your First Wives will gather in the training area, when you are ready."

"As usual, my loves." Chen-Li smiled. "Thank you."

Chen-Li slid the western door closed, then he was alone. He grabbed a peach from a bowl and, walking across the room, slid the eastern door open.

A man stood in the doorway. One of Chen-Li's spies stood there waiting; he was escorting another man, a prisoner with a bag over his head.

"Were you seen?" Chen-Li asked the spy.

"Not until I reached the temple," was the reply.

Chen-Li motioned the spy to come in, and the two men entered the room. Chen-Li lingered at the door, looking for any trespassers. Seeing none, he slid the eastern door shut and turned to face them.

Chen-Li put his finger to his lips, instructing silence. The spy nodded and took a step back from the prisoner. Chen-Li circled the prisoner and looked him over in silence. He wore a black uniform with a crescent moon in a silver circle on the front. Chen-Li finally nodded, and the spy took off the hood in one quick motion. The prisoner squinted, not accustomed to the bright light.

"Do you know where you are?"

Adjusting his eyes, he shook his head.

"You are in the house of Chen-Li. You are in my home."

Chen-Li produced the piece of fruit.

"Untie him." Chen-Li motioned to his spy, and he untied the prisoner.

"You must be hungry," Chen-Li said, extending the fruit to the prisoner, but the man hesitated.

"See? Not poisoned," Chen-Li said, taking a bite from it. "Take it."

The prisoner took it and ate it while Chen-Li turned his back.

"I see you are a cultist of the Zornastic Order, are you not?"

"Yes," he answered between slurping sounds.

"So, you serve the Zorn?"

The man stopped slurping the peach and gave Chen-Li a worried look.

"I see," Chen-Li told him. "Then we have a lot to talk about."

Chen-Li motioned to his spy. With that, the spy sat at a table, producing paper and ink. The spy received a favorable look from Chen-Li as he observed him, ready to take notes.

"I will find out what I can," Chen-Li told him. The spy nodded.

Chen-Li approached the prisoner, taking what was left of the peach from him. Instructing the prisoner to sit on the floor, Chen-Li sat across from him and began his meditation. They sat cross-legged, facing each other in the middle of the room. Soon Chen-Li drifted into a deep hypnotic state while both the prisoner and the spy watched. The prisoner looked at the spy, but all he did was put his finger to his mouth, instructing silence.

Outside, the clash of fighting carried on the wind up to the open windows of the wooden house as the training hours began in the Temple of Chen-Li below.

A few minutes passed, then Chen-Li's body started glowing with a soft, white light. As he became even brighter, his body levitated off the ground until it hovered five feet from the floor.

Chen-Li could always feel a little pressure on the top of his head, just before his spirit would split from his body with an audible *pop*! The prisoner watched in fascination as Chen-Li's spiritual body ascended above his physical form in dull colors, floating to the ceiling as if treading water in an unseen ocean of air.

The Li looked down upon his body still in meditation. Then his spirit leaped toward the prisoner like a bolt of lightning. It slammed into the prisoner's chest with a pounding *thump*! The prisoner now had two spirits inside his body, and a battle ensued while the Li wrestled for control of the prisoner's body.

The spy watched in wonder as Chen-Li's body remained floating above the floor, but the prisoner's body trembled. The prisoner opened his eyes, and the pupils were rolled up in their eye sockets, a sign that the spiritual combat between the two spirits had begun. Chen-Li had long perfected combat in his Li form, and the untrained prisoner was no match for him. It took mere seconds until the prisoner's eyes rolled back into their place.

"Can you hear me?" Chen-Li called out to his spy from the body of the prisoner.

"Yes, I am ready to begin," the spy answered.

When his Li inhabited the prisoner, it was Chen-Li commanding the body; the voice heard in the prisoner's throat was not the prisoner's voice, but his. It made Chen-Li's voice sound deep, hollow, and far away—an unfortunate side effect of his ability of possession.

"This man was a painter. He and his young son, they were from the village of Estes."

The spy scribbled ESTES and PAINTER in his notes.

"His paint buckets were empty. He placed them in the wagon. The sun was going down, they were going home—wait, there is something in the bushes, a noise. A baby crying there, in the bush. How did a baby get there? Why is it lost? The wagon stopped. Who allowed their baby to be out here alone? We must save it."

Chen-Li turned the prisoner's head as if to look around the scene in his trance. The spy continued taking notes of the exchange.

"By the gods! It is not a baby, but a beast. It tricked us, mimicking the infant's cries. It attacked my son. Fangs and claws cutting him. Blood everywhere. I try but cannot get the creature off my son. It is a serpent. No, it is a woman. Yet it is both; this is a demon. My son is dead now. The demon looks at me. Her eyes search me, they know me. She knows I desire her. She touches me now. I feel no pain, only pleasure. I am getting dizzy. Must sleep for a moment."

The spy paused briefly and looked up. Then the prisoner spoke again with Chen-Li controlling the body.

"Now, I am awake. In a dark place. It's cold here. I am chained in metal to stone. There are other people, chanting:

'Your days are gone, never to return
Your days are gone, never to return'

"They offer a glass to me. I look inside. It is filled with dark red. It is blood. But I drink it anyway. I can taste the blood. I am feeling strange. The blood is foul; it is the Zorn's blood. I am now a part of him. He is now part of me. I see her again. The First Lady of the Zornastic Order. Langula the demon, the Zorn's demon."

Everything he said, the spy hastily scribbled down. Chen-Li continued in his trance.

"The Zorn is on the move in the Mid-Run Valley. He continues to gather forces of prisoners, captives, through fear and intimidation. He is forming a cult he calls the Zornastic Order. They hunt at night and worship the darkness."

The prisoner's face twisted sourly with Chen-Li's disgust. Licking his lips, the possession continued.

"They feast on the blood of sacrifices. Why are they doing this? They are hoping to lure the White Eminence out into the open while we are weaker than they are. They will try to defeat us by a thousand cuts instead of open war. The temple must be completed soon. Here, we can make a stand. He knows we will grow stronger—both in numbers and in skills. He knows in open combat we will overrun them!"

Suddenly Chen-Li, inside the prisoner, turned an eye behind him.

"Wait! We are not alone! I see a pair of eyes, yellow eyes. I have seen those eyes before. The Zorn is here."

In the mind of the prisoner, Chen-Li could see the Zorn, to whom the prisoner was connected through blood. The Zorn began to speak using the prisoner's voice as well.

"Brother, brother, how long has it been now? Ten years or so? I have missed you. But now why do you offend me? Why are you abusing one of my priests of the Zornastic Order?"

"Hazor! Or shall I call you the Zorn?"

"Do as you wish, Marus. I see you are now calling yourself Chen-Li, the meaning of body and soul. What arrogance! Naming a temple after yourself! Remarkably shallow, even for the likes of you."

"What are your designs in summoning a demon to serve you?"

"Everyone needs friends, dear brother. I have not had the benefit, nor the privilege, of the simplest charms and blessings that you have had. Since my birth, when our own mother looked upon me in disgust, and you in love, I have been the hated one."

"Stop it, Hazor! That is an excuse for your scorn, and you know it. Where are you?"

"Where am I? Where are you? I see wooden walls and sliding doors there; where are you, my dear brother? It's been so long, I feel the need to pay you a visit. I can also see a magic feather around your neck. Now, where would you have gotten that from, I wonder?"

"He can see us," Chen-Li told his spy. "Hide your face." To his brother, he said, "I see you in a dark stone chamber somewhere. Where are you?

"You can tell your spy to hide from me, but I do not hide from you, Marus. Here, look upon your destiny. Look at Langula!"

The Zorn pulled someone else in front of him, and Chen-Li gazed into a demonic face with silver eyes and blood-red lips. The demon Langula bared her fangs.

"We will meet again soon, brother," the Zorn told him. "Please give him a proper burial."

The Zorn motioned with a flourish of his hand, and the prisoner's heart stopped beating at his command. The prisoner's body dropped to the floor and Chen-Li was forcibly ejected out of the host with a loud popping sound.

"You must get back to your physical body, Chen-Li," the spy shouted.

His Li flashed back to his Chen, meditating there across from the dead man. Squeezing his spirit back into his physical body, his Li slipped back inside through the top of his head with another stretching *pop*! Then Chen-Li became whole again. He sat cross-legged, still in meditation, then began a steady descent back down to the floor. Eventually, he came out of his trance, breathing heavily, and shakily got to his feet.

"Farewell, Hazor." Chen-Li looked upon the dead prisoner. "We will meet again soon."

The spy kneeled by Chen-Li's side to help him up. He looked his spy in the eyes and told him, "We all are targets of the Zorn. We must always be on guard. I need to rest now." Holding his head with one hand, he thanked the spy and turned to go. "Have a detail fetch the prisoner. Give him a proper burial."

"I will see to it. It will be done."

Chen-Li stumbled into his bed to rest. That was where Tyla found him after her training with the White Eminence. The rest of his wives were looking in on him, murmuring to each other. Some giggled, failing to grasp the seriousness of the situation. Tyla alone walked into the room and, turning to the others, slid the door shut without a word. After laying a blanket over him, she slipped under the covers next to him.

There they remained resting for hours.

As he slept, the first shovel of dirt landed on the prisoner's face.

"It won't go away
And there's no reason to stay
When I find my mind's gone deep
Slowly sinking underneath the surface."

Excerpt from *The Witch's Songbook*

THE BALANCE

THE GREAT MAPES FOREST IN THE YEAR 826 HRT

The Witch noticed the Timmutes stirring, as if readying for an attack. A steady torrent of red streaming orbs rushed outside her window. They moved in such a large force she had seldom seen before. *It must be something big*, she thought, *maybe as big as a bear.* Opening the door, she stepped out to see what all the commotion was about.

That is when she saw him. Even from a distance, she knew exactly who it was.

The man standing in the Great Mapes Forest was Hazor the Zorn, all grown up. He was dressed very properly, with a black coat buttoned up to the chin and his dark hair combed back. Overall, he presented a striking figure. He saw the Witch and his yellow eyes flashed with an unnatural sparkle.

The Timmutes swarmed, changing their color of gold to an angry crimson. Thousands of them circled, but only in curiosity. Sensing the Witch's blood in him, they slowed until they ultimately changed back to their more pleasant golden color. They let him pass without any harm, in honor of the blood oath. Yet they watched and listened and waited.

Hazor continued walking past the Timmutes, unimpeded, ignoring the little golden orbs. He walked with a confident stride, deliberately, unmolested, without any hesitation. The Witch stood her ground defiantly as he neared. He maintained eye contact with her, giving her a little smirk. The closer he came, more of the orbs floated away.

At last, the two stood face to face.

"Mother," Hazor said. "You are looking lovely."

"What is it you want? Why are you here?"

He looked hurt. "Can't a son have a reunion with his long-lost mother?"

The Witch did not answer.

"I see. But that has already happened, has it not? Of course, I am referring to the other son. The one you wanted to see. The one you love."

He took a step beyond her, advancing shoulder to shoulder with her. He looked over the scene: Her little cottage resting in the forest by the big white oak.

"Nice place you have here. Very quaint and cozy. It looks like the Great Mapes Forest has been an excellent ally for you. So, this is how you spent your time, after all those years, after abandoning your children." He looked her up and down. "You can't hide from the truth forever, can you? But something is different here.

"I do not have the hateful eye of my father. Yet, I see that life is all around us in the Great Mapes Forest. What have you done here, Mother? You certainly have been a real busybody, haven't you? I see you have been doing a little creating, as evidenced by your little orb friends. Timmutes, you call them? That is nice. We all need friends. At least, that is what I told someone recently.

"But Mother, your friends—they got a little out of control, didn't they? Like drunken party guests, they started to run roughshod through your forest, didn't they? But still they were your responsibility because you invited them to the party. They lost control, which means you lost control. No surprise there. As my most excellent father said about you—before your ogre of a husband attacked him—you do not deserve to be in this world because you are weak." Hazor leveled a stern look at her and shouted. "WEAK!"

"Get out!" the Witch told him.

"All in good time, Mother. But first things first. What is that thing that hangs where your left arm should be? It shines with a different light in my eyes. What is it made of, because it certainly is not flesh and blood? Looks to be made of white oak and little orbs? Fascinating. But do you know what I think? I think you have grown complacent and sloppy, leaving parts of yourself lying around. Mother?"

"No, Hazor!" the Witch said nervously. Anxiety grew inside her.

He pointed to the ancient white oak. "What I mean to say, Witch, is that if you have no need of it, I do."

The Zorn approached the Master Tree, plunging his hands inside a crease in his trunk. Then he spread his hands apart, stretching a wide hole in the trunk, and holding the knothole open.

"Stop it!" the Witch said, quickly casting a spell to speak to Ulrig. The Master Tree suddenly called out to her.

"Help me!" he said in a scream. "What is happening? This man is hurting me!"

Despite the Witch's' spell, Hazor spread Master Tree's trunk farther until it became wide enough that he could jump in. He leaped inside the knothole of Master Tree, and once inside, the knothole slammed shut behind him.

"Good heavens, there is a man inside me! What is he doing?" Ulrig shouted.

"Leave him alone, Hazor! It's me you want!" she said with tears streaming down her face.

After a moment, Hazor's fingers appeared poking out from inside the trunk. Again, he forced the knothole open from inside of the Master Tree. But this time, Hazor exerted a tremendous force tearing it open, splitting the tree apart, splintering it into thousands of pieces. Master Tree broke down and toppled over with a loud crash. Hazor emerged from Ulrig's trunk, holding the petrified arm of the Witch.

"You are right, Mother, it is you that I am after, and now I have you!"

"Master Tree!" the Witch screamed. "Master Tree! Master Tree!" But the great white oak answered no more. The Timmutes changed color to red again and swarmed around Hazor but still they did not attack him because of their shared blood.

"RECOMPENSE!" Hazor said, holding up her arm. "RECOMPENSE, I say again! This is the price you pay for welcoming my brother Chen-Li and giving him the gift of flight! Did you think I would not find out about the feather? The magic you gave your favorite son in an attempt to alter the balance and tip the scales in his favor?"

The Zorn shook her arm in front of her. "RECOMPENSE!"

"You have what you came for, Zorn. Now go!"

He pretended to look hurt. "You, of all people, should know. The balance must be kept. It is not to be trifled with. The balance has consequences, always consequences. Like the consequences your actions had for our fathers. You, of all people, you should have known better!"

The Witch cried, trying to collect the pieces of Master Tree, but he was now in fragments and far from repair. Hazor looked at her in contempt. He considered the Timmutes circling fast around him. They had only a minor power, but the real power was in their numbers. There were so many of them. Hazor could not physically harm the Witch without incurring their wrath, and he could not survive a Timmute red swarm.

He tucked the arm under his.

"I will leave you to play with your little sticks," he said and turned to go. After walking a few feet, he turned and asked a question. "Oh, I nearly forgot. Before I go, I would like to ask your opinion on something. It is another matter entirely."

The Witch refused to look at him. With equal parts anger and hatred, she stared through her tears at the Master Tree.

"Do you think what happened to Heironomus and Hexor could happen to Marus and me? If we engaged in a direct combat with each other? Do you think the Great Negation would claim us in eternal combat, like our fathers, in the Cosmic Creation?"

"You said it yourself, Hazor," the Witch said through clenched teeth. "The balance is not to be trifled with."

The Zorn nodded silently in agreement, in deep thought for a moment. Then he turned to look at the Witch again. She was on her knees amidst a scattering of splintered wood that used to be the great white oak Ulrig, the Master Tree.

"Goodbye, Mother."

"Look upon me for the last time. For if I ever see you again, Hazor, I will kill you. Balance be damned."

"That's my girl," he said, chuckling. With that, the Zorn left the Great Mapes Forest with the petrified arm of the Witch.

The Witch had no interest in watching him go. Only when she saw the Timmutes return to her did she realize that he had departed. That meant, for now, the danger had passed.

The Witch kneeled before the fragments of the broken trunk. She sobbed. "Master Tree? Are you well? Ulrig?" But no life remained in the Master Tree.

Yet she did hear the soft voice of another behind her. "I wish you never came here."

She turned. A little green sapling was speaking to her.

"I was raised from just an acorn from the Master Tree's branches, and would have grown beside him, as the next generation of Ulrig. Now I must learn to survive without the wisdom of his teaching. You have shamefully brought great harm to the living things of the Great Mapes Forest. You have brought us nothing but danger when you were supposed to protect us."

"I am so sorry, Little Sapling. I am so sorry."

"Go before you do more harm. Ulrig, our patron, is dead. Just leave us with whatever we can salvage." The Little Sapling spoke what was in the hearts of all the living things. A deafening silence filled the forest for the first time.

The Witch looked around the Great Mapes. She could feel the eyes turning away from her. She no longer had the confidence of the living things, the bushes, vines, moss, and especially the trees. She was no longer welcome here.

"I will leave. But where I shall go, I do not know."

Little Sapling made no reply. The Witch would find no sympathy here. All the others in the forest agreed with Little Sapling.

She stood and left that very minute. Without going back into her house, without collecting any food or possessions, she took nothing with her: no magic, no ingredients, no notes, no recipes, or anything else. She left with only the clothes on her back.

After she left the Great Mapes, her home fell into decay. Over time the Great Mapes Forest reclaimed the Witch's house as its own.

The Timmutes continued to multiply. Many of them stayed in the Great Mapes, assisting all the living things in the forest. The early animosity between the Timmutes and the Great Mapes had gone away. A sub-section of the vast Timmute society remained inhabiting and helping the woods, but it was never the same after that. Darkness descended over the Great Mapes Forest. The very air became heavy and foreboding. The Great Mapes remained a place to be avoided, not because of the existence of the Witch, but now for the living things' deep sense of resentment and betrayal. The feeling lingered there for all time in all the living things themselves.

The Witch wandered away utterly broken. She had no plan, no home, no hope; she could not even cry anymore. Once again, her appearance changed for the worse. She became even more hideous than before. Her eyes changed in color from milky to gray. The hump on her back grew larger and heavier, until it became so extensive that moss and weeds grew on top of it. The Witch lost any resemblance to a living being. When she came to a rest, it was hard to determine the difference between her and a stone covered in moss.

Lots of memories haunted her. She loved to sing and play music on her lyre, but now she found no joy to sing about. Eventually she would pick herself up and shuffle further away again, looking more like a monster than the former Goddess of Beauty.

She wandered unseen in the world for years, her melancholy overwhelming her. Through her remaining days, she was dimly cognizant of conflicts and wars going on around her. She took no interest in them, as she could do nothing about it, and quite frankly did not care. She lost interest in the affairs of gods or men. Yet she lingered, living on as the matters of the world pressed on through the generations.

The Timmutes remained faithful to their blood oath, staying close to her and serving her. They assisted in her care, giving her everything she needed to stay alive. They provided food and water for her. As she lumbered away from the forest through the countryside, they ensured nothing harmed her.

Years later, the Witch saw Chen-Li once more quite by accident. He came flying overhead and landed nearby. He remained there for a time, far enough away from her as to not notice her presence. He was older now, fully the fierce warrior he was meant to be. But she took no pride in that. She had no memories of him, and it amazed her that she felt nothing by seeing him again. Chen-Li kneeled and studied the ground, tracking someone or something in the grass. Then he stood up again, and when he did, his gaze passed right over her. Lingering there for a moment, he finally took to the sky once again, bounding away. As he flew off, the Witch watched, her eyes following him as he flew on his way. She knew this would be the last time she would ever see him, and she followed his flight. But along the arc of his path, she noticed something else that she had long forgotten.

The Witch's gaze stopped on the large mountain on the horizon. She focused on the high summit of the Dragonbreath Mountain, glistening in the sunshine.

That is where I can go, she thought. The highest mountain would elude the grasp of the humans. There, she could escape. She had a new goal.

It took her years, for she moved slowly, dragging her feet. The trek to the mountains was long and hard but it gave her purpose. Most times, the Timmutes carried her through it, over the heights, and let her limp through the valleys. She could only accomplish the journey with the assistance of the Timmutes. They lifted her higher and higher, closer to her goal. As the air continued to thin, they helped her further by providing a thick cloud of air at the top of the mountain.

The Dragonbreath cloud was born, and it would remain there for the rest of time.

They carried her up until, at last, she reached the top. The Timmutes stayed with her, creating a cabin she could call home. They made her as comfortable as they could and provided a continual supply line of fresh food and water to sustain her.

She sat on the summit of the Dragonbreath for years, obscured from prying eyes as the Timmutes cloud supplied her with oxygen to breathe. The cloud obscured her body as much as her memories obscured her mind. Her feelings of guilt were a massive burden and a constant reminder of all she seemed to bring to ruin. She acknowledged that she had been weak and that she had destroyed everything she touched.

After years of being imprisoned by guilt, her tortured mind had reached its limit. She could no longer live with it.

She shuffled to the edge and looked over the abyss. Peering down, she could not see through the white cloud to the bottom, but she knew it was there. A drop sufficient to end even a god's life. There were no longer any fears or doubts, just anticipation of getting it over with.

She turned to face the Timmutes, her faithful creation. "In all the world, I think you were the only thing I managed to do right. Thank you, my friends. You were my noble companions and able providers. Where I go now, you cannot follow. Please let me go. I bless you with peace. I love you all."

The Witch stood as straight as she could. It surprised her that she could stand taller now than she had in years. She spread her arms wide and looked up to the heavens.

"Back to the Cosmic Creation I come."

These were her last words, as she tipped backward off the summit and disappeared into the fog. The air raced by her as she fell for a long time. With no fear, expectancy, or distress, she plummeted down the Dragonbreath Mountain. Her gaze ever up toward the heavens, she smiled.

In the end, her body smashed against the rocks below, splashing in dusty debris. But her spirit continued her momentum down through the solid ground, like a diver in deep water. Her spirit slowed arced back to the top. Her soul had changed, no longer possessing her previous form; there was no more Ehlona, no more Witch. Erupting from the rocks where she struck, her spirit shot from the ground, soaring out, and skyrocketed upward, toward the heavens.

This spirit was no ordinary one. Hers had been created, designed, to be a goddess. Her self-destruction affected only that part of her that contained her physical body, which had long become practically useless. But her spirit, or the magical energy it contained, that would live on forever, just as she told the Sisters of the Orphans. The fabric of her spirit had been recalled, absorbed back into the cosmic shuffle from where it came. From the same spirit that created the world, the energy of hers would experience a rebirth, a renewal, a recycle. It would be washed clean, to someday get a fresh start.

And so, with the death of the Witch, the age of the gods ended.

Her spirit had departed the world for now, but it would not be gone forever. The world had reason to watch the heavens for the sign that would signify her return.

"So, go ahead and raise your mighty sword.
Lift it high. High before the Lord.
You smile and grin and crown your head.
Well, he better not find you, or you'll be dead."

Excerpt from *The Witch's Songbook*

THE SWORD OF KILMER

THE DRAGONBREATH SUMMIT IN THE YEAR 1041 HRT

Almon had fallen asleep after a day of transcribing notes for Aberfell. He was resting on Aberfell's little sleeping bench against the northern wall. Draped across the beam of the bench hung Almon's scabbard, the pommel of the sword facing his head while he slept. It was an old habit Almon picked up from his father, to always stay on guard and have steel within arm's reach.

As Almon slept, his sword lifted slowly out of the scabbard, giving the slightest squeak of metal on metal—a sound Almon had trained himself to listen for, even in his deepest sleep. He woke with a start, and in one fluid motion instinctively reached for the hilt of his sword. But surprisingly in his grasp, instead of cold steel, there was a warm hand.

Almon opened his eyes and turned to see Aberfell, with his hand on his sword, lifting it from the scabbard.

"What are you doing?" Almon said with his hand on Aberfell's.

"My, you are fast! It has been a long time since I held a sword. I just wanted to look," Aberfell told him. "May I?"

Almon considered Aberfell for a moment. "Don't go swatting any Timmutes with it."

"Sorry I woke you," Aberfell whispered. "I'll be careful."

Almon released his hand upon Aberfell's, allowing the old man to pull the sword entirely out of the scabbard. Although Almon had nothing to fear from Aberfell, he could not just go back to sleep knowing his sword was out in the open. So, he rolled over on the little sleeping bench and turned to face the interior of the room. He kept one eye watching the old man—just in case he was wrong about him.

Aberfell lifted the sword with care, moving it up and down.

"Heavy," he whispered. He moved it gently from left to right. "Good balance."

Almon watched him dimly under a half-closed right eye. He thought the old man probably had a sword master's proficiency somewhere in his ancient memory.

"Eh, needs sharpened," Aberfell said with some disappointment, running his thumb across the edge. Running the flat side of the blade in his open palm, he drew his face closer to get a better look at the inscription. He brought the sword so close to his face that he could see his reflection in the polished steel. Examining the decorative scribes upon it, he saw a vine of oak leaves running up from the base to the point, scenes of the hunt for elk and deer, the Plum-Kilmer family crest. The inscription of the maker upon its blade read "Haverhill."

"Haverhill," Aberfell whispered. "Pure Haverhill. The finest maker of swords."

Almon gave up pretending he was asleep anymore and came to a sitting position on the sleeping bench.

Aberfell now turned to face him. "A fine sword is a sign of wealth, privilege, and power. This sword possesses all three; it is no poor man's blade," he said with a slight thrust of the blade.

"It was my father's sword."

"Ah! An heirloom," Aberfell lifted it in front of his eyes, still studying it. "Do you know how old it is?"

"My father said it had been passed down from the original Kilmer."

"Magnificent," Aberfell said, returning a look to Almon. "Thank you for letting me see it. Kilmer's sword is as much a piece of history as I am. Kilmer wielded this sword before I was born. It was an honor to hold something older than myself. Thank you, Almon."

Almon rubbed the sleep from his face as Aberfell gently slid the sword back into its place inside the scabbard. He then returned to his rocking chair by the window. Almon touched the handle on his sword in reverence.

Aberfell continued talking about the fate of the Witch.

"When the soul of Ehlona would return, it would indicate a significant cosmic re-alignment, enough to cause a star to erupt in the sky, but that would still be later. The Witch knew about it, she knew the star would be visible to the whole world, and wrote about it in her books."

Almon returned to the table, dipped the quill in ink, found his place, and continued writing.

"In the days after the Witch left her home in the Great Mapes Forest, Chen-Li founded the Star Prophets. These were people dedicated to watching the skies, searching for the sign of her soul reborn. That was their primary purpose, but there were other signs too. The Star Prophets would watch the heavens for any stellar movements, alerts or warnings, anything that could foretell the future. They watched and waited for her star to return, and for other things significant to humanity. Ever watchful, the Star Prophets spent generations waiting for these signs. The world's destiny depended on it."

"After the Witch leaped from the summit of the Dragonbreath Mountain," Almon said. "Why did the Timmutes continue to make that cloud of air to the top of the mountain?"

Aberfell nodded. "In tribute to their creator, the Timmutes determined that the summit was holy ground to them. They kept the house she lived in, this very house. They continued making the cloud. Then they formed the Praying Lady tree. It is not a real tree, you know; it is made from a Timmute society just as this house is." The golden orbs went about their business all around them. Aberfell watched them for a moment, then continued.

"They modeled the white oak in the image of her as the younger Witch but posed in her final moments. The Praying Lady sits on the exact spot where she last stood before plunging over the side. They gave her branches to look like arms outstretched to the heavens, her roots formed as crossed legs, and the trunk gave her feminine features. As the last addition, a section of the tree resembled her face looking skyward in prayer. It is how their society wanted to remember her, looking up to the heavens, arms wide open, right before that final step backward to leave the world."

"It is a beautiful tree, and a fitting tribute," Almon said.

Aberfell spoke softly. "All the Witch ever wanted to do was take a step backward. She always had a desire to make things right. But of all her powers, which were many, she did not have the power to go back in time. Sadly, none of us can.

"She had to live with the consequences of her actions, like all the rest of us mortals. Not a very god-like quality, is it? Living with the consequences was not something she was prepared for. None of the gods could undo their cataclysmic decisions. And so, their era came to a close. But when one era ends, another one begins," Aberfell said, taking a deep breath and closing his eyes briefly.

"Are you tired?" Almon asked him.

"Always these days," Aberfell said. Opening his eyes, he continued. "Then, the word spread throughout the entire Timmute society that the Witch was dead. To this day, every living Timmute is encouraged to visit the mountain at least once in their lifetime. They all want to see the Praying Lady on top of the mountain, to honor their creator. While they are here, they serve. Either as structural Timmutes, or service orbs, or warriors."

"Maybe that is why they maintain the artificial air?" Almon asked.

"It did provide oxygen for both the Witch and their society. From the moment they brought the Witch up here to the summit of the Dragonbreath Mountain, the cloud obscured the summit, keeping the wind at bay, and then later provided the Timmutes with a degree of privacy which is so important to them."

"So, the Witch was dead, and the world watched and waited for the Star of Ehlona to shine?" Almon said.

"The Star of Ehlona would shine again, and her soul would return. But nobody could have predicted when or in what way. That is where you come in. That is why you found safe passage through the Timmutes as you climbed this Mountain. It is why they helped you. It is why they came to your aid when you needed them. It is why they did not kill you."

"Me? What are you talking about?"

"Your ancestor, Kilmer, and the Star of Ehlona, would end up being closely related. That is how I met him, and why it was such an honor to touch his sword. That is why so many Timmutes have found it fascinating as well."

Almon turned to look; he had not noticed, but the golden orbs swirled and took turns swiping past the sword, touching it, getting the same honor that Aberfell had. The Timmutes' desire to touch it made Almon smile.

"The Timmutes have an appreciation for history. The sword of Kilmer has plenty. But yours is not the only historic weapon, or the most highly sought. There was one above all the rest, one considered to be the most righteous, not a sword, but a dagger. An instrument of vengeance, it started as a sacred relic of the Zorn, created in Castle Orlo. But its legend was more than anyone could have possibly imagined."

"The blade Soothsayer," Almon said.

"When I'm down and out
When it all comes crashing down,
When it's dark, and I'm low
I will keep you close. I won't let go."

Excerpt from *The Witch's Songbook*

THE GOLDEN DAGGER

Castle Orlo in the Year 826 HRT

The Zorn hated this part of Castle Orlo: The furnace rooms. The odor of carbon and burned fuel offended his sense of smell. Deep below the upper chambers, these hot smelly maintenance rooms kept the drafty castle warm. The furnaces belched smoke and fire, endlessly burning, so that the walls were caked with dirt and a thick black soot covered everything. Behind the furnace room were the smelter and the armory forge. That was his destination.

The Zorn found the Master Smelter standing by the forge, feeding the fire through the bellows. Brilliant yellow and crimson flames roared with each breath of oxygen. The Zorn walked in with a handkerchief covering his face, protecting him from breathing in the dust.

"Did you get the arm?" the Zorn said, walking up to the Master Smelter, a large man wearing a dirty, stained apron.

"Yes, Your Excellency, I have it here." The Master Smelter held up the petrified arm of the Witch.

"It must be gold," the Zorn told him. "It must be pure."

"Yes, Your Excellency," the Master Smelter said, flipping a tarp from a wheelbarrow, exposing a stack of gold nuggets. "I have more than what is needed."

The Zorn took his hand from his face and placed it on the shoulder of the man. "Take extreme care, Master Smelter. For this artifact, there is only one, and there will never be another. It is a valuable treasure, rarer in quality than gold." The Zorn looked deep into the face of the Master Smelter with swirling yellow eyes. "Understand?"

"I understand, Great One. This will be the greatest weapon ever created."

"Very well, Master Smelter. I will leave it to you then." Just before he left, he started to sweat. The Zorn hurried up the steps, opening the door at the top, and swiftly entered the fresh air of the corridor.

The Zorn took fresh linen out of his pocket and cleaned his hands and face. He dropped the linen and walked away. His servants caught it before it had time to hit the floor.

Langula waited for the Zorn in the throne room. He was still giddy about how his visit to his mother went. Now his concern shifted to his brother.

"I know my brother is looking for me. He is trying to locate Castle Orlo. I also know he will continue to spy on us at every turn."

"Let us attack him, my love," Langula told him, "before he attacks us."

"He knows that we cannot engage each other. He has to know that, doesn't he? He must have the instinct like I do, that the fate of our fathers hangs in the balance between us still. Let us send him a message."

Langula looked bored. "Why can't we just kill him?"

"I'm afraid you haven't been listening my dear. Find us a messenger from the Zornastic Order and bring them to me."

"I shall obey, Zorn," Langula said, leaning closer to him, examining his face. "Hazor?"

The Zorn turned to her. "Yes, my love?"

Langula stroked his face. "What is this on your face? Are you wounded?"

Realizing that there were sores on his cheek, he shouted, "Bring me a mirror."

A servant brought one straight away. Langula backed away from him while he inspected his face, knowing better than to crowd him, especially when bad news was inevitable. The mirror revealed deep, pockmarked, and bloody sores across his face.

Looking at his reflection from a variety of angles, at length, he put the mirror in his lap.

"What is it?" asked Langula.

"The mark of the Witch," he said, grimacing.

"She cursed you?"

"I think it's rather more than that. Remember, she is my mother, and her wretched blood is in my veins as sure as my own."

Meanwhile, down below the castle, the Master Smelter was busy at work. He placed the gold into a cauldron, super-heating it until it dissolved into a thick liquid. When the gold was ready, the Witch's petrified arm was carefully dipped into the molten gold. It lingered on top for a moment, then dissipated into the glowing precious metal. As the Witch's arm dissolved, it released magic into the gold. The cauldron rocked as the gold turned a light blue and white color. The Master Smelter stabilized the cauldron and continued to stir as white and blue sparks crackled upward. The molten gold vibrated as if it were alive.

The Master Smelter aligned the cauldron with the foundry mold. Once he was positive he had it perfectly aligned, he began to pour.

Even though the molten gold looked light blue in the cauldron, the pour was pure gold. It rolled into the mold of a large dagger. It took the entire mixture to fill the mold.

Once every drop ran out of the cauldron and into the foundry mold, the Master Smelter worked quickly. With hammer and water, he cooled the red-hot metal and worked it on the anvil, hammering it into a refined sharp blade.

Once the Master Smelter completed his tasks, the dagger went to the artisans. They added ornamental decorations worthy of a magical artifact, including the deer leaping over oak leaves on its blade.

Next, the dagger went to the weaponeer, who attached a sturdy handle and hilt with precious jewels to its pommel. They buffed it thoroughly, bringing it to a bright, fantastic sparkle.

The only thing left to do was to present it to the Zorn.

The moment he heard the golden dagger was finished, the Zorn called for it. He would have a private ceremony in his throne chamber, without the normal onlookers and courtesans, for this weapon and its magical properties were not for prying eyes. Hastily the throne room was prepared for the people responsible, the Master Smelter, the artisans, the weaponeer, all who took a part in making the blade, all worthy of praise.

The impromptu ceremony began. The Master Smelter, the artisans, the weaponeer, all were given the honor of presenting the weapon to the Zorn. With as much pomp as possible for a small ceremony, the blade was given a name by the Zorn. He called it Soothsayer.

Through the red-carpeted center aisle, Soothsayer made its way to the foot of the throne. The Zorn stood in front of his throne with his hands behind his back, waiting to receive his masterpiece. The Master Smelter approached the throne and took a knee, cradling Soothsayer like newborn infant, and lifted to the Zorn.

"Well done, Master Smelter. This is the most beautiful thing I've ever seen," the Zorn said, seeing his reflection in Soothsayer's blade. He turned it over many times, watching it glisten in the light.

"My, my. All of you, thank you for the quality of your efforts. I want you to know you have produced the rarest artifact in the world. No words of mine can adequately express my gratitude. To the artisans and weaponeers, you have given a life's worth of great beauty. Well done to all of you. For your efforts I shall greatly reward you."

The Zorn smiled, then he abruptly stopped.

"Now kill them," he ordered.

A black flurry of arrows erupted from arrow slits in the sides of the throne room. The Master Smelter, the artisan, and all the weaponeers fell to the ground, dead, multiple arrows sticking out of them. The Zorn stepped through the bodies, careful not to get blood on his shoes. Langula slithered behind.

"You might find this hard to believe," the Zorn told Langula, holding Soothsayer, "but I have never held a dagger in my hand before."

"No one has ever held one like Soothsayer," Langula told him.

"I can feel its power," he said. Then he leaned to Langula so only she could hear. "Gather up all the archers and have them killed."

"Of course, mighty one," Langula hissed and slithered away.

The Zorn marveled at Soothsayer, knowing that it had been crafted from the left arm of the Witch. Then the strange tingling where the mysterious sores appeared in his cheek returned. He reached up and touched the place on his cheek, feeling a strip of skin peel away from his face. Something was happening to him. He was changing; he knew it.

But for this day, it became known as the day of Soothsayer, the golden dagger.

"The best that I can do, is stand in front of you
with my hand over my mouth.
All this simple conversation, is now bleeding in my ears,
Quiet hope and desperation, reflected through the years."

Excerpt from *The Witch's Songbook*

THE PARLEY

The Temple of Chen-Li in the Year 827 HRT

A White Eminence patrol of three warrior priests captured a boy riding a mule about ten miles from the now completed Temple of Chen-Li. The young boy wore the familiar priests' clothes of the Zornastic Order, a black uniform adorned with a crescent moon inside a silver circle. The boy offered no resistance.

"My master, the Zorn, said I am to parley with your master, the Chen-Li," the boy told the patrol. The patrol looked at each other.

"What should we do with him?" one of them asked the others.

"Let's search him and take him to the captain," another one said.

They told him to dismount and searched him, finding nothing on him except for some partially eaten bread and an empty bottle. They tied his hands behind his back with twine and lifted him back up on the mule.

"Follow us," they told him. "We are taking you to the Temple of Chen-Li."

"Can I ask you a question?" the boy said. "What's a parley?"

The guards smiled and told him that a parlay is a peaceful discussion.

"See?" the boy said. "I can do that."

An hour later, the White Eminence escorted the boy to the ramp leading up the mountain to the Temple of Chen-Li. The temple stood on the top of the Fangs within view of the summit of the Dragonbreath, in all its white marble brilliance, shining in the sun. Its design would be unmatched for generations, and the temple stood as a landmark as the farthest location to the east.

The emblematic Temple of Chen-Li served multiple functions. First, as a defensive structure; the temple's heights were unassailable. It stood as a rallying point for the warrior priests of the White Eminence. Second, it provided a training area for martial defense. Third, it housed the warrior priests as a barracks. And lastly, it served as a holy place where the White Eminence could practice astral travel. Chen-Li had formed an idyllic and iconic structure to serve his organization of warrior priests inside an indestructible headquarters.

Further up from the temple, the humble home of Chen-Li straddled a long, rocky waterfall.

As the patrol got closer to the Temple of Chen-Li, the boy beheld its spectacle. Rocking with the stride of the mule, he could not hide his excitement as the patrol scaled the heights.

A short time later, they reached the temple grounds, high on top of the first of many mountains. After a series of initial interrogations, and three or more searches, the boy was taken under armed guard to a private chamber, where he would later meet Chen-Li himself.

The boy was told to sit cross-legged in the middle of the room. Observing the barren chamber, the boy pleasantly did what he was told without objection. There, he had to sit for hours, aimlessly staring at the white papered walls.

Finally, some dinner arrived, a bland meal comprising a slice of bread, a dollop of butter, a cup of stewed meat with vegetables, and a glass of pomegranate juice. The boy did not care about how plain the meal seemed to them. For him, the dinner was the best meal he had in months. Once fed, he waited some more.

About an hour later, with a sudden, loud clang, the door opened, and several guards with spears poured in. Lining the walls, they remained at attention. Several more minutes passed, then Chen-Li himself walked in and faced the boy, who watched all these events happening with bright eager eyes.

Chen-Li looked him over. "How old are you?"

The boy swallowed. "Fourteen years, or so my brother told me."

"What is your name?"

"Nantz."

Chen-Li nodded, sitting in front of the boy. Chen-Li told the observers to come in with their writing equipment, quill pens, paper, everything needed to take their notes. As they came in, he got settled on the floor. Smiling at Nantz, he asked, "Did you get enough to eat?"

Nantz quickly nodded, gawking at everything around him with a sense of wonder.

Chen-Li looked at one of the guards. "Did he drink all of it?"

The guard nodded and turned over the empty glass that once contained the pomegranate juice.

"Let's get started then, shall we?" said Chen-Li to the boy.

Nantz seized his opportunity.

"My master, the Zorn, said I should parley with Chen-Li. I know that parley means a peaceful conversation." Nantz gave an affirmative nod to those in the room.

"And you will parley," Chen-Li reassured him. "I'm sure of it. Now for the next few minutes, I need you to be quiet, not a sound. And the parley will begin. Do you understand, Nantz? You certainly do not want to upset your master now."

The boy smiled and nodded at Chen-Li. "Good boy."

Chen-Li began his meditation. The chamber soon became electrified as Chen-Li emitted a soft light from his body. The light intensified, and at length, he rose off the ground. He floated up until he was a few feet off the floor.

Nantz watched Chen-Li rise from the floor with an open mouth and wide eyes. He strained to remain silent.

It did not take long; soon, Chen-Li's head elongated slightly. Then, with an audible *pop!* his Li levitated above his body. The Li looked like a copy of Chen-Li, only dull and translucent, with glowing golden eyes. The Li thrashed its arms and legs, trying to gain leverage in the air, finally rotating to face Nantz. Hesitating only long enough to coil in preparation, like a lightning bolt, his Li buried itself deep into Nantz's chest. The boy recoiled, as if being hit in the chest with a hammer, and dropped his head.

Now inside the boy, the Li had a brief struggle for control of the body. It took only seconds, then Chen-Li used the boy's throat to speak. The real parley had begun.

"This boy knows nothing useful; his mind is simple, that is why the Zorn sent him." Chen-Li's voice sounded dull and distant from inside the boy's throat. "I'm going to look for the Zorn now."

It did not take him long. Chen-Li swirled through the tunnels of the boy's mind. Soon, he found the image of the Zorn standing in the middle of a swirling cloud of reality. There, the Zorn had been waiting for Chen-Li.

"Ah! There you are. I can sense your Li, brother."

"I understand you sent the boy to parley. What kind of treachery are you up to?"

Chen-Li could see the Zorn's face. Something looked wrong about it, but he had not the time to get into details about that just yet.

"No treachery, Marus. I just wanted to provide you with a service. But admittedly for a selfish reason. I want us both to survive in this world. Me, for my purposes, and you, for whatever you do."

"My only purpose is to oppose you."

"Yes, exactly my point."

"What is the point, Hazor? And what has happened to your face?"

"Do not worry about that, it's just a temporary malady," the Zorn said, rubbing his cheek, and turning more to the side, shielding the worst of his face. He was too absorbed in his vanity for the criticism. "The point is, I wanted to tell you, I confirmed that any direct battle between you and me will have devastating results for the both of us. You do realize that, don't you?"

"You are afraid that we will negate each other?"

"I really want to avoid staring into your face for all of eternity. And I am sure you have better things to do than stare into mine."

"Like Heironomus and Hexor?"

"Like our fathers? Precisely. I wanted you to know that I asked the Witch about it, and she agreed with me. She confirmed, the balance is not to be trifled with."

"You saw the Witch? When?"

"Oh, my!" the Zorn said. "We might need to catch you up a bit. Understandably, you have been rather busy with your little temple and all. Yes, I visited her, the Witch of the Great Mapes Forest. I visited her at her home. Cozy little place. But I don't need to tell you, do I?"

"What did you do, Hazor?"

"Oh, Chen-Li! You cut me to the quick. I was there for another reason entirely; it was purely by accident that I ran into her. I was looking for something else. Something that was misplaced. Please believe me, Marus, with her accursed little creatures buzzing all around me, I could do her no harm. I couldn't if I tried, but I did find what I was looking for."

"What did you find?"

"Turns out the missing item was found in an old tree. In it, I found a missing piece of history for my collection."

Chen-Li realized what the Zorn was looking for and had found.

"What did you do with Mother's arm?"

"I just turned it into this little dagger here." He produced Soothsayer. "A beautiful blade. Let me show you, Marus. A little demonstration if you will. You remember Langula?"

Chen-Li could see the Zorn standing in the room at Castle Orlo as Langula slithered in. Three prisoners, dressed in rags, dirty and scared, were thrown down to the floor. The Zorn grabbed one of them and stuck Soothsayer in the side of his neck.

"No! You're killing him!"

The prisoner crumbled to the floor, but Soothsayer crackled with blue energy, vibrating as it absorbed the prisoner's spirit into the blade. Wasting no time, the Zorn repeated the executions, killing two other terrified captives in the same way. With each kill, the dagger crackled, absorbing the souls of its victims, and growing in size.

Chen-Li watched in horror.

"The blade is alive, Marus," the Zorn said. "It grows more powerful the more it kills and the more souls it takes, and I have plenty of souls to take."

But then something else happened: as the blade grew, the Zorn's face became marred with more blisters on his cheeks, as if he aged by applying the magic of the blade.

"This weapon is an abomination, made from the same flesh that created your flesh. It is nothing more than a sacrilegious, morbid desecration of the body of the goddess. A misguided attempt at magic you do not understand."

"It's not an abomination. It is Soothsayer. And you are just jealous because you did not think of it first. But I always win, Chen-Li. Remember that. I always win." With those words, the Zorn motioned with his hand to stop the boy's heart, to kill Nantz. But his spell did not work. He concentrated again, trying to stop the boy's heart and break the spiritual connection between him and Chen-Li. Again, it did not work. Flustered, he concentrated harder. Still, the boy's heartbeat continued without interruption.

"Something wrong, Zorn?"

The Zorn knew that Chen-Li was learning. "You gave him your blood."

Chen-Li showed the Zorn the guard holding the empty glass of juice—the one that Nantz had enjoyed so much with his lunch.

"You don't always win."

"We'll see about that. But maybe with you, I have met my match."

"I have always been your match. Never forget."

"Keep the boy then, but remember this Chen-Li: any direct conflict between you and I will lock us in a Great Negation. So, do what you must. I will do the same. But keep your distance, and stay away from me."

With that, the connection ended as the Zorn blocked any more remote viewing into his mind. This time, instead of being kicked out of inhabiting his host, Chen-Li left on his own. His spirit squeezed out through the top of Nantz's head with a loud *pop*. His Li tumbled out above Nantz, floating overhead, close to the ceiling of the chamber. Nantz dropped his head; otherwise, he was unharmed. The Li leveraged its way back into the body of the Chen. Being rejoined in both body and spirit, Chen-Li remained levitating off the floor for several moments. Then, his light started to fade, as he slowly drifted back to the ground. Coming out of his meditation, Chen-Li opened his eyes, whole and unharmed.

Nantz slumped in front of him, and Chen-Li kneeled beside the boy, caressing his head, and caring for him until he recovered. When he revived, the boy had no idea, no memory, of what had happened, but he felt very strange.

"I am so thirsty," the boy said. "Do you have anything other than pomegranate juice?"

"Bring a glass of cold water for Nantz," Chen-Li said with a smile.

"Did I parley?" he asked.

"Oh yes," Chen-Li told him. "You parleyed very well. Your master will be very proud of you when you return."

Nantz smiled and took a deep breath. It was an enormous relief.

"It doesn't feel much like hunger, the spell you put me under
And now you want to break it, I don't think that I'll face it,
So, I've locked myself in, these memories that I've lived in,
I've pulled the shade and cursed my light away."

Excerpt from *The Witch's Songbook*

THE ZORNASTIC ORDER

CASTLE ORLO IN THE YEAR 828 HRT

Though he had just produced the most dangerous weapon in the world, things were not going well for the Zorn. Locked deep inside his castle, he helplessly watched as his flesh was dying. His skin had turned yellow; the fleshy parts of his face had already fallen away. His nose deteriorated, leaving him with two vertical gashes to breathe from. Some of his teeth had fallen out; those that remained moved into unnatural positions. His entire body had become deformed and hideous. He was changing into something more skeletal in nature. Finding nothing in his immediate power to stop it, he locked himself into his throne room. He neither came out, nor did he receive anyone. He even pushed away Langula, his most trusted advisor and companion. He had become so vain that instead of trying to find a cure, he hid himself away and gave orders by shouting or writing commands on slips of paper that he passed through the door. All of this led to speculation: What was happening to the Zorn?

Even though he created Soothsayer, he could not capitalize on its power. All he could do was look upon it as a possession. He kept it near to him, keeping it in his throne room in the heart of Castle Orlo. He suspected that it somehow fed off his life force. His greatest decision would be whether he must now feed the dagger or heal himself.

This is the revenge of the Witch, he thought.

Maybe he had gone too far. Privately, he thought he might have put the balance in jeopardy. The blood in the blade was the blood in his veins, and it was co-mingling, reaching out for vengeance because of what he did to the Witch. Yet he held on to the blade. He did not have the strength to get rid of it.

Chen-Li told me I was dealing with magic that I could not control or understand. That son of a buffoon may have been right. The thought hurt his head. It was like a nightmare.

How do I wield the most arcane weapon in the world? he thought, and he knew it was killing him; he had to decide. Whatever that decision was, he had to do it fast. He felt his time was running out.

What does one do when the ship is about to sink?

You dump the ballast. I must lighten my load.

The Zorn sneered in his thoughts. He knew what he must do.

But the Zorn was not the only one thinking of bold ideas.

At the Temple of Chen-Li, his brother sensed something was wrong him, and saw it as an opportunity. It had been weeks since they had parleyed through the boy Nantz. He speculated that the last thing the Zorn expected, especially after unveiling a new powerful weapon, was an all-out attack by the White Eminence.

So, an attack was precisely what Chen-Li had in mind for his warrior priests. Even though he still could not locate Castle Orlo, Chen-Li gave the order for a deployment of a large, sweeping skirmish line toward where most of the Zornastic Order activity had been reported, to the south of the Blue Mountains. Castle Orlo had to be close, but even if they could not find Castle Orlo itself, they would hit the Zorn where it hurt him the most: His Zornastic Order. If the White Eminence could kill or capture many of them, right there and then, Chen-Li would cripple the Zorn from further attack. The element of surprise would be the great equalizer to a newly formed weapon such as Soothsayer.

Chen-Li drew up the plans and sent out the order to deploy the White Eminence into the Mid-Run Valley in force immediately. They were to spread out over a fifty-mile front and start their sweep down through the grasslands of the Mid-Run Valley. Their orders were simple: Kill or capture as many of the Zornastic Order as they could find.

There was one exception. Chen-Li ordered that no harm should come to the boy Nantz, who would be riding out with the White Eminence dressed in the black uniform of the Zornastic Order. Chen-Li was returning him to his master, and he was adamant that no harm should befall the boy.

As the warrior priests of the White Eminence took to the field, Nantz rode out with them on his mule, finding the maneuvers extremely exciting.

While Chen-Li planned the attack of the White Eminence, the Zorn was thinking of his own survival, and had decided on his plan that would be equally shocking.

The Zorn scribbled his orders in a quick note to Langula, then slid it under the chamber door.

The note made its way to her, but after reading it, her brow furrowed as she struggled to understand it. The order was recalling the entire Zornastic Order back to Castle Orlo, taking them out of the field. It made no sense to Langula. The entire Zornastic Order?

The Order fulfilled a variety of duties, tasks crucial for Castle Orlo's operations. Their priestly duties were not just to fight but also to pillage the materials and resources necessary to run the economy of Castle Orlo and the Zornastic Order. They provided prisoners, food, riches, supply lines, and slave labor for the care and maintenance of the castle. Why recall all of them back to Castle Orlo? She read the Zorn's command again, and it clearly included the entire Order.

While the command was still in her hands, she received word that the White Eminence were no longer hiding in the Temple of Chen-Li but rather were coming down out of the mountains in force. It seemed an attack was imminent. The Zornastic Order braced for a fight and talked bravely about turning Chen-Li's white robes to scarlet with blood.

Langula did not know where the forces of the White Eminence were headed, but she had no illusions that they were going anywhere except straight for them. Still, with this recall order, the Zorn must know what he was doing. He had accomplished so much so fast. Still, she wondered if he knew the full impact of this order. Despite her concerns, she sent the command. With the order sent, the recall was out, and those in the field began returning to Castle Orlo.

For many, the order was received just in time, as some of the Zornastic Order were in line of sight of the enemy. The White Eminence and their approaching forces neared their positions. It relieved some to hear that retreat was preferable to battle.

They obeyed the Zorn's command for retreat as they obeyed him in all things. In the field they only had one desire: To prove their loyalty to him. That included either killing the White Eminence or laying down their lives in sacrifice for the Zorn. Wave upon wave of black priests crowded into the spaces of Castle Orlo.

Simultaneously, the spreading skirmish line of the White Eminence became a single force moving in a fifty-mile front and getting closer.

The Zorn called Langula to the throne room. She came to him, and upon entering the room she saw the Zorn's face for the first time in weeks. She saw what was happening to his flesh. It delighted her.

"What is happening to you? It is splendid, perfectly demonic."

The Zorn sat on his throne with a look of gloom. He sat in flickering torchlight; shadows danced across his face. He wore a crooked crown on his head and a black-and-white robe buttoned up to his chin. He said nothing to Langula at first, he just breathed heavily.

"I cannot stop it. I think I might be dying," he told her at length.

"No, Zorn, this cannot be."

"Have you obeyed my orders? Have you gathered the Zornastic Order in the castle?" Langula nodded that they were.

"All of them?" the Zorn asked. "How many?"

"About twenty thousand dark priests," Langula told him. "They barely fit. They stand shoulder to shoulder in all the available space. The castle has never held so many at once. It is a grand spectacle."

"Then send my Grandest Command," he said. "The Zornastic Order are to die. They will either kill each other, or commit suicide, but none must be allowed to leave Castle Orlo alive, and this must be done now, immediately."

Langula's eyes widened. "Hazor, if you give this command, they will have no choice but to obey it. Your blood runs in their veins; they are defenseless against it."

All the Zornastic priests had been coerced to drink a concoction containing the Zorn's blood to complete their initiation ceremony. This gave the Zorn power over their blood while they lived.

"All of them, right now!" the Zorn thundered, standing up. "All of them must die! None must be allowed to leave. None must be allowed to live! Now give the order! Send it now!"

He turned his back on her. Langula hesitated, tears welling up in her eyes.

The Zorn turned and saw her. "Are you crying?"

"It's just so beautiful," she said gushing. "It's the most beautiful thing I've ever seen."

The Zorn's Grand Command echoed through the hallways and corridors. The dark priests stood looking at each other in disbelieving shock. Then the first scream pierced the mumbling. The first faithful priest sunk a dagger into his own heart. There were more screams, and bodies started to fall throughout the ranks.

The chanting started.

"Your days are gone, never to return.
Your days are gone, never to return."

Unexpectedly, vials of poison, normally reserved for tainting their weapons, passed down the line; those who drank from the vials collapsed on the floor, foam spraying out of their mouths. But for some, they considered poison the cowardly way. The more dignified priests opened their veins, cutting their wrists, slicing their own throats, or running themselves through by falling on their swords.

"Your days are gone, never to return.
Your days are gone, never to return."

Some priests lacked the nerve and could not find the courage to take their own lives. For these, they offered their swords to another, maybe a friend or superior, asking them to do what they could not do themselves.

The bloody onslaught heightened now. Some of the priests went into a murderous rage before killing themselves. The hesitant were not given a chance to think or given a choice to act on their own. The priests were turning on each other, putting the others to death in a murderous fury. All in the name of the Hazor the Zorn.

"Your days are gone, never to return.
Your days are gone, never to return."

Those who questioned the Grand Command, those who begged for their lives, were considered cowards and were instantly destroyed, killed immediately by priests who later joined them in death by their own hands.

They fell inside the castle in a cacophony of screams. For hours, death reigned as the priests cut, sliced, and poisoned themselves, ending their lives just as the Zorn's Grand Command ordered them to. They died on the floors, fell over balconies, tumbled down the stairs. Bodies of twenty thousand collapsing in piles on top of one another. They considered it a privilege to do their master's will and demonstrate their unwavering loyalty.

The chanting started to fade away, too, as there were fewer of them every minute that passed.

As a result, blood ran deep in the hallways of Castle Orlo. In some places, it rose to waist-deep, fulfilling the prophecy given by the Goddess Ehlona to the Sisters of the Orphans.

Blood will flow in rivers waist-deep because of this child.

But there was one priest who did not commit suicide, and he was particularly successful in fending off the other murderous priests, fighting like a tiger to stay alive, in a flurry of lightning-swift strikes.

This priest struck down any that approached him with murderous intent. He reversed the blades that attacked him to strike down his attackers. One by one, he watched them all hit the floor to bleed out.

It was Nantz, fighting like a man possessed. He ran through the blood-soaked puddles making his way toward the throne room. Using an expert knowledge of martial arts, swiftness, and stealth, he managed to sneak past Langula, who was distracted watching twenty-thousand men take their own lives in the suicidal Grand Command. Morbid delight blinded her, allowing the boy Nantz to slip by.

The Zorn stood in his throne room, the doors now open, absorbing the energy of the dying priests. Their newly released spirits rushed into his body, providing the rejuvenating energy to cure his malady, repairing the decay of his dead flesh. With his arms outstretched in a feeling of ecstasy he had never known before, he did not notice that Nantz had slipped into the throne room. The Zorn felt the power of the priests' energy working on him; he could feel his skin growing, healing over, covering his lesions, his face reforming, his vanity returning. He chanted.

"In Zornastic fire, your soul will burn!
In Zornastic fire, your soul will burn!"

While the Zorn basked in a new feeling of renewal, Nantz located the golden blade on his throne and took it. While the Zorn was distracted in receiving the healing energy of the suicidal priests, Nantz snuck in and stole Soothsayer.

Staying in the shadows, with Soothsayer tucked in his belt, he snuck back out of the room. He maneuvered around the weeping demon, over the dead, through the dying, and handled any murderous priests still living. Eventually, he found his way out of the castle, and once outside, he ran away from Castle Orlo as fast as he could.

The sun was setting, and the White Eminence waited in every direction he looked. But Nantz did not run away from them, he ran toward them, trying desperately to reach their lines.

Running on his way, Nantz suddenly doubled over, as if shot by an unseen arrow; the spirit of Chen-Li tumbled out of him. Nantz collapsed on the ground, now suddenly free from his possession. The spirit of Chen-Li looked back in shock at being suddenly ejected out of the boy's body. He immediately struck the boy to inhabit him again. But this time when his Li re-entered Nantz, Chen-Li discovered that another spiritual entity was already inhabiting him. It was the Zorn occupying the boy's body now! Chen-Li forced himself inside, squeezing his Li into Nantz, where the Zorn's spirit was too. Inside of Nantz, Chen-Li and the Zorn engaged in a spiritual battle for control of the boy's body.

Three spirits battled for control. Sporadically, Chen-Li would take control, then the Zorn. When the spiritual battle between Chen-Li and the Zorn drew to a stalemate, Nantz assumed control of his own body. As he went through several reiterations of influence in the three-way struggle, the boy's body stumbled in various directions: Toward the mountains, toward the valley, toward the sea.

They boy continued to run haphazardly in front of the White Eminence. They were given strict orders that no harm should befall Nantz, and they let him pass, giving the boy unimpeded freedom to go wherever his feet could carry him.

The randomness of control continued for hours, until well into the night. In the meantime, the boy ran as fast as he could into any direction. Sometimes by his own will, but mostly from the will of the brothers.

They were equally matched; neither Chen-Li nor the Zorn could defeat the other. The Zorn worried that at any time they might be swept up in another Great Negation, as he had warned about weeks ago. But because of the presence of the third spirit, the boy Nantz, they were not swept up in the Cosmic Creation. However, there were no winners in this conflict.

Sometime around midnight, all three of them felt the sensation of falling. Nantz had run so long, and so far, that he blindly fell into a deep hole in the ground. They fell for a long time, until the body of Nantz smashed at the bottom. It suddenly ejected both Chen-Li and the Zorn from the boy's body. Their Lis returned in a flash to their own bodies.

With their spirits reunited to their physical bodies again, they both fell to the ground, exhausted in their respective places, both wide-eyed and frightened about what they just experienced. And somewhere out there, they knew, the boy Nantz was dead. Soothsayer, the most dangerous weapon in the world, was lost with him.

The Zornastic Order now lay destroyed, the entire twenty thousand of them dead in Castle Orlo. Their spirits siphoned into the Zorn's decaying body, restoring his flesh and his vanity.

The White Eminence had not a single casualty. However, their mission was unsuccessful. They neither found, nor killed, nor captured a single priest of the Zornastic Order in their fifty-mile-long skirmish line. They were all dead just the same, but they did not know it at the time. They did not find Castle Orlo or have any knowledge of the scene inside.

The White Eminence returned to the Temple of Chen-Li frustrated, with a sense of failure. It was not until later, when Chen-Li reported to them what he had seen as he inhabited Nantz body—the mass suicide, the Grand Command, the elimination of the Zornastic Order by command of the Zorn—that the White Eminence felt compassion and sadness for their one-time enemies.

Chen-Li, however, was partly successful on his own: He had deprived the Zorn of Soothsayer. Yet Nantz, whom he had grown so fond of, was dead. He had wanted to save him and instead had killed him.

That poor boy.

Langula was the only winner that night, as she fed upon the fearful emotions caused by the mass suicide. The scene had her demonic senses simply ticklish. She was giddy that so many lives, so much blood, was shed in such a short period of time. It would be the premiere event she would remember fondly throughout all time. At that moment, her love for the Zorn had never been stronger. She had watched him as a ten-year-old boy grow into adulthood and now into this diabolical destiny. She found it simply marvelous.

Deep in a hole somewhere, the boy Nantz lay dead, in his black Zornastic uniform. Nearby, also tucked away in whatever hole he had fallen, lay the most powerful weapon ever created.

Soothsayer, lost.

"Killer after me, and his blade knows it's stuff
And I can't get away, or run fast enough
My blood's chilling cold, as he catches up with me
I take my last breath, and fly for eternity."

Excerpt from *The Witch's Songbook*

BLACK SCAVENGERS

CASTLE ORLO IN THE YEAR 829 HRT

One hundred prisoners remained locked away in the dungeons under Castle Orlo, would-be sacrifices for the next blood feast. They heard the commotion, the screams, the pleas, the chanting, as twenty thousand Zornastic priests took their own lives as ordered. The screams had started low, then grown into a cacophony of agony, swirling down through the dungeons. The prisoners trembled in fear, huddled together, but had no idea what was happening above. After many hours of terror-filled screams, the sounds gradually began fading away to a final dreadful quiet. None of the prisoners slept; it was their longest night.

In the afternoon of the next day, a shadow appeared slithering in the doorway of their cells. None of the prisoners saw Langula come down the stairs, but they sensed her malevolent presence and moved to the back of the cell in unison.

Langula watched them for a moment, then at length crawled over to their cells. She caused a wave of panic, a general gasp of anxiety.

She produced a set of keys on a brass ring and causally went down the line unlocking all the cell doors. Remaining huddled together, the prisoners watched as the cell doors creaked open with a metallic screech, but none of them dared step out.

"Come, come," Langula said, turning her back, leaving the doors open. They looked at each other, afraid to move. When she reached the staircase, she turned to face them again. She was not surprised no one followed. She gave them an impatient look, and slowly they started to shuffle out of the cells, expecting the worst.

"Follow me," she said, beckoning them with a bony finger. She turned to go up the steps. Afraid of angering her, the prisoners paced out more quickly now, reluctant to be left behind. They caught up to her on the stone steps to the castle's upper reaches.

The prisoners gingerly followed her up the stairs, stepping around a slippery, congealed, dark grease on the stones. They came upon the body of a Zornastic priest, face down on the steps. Stepping over it, the first few prisoners continued after Langula.

"Pick it up," Langula said casually. "Bring it this way."

The stairs had turned treacherous, and the prisoners slipped on blood, dropping the dead priest several times, desperate to pick it up just to drop it again. Langula pretended not to notice. As for herself, she had no problem navigating the slippery steps with her serpent bottom half.

The prisoners picked up the dead body, each taking a limb, and carried it further up the stairs. After a few more steps, there were more bodies; three of them this time. "And these too, pick them up, bring them along," Langula instructed.

Every time they passed new piles of bodies, the demon ordered the prisoners to pick them up.

They carried the bodies as they followed Langula to the upper regions of Castle Orlo and emerged at the top caked in sticky blood.

They entered the corridor and stared for the first time at the piles of dead bodies lying on top of one another like bricks forming a wall of the dead.

"Stop!" Langula commanded. "Drop the dead."

The prisoners gently laid the dead priests on the floor, afraid to disrespect or damage them further in her sight. Langula turned to face them.

"Listen up, all of you. You are prisoners of Hazor the Zorn. We know where you came from, we know where you lived. We know where your families still live. The Zorn's plans consist of torturing and murdering every one of you, and killing every man, woman, and child from your family clans."

She ignored the prisoners' screams.

"After this, the bodies of you and your family will be mutilated and fed to the crows. Your homes will burn; we will take your family treasures, and desecrate the graves of your ancestors."

The prisoners gasped, crying out loud, murmuring to each other, all in tears.

"Unless… Unless, you would rather be granted your freedom, to be returned to your homes and families, and live out the rest of your lives in peace and comfort until a ripe old age with your grandchildren. Hmm?"

The prisoners fell to silence.

"Have I got your attention?" She slithered through the dead bodies. "As you can plainly see, our priests have been tested for their loyalty. What you see before you are the depths of that loyalty. These honored dead, these priests of the Zornastic, were faithful until death. They passed the test. They followed the Zorn's desires as his Grand Command went forth. Now you prisoners follow orders. You will consecrate the ground around Castle Orlo. You will commit these priests to graves outside around the castle. This is the order I give you now. You will obey without delay or hesitation."

Every man, woman, and child nodded fearfully at her words, cowering under her gaze. Perhaps if they did as she asked, they would avoid the priests' fate. "And in return for your service, the Zorn will grant you your freedom."

The prisoners could hardly believe it. They gaped at her, many of them narrowing their eyes. What was the catch?

"Also, the Zorn has decreed that any treasures you find, you may keep. A token of his gratitude for your service."

An excited and hopeful buzz grew among them

"A word of warning though: If you try to escape, if try to run, we will catch you. Your judgment will be death. But the price the Zorn demands is ten-to-one. For every prisoner that escapes or even attempts to escape, ten prisoners will die. Also, your families will be terrorized in their villages for your insurrection. So, convince each other to work and not run. Now, here, take this." Langula threw a shovel on the floor with a loud clang. "Find more of these and get to work."

Langula pulled a long wooden lever, releasing the counterbalance, and Castle Orlo's heavy double doors slowly creaked open, flooding the corridors in smoky light. She gave them one last stern look, knowing it would take them a month or more to drag the bodies all out. Then she turned to go, leaving them behind. Slowly they scattered to find more shovels and begin to move the dead.

Langula left to the throne room. The path was littered with the dead, and after twisting, turning, and climbing over stacks of dead bodies, eventually, she opened the door. She found the Zorn slumped on his throne, still wearing his crooked crown. His appearance was whole again—black hair, yellow eyes, flesh on his cheeks—but his mind was a tangle.

"The stink is awful," he said.

"Really?" Langula sniffed. "I rather enjoy it. I see you are looking more together. What's wrong?"

"It only took twenty thousand priests and the destruction of my Zornastic Order."

"So, is it over?" Langula asked, running her hand across his shoulder while slithering around his throne.

"I won't know until later. I can only hope so. Are the prisoners disposing of these stinking bodies?"

"Yes. They are also collecting up treasures for us."

"Shut all the doors to my throne room while they are roaming around. I do not want them nosing around in here, looking at me. Plus, the stink is only going to get worse. Once these accursed dead bodies are out of the castle, round up all the treasures. Tell them we are re-distributing the wealth. Then, bring half of captives inside and put them to death. Give the other half a bauble to clean it up."

"Are you thinking you will need more souls to keep your flesh restored?"

The Zorn ignored her. "Keep working and killing the prisoners in halves until it becomes unmanageable. Watch which ones escape. You are free to hunt them down."

"Of course, my Zorn," Langula said behind him, bringing her face flush against his, purring like a cat. She breathed into his ear. "And what of Soothsayer?"

"I must find it!" he said, raising his voice. "But right now, I cannot even walk the halls with all these stinking, dead bodies stacked in every direction! GET THEM OUT OF HERE! GET THEM OUT OF HERE RIGHT NOW!" The Zorn stood and paced while Langula recoiled at the rebuke.

"I told you the prisoners are working!" she said, slithering away.

"Where could it be?" the Zorn said with a sigh. "As master of my own blood, I ought to sense where it would be. Oddly, I sense nothing. That boy must have fallen into a deep hole, or else a rock fell on top of him. Something must be interfering with my ability to sense Soothsayer. But wherever it is, it is hidden from me. For now."

He knew that he was not the only one looking for it; his brother would want to find it as well. The race was on to locate it. Chen-Li was watching his every move. If the Zorn could not think of an alternative plan, he would become a prisoner in his own castle.

But then again, Chen-Li would have the same problem.

"The destruction of the Zornastic Order was necessary. Not just to restore my health, but it eliminated the only object the White Eminence could focus on. My power is best served in secrecy. But now, I need something else, something indirect, something that will not lead to any direct conflict between me and my brother."

He worried how narrowly he avoided another Great Negation between them. The only reason they were not locked in one was because of the spiritual presence of the boy Nantz. The boy's fragile spiritual presence provided only the thinnest membrane separating them from an eternity of perpetual combat, like their fathers.

It was a very fine line that separated us this time. How fortunate for us, he thought. But then, that gave him an idea.

"Langula, we have grown accustomed to intimidating captives to serve us. But why couldn't we entice people to join our cause willingly? Not as a direct force of the Zorn, but as unknowing puppets of indirect power."

Langula listened intently. "You mean, instead of terrorizing surrounding villages, you want to empower them? Where is the fun in that?"

"The fun is in the victory, my dear. Who can stop us? We will entice them, keep them in ignorance and control them." The more he thought about it, the more he liked it. More of the idea was beginning to take shape in his twisted mind.

"But first, I need a leader, someone to lead an empire of men. I could rule the world by manipulating just one man. And I think I know of just the right person."

But his plan would have to wait. After a few days of sitting in his throne room, he could not endure the stink of the dead any longer. The prisoners had cleared a path to the outside by now.

He opened the doors, held his breath, and put a cloth over his mouth. Rushing past the prisoners and the rotting corpses, the smell was unbearable. For the first time he saw the results of his Grand Command. The destruction was so vast, so complete, he could not hold his breath long enough. He wanted to take more time to admire the extent of it, but he was running out of time. Unable to hold his breath any longer, he had to exhale abruptly; when he did, he breathed in the fume of the sickly sweet, rotten flesh in his nose. It made him gag. Choking on the smell, he made it through the passage and stumbled into the clean air. He could never be free from that accursed smell now. The stench clung to him, permeated his clothes. Everything seemed to have that same odor now.

The prisoners watched him, but only briefly and never directly, sneaking a quick look from the side for fear of being put to death themselves. The Zorn felt their eyes upon him and wanted to show no signs of weakness. He turned his back, closing his eyes, and held his nose high in the air, breathing in as much of the sweet air as he could. He lingered outside with his hands clasped behind his back, watching the prisoners work.

They were digging shallow graves, some only inches deep, covering the bodies with just a scattering of dirt or just laying them on top of the ground. The Zorn cared nothing about the dead priests. But by observing, he saw something else. The crows.

Thousands of bodies, still exposed on top of the surface, were food for hundreds of black scavengers. He watched them with interest as they pecked at the dead flesh.

The Zorn's yellow eyes swirled as he stared at the crows, his body trembling as one by one they stopped their feeding to turn toward him. The Zorn was manipulating their minds, connecting one with another, then another, until all the crows were connected to him as a single entity. As he channeled their energy inside himself, he felt himself changing. The more of their power he absorbed, the more he became one of them. Black feathers appeared on his skin, his arms turned to wings, his feet to claws, and his face to a beak. Finally, he spread his black wings and pulled. He caught enough air to propel him off the ground. The Zorn was flying in the form of a giant, black crow.

The prisoners dove on the ground as he swooped over their heads. At first, he stayed close to the ground, flapping his wings awkwardly, turning erratically in circles, up, down, and around the castle grounds. But once the Zorn got his feel for the aerodynamics of flight, his confidence lifted him higher. He took to the clouds and headed west, where he thought the boy with Soothsayer might have been lost.

He glided low now, far from his castle, scanning the horizon of the Blue Mountains with the vision of the crow. High above, he could still not sense Soothsayer anywhere. He continued flying through the Mauveguard Pass and still he had no sense of where it could be.

But ah! Up here, high in the air, the stink of the dead had finally gone. He wondered if it was the fresh air or the crows' lack of ability to smell. Nevertheless, for the first time in weeks, that awful stench of the dead was gone.

He returned to Castle Orlo, circling high among the high towers and spiraled peaks. He flew over the prisoners, then soared to the top of Castle Orlo. Perching on the tallest tower, he enjoyed a splendid view of the valley.

From the top of the tower, he flew into an open window. Then he broke his spell, becoming the Zorn once again. Returning the spirits back to the crows, a few feathers clung to him as he stumbled under his sudden weight in the high chamber. Looking below, the crows had suddenly rejoined with their spirits and took flight in fear, getting away as fast as they could, despite the abundance of flesh to eat. Most of them never came back.

Unable to locate the magic blade, he thought more about how to best execute his new plan. He knew where to find who he needed. Only, for the time being, staying here in the high tower, he could avoid the awful stench of death below. He would wait.

The prisoners worked night and day for months removing bodies, but never all of them. They cleaned up some blood and dragged the dead outside, burying them around Castle Orlo. Two months passed before the prisoners removed enough of them that he could freely navigate its corridors. By now, the numbers of prisoners dwindled, until eventually, there were no more of them; they had either been paid, worked to death, killed, or run away. Nevertheless, they were gone.

Castle Orlo was never the same after that. It stood quiet and still, its hallways dark and foreboding. With its furnaces silent, no longer stoking warmth throughout, it became drafty, cold, and in disrepair. The worst of it, though, at least for the Zorn, was the everlasting stench of the dead. For years to come, he would continue to find more dead bodies, a skeleton here, a corpse there, flesh moldering in some out-of-the-way place. No matter what he did, he could not sanitize it, he could not purify it. Remains of the dead priests would haunt him for the rest of his time in the castle.

Castle Orlo was now home to only the Zorn and Langula. He continued to watch his reflection in the mirror often. His appearance started to slowly deteriorate again. He ran his fingers through his thick luxurious hair only to realize it was falling out. The reflection of his infamous yellow eyes, now deeply set into hollow sockets, were losing their symmetry, becoming different sizes. In his mouth, the gums exposed rotting teeth. Skin stretched tight across his forehead, carving deep lines in his face, and sagging under his chin. Painful sores spotted his skin, which was turning gray and purple.

Hazor was permanently turning into the Zorn, the Skeletal King.

Langula simply loved it. She told him how utterly demonic he looked. But from his reflection, he could clearly see that his days of looking even remotely human were over; he would soon be dead in that realm.

In the meantime, the dead bodies of the priests lay on the ground, attracting anything that fed off the dead flesh. Eventually, these creatures brought with them the digested seeds in their droppings. Soon little saplings appeared. Fueled by the spoiled blood of the priests that had been tainted, these trees grew suddenly to full height. In less than a year, they grew and multiplied to form a forest. But these trees did not resemble anything healthy with green leaves and branches. Instead, they all looked dead, with sharp branches like menacing claws and blackened trunks. Where each priest had been buried, a sapling rose unnaturally fast, twenty thousand of them.

A Sanguine Forest soon formed around Castle Orlo. The forest gained a fatal reputation: None who entered ever ventured out. Legends said that it was haunted and should be avoided, especially at night, when it was most dangerous. Rumors of its evil grew. Soon, people talked about how the Sanguine Forest was a suicide forest, where people would go to die.

Little did anyone know that Langula and the Zorn were behind it all.

"Listen, listen, listen!
We say so much but don't have to speak.
The language of our devotion
Is took to heart."

Excerpt of *The Witch's Songbook*

THE SEARCH FOR THE WITCH

THE GREAT MAPES FOREST IN THE YEAR 829 HRT

Chen-Li had other concerns while the Zorn planned his next move. He had to find out what happened to his mother. He worried about the visit the Zorn said he paid to her. He needed to search for the Witch of the Great Mapes Forest.

The fastest way for him to do this was to use his Li. His spirit raced away from the temple, through the mountains, down to the Great Mapes Forest. There, he moved among the white oaks searching for a sign of her, anywhere. The Timmutes filled the forest as before, moving as golden orbs through the trees, but everything was quiet, too quiet. He could feel an oppressive heaviness. Something bad happened here, he could tell; something was wrong.

He traveled to the place in the woods where he last visited her in the little house. He found it and discovered that it had not been lived in for some time now. Vegetation had overgrown into it; the door was broken, as were the windows. The forest had been reclaiming the materials that made up the house once again. Outside her door, fragments from a broken white oak tree littered the area.

Chen-Li thought back to his conversation with the Zorn:

"I found what I was looking for—an ancient relic, hidden in an old tree. There, I found a missing piece of history for my collection."

He knew this was the work of the Zorn. His Li floated around the area, searching for the Witch, but found no evidence of her. In spirit form, it was easy for him to squeeze through the open spaces of the broken window. The inside had become a jungle of plants, dirt, and debris. He spotted her lyre there in the house, but being in this form, he lacked physical hands to secure it. Inside he discovered other personal things that he knew she would not have left behind given a choice.

He resolved to come back, but for the moment, he needed to return to his body. Like a flash of lightning, he traveled across the mountains, arriving at home to find his Chen waiting for him in meditation. After a moment, the Chen and Li now joined, he walked into the inner rooms of his home.

"You look troubled," Tyla said to him as he closed the door behind him.

"I fear the worst for my mother. She is not dead but missing." Chen-Li looked at Tyla. "If she were dead, I would feel it. No, she is out there, still alive, but where is anybody's guess."

"Maybe she wants to be missing," Tyla told him. "Maybe she does not want to be found."

Chen-Li looked surprised, but only momentarily. He knew she spoke the truth. Ehlona's need for privacy had kept them apart all these years.

"I don't know her, Tyla. I wish I did."

He stood up now and looked out the window. "Maybe there is some truth in what Hazor says. She took no interest in us. She took a little more interest in me than him, but just barely. What possessed her to abandon us like she did?"

"Reality can conflict anyone," she said, standing behind him, rubbing his back. "She tried so hard to make things right."

"She only made things worse."

"Perhaps. But maybe it could have been worse still."

"It's hard to imagine." Chen-Li continued staring into the night.

"True balance is hard to achieve. Especially with all the troubles that seemed to find her."

Chen-Li nodded, then shrugged, turning to look at her.

"She did the best she could," Tyla told him. "She did what she thought was right."

Chen-Li kissed her. "Thank you."

The following day, he was up at dawn, staring at the feather the Witch had given him. He imagined all those years of it being in her presence, even when he was not. He wore it on a chain under his white uniform. He went outside and climbed to the top of his little home. Then he confidently leaped into the blue space of the mountain chasm. He sailed from mountaintop to mountaintop, flying over the trees, looking for any sign of the Witch. Following the brook, he searched all day for her, reasoning that she would need water to drink.

Finally, it paid off. Perched atop a tall pine overlooking a small brook, he picked up on her trail. The path looked as if a stone had been dragged through the woods. The trail led from the Great Mapes to a running brook. After a careful search, he observed the Witch, or what was left of her.

She was nearly impossible to detect in her advanced deformity. She resembled a large rock more than a human figure, covered in dirt and moss with little saplings and weeds growing on her back. From his perch high overhead, he could see her, but she could not see him. His hands curled into fists; this was all the Zorn's fault. But Chen-Li could not reverse what had been done. He could see she was struggling. If she needed his help, she knew how to get it, but it seemed to him that she only wanted to live in complete solitude. Chen-Li had to respect that. He bowed his head from atop the tree and gave silent praise for Tyla and her wisdom.

Her time has come, he thought. He wanted to honor her desires, but he had to make sure.

He resolved to make his presence known and show himself to her. If she called for him, he would gladly help. But if she stayed hidden, then at least he could express a final farewell. He leaped from the treetop and glided down a distance in front of her.

Chen-Li stared directly at the Witch. His gaze remained on her for a long moment. There was a strange calm about her, she did not look in any distress. Her eyes conveyed no emotion—her power, like a candle, had faded away, longed burned out.

He wanted to wave to her. But if he did that, he would acknowledge that he could see her. It seemed like a boundary that need not be crossed. He remembered her song:

You cannot see me since I have wished myself away.

The Witch made no move toward him, no acknowledgment. Chen-Li had accomplished what he wanted. Their eyes would look upon each other for the last time.

Then the moment was over. Chen-Li found it hard to breathe, but he forced himself to look away. He bounded above the treetops and began his journey back home.

He could not avoid the emotion. It confused him, but tears streamed from his face, faster than the wind could dry them.

The next day, Chen-Li would return to the house in the Great Mapes before the forest reclaimed the last of her home. He went back to retrieve some of her things, her books, her papers, her lyre, some magical ingredients, and maybe most important, a small book of songs.

Even though she still lived, Marus knew his mother was no more a part of this world.

"I grabbed the prism, and I held it tight
I won the war, but I lost the fight
A valley conquered, one mountain score
I showed them something they never saw before."

Excerpt from *The Witch's Songbook*

THE WITCH'S SONGBOOK

THE DRAGONBREATH SUMMIT IN THE YEAR 1042 HRT

Almon put the pen down, wiping a tear from his eye.

Aberfell looked at him. "Do you need to take a break?"

Almon rubbed his face with both hands. "Aberfell, I have been here over a month now. That story made me think of Mose and Jacko. I wonder what they would say if they could see me now?"

"Friends of yours?"

"They probably think I am dead," Almon said, squinting his eyes in thought.

"Good heavens," declared Aberfell. "If you were, I would know it."

Almon nodded. "If you say so, I'm convinced."

Aberfell said nothing, he just chuckled and continued whittling.

"What was the disease affecting the Zorn?"

"His use of arcane magic. He had turned from life; he was changing into something else. Just as the Witch had before him, the Zorn was becoming less a part of this world, and more isolated. In the beginning, he was Hazor, the mischievous son of the God of Darkness. He grew up to be very dashing, prim, and proper. And as you have heard, he hated the sight of blood, hated the stink, hated the heat, groomed himself impeccably, his vanity supreme. But as he changed, he turned into what the legends would later call him: the Zorn, the Skeletal King of Orlo, the Master of Evil."

"And what of Chen-Li?" Almon asked. "How was he not effected by the flesh-eating disease?"

"Chen-Li gave back to the world more than he took from it, maintaining a positive deficit. He tried to warn the Zorn about mishandling magic he did not understand, but the Zorn always took more than he gave, producing a negative deficit. But even Chen-Li, in his isolation, waiting to battle his brother, was losing pace in the affairs of men. To maintain connection, he gave the world two books he found in the Witch's house. One book, called *The Constellation Volume*, contained the Witch's notes on prophecy and star movements. The other, simply entitled *Songs*, would be referred to later as *The Witch's Songbook*. It held several songs and poems she liked to sing during her life. In time, they both became just another legend attached to her name. She was known as Saint Ehlona for her orphanages, and the Witch for her songs and prophecies. Just more of her treasures left behind."

"Was she the first to summit the Dragonbreath?"

"Probably so," Aberfell said. "But she did not climb it; the Timmutes carried her up. I told you that about ten million Timmutes were here before you. Plus, she never wanted to claim that title, anyway. The last thing she wanted was more fame. No, she only wanted a place to be left alone in peace and quiet. She was not part of this world anymore, and the mountain served her purpose. At least for a little while. Then, when the time came, and she wanted an end, the mountain served her purpose again. She had gone through enough. The legends say Ehlona was a saint. Far from it; she was one to be pitied."

Almon thought out loud. “To think that she started as a beautiful goddess and for it to end in such a tragic way.”

The only sound in the house was the rasping of steel on wood as Aberfell continued whittling away.

“Where do you think she is now?” asked Almon, breaking the silence.

“I don’t have to think, I know, but I can’t tell you now. It is not time. Even if I did, you would not understand. You would not comprehend yet with the information you have.”

Almon looked at him with disappointment.

Aberfell tilted his head at Almon. “Well, do you have somewhere else to go?”

Almon shook his head.

“Good,” Aberfell continued. “So, just pick up your quill there, and keep writing. Listen and write.”

Almon did as he was told. “What’s next?”

“The Empire of Men.”

ACT III

The Empire of Men

Put on Your Blood Colors!

"It's in the way that you touched me.
Deep inside this strange heart of mine
Look outside of your window!
Now, it's your time."

Excerpt from *The Witch's Songbook*

THE ORPHAN WHO WOULD BE KING

THE VILLAGE OF UMBRICK IN THE YEAR 820 HRT

The baby was abandoned at the orphanage of St. Ehlona in the village of Umbrick, dropped there by someone he never knew, discovered on the doorstep by Sister Luna of St. Ehlona. She found him and took him in. And there he stayed for many years.

As the Sister in charge, Luna, saw to it that the Orphanage in Umbrick of Saint Ehlona provided a structured way of life for the orphans. Life there could be harsh; Sister Luna tolerated no foolishness. There was no privacy of any kind. The orphans were not allowed a sense of personal identity; they all had to conform to the rules. The orphans grew their own food, fetched their own water, tended vegetable gardens, took care of the livestock, and performed any other chores Sister Luna could think of.

What the orphanage really stood for was a profitable front for a forced labor camp, resourced by the slave labor of the young orphan boys. He was not the first, nor would he be the last, to experience this type of suffering at the orphanage of Umbrick.

The orphan boy grew out of his infancy and into adolescence. What they called him then, what his name was, is unknown to the world today. Like the other orphans, he went to work on the farm at an early age, and like the others, he lived his life without any intimacy and little personal affection, and what attention he did receive was only negative. He endured some physical beatings. He was ridiculed, mocked, and degraded, all designed to break his will.

But the boy had an unusually forceful will, and they did not break him. In fact, they hardened his resolve. He grew in a world of hate and pain, as did all the orphans in Umbrick, but he handled it differently than all the others.

There was something more to him, something lurking just under the surface. Maybe it was an overreaction to the severity of the discipline. Perhaps it was some yet undefined personality trait. Whatever it was, he vowed revenge the only way he knew. Whatever happened to him there, either real or imaginary, he grew up with an intense hatred of the St. Ehlona's orphanage of Umbrick. He never spoke of his formative years in the orphanage to anyone; it was not in his nature, and for him, actions spoke louder than words. It did not take him long before he ran away.

Vowing never to be powerless again, he escaped Umbrick and ran through the streets of the nearby village of Hammerville. He took to a life of crime naturally, stealing his meals, and taking what he felt was rightfully his but only temporarily in the possession of others.

Violence became a crucial part of this environment. He roughed up those easier and weaker marks, victims to the power of his will. By the age of eleven, he killed a man who double-crossed him. When the deed was done and he stood over the dead man, he felt no regret for stabbing him. No more than he would feel about staring at a dead rat caught in a trap.

A life of crime might have been his final calling until he found eventual reckoning on the hangman's gallows. Maybe that would have been the final judgment for a life that, perhaps, never should have been born in the first place. That would have been his fate, if not for a chance encounter.

In folklore, having a crow outside of one's house in the morning was a bad omen, meaning someone in the home was about to die. The orphan knew about the omen, but when he saw the crow outside his door, he thought it could only be an omen of questionable origin, since he would not be staying in that house any longer. Running through the forest in search of a new place to stay, on his way to the town of Bowling, he heard a baby crying in the far-off woods. In those days, when a mother did not want to raise a child, they left the babe in the woods. He was eighteen years old now, and although he'd had a troubled past, he felt compassion. Especially for the weak or helpless, and nothing was weaker or more helpless than a baby. His memory flooded back to his beginning, not what it was, but what it could have been and what it should have been. He searched for the baby, determined to help it.

"Hello, hello," he called out. "Where are you?"

He followed the sound of the baby going deeper in the woods. But when he found out where the sound was coming from, it was not a real baby: A demon had been making the sound, setting a trap.

Through the mist of the streaming daylight, filtered through the trees in sparkling rays, he came into a clearing. In the middle of the clearing, a black crow with yellow eyes stood on clawed feet, towering over six feet tall and staring at him at his own eye level. The crow's large beak snapped shut, and the baby's crying stopped. The crow cocked his head to one side, then the other. Likewise, the orphan considered the bird. He spread his massive wings and hopped on one foot before planting himself firm again. Then the crow spoke.

"You do not run," the crow said in an even tone. "Do you not fear death?"

The boy stood there looking at the massive crow, bewildered by its presence, but mostly at the bird's ability to speak. Even so, he did not run away. He did not show any fear. Instead, he addressed it, unnaturally calm.

"Why should I fear you? I have never seen a bird like you before."

"Nor will you ever see one like me again," the crow answered.

"A bird as large as you, one that has been given the power of speech, must be either good or evil. Which one are you?"

"You should know," said the crow, inching to the orphan's left.

"Demon it is then. Still, I have no fear of you. Why should I? What can you do to me that hasn't already been done to me at the hands of men?"

The crow walked beside him, but the boy did not turn. "With my beak, I break bones. I pierce flesh plucking out the hearts of men."

"I see that you have a powerful beak; that much is true."

"I eat the flesh, in my own sweet time," said the crow, standing beside him now.

"I believe you. But while you have one beak, I have two hands," the boy said as the bird walked behind him. Still without turning to face the bird, he spread his hands out before him. "With my left hand, I can grab your beak and hold it closed. And with my right, my fist is like an ax to break it off."

The enormous bird cawed in laughter, cocking its shiny head to the side, and came around to the right of him.

"Then, demon, I'll bust your beak right off your head," the boy went on. "And it will be you that feeds my belly tonight, as I will eat your flesh in my own sweet time."

"I have never been spoken to like this before," the crow told him. "But we mustn't fight like that. That is not my purpose here today."

"Then what is your purpose in this realm?"

"I know who I am. I am Hazor the Zorn. Do you know who you are?"

The boy did not answer the crow. He could not answer, because he did not know. But instead, his lips curled in growing fury.

"Your name is Leopold, and soon the world will know it," the bird said.

"That's fine by me, demon," Leopold said. "Any name you want to give me is as good as any other."

"True, but with this name, you will come into your empire. They will fear the name of Leopold, and they will dread you."

"So be it," said Leopold. "Now begone, you foul crow."

"You will be the orphan who would become king."

"Do not mock me," Leopold warned, "or so help me, I will kill you."

Leopold thought he saw the bird smile. Then the crow spread his wings wide and turned itself into a black mist. The crow disappeared, then reappeared twenty feet away from him. Leopold had never seen this type of magic before. But no matter; he tried to follow.

With a sudden thrust of giant wings, the crow's claws came off the ground and slashed at Leopold in a swirling cloud of dust. Leopold reached out to grab the foot of the crow, but he missed, and the crow flew off, soaring over the forest and out of sight.

The encounter left Leopold with a cut upon his left cheek. It would stop bleeding over time, but it would never heal completely. For the rest of his life, every time Leopold looked at his reflection, he saw the scar, and it would remind him of the encounter with the giant crow. It was there to convince him later that the meeting with the demon was not a figment of his imagination. The scar never allowed him to forget it.

Now the boy had a name, and at eighteen years old, Leopold had finally been born.

"You knock me out

No punch worth pulling

No teacher's doubt

No fools a-fooling"

Excerpt from *The Witch's Songbook*

CONTEST OF FISTS

In the Village of Hammerville in the Year 832, HRT

LaNew was his name and he liked to fight. He had established a reputation as a barroom brawler, getting drunk and fighting with anyone no matter how big. Standing just slightly over five feet, LaNew thought everyone was big. His blond hair was always in need of a comb, but his yellow sideburns darted in at an angle of ninety degrees, requiring some precise shaving sculpturing. He was known for dirty fighting; he would scratch, bite, claw, and if he could get away with it, a swift kick to the nether regions was never out of bounds for him. He never lost a fight, at least none that he would be willing to admit, and was confident he could take a beating as well as dish one out.

"LaNew, LaNew!" some cheered.

One of the onlookers patted LaNew on his back and said, "I think Amtor killed the last guy! You go get him, LaNew."

The closer he got to the ring, the louder the crowd roared; his reputation preceded him. He received slaps on the back as he made his way through the raucous gallery of onlookers. One patron handed him a bottle. Not knowing what it was, he tipped it back and drank deeply anyway, spilling the contents all over his face. He was pleasantly surprised to find out that it was full of spicy ale. He smashed the bottle on the ground with a growl as beer dripped down his chin. He was ready for a fight.

His opponent was the champion, Amtor. Already in the ring, the large burly man with the thick, barrel chest calmly rested his elbows against the ropes. He was covered from head to toe in dark, curly body hair, looking more like an animal than a human being. At six foot four, maybe taller, he seemed larger than life. He had bushy, dark hair and a thick beard trimmed to a square down to his chest. Fighting his second bout of the day, he leaned against the ropes, taking a break from the last fight.

LaNew received no interest from the champion as he made his way through the crowd. Finally, he ducked under the ropes and entered the blood-splattered ring. Amtor turned his back to the challenger as he entered, exposing a broad back as big as a wall. The crowd closed in behind him.

The crowd cheered their champion.

"Amtor! Amtor! Amtor!"

LaNew strutted around the ring, making a big noise, bounding upon the ropes, trying desperately to get the big man's attention.

Amtor took a sip of water, then spit it out over the ropes. A beautiful woman in the gallery climbed the apron to wipe the sweat off his face and beard. Then she faded back into the crowd with a giggle. He took a thumb and cleared his nasal passages by covering one nostril while blowing his nose on the ground inside the ring. Then, finally, he turned to face his challenger. Amtor watched LaNew energetically thrashing in the ring. He smiled.

LaNew had heard of Amtor, but never seen him up close. He had heard of his size, inexhaustible vigor, and prodigious skill, and he was even larger in person. Amtor had been fighting in Hammerville for over a month and had never lost. LaNew wanted to prove his worth by showing that Amtor was not so tough.

Amtor, as big as a grizzly bear, stood across from him. LaNew needed to put on a show. He danced on sure feet, demonstrating his quick footwork, throwing punches in the air with a quick one-two. He mocked the big man, sizing him up, shaking his head. Nothing affected the big man, who continued to rest against the ropes without a care in the world.

The referee called both men to the middle of the ring. LaNew was fighting above his weight class. Against Amtor, everybody was fighting above their weight class. Amtor had a lot more talent and size than him, but LaNew always found a way to win.

The excitement in the crowd rose to a fevered pitch. Gamblers shouted bets and accepted a flurry of wagers. LaNew, considered the long shot, attracted bets on whether he could survive to the third round or not. But the smart money was placed on Amtor for a first-round knockout.

The referee briefly explained the rules, which were very few. A count to ten while on the mat would end the fight. The referee separated them, and the opponents went to their assigned corners to wait for the bell.

Each of them acknowledged they were ready.

Then the bell sounded, and the crowd went wild.

LaNew stormed out of his corner, punching with vigor. Amtor cautiously walked out of his. LaNew threw a flurry of punches, one-two-three, scoring first blood, connecting with three quick strikes: Two to the big man's body and a roundhouse to Amtor's head. Amtor protected himself with his hands up; he made a large target and had a lot of mass to protect.

LaNew circled to his left and lunged at the big man again. This time Amtor quickly dodged with his head, then evaded two more punches. LaNew lunged at him again. Amtor stepped into the punch with a block of his right hand and landed a left on his opponent's jaw. LaNew took it, then pressed the advantage.

LaNew landed another punch to the side of Amtor's temple. It left the big man unfazed, and a counter-punch sent LaNew's head rocking backward. Then Amtor followed with a right that repositioned LaNew's skull, leaving his brain behind.

LaNew wobbled. His whole world seemed to turn sideways, like the mat reached up and hit him. Suddenly, he found himself flat on his back with the referee counting over him: one, two three.

"Stay down. Stay down, LaNew!" the crowd cheered. He awkwardly scrambled to his feet just in time. Amtor was just a predatory blur to him now. The big man moved so fast, so brutal. LaNew was not sure what happened next, as darkness replaced any memory of it. LaNew could only manage to take a single breath before his opponent's enormous fist hit him square in the nose, splattering it across his face. A flurry of simultaneous blows pounded him all over his ribs, his face, left, then right, then right again. Once again, LaNew never saw the ground coming up to meet him, but there he was, sideways again. Then darkness.

LaNew struggled up again. This time, though, it was about an hour later. He was not even in the ring anymore. A cadre of men had carried him away, unconscious, to the dressing room. They had laid him on a table and left him alone. Healers were there to watch over him, glad he was not dead and finally showing signs of reviving. His eyes were swollen, his nose and ribs broken. The only thing that did not hurt on him were his fists, mostly from the lack of use. When LaNew realized the fight had been long over and he had been soundly beaten, he relaxed back on the table. He had survived the fight with that monster.

After the fight, while they were still carrying LaNew away, Leopold walked through the crowd to Amtor's corner.

Amtor wiped the sweat off his brow and LaNew's blood from his face with a small towel. He fought two fights and gained two wins to his long record. His fans were satisfied, and he prepared to leave the ring. Many well-wishers wanted to touch him just to say they were so close to such a brutal man. Leopold pressed his way through the crowd and managed to get Amtor's attention.

"Great fight," Leopold told him. "You are an impressive fighter."

Amtor thanked him with a nod and acknowledged the gathering crowd with a wave.

"Are you ready for one more?" Leopold asked him.

"That's all for today," said the champion, gathering his water bottle and draping his towel over his shoulder.

"Do you have one more in you?" Leopold asked, standing in front of him now.

"Haven't you seen enough?" Amtor laughed, ducking out of the ring and wiping his face. "There is no one left to fight anyway."

"I want to fight you," Leopold told him, "right here and now. Unless you are too tired; then I can come back another day. After you are rested."

The crowd heard Leopold's challenge, and they became silent.

Amtor looked him over. "You have got to be joking."

Leopold was not much to look at. He was tall, though not as tall as Amtor, leaner and not nearly as muscular.

"You should go home before you get hurt," Amtor told him.

"They call me Leopold."

"Eh? Leopold? Never heard of you."

"Let me make a wager with you. If you win, I will be your servant for one full year."

"And if I don't?" Amtor said. General laughter followed this statement. Amtor diffused them by spreading his hands. "No, no, no. I want to hear it. I like to know what the bet is before I take it."

A general hush fell over the crowd. Now all eyes were on Leopold.

"If I win, then you serve me for one year," Leopold said.

"A year of servitude?" Amtor said. "That's a big wager."

"Would you be more comfortable fighting me for less?" By now the big man had heard it all: Fools with false bravery, the arrogant attempts to intimidate him; most people did these things, at least before the first fist landed. But Leopold did not mock him; the boy had a calm demeanor, determined but not impassioned. The silence of the crowd seemed to slow time.

Leopold extended his hand for Amtor to shake.

"I want no man as a servant," Amtor said and continued. Yet Leopold asserted his hand again and would not go away. Then the crowd laughed, mocking Amtor. Somehow this boy had scored a short-term victory that could not be overlooked. Amtor gave a stern look to his ever-fickle fans. They hushed again, waiting for Amtor's final reply. Wiping his brow, he glanced up to look into Leopold's eyes. They boy stood without a trace of fear. Then Amtor gave his answer.

"I don't know where you came from, boy, but your courage is to be admired," Amtor said and shook Leopold's hand. "Don't say I didn't warn you, though."

The crowd cheered and took up their chant again. "Amtor! Amtor! Amtor!"

Leopold stepped into the ring; Amtor could get a better look at him now. He was not dressed for fighting: His coat was threadbare, his pants ripped, his shoes had holes in them. Under his old coat, he wore a tattered, white shirt. As if his coat were a noble cape, he calmly draped it on the cuff buckle. Amtor could see Leopold was nothing more than a young kid, probably with more ego than common sense.

He resolved to teach the kid a lesson, come at him hard, and make quick work of this Leopold. Once he'd given this boy a beating and the crowd had dispersed, he would let the boy go his own way. Amtor had no desire to hold him to any servitude. Amtor had grown up in the streets of Hammerville. He only knew poverty and exploitation; he knew how oppressive it was. He would not be any man's slave, nor would anyone be his.

The contest began as before. The referee called them to the middle. Amtor looked the boy in the eyes, and Leopold returned it. The boy displayed neither any false nervous energy, nor any perceivable fear. Leopold was oddly different from the amateur opponents Amtor had faced in the past; he seemed overly calm and confident. The referee separated them, to their corners. They turned to face each other. Amtor relaxed in his corner, elbows against the ropes; Leopold stood upright fists together.

The bell rang. Amtor walked out of his corner in a boxing stance and approached Leopold as the crowd went wild. He tested the boy's reaction by moving left, then moving right. But Leopold did not react all, he merely watched Amtor.

"Knock him out!"

"Hit him!"

Amtor landed a quick left jab, but Leopold absorbed it without moving to defend himself. Shifting his head left, he tagged Leopold with a right. Leopold wobbled, but still did nothing in return.

Amtor dipped to the right, swung with his left, but never landed the punch. Leopold dodged with his head as Amtor's massive fist blurred past. He caught the big man's arm and with a twist used Amtor's strength and speed against him. Momentum lifted Amtor up in a sweeping arc, and with a violent thump he hit the mat hard on his back. He lay there, stunned, grimacing at how much his weight hurt when used against him.

The crowd gasped. They had never seen their champion on the mat before.

But before Amtor could react, Leopold performed a spin and came down hard on his throat with his elbow. Scrambling on the mat, Leopold swung his legs around, locking Amtor's neck, then leaned back and pulled his arm in the opposite direction. Amtor's arm was dislocating from his shoulder, his windpipe was being crushed, his lungs burned in agony. Stuck and running out of air, he was passing out under the pain.

Incredible as it seemed, through clenched teeth, Amtor conceded.

"Stop! No more. You win!"

The crowd fell silent. Their champion had been beaten.

Leopold let the big man go. Amtor knew if he had not, he could have killed him. Making sure Amtor was not seriously hurt, Leopold kneeled on the mat and smiled, patting him on the back.

Amtor sat up and ran a hand over his throat, trying to rub the pain away. The audience was silent, stunned.

One voice crowed. It seemed one single person held the winning ticket for betting on Leopold to win. He received sneers from the crowd and stopped cheering.

"Are you all right, Amtor?" Leopold asked.

Amtor nodded in silence, trying to catch his breath. He considered Leopold through a side look. Leopold stood, extending his hand to the former champion and helping him up. The crowd cheered wildly for the new champion. They stood together in the ring as Leopold continued to pat him on the back.

Leopold put up his hands, stepping up and addressing the crowd.

"Friends, power is an illusion. This was a demonstration of how we can fight. Not just in a ring for sport, not just for amusement or profit. We are all part of a system where small village aristocrats dare to rule over us. They dare to keep us in poverty. They take the food from our mouths while they get richer. Who are they to use their power against us? Against us, the people! What power do they really have? The only power they have is the power we give them. If we stand together, if we can stay together, then together we will keep our power instead of giving it away to these aristocrats. We will shatter their illusion and take our power back! Join us. Together, we strike at the heart of tyrants!" It was not the best of speeches. But the crowd politely cheered, and it was a compelling enough initial demonstration.

Leopold and Amtor walked away, together. After that, Leopold gained a popular following of men who demanded change. That was all Leopold needed to start. Shortly after that, Leopold started waging his war.

"You've got a reason to hate me.
I'm not the kind you just forget.
You're dealing with a feeling
Of fear and regret."

Excerpt from *The Witch's Songbook*

THE CASE OF THE SICK PIG

THE VILLAGE OF BOWLING IN THE YEAR 833 HRT

It was just before noon when the council was called to order. The Head Council, the Honorable Jakob Whitney, presided over the town meeting. On the agenda today was the case of the sick pig. The case involved a man who refused to refund the costs of a pig that died prematurely. Jakob Whitney felt that the pig was a personal slight.

"All knew that pig was sick. Knowingly selling a sick pig is not only unethical in Bowling, but also illegal, according to the village ordinance," Jakob said.

Through public and official correspondence between the Villages of Hammerville and Bowling, it was the Honorable Sulli Whitney who sold the pig in question. Sulli disavowed any foreknowledge that the pig was sick in the first place. He asserted that the pig developed the illness after it arrived in the village of Bowling and not before. This was an assertion Jakob Whitney denied vehemently.

The Head Council gaveled the council to order to introduce evidence regarding the pig's health prior to arrival in Bowling. But before he got the chance, something quite out of order happened.

The heavy double doors of the chamber burst open. Without fanfare, Leopold and an armed entourage stomped unceremoniously into their council in heavy boots. The chamber suddenly filled with thirty soldiers of Leopold's colors, called the army of the Red and Blue. His forces wore makeshift armor and were armed with swords or spears.

Leopold walked in, moving to the front. At his side stood Amtor and LaNew.

"Excuse me," Head Council Jakob Whitney said. "What is the meaning of this?"

"I am Leopold. I claim this village for the Empire of Odessa. Will you vacate?"

"You are out of order, sir!" the Head Council shouted back. "We are holding an important village council meeting here!"

"The council is dissolved and you are no longer Head Council," Leopold told him. "I ask you again, do you surrender?"

"Dissolved? Vacate?" the Head Council said, stammering. "Try to understand, this is a preposterous outburst. We do not recognize you before this council. Who did you say you are?"

"I am King Leopold."

"King? Who?"

"Take them!" Leopold motioned with a sweep of his hand. The soldiers marched behind the bench with military precision. Each council member was seized by three soldiers.

"You are under the custody of King Leopold," Amtor announced to the council.

"You can't arrest us; you have no authority here!" Jakob Whitney objected.

"Can you stop us?" LaNew said, holding up a sword. "Then you have no authority here!"

Leopold's men tied the hands and arms of each council member. Despite their protests, they were led outside into the village streets.

Outside, it was a beautiful day, warm with just the odd cloud. The people of the village came out of their shops and homes to watch in fascination.

Leopold's men quickly dug round post holes. Soon they erected tall poles in the town square. Each of the council members was tied to a stake, with the Head Council tied to the center one.

"This is disgraceful!" he objected.

Leopold reached into his coat pocket and produced a folded paper. He walked up to the Head Council.

"I most sincerely apologize for this inconvenience, sir," Leopold told him. "I understand the awkwardness of all this."

"You will pay for this humiliation!" Jakob Whitney said in a huff.

"I need you to sign this paper." He held it to Jakob's face.

"I will not."

"You haven't looked at it, sir," Leopold said patiently.

"And I will not look at it."

"Then I will read it to you." Leopold turned the paper to himself. "I grant all titles, privileges, and conveyance of rank, and the resources of the village of Bowling in their entirety to King Leopold. Signed, the Honorable, and here, the name is left blank. Your name will go here.

"This document effectively surrenders the village to me. Will you sign it, sir?"

"I will do no such a thing! Now release me!"

Standing in front of the Head Council, Leopold took a deep breath, then slowly folded the paper and put it back in his coat pocket.

"I'm afraid that is impossible." Leopold shook his head. "Very well, then."

He motioned to LaNew, nodded, then turned away. A cadre of soldiers stood nearby hustled to stack a load of kindling around their council's feet. LaNew held a large bottle filled with a bluish fluid. He came forward and poured it onto the kindling.

"What is that?" the Honorable Jakob Whitney said as the first sweet-smelling fumes hit his nostrils.

"It's called an accelerant," LaNew told him. He backed away to a safe distance. "Light him up," he shouted.

"Wait! Wait! NO!" the Head Council pleaded to Leopold.

"Why are you speaking to me? You said I have no authority here," Leopold told him. "I can't help you."

"I will sign, I will sign," he cried. "Anything you want."

"The time for negotiation is over."

Leopold backed away and addressed the other council members tied to the poles. "Let this be an example to the entire world. King Leopold's authority is the ultimate authority."

After a brief silence, he nodded to LaNew, who produced a torch.

"Now wait just a minute! No, I'll sign! I'll do whatever you want!"

He applied the flame to the kindling.

The fire roared underneath the feet of the Head Council. Thick black smoke filled his lungs, choking out his screams. His clothes blazed, his flesh roasted, his body struggled against the bindings. The fire only strengthened, and soon his movements ceased altogether.

"Now, to the rest of you," Leopold told the others. "I will give you a choice."

He called for Amtor, who stepped forward. "Offer them the papers."

While the remains of the Head Council continued burning, Amtor went down the line. Each council member frantically signed the papers, making the surrender of the village of Bowling legal and binding. They could not sign fast enough. King Leopold had taken his first village in the Mid-Run Valley.

"Have they all signed?" Leopold asked Amtor when he returned to him.

"They have," Amtor said, holding the signed papers under his arm.

But then Leopold gave Amtor a stern look.

"They have, *Your Majesty*," Leopold said. "How can I expect respect from the Red and Blue when my own Minister of War addresses me so causally?"

"Yes, they have all signed... Your Majesty," Amtor said, adding a slight nod. Surprised at the rebuke, he tried to hide his embarrassment. Leopold acknowledged Amtor's loyalty and made sure the rest of the Red and Blue heard and saw it.

"LaNew!" Leopold now commanded.

"Yes, Your Majesty!" LaNew jumped.

"Order your men to assemble kindling under the other four poles."

"Yes, Your Majesty!" LaNew said quickly.

This order shocked and perplexed the captives tied to the poles, who thought by signing the papers their lives would be spared.

"Wait, what are you doing?"

"We did what you wanted!"

"We surrendered the village!"

"I am my own authority," Leopold told them.

One by one, each council member was burned at the stake. Their screams and thick black smoke drifted up to the sky. The smell of burned flesh putrefied the air.

The streets of the village had long been deserted. No one had the courage to come out. The villagers of Bowling were crying in shock. Some would sneak away as fast and as far as they could. Those who got away left without any of their belongings. Through a steady stream of refugees evacuating Bowling to surrounding villages, word spread of what happened, though the other villages simply found it too outrageous to believe.

Leopold took the signed documents from Amtor, returned to the flames and let all the papers slowly fall into the fire. He watched them burn.

As the papers and the bodies burned, the Red and Blue were plundering Bowling for anything and everything of value.

Amtor watched Leopold calmly walk alone toward his horse. A crowd of onlookers ran out of his presence, wherever he would go, and no one dared challenge or mock him—with one single exception.

A small black dog barked at him. Leopold stopped and considered the little dog, a black furball with brown eyes and a long tail. It had one sharp ear and one folded in half. Laughing at how funny it looked, Leopold kneeled by the dog and reached into his jacket pocket for a piece of dried beef.

"Hungry, little fella?" Leopold said, encouraging him. "Go on, take it."

It saw the dried beef. The barking was replaced with exploratory sniffing. Hesitantly, the dog cautiously approached and slowly took the dried beef from Leopold's hand.

Leopold patiently let the pup come on his own, then watched him eat it.

"Do you need a name?" he asked the little furball. The dog wagged his tail, allowing Leopold to pet him. "I will call you Babbit the Magnificent."

Leopold laughed as the bodies behind him turned to charcoal. Smiling, he mounted his horse with Babbit the Magnificent stuffed into the opening of his uniform.

Amtor watched Leopold in amazement. How could any man casually burn five people to death, conquer a village, terrorize the population, then befriend a pet dog all within the same hour? Amtor did not know what to make of this man. Leopold's unpredictable behavior presented a mystery that Amtor could not decipher. It made him a very dangerous man.

"Let's go, Babbit," Leopold said, as the dog peeked out of his coat jacket. They rode out of the village of Bowling with five black smoke columns rising from the town square. The surrounding villages could see the sign, the declaration, a formal notification of war. Leopold had arrived.

As for the case of the sick pig, the last entry in the village of Bowling's council was marked UNRESOLVED, never to be discussed again.

"All my dreams went up in smoke.

When those four queens robbed me of my hope

The bouncer showed me the door

Then he broke my nose.

Isn't that the way my luck sometimes goes?"

Excerpt from *The Witch's Songbook*

THE RETURN OF LORD WHITNEY

The Village of Bowling in the Year 833 HRT

"Red Guard!" LaNew ordered. "Put on your blood colors!"

At his command, the Red Guard produced red ribbons and tied them to their foreheads, just as he did.

This was the forming of the Red Guard. LaNew handpicked these men. Most of them were ruffians and scoundrels, now reforged into elite shock troops. Not foot soldiers of Leopold's Red and Blue, but a special force for a special purpose. By order of Leopold, the Red Guard was to be the military intelligence force, and LaNew would be their leader to obtain intelligence in any way he could. A job that LaNew had definite ideas about.

"This red band symbolizes the blood of our loyalty. Look around you, at all your brothers—we are all joined by this blood, and blood is the price you pay for disloyalty. The blood that flows through your veins is blood you will owe your brothers if you ever betray them. We pledge a bond of secrecy, and this secrecy we take with us both to the grave and to our glory! Today, the Red Guard is born. We will unite this land under one rule: The rule of King Leopold! We have our orders. We are to march upon the village of Plum. Now, are you ready, Red Guard?"

The Red Guard cheered. Then another cheer went up.

To Plum!

To Plum!

To Plum!

The spoils and the significant wealth of Bowling were now in the hands of Amtor. Anything of value—food, water, wine, gold, maps—and other resources were plundered from the village. All to help create Leopold's fledgling Red and Blue army.

With the village taken, Leopold's army grew to four thousand. Potential soldiers were recruited daily, either voluntarily or conscripted against their will. The Red and Blue expected all able-bodied men to join or swing at the end of a rope. It was effective recruitment: Their numbers swelled.

Amtor was in charge of training and became an efficient administrator. Daily he reviewed staff numbers and trained the army in military maneuvers, instructing the soldiers how to ride horses, swing swords, attack with spears, shoot arrows, march, and follow orders. He had the respect of his men, and over time, he earned their trust.

With the Red Guard developing maps of the area and supplying intelligence, Leopold studied in private to develop strategies. In this regard, Leopold had sent a plan to Amtor for a castle to be built, with a specific location and schedule.

It would be a complex engineering project. But Amtor did not have the expertise himself, or any skilled engineers on hand, and so he began an inquiry. Through his inquiry, word got to him of an engineer in Bowling.

His name was Oskar Whitney, and he was a cousin of Jakob Whitney, the Head Council burned at the stake. He went by the title of Lord Whitney. He had completed advanced studies in mathematics and construction, exactly what Amtor was looking for, but would he serve Leopold? Amtor summoned Lord Whitney to him, and not surprisingly, he agreed to meet, since the Red Guard escorted him under arms to the meeting.

Amtor had the guard escort Lord Whitney into the little office he used as a temporary headquarters, then dismissed the Red Guard. Amtor alone would meet with the man.

Lord Whitney made quite a first impression. He was tall and lean, with short-cropped blond hair, almost tinted to the color white. He walked with an unintended swagger. He was very polished in a luxurious double-breasted uniform. Amtor could see he came from a long line of wealth.

"Lord Amtor, I am Oskar Whitney, at your service." He gave Amtor an amiable smile and his green eyes sparkled.

"I have heard you called Lord Whitney?"

"Times change, Lord Amtor."

"You are still aptly named Lord Whitney," Amtor said, walking closer to him. "I am not a lord myself. So please, just refer to me simply as Amtor. I come from common stock, not from the ruling aristocracy."

Whitney needed to tread carefully here. This line of questioning had all the intrigue of class warfare, and his situation now could be a detriment. There could be nothing more satisfying for commoners than to humiliate a member of the ruling class. For Lord Whitney, this was no time for pride.

"As you wish, sir," Whitney told him with a slight nod.

"But, just to be clear, if you were Lord Whitney last week, then you shall remain Lord Whitney this week. I am not here to see you harmed, Lord Whitney. We are trying to establish a kingdom here. What kind of kingdom would we have if we eliminated all the valuable people in it? I simply wish to learn more about you. I understand that Jakob Whitney was a relative of yours?"

"A cousin, yes. A more senior member in the Whitney clan than I, but a cousin just the same."

"I see. I also understand that you have experience with large-scale construction."

"That is true as well. I have building experience, in stone block mostly. But I have also worked in wood and some subterranean structures."

Amtor looked Whitney square in the eyes. Lord Whitney held his look. "How do you feel about the death of your cousin?"

"I am sorry that he is gone, naturally. A horrible way to go, to be burned like that. But I had told him many times."

"Told him what?"

"To prepare for such a contingency. For the common defense and fortification of the village. To prepare a security force. If he had listened to me—and please forgive me, Amtor—you might not have been able to take the village of Bowling so easily, and without any resistance. At least, that is what I told him."

"Why didn't he, then?"

"Jakob could be stubborn; he was hardheaded. Anyway, he would not listen. Fortifications cost money. Armies cost money. He could not part with his wealth for something he thought he would never need. A practice he extended to the village defense when it came to funding projects. I understand he would rather argue about pigs."

"I could use a man with your talents, Lord Whitney. Unless..." Amtor said, hesitating.

"Unless I am to be tied to the stake as well, like Cousin Jakob?"

"Unless you find that you cannot serve King Leopold. Yes, precisely because of how Leopold's forces dealt so harshly with your cousin. That was what I was going to say."

Amtor broke eye contact, looking down at the floor. "I am from a poor family myself. I never knew my father. My mother, well, she ran with a rough crowd. She was a whore you see. I raised myself on the street; it was my home. You see, when you have wealth, you can be more like the rock: More unmoving. But when you have nothing, you become more like the water, leveling and filling the empty spaces. This proposition is more like one of those empty spaces that begs to be filled, and less like a challenge to those who remain unmoved. I don't know about you, Lord Whitney, but my hope for you is far more than a burn stake, or a prison, or a rope around your neck."

The smile left Lord Whitney's face. "I have offended you, Amtor. I am sorry. How may I serve you?"

Amtor walked behind the little desk.

Lord Whitney looked the room over and remarked, "You know, this used to be my office, once."

Amtor looked up through his eyebrows. "Oh really? I had no idea."

Lord Whitney gave a quick chuckle. "That was a long time ago. Before I left Bowling for the village of Connor and my studies, about seven years ago."

"Interesting," Amtor said as he produced a sizable rolled-up map. He placed the map on the desk and unrolled it. Placing small weights on the four corners. He motioned for Lord Whitney to approach. "Come, look at this, Lord Whitney."

Lord Whitney had always had a fascination with maps. He narrowed his eyes, getting his bearings. Amtor showed him. "Now, we are here, in the Mid-Run Valley, in the village of Bowling."

Amtor ran his finger across the map, pointing out landmarks. He moved his finger to the west. "Now due west, the Blue Mountains. They block any straightforward route to the land beyond, except for here." Amtor pointed to the break in the Blue Mountains' peaks. "Here is a way through the Blue Mountains, a cut in the ridge, called...."

"The Mauveguard Pass," Lord Whitney interjected.

Amtor looked up at Lord Whitney. "Exactly. The Mauveguard Pass. This is where we need your service."

"What would you have me do?"

"Those defensive fortifications you spoke about earlier. Leopold knows the value. He wants us to establish a strategic position here at the Mauveguard Pass. Somewhere at the western end of the pass occupying the high ground."

"What sort of fortification did you have in mind?"

"A stronghold. Castle Odessa. Leopold has the plans already made up. Here they are."

Lord Whitney straightened them and looked over the plans. "Interesting construction," he said at last. "When does he expect it?"

"In two years."

"Oh no. That is too aggressive a schedule. It can't be done. I would need twenty years ordinarily."

"You will find Leopold aggressive in all things."

"I see. How many resources will I have to do the work?"

"Seven hundred. All at your discretionary command, of course," Amtor said. "You will be commissioned with high rank in Leopold's army. What can you accomplish in two years, and are you willing to do it?"

Lord Whitney did not answer but continued to look over the plans.

Amtor broke the silence. "You will be greatly rewarded if successful."

"I have heard rumors about how compensation is rewarded, Amtor. With a thank you and then an escort to the grave. What about this man, LaNew, and the Red Guard?"

"Leopold is prepared to entitle you with rank in his new army. You'd be wise to accept."

Searching Amtor's face, Lord Whitney felt he had little option.

Amtor wanted to say more. "Look, Lord Whitney, to accomplish this task, it will not be enough to just accept it. I need you to believe you can do it, that you can build what defensive fortifications we can in the time frame given. The door is there. If you want to walk out, you can. I can guarantee you; no punishment will follow. On that, you have my word. No harm will befall you, despite your decision. But if you decide to do this, I need you to have confidence that you can do it and bring as much motivation, creativity, and innovation to the project as you can. You'll need it, because you'll be on your own."

"It must be accomplished in phases. With the castle stronghold constructed first, completed as a war fortification in two years. The towers and some of the other, more decorative features, will take longer."

"That is reasonable and acceptable to His Majesty."

Lord Whitney looked back at the map and gave it some thought. "I would like to select the men myself."

"Of course. I will see to it," Amtor reassured him.

"Then please tell His Majesty Leopold that his fortifications will be waiting for him when he arrives at the Mauveguard Pass in two years. I will start immediately."

"I see my life before me
as the paper catches fire in the wind.
Still got some strength left inside
And I'm never going to fall again.
Can't you hear me say?
I'm never going to fall again."

Excerpt from *The Witch's Songbook*

THE UMBRICK MASSACRE

THE VILLAGE OF UMBRICK IN THE YEAR 833 HRT

LaNew came out of the tent with blood on his hands. He placed the straight razor aside and washed his hands in a white ceramic washbasin. As he washed, the water turned pink with the man's blood. Behind him, through the open tent flap, the man tied to the chair begged to be put out of his misery. LaNew left the prisoner in the hands of other men in his Red Guard, who would take turns working on him. Unfortunately for the man in the chair, there would be more suffering, more torture, more confession. It was another one of the Red Guard's interrogations, and LaNew looked back at his handiwork with a little smirk.

LaNew, with thick yellow hair and wide sideburns that turned in at right angles across his cheeks, had a violent temper. He was the shortest of all of Leopold's officers but had the longest history of fighting and drinking. He took valuables for himself, fashioned from gold, beautiful rings, and elaborate jewelry. He and the Red Guard committed atrocities and torture, sometimes just to pass the boredom of the day.

He drank too much, cheated when he played cards, and did not have a friend to his name prior to Leopold putting him in charge of his intelligence and security forces. Leopold saw something in him, but most others only saw him as a loose cannon, encouraging fear and intimidation from the Red Guard. Once LaNew was chosen for his prestigious role as captain, he found he had more friends than ever—all of them with similar sadistic tendencies. They all wanted something, and treachery was not beyond any of them.

He had orders to march on three villages of Darby, Plum, and Blaize. He was to plunder them, collect intelligence, and claim them all in the name of Leopold. At the same time, Amtor was to sweep through three of villages of his own: Hammerville, Olzen, and Chase.

Amtor was Leopold's Minister of War, the most formidable and fiercest warrior in the ranks. But he was not a killer like LaNew was. Amtor fought for survival, for honor, for what was right in his heart. But if he had his way, he would have never hurt anyone, unlike LaNew, who enjoyed hurting people.

Word in the villages had been spreading that Leopold was coming. But with the slowness of their village bureaucracies and their petty internal power struggles, they blinded themselves, refusing to see what was to come.

Leopold's strength was in speed, and he was moving fast. With the orders given to LaNew and Amtor, he ordered two sweeping flanking movements through the Mid-Run Valley. Leopold aimed to take six villages in their combined arc, each of them defenseless to stop him. His forces would encounter minimal resistance while forcing them to surrender. Each village would increase the Red and Blue's resources of materials, swords, armor, horses, shields, food, tools, clothes, and shoes.

LaNew deployed the Red Guard, marching on Darby, Plum, and Blaize, leaving burned bodies and destruction in his wake. Amtor likewise swept through Hammerville, Olzen, and Chase with the army of the Red and Blue. They plundered the villages for everything they could get their hands on.

Leopold did not accompany either army. He had another mission of his own in mind, one of a more personal nature. He took a small contingent of the Red and Blue to the village of Umbrick, the village where he grew up. He was not after riches or materials in Umbrick. No, he wanted revenge.

He and his soldiers wasted no time. Soon, the entire village of Umbrick was burning. Leopold rode with four soldiers to the Orphanage of St. Ehlona.

Sister Luna was sitting inside the orphanage when the smell of burning filled the air. Then smoke drifted into the room. Sister Luna rose out of her chair in a panic, covering her nose.

"Fire! Fire!" someone screamed.

"Get out of the orphanage!" Sister Luna screamed.

The whole orphanage jammed against the door trying to get out; it was sealed from the outside. Sister Luna, the children, all of them were trapped within the thickening smoke. Their screaming, coughing, and pounding on the door rose in the air as the flames devoured the walls of the orphanage.

Leopold stood back watching the orphanage burn. He knew what the scene must be like inside. He took no satisfaction in it. It was a grim and tragic ending to a painful chapter in his life.

Just then, he was knocked to the ground by a massive gust of wind. His horse reared, spooked. Leopold lay on the ground only to find himself in the presence of a spiritual being—Chen-Li.

His Li had soared over a hundred miles in seconds to slam into him, knocking him off his horse. Now he appeared above Leopold, floating in the air in front of him. Despite his dulled colors, his eyes glowed yellow and furious.

"How dare you burn the orphanage! There are women and children in there!"

But Leopold stood his ground. "How dare the orphanage do what it has to me!"

Wrinkling his brow in anger, Chen-Li coiled to strike. He shot like a lightning bolt into Leopold's chest. Recoiling, Leopold's eyes rolled back in his head as Chen-Li battled for control of his body.

But Leopold was not a commoner or a simple spy of the Zornastic Order. This was Leopold, whose willpower was as strong as a hundred men. Leopold and Chen-Li wrestled spiritually to the task, for neither one could gain control of the other. Chen-Li had not expected such a fight. Leopold was every bit as strong as he was.

In the physical world, outside their spiritual battle, Leopold's body trembled on the ground. His troops had no idea what was happening to him; he seemed as if he was dying. They could do nothing to help except watch and wait.

Chen-Li could not inhabit Leopold's body, and Leopold could not force him out of his. Inexplicitly, Leopold proved to be an equal match for Chen-Li. He stayed in control of his own body as Chen-Li's spirit popped out of it and floated overhead.

Leopold's soldiers tried attacking the Li with spears, but their spears went harmlessly through the spirit. They backed off in fear.

Leopold recovered faster than Chen-Li had ever seen anyone recover before. Not only could Chen-Li not win control of Leopold's spirit, but he could not find out any information about him either, as he had done with all others before.

"You are Leopold?" Chen-Li said in a distant voice. "The killer running amok in the Mid-Run Valley?"

"And you are the Chen-Li that I have always heard stories about?"

The two considered each other breathlessly after their stalemate; behind them, the orphanage burned. The screaming had stopped long ago.

"Stay back," Leopold's said to his soldiers. "You are helpless against him anyway."

They retreated at his command.

"Chen-Li, you are enormously powerful. I am fortunate to have regained control of my body against your spirit. But I know you could take any of my men with ease."

"Just to have you kill them?" Chen-Li never took his eyes off Leopold. "No. I will not give you the chance."

"I have no quarrel with you, Chen-Li."

"You just murdered innocent women and children."

"Innocence died here long ago, while you stood by and did nothing. You, of all people, should have known what was going on here. If you did, not only would you have known I was settling an old score, and you would have been complicit. If you did not know, then you should not judge me now."

"You murdered those people. I can't allow it!"

"What happens behind the doors of other St. Ehlona orphanages is not my concern. I do not know about them, and I don't care about them. But I do know what went on here, behind these closed doors—that is why I sealed them shut! In this orphanage, and for the greater good, I have destroyed it."

Chen-Li considered if there had been any truth in what Leopold had said. He was powerless in his Li form anyway.

"But I pledge this to you, Chen-Li, I have no designs to do harm to any other St. Ehlona orphanage. Can you pledge to me that you will no longer try to defend what is indefensible?"

"All those people burned alive." Chen-Li glared at him for a long moment. "I have heard you out, Leopold. Don't disappoint me."

With a sudden rush of air, his Li returned to the temple as fast as Leopold could breathe.

Leopold and his soldiers watched Chen-Li's blue flash rushing away from them. They looked at each other, amazed that they had seen the spirit of Chen-Li firsthand and lived to tell the tale. Leopold had now held audiences with both the Zorn and Chen-Li, the only human being to do so.

"Your Majesty," one of the soldiers said. "Would you really have killed us if Chen-Li inhabited our bodies?"

Leopold shifted his gaze from the horizon to the burning orphanage. He looked at it with a grim expression. Hearing the soldier's question, he just looked at them with the same grim face.

"Mount up," Leopold said. "Forget this place."

Meanwhile, back at the Red Guard tent, LaNew washed his hands in bloody water once again. The Red Guard carried away yet another dead body from the back of the tent.

LaNew gave the order.

Send in the next prisoner for interrogation.

"The days of tomorrow are blowing in the trees.
They fall like the mourning but are too afraid to leave.
A love, lost and dying, and too afraid to breathe."

Excerpt from *The Witch's Songbook*

THE AMALGAMATES

VILLAGE OF HAVERHILL IN THE YEAR 834 HRT

A man ran out of the tent and threw up on the grass. Gruesome. Shocking. Horrific. These were just a few adjectives describing the morose scene inside the tent. Even the seasoned Death Wardens, accustomed to preparing the dead for burial, were sickened at what they found inside.

"These are not human beings," he said over a buzz of flies. "A human being could not do this."

Blaize Plum was the Head Council of Haverhill, sent to the village of Plum to inspect the atrocities. He watched the Death Warden puking. Even from outside the tent, the smell of death invaded his senses.

A young boy of about twelve years old stood nearby with a darkened look on his face. He spoke to Blaize without being prompted.

"It was LaNew, and his Red Guard. At first, they were asking questions. They wanted to know what they could take, where things were hidden, and stuff like that. They wanted names, always more names. Then they stopped asking questions after they got what they wanted and just started killing people. Torturing them, laughing, they thought it was fun."

Blaize looked away. "I'm glad you are unhurt."

"My father and brother went into that tent. They never came out. What if these monsters come back? Who will protect us if they come back?"

"These monsters are real, but we will protect you; we have to," Blaize told him. "I am sorry I could not come in time to save your father and brother."

With that, Blaize turned to go, telling an assistant, "Send that sick Death Warden home for the day, and make sure this boy is given everything we can give him."

Blaize returned to Haverhill haunted by the nightmares of the massacre he saw in Plum. LaNew and the Red Guard had left the destruction in the tent in their wake and the burned bodies tied at the stake in the town square. He determined to set the wheels in motion for the first defense against Leopold.

Blaize called for an emergency conference of all the villages in the Mid-Run Valley, requesting representatives from each village to come to Haverhill immediately to discuss a common defense.

It took two long weeks before the emergency council convened for its first meeting, attended by over fifty representatives of the Mid-Run Valley villages. The meeting was held just outside of Haverhill on a nearby hilltop, in a strategic location, to remain on guard against any sudden attack by Leopold or the Red Guard.

Haverhill was the first village to provide an armed security force, fielding the first one hundred troops, arming it with swords, shields, armor, and spears. For the meeting, twenty archers were posted in overlooking strategic positions. Haverhill's initial forces provided the council's primary security, but soon other forces joined them. The total number of forces for the event totaled five hundred.

A large tent on the hilltop displayed large streaming banners of green and yellow. Inside the tent, about one hundred and fifty people milled around, discussing the same topic on everybody's mind, forming an army to strike back at Leopold. Some discussions were animated, some angry, some decisive with resolve, yet some others were panicked and willing to consider surrender and pacifism. Over the loud discussions, a multitude of voices resounded throughout the tent.

The sound of a wooden gavel called order to the chaos. The gavel struck repetitively with a slow but steady regularity.

"Order!" the speaker shouted. "I call the Council of the Amalgamates to order!" The speaker shouted. Slowly, the cacophony subsided as the members took their seats around tables. The gavel continued pounding even in silence. Finally, it stopped, and the speaker addressed the group. "The Honorable Blaize Plum presiding."

Blaize Plum stood and addressed the council.

"Colleagues. Members of our Amalgamation of Villages in the Mid-Run Valley, thank you for coming here today, and welcome to Haverhill. We come together for the first time as an amalgamated council of the Mid-Run Valley. Never have we come together as a single council before. Never have we had the need. Now we find that the times require it. Two weeks ago, I traveled to the outskirts of Plum, the traditional homeland of my clan. What I found was the destruction of the village after an enemy conquest and occupation. All my life, I have visited Plum freely and as often as I could. I would go to visit my cousin, the Honorable Justus Plum, the Head Council of the village of Plum. Only when I arrived on the outskirts two weeks ago, I was not permitted to go into the village. Because it was still burning and not safe. Even from miles away, I could still see the columns of black smoke. I did not know until later that the black smoke rising from the town square was the body of my cousin,

Justus Plum, forcibly tied to a stake and burned alive, in the same familiar place where we used to walk and eat our lunch together."

At this a gasp erupted in the tent. Fighting back the tears welling up in his eyes, Blaize Plum briefly choked up. He cleared his throat and continued.

"What was his crime? He refused to surrender the village of Plum to Leopold's killers. He refused to surrender and after his own death, innocent men, women, and children, were later brutally tortured and murdered."

"Head Council Blaize Plum," a man said, standing up. "Will you yield the floor?"

"Of course," Blaize told him. "The chair recognizes the Head Council of the village of Chase, the Honorable Alton Whitney."

Alton Whitney gave Blaize Plum a deep nod. "I deeply regret the loss of the Honorable Justus Plum. I knew your cousin well. I knew him to be an exceptionally decent man, and no finer Head Council in the Mid-Run Valley. His murder is a terrible loss to all of us, and we are so much less a council without him."

He took a deep breath, as the council resounded with fists knocking on the tables in agreement. Then he turned to the face the others in tent.

"In my village of Chase, we too have experienced the Red and Blue banners of Leopold. They suddenly appeared, taking us by surprise and invading our land. Our village was ransacked. These warring brutes of Leopold stole our treasures, our food, our supplies. But here is the difference: When allowed to surrender the village, I did it. I surrendered. Now, I am not proud of that. But it was the right thing to do. It saved lives. In Chase, we suffered brutality and violence, but not one of our citizens was killed. When the invaders got what they wanted, they left our village in shambles, but everything they damaged can be rebuilt. Because of our compliance, no one in Chase was burned alive, and nobody got seriously hurt. Now, I loved the Honorable Justus Plum, loved him like a brother, but we all knew he was a willful person. As he should be! His priority was protecting the village of Plum in the best way he knew how. He fought back, but he lacked the resources to do so, he lacked good fighting men and equipment. It was not the time for fighting back, but for surrendering. And for fighting back, he incurred the wrath of Leopold's army."

Loud murmuring interjected. Alton Whitney said louder, "Now, that's not a pleasant fact, but it is a fact nonetheless."

Several shouts from the crowd:

"You dealt with Amtor!"

"Amtor entered Chase!"

"It was not the Red Guard!"

"LaNew is a murderer!"

"We should consider all possibilities is all. Appeasement should not be taken off the table of discussion. That's all I have to say." Alton Whitney bowed and sat back down.

More voices erupted around the room:

"Objection!"

"Appeasement?"

"What is the meaning of this council?"

The gavel sounded again, eventually restoring order. Blaize Plum extended his hand to quiet the crowd.

"I respect the views of the Honorable Alton Whitney. I appreciate your words for the Plum family and especially for dear Justus. I deeply regret the losses that occurred in the great village of Chase. I am sure the brutality and intimidation you experienced was humiliating and hurtful." Here, Blaize looked down, a solemnness covered his face.

He spoke softly. "Let me tell you about a tent we discovered in Plum, smaller than this one, but not for a lesser purpose. It was just a small tent on the banks of the Plum River, located on the outskirts of the village. This was the center of activities for the red banners of LaNew and the Red Guard. For several days they were there, conducting what they called interrogations. When they left, the river ran red for days as the blood that drained from inside the tent ran down the banks and into the water. What LaNew and the Red Guard did inside that tent defies description. Men, women, children, no one was exempt from it. But not just death. Torture. Slowly and painfully, they were mutilated while still alive."

He looked back up at the council. "Now, I know what happened in Plum, and in Bowling, was not the same as in Chase. But what is at issue is this: All of our villages of the Mid-Run Valley lie undefended. Appeasement might be the right choice for some, but no one can predict if Leopold will decide to send Amtor's Red and Blue or LaNew's Red Guard to your village. We must establish a common defense. We must take the fight to Leopold, defend our villages, and those who stand defenseless against them."

Considerable applause indicated the council's general acceptance, but not all were clapping; some were still unconvinced, or scared.

"What I propose, friends, is the creation of the Army of the Amalgamated Villages. To form our army of the Amalgamates, we must pull all our resources together, a consolidation of all our villages in the Mid-Run Valley. We establish a force to fight. A force to protect our families, our property, and our dignity."

Applause and knocking on tables burst out spontaneously.

Blaize Plum held his hand up and silenced them once again.

"I saw a boy there, he was about twelve years old. He had lost his father and brother in that tent. The boy's family were tortured before being put to death. He asked me, what would he do if they decided to come back? Could we protect them from the monsters? We have no greater duty, colleagues, than to protect our people from the return of these monsters. Now how are we to do it?"

More applause and pounding on tables ensued.

"Will you yield the floor?" a voice cried out.

"The chair recognizes the Honorable Hoyt Whitney," Blaize announced, then sat down.

"An army is crucial for our protection. No question," Hoyt said. "But who will lead such an army? We need willful leaders—a leader of the Amalgamates that can win against the forces of Leopold and drive them to their knees. I know a leader like this—a leader who dares to organize a council of this size and purpose. I nominate the Honorable Blaize Plum to lead our armies against Leopold. Blaize! Blaize Plum to lead the Amalgamates!"

Alton Whitney stood up again and shouted. "I second the motion!"

Blaize Plum looked at them with wide eyes. At length, he stood up, addressing the council. "Friends, thank you for your motion of support, but I am not sure I am the best choice to be your general."

Alton Whitney spoke up. "Chairman, a motion is on the table. A vote for the motion!"

The entire council applauded this sentiment.

Blaize held up his hand again. "We have a motion on the table for a vote. With an oral vote, all in favor of Blaize Plum to lead the Amalgamates, say Aye!"

With that, the council resounded with a loud "Aye!"

"All opposed, say Nay!"

Not a single Nay.

Blaize Plum shook his head, realizing what just happened.

"With an overwhelming vote, the motion carries. Blaize Plum will be commissioned to lead the Amalgamates and the forces of the Mid-Run Valley defense! May the gods divine me."

The council erupted in applause and broke out chanting for several long minutes.

"Remember Plum!"

"Remember Bowling!"

"Death to Leopold!"

"Death to LaNew!"

Soon after, a war committee was quickly convened to further establish plans for logistics concerning the establishment of the Amalgamates. The war committee lasted for two weeks, ironing out details under General Blaize Plum's leadership. After the time spent in committee, they closed the council with the gavel. By the time the gavel struck, the Amalgamates were already up to four thousand armed soldiers and growing rapidly with volunteers. The Amalgamates were in the fight.

The army of the Amalgamates would be identified by colors of green and yellow on their banners, adopting these colors for armor and for their uniforms. Shortly afterward, the Amalgamates' army took to the field in force, eager for battle, wearing the green and yellow to distinguish themselves from Leopold's Red and Blue.

The villages of the Mid-Run Valley were now in a state of war against Leopold. They had growing resources and conducted military operations, meeting him in the field outside of the villages, not in them. The formation of the Amalgamates ended Leopold's easy conquests on unsuspecting and indefensible villages. From this moment on, the entire Mid-Run Valley organized against him as a single fighting entity.

Under General Blaize Plum's leadership, the enemy was joined. General Blaize Plum fought with surprising skill, earning a steady string of victories over Leopold in rapid succession. Each battle improved the Amalgamates' supply line of materials and made available more soldiers liberated from Leopold's service. As a result, the Amalgamates were growing more powerful as Leopold gradually became weaker, unable to replace his losses.

Under Blaize Plum as their general, the Amalgamates had turned the tide against Leopold. Soon the Amalgamates outnumbered him.

It was all going according to plan.

"She makes mountains,
Mountains that run so high.
She don't believe me
But she makes mountains, then she cries."

Excerpt from *The Witch's Songbook*

THE BLUE MOUNTAINS

The Blue Mountains in the Year 837 HRT

As a high-ranking officer in Leopold's Army of the Red and Blue, Lord Whitney had his mandate to fast-track construction of a stronghold for a castle at the highest part of the Mauveguard Pass in the Blue Mountains.

But first, he needed manpower. He began to conduct a series of interviews, looking for a wide array of experience. Throughout the ranks, the call went out for experienced stonecutters, masons, builders, mortars, loggers, mountain climbers. He needed people with experience in ropes, pulley systems, hoists, and a variety of other tasks that would be needed. Authorized to take seven hundred builders with him, Lord Whitney took the time to find the necessary skills he would need on the journey.

Within a month, they assembled a convoy and left Bowling on horseback; a long trail of rugged men, rattling gear, and boxed supplies headed west into the Blue Mountains. All of them, regardless of their specific skill, would take up arms to fight in the face of the enemy, although a hundred fighting soldiers, skilled in sword, spear, and arrow, followed the convoy to provide security.

They traveled along the road to the Blue Mountains without incident. These were the days before the formation of the Amalgamates, so there had been no organized resistance yet.

The convoy reached the base of the Mauveguard Pass. The Blue Mountains formed a range of peaks demarcating the western lands from the Mid-Run Valley. Beyond the mountains lay the land of the Wilds, where the ground dropped abruptly, forming steep cliffs above the marshes that stretched to the western coast of the Endless Sea. The mountains created a natural obstacle, isolating the native people of the Wilds, who roamed and hunted game there. The way between the Wilds and the Mid-Run Valley was impassable except through a single narrow cut through the mountains that the God Heironomus forgot to fill, the Mauveguard Pass.

The Mauveguard Pass opened a corridor through the steep cliffs, approximately three hundred yards wide at its base, but narrowing to only fifty yards at its crest. The pass consisted of a three-mile-long incline running uphill from east to west. Appearing as an upward slope, the pass sat in between two dramatic cliffs of the Blue Mountains.

Lord Whitney and the convoy reached the foothills without incident and got their first view. They had no trouble locating the Mauveguard Pass or ascending its gentle slope to its fulcrum. At the highest point, three-quarters of the way, Lord Whitney pointed to a peak that presented no finer strategic location to build Leopold's Castle Odessa.

"That is where we build," he said, pointing at the location.

There being no time to waste, this declaration from Lord Whitney began a flurry of activity over the next two years. Immediately the sounds of pickaxes and hammers echoed in the canyon as carpenters hammered scaffolding, and stone cutters and masons carved limestone blocks to exact specifications. Once quarried from the mountain, massive stone blocks traveled to the construction site fastened onto wooden carts and sleds, pushing them through the peaks and valleys. Massive wooden levers, cranes, and a system of pulleys guided the heavy stones into their proper place. Lord Whitney oversaw the whole construction, placing each numbered stone in its place according to his detailed project plan.

"Build the ramparts high," Lord Whitney ordered them. "Fortifications on each side of the mountain cliffs."

Two years passed on the mountain in intense labor. Progress was excellent, but time marched on quickly. They completed the lower sections of the stronghold, its walls well-constructed. The interior rooms for ceremony, such as the throne room and the connecting antechambers, anything not immediately important to defense, were delayed. Especially the towers; they would be saved for later. The areas completed first were the most defensible part of the stronghold.

Lord Whitney looked favorably upon the work. He corresponded regularly with Amtor in the field through courier. Through their communications, Amtor passed information to Leopold about their progress in the Mauveguard Pass. In return, Lord Whitney learned from Amtor that the armies were on the move through the Mid-Run Valley. The Amalgamates were pushing the Red and Blue, fighting, retreating, counterattacking. Leopold had been bogged down in fighting defensively, mostly to stalemate, after suffering an initial defeat at the hands of the Amalgamates. Defeat was a common occurrence for the Red and Blue these days.

Leopold's army now dwindled in number to around thirty thousand. The armies of the Amalgamates were swelling to forty-five thousand. The Amalgamates did much more than defend themselves: They were on the offensive, striking back, and to no small degree, they were winning. Leopold suffered defeat after defeat at the hands of Amalgamates, and his forces were on the run. The Amalgamates could recruit more soldiers daily and grew in numbers while Leopold could not replace his losses.

Lord Whitney knew that here, at Mauveguard Pass, Leopold was leading the Amalgamates to these fortifications. If they suffered a defeat here, then every officer in the Red and Blue, including himself, would hang from the gallows. He feared the end was near, his head practically in the noose.

Two years had gone by, and Lord Whitney did his best, constructing a stronghold to the extent of his skill. Not only had he worked diligently on the fortifications, but he motivated the workers to give the project their utmost efforts. Throughout the hard work, the men grew to admire him and each other.

Without warning, a rider came galloping up the Mauveguard Pass in a plume of dust.

"The armies are coming! The armies are coming!"

"What's this all about?" Lord Whitney came out of his tent adjusting his red suspenders. He intercepted the rider; he was one of Amtor's Red and Blue. His face was blackened in ash and dried blood; his eyes were wide as he excitedly gave Lord Whitney his report.

"The armies are ten miles east, advancing west to the Mauveguard Pass. The Amalgamates are close behind."

Lord Whitney turned to look at the horizon. He knew this day would come, but hearing the words stung his ears. Donning his blue jacket, he buttoned it while shouting the command, "To arms! To arms!"

Bells tolled, loud and shrill, warning all of imminent invasion.

"To arms! To arms!" the shouts echoed down the lines.

"Come on, men!" Lord Whitney said. "Look for the Red and Blue banners. They will be coming first. Do not engage the wrong troops, boys! Let the Red and Blue pass, then close around behind them."

Lord Whitney attached his scabbard and sword, scanning the scene. It surprised him to see some of his workers still hauling supplies. He pointed at them, shouting.

"Put those supplies down. Everyone stops work. Stop work! Today you are soldiers! Take up your swords! Take up the steel! To battle! Everyone, to battle!"

Rocks, ropes, and supplies were dropped where the men carried them.

"Put on your armor! Grab your swords!"

Taking out his spyglass and scanning the horizon, he could see a plume of dust rising in the distance.

That is them, he thought. *It is time.*

"Come on, come on, what color are the banners?" he whispered to himself, looking through his spyglass. "Let me see the banners."

At last, he could make out the Red and Blue banners of Leopold's army, kicking up dust on the road. He cried, "I see them! Leopold is coming!"

"Commanders! Form your units," he shouted over his shoulder, folding up the spyglass. "Form your units!"

Commands from the various commanders echoed down the line in reply. *Report! Report!*

A staff officer came running to Lord Whitney. "All accounted for, sir!"

"Excellent! Excellent! Take your position!"

They positioned themselves behind their fortifications as they had drilled many times.

The thundering of hooves came charging up the pass as the first of Leopold's forces came. Lord Whitney saw Amtor pull his horse to a stop, then watched him dismount. The lumbering giant took off his gloves and looked over at Castle Odessa. Lord Whitney met him there.

"Lord Whitney," Amtor said. "Outstanding work, what fortifications! You have done well."

"I apologize that the castle is not yet complete, Amtor."

"Nonsense! You have completed the most defensible parts of the stronghold. You have given us the best chance to be victorious in the Mauveguard Pass."

Amtor turned from Lord Whitney as the full complement of Leopold's army marched up Mauveguard Pass. Arriving somewhere in the middle, Leopold made a spectacular entrance. LaNew and the Red Guard came up the pass last, protecting the retreat.

Lord Whitney had prepared a battle order detailing how Leopold's forces should be placed throughout the fortifications to provide maximum resistance with minimal risk. He handed the battle order to Amtor, who quickly reviewed it. Finding it sound, Amtor walked over to Leopold, still mounted on his warhorse. The two reviewed the battle plan, Leopold pointing with a sweeping motion of his hand. Then he kicked his horse in the ribs, and they were off again.

Amtor came back to Lord Whitney. "Leopold has utmost trust in your plan. He told me to tell you, well done."

Lord Whitney briefly felt humbled and honored to hear such words, but with little time to prepare, he said nothing in return.

The soldiers scrambled into position, spears to the front, archers in back, swords in between. Then, once settled in position, a general hush filled the air, an unnatural quiet. The only sound was heavy breathing and the occasional rattle of armor. No one spoke.

General Blaize Plum halted the Amalgamate column at the bottom of the pass, gathering his forces, while he looked the situation over. His force was strong; he knew they outnumbered the Red and Blue. Confident after a long string of victories that put them hot on Leopold's retreat, the Amalgamates filled the pass in what seemed like an endless number of soldiers.

On top of the pass, Lord Whitney pulled out his spyglass again. He could see the massive numbers of Amalgamates, wearing green and yellow, their banners unfurled, their bloodlust heightened. Lord Whitney heard the Amalgamate battle cry at the eastern end of the pass that echoed all the way up the mountain. The dust their army kicked up created a massive cloud obscuring most of their numbers.

Then, just as if by divine intervention, it began to rain.

A scout returned to General Blaize Plum, saluting as he delivered his report. "They have fortified positions in the pass, sir."

"How many are up there?" he asked.

"Less than thirty thousand," replied one of his captains.

The Amalgamates had been chasing Leopold's army across the Mid-Run Valley; now, finally at the gate having them cornered, an impatient rumble came from his troops.

"What are we waiting for?"

"There they are, let's go get them."

"A strike for Plum, a strike for Bowling!"

Feet shuffled angrily; grumbles rose in a heated chorus. General Blaize Plum's captains urged him to attack—they had come all this way; the time was now.

But the general stared at the fortress with narrowed eyes, as if he could see directly into his opponent's eyes and read his mind.

"No," he said finally. "It's a trap."

"General," his captain said. "Give us the order. Can't you hear the men? It is what they want. It is what they have been waiting for. An end to this war. An end to Leopold."

"Attack! Attack!" cried the troops. "Give us the order!"

If not now, when? They had not pushed Leopold halfway across the Mid-Run Valley just to let them escape now, so that he could terrorize them another year.

The wait was agonizing. Mauveguard Pass was as quiet as the grave as eighty thousand men squared off, waiting for one man's decision.

All it would take to cut the tension was one arrow—but who would take the first shot?

"Units!" The general gave the preparatory command. It echoed down the Amalgamate line.

"Forward! March!"

Lord Whitney heard the distant commands from the Amalgamates' leaders. The commander's voice was almost too far away for him to hear. But far away as the order echoed, the total of the Amalgamates' spears and swords started to move up Mauveguard Pass. Thousands of marching feet shattered the silence. The force of heavy boots and iron chain clanking together mixed with the shouts of fury. Slowly up the pass they came to meet Leopold's force.

"They are coming!" Lord Whitney shouted. "They are attacking!"

The faraway voice of the Amalgamate commanders sounded again, and the troops gained momentum at the double quick. Lord Whitney could not believe his eyes. The whole Amalgamated army filled the void of the pass in attack formation, spears glinting, thrust forward.

"Here they come!" Lord Whitney said, trying not to panic. He turned and ducked below his stone rampart. His thoughts raced.

The Amalgamates will overwhelm us. Their numbers are superior. We are going to die. What did I do wrong? How did I get here? There is no way out!

Where does courage come from? Lord Whitney thought. These could be his last moments alive. He had a strong desire to run. But he stayed nervously behind his post. Each breath he took felt sweeter than the last. He swallowed hard; he was feeling very weak. His thoughts raced to his fortifications; would his efforts be good enough? His mind flooded with the thought that he could have done much more, and would have, if he had fully understood the terror he would be feeling this hour. He thought he had been a fool to allow himself into this situation.

But everybody was just as scared as he was. He felt the eyes of the soldiers upon him, searching him for strength. He knew they wanted to run too. Looking into their eyes, he found the words.

"Be brave, lads. Fear will not defeat us here today."

He turned and faced the enemy coming up the pass. Then Lord Whitney stood and jumped on top of the stone block he had been sheltering behind. He raised his sword over his head. "Come on boys! Let them hear what waits for them here! Show me your swords!"

A loud cheer went up with a multitude of swords waving behind stone blocks.

"That's it! That's it!" Lord Whitney became possessed in a fury most unexpected.

With their green-and-yellow banners streaming behind them, the whole Amalgamate army moved in a column up the pass. Chanting as they marched, they shouted with a loud grunt with every step.

Omphf! Swords up!

Omphf! Here we go!

Omphf! Spears ready!

The rain continued and turned the dust to mud. The footing became slippery, then treacherous. The chanting, so fierce, now became out of unison and disconnected as the men were slipping, skidding, and tripping up the hill. They could not stay in formation. Yet they did not stop.

As the Amalgamate army struggled for traction, commands were coming fast and loud from Amtor on top of the pass.

"Spears to the front! Swords at the ready! Archers! Nock arrows!"

The battle of Mauveguard Pass had begun.

"All the sharks are swimming closer,
And the beach is too far to see.
We've all got to work a little harder
To live in perfect harmony.
When all the horses are laughing, at the cavalry."

Excerpt from *The Witch's Songbook*

THE BATTLE OF MAUVEGUARD PASS

THE MAUVEGUARD PASS IN THE YEAR 837 HRT

In the next few hours, legends would be born at Mauveguard Pass. The battle would be at the center of a thousand stories. And it all started with Leopold's archers.

Amtor screamed commands mounted on his black warhorse.

"Archers! At the ready! Arrows, thirty degrees!" All down the line, the bowmen leveled their arrows at the same angle.

"Archers! Release!"

These were the first shots of battle at the Mauveguard Pass. The Red and Blue archers unleashed a barrage of arrows down the pass, arcing overhead, blotting out the sky. But the angle did not take into consideration the steep downhill slope. The Amalgamate spears in the frontline ducked, holding their shields over their heads, as the arrows went over them. Many shots in the first volley missed their mark, landing harmlessly in the void between the Amalgamates' first and second formation.

Amtor was quick to correct.

"Archers, eighteen degrees!" Once again, all down the line, the angles of the arrows dropped lower. "Archers, release!"

Another swarm of arrows sailed down the pass. This time the arrows slammed into the Amalgamates' frontline of spears. Most of the arrows thudded into their shields, but still, soldiers fell. The dead now hampered the column's forward movement.

Another round of the deadly missiles stacked up more bodies in the mud, causing the next wave of foot soldiers to climb over the dead.

Confusion started to permeate the Amalgamate line, though their column doggedly continued to press on up the pass. These were hardened soldiers who had seen death and gore. They had been fighting now for going on two years. These were determined men not deterred by the sight of blood or the presence of hardships. For some, the casualties fortified them, and a general shout resonated over the column:

Strike for Bowling!

Strike for Plum!

Leopold countered with a rally of his own. He grabbed a banner of the Red and Blue and stood on an archway of the incomplete stone tower. Precariously balanced, he waved his banner for all to see, inspiring his men. They started their own war cry.

For Leopold! For Odessa!

"Archers! Release!" Amtor shouted again.

Volley after volley of arrows rained down on the Amalgamates. Time after time, they found their mark striking down the green-and-yellow clad soldiers. The bodies were stacking up in the mud and rain.

In range now, the Amalgamates unleashed their own archers. Their arrows shot up the pass. Soon, it was Leopold's spears that were falling over in his front line.

"Spears, steady! Swords at the ready!" Amtor bellowed.

"Keep moving!" The order came from the Amalgamates. "Keep moving!"

The two armies closed ranks in the Mauveguard Pass. The first of the Amalgamate spears reached Leopold's frontline, and the fighting broke out, each side suffering losses at the tip of the spear. The fighting turned to hand-to-hand.

"Swords, prepare to attack!" Amtor said with shout. He looked up at Leopold standing on the tower's arch, still waving the banner. Leopold, in a strategic vantage point, looking across Mauveguard Pass and down at his enemies' advance, suddenly stopped waving the banner, and thrust it forward as a signal to attack.

"Attack! Attack!" Amtor shouted at the top of his lungs, and a loud battle yell erupted from the field. The Red and Blue poured over their fixed fortifications and rushed the Amalgamates.

Leopold's swords rushed forward to take the fight to the Amalgamates. In a downhill charge, the two armies smashed into each other at spear and sword point. Immediately, blood spattered on both sides. The downhill sloping terrain pushed the Amalgamates crumpling backward, collapsing under the weight of Leopold's onslaught. The battle was the most vicious and deadly contest these warriors had ever seen. Men on both sides lay dying, crying, screaming. Men were impaled on spears, cleaved with axes, slashed open with swords, pierced by arrows, stabbed with knives, pummeled with fists, and stomped with feet. Weapons were dropped, piles of bodies were stacking up. Through the mayhem, the rain kept coming down and blood ran down the pass in rivers of scarlet.

General Blaize Plum watched as his Amalgamated forces fully committed to the battle. At the two-hour mark, both he and Leopold knew the contest could end either way. It became immediately apparent to both leaders that, whatever the outcome, this would be the decisive battle. The victor here would be the victor of the war. The two armies were consuming each other, devouring each other, like two hungry wolves.

The fight continued to grind on for another hour. Across the battlefield, the bodies in writhing masses crawled in mud and blood.

Leopold gave the order. "Amtor! Send in the Red Guard."

LaNew and the Red Guard waited in reserve. Amtor knew what unleashing them meant. Leopold used them as shock troops; their atrocities struck fear in the hearts of their enemies, a tactic the Red Guard were all too willing to supply. Amtor reluctantly gave the order.

"Red Guard at the ready!" Amtor shouted. "Red Guard attack at will!"

With that order, the Red Guard rode down the muddy slope, picking through the survivors and doing their absolute worst.

Sending the Red Guard in worried Amtor. He had become an honorable man of war. He had respect for the enemy, not hatred. What started out as one year of service had made him into an accomplice in something other than war—and all because he'd lost a bet. After contributing to the cold brutality and vicious atrocities for years, he'd had enough. Looking over the battlefield, he knew this war was over. Sending in the Red Guard seemed like a criminal act now.

"Red and Blue, with me!" he said. With a small contingent of his own, Amtor went out to accompany the Red Guard; maybe he could save someone.

Likewise, a small contingent of Amalgamates circled around General Blaize Plum, who by now was holding his head low, knowing his army was in defeat.

"I'm sorry, I'm sorry," he told any soldier that could hear him. A steady stream of horrifically wounded men filed past him.

"What should we do now, General?"

That is the question, he thought. *What do we do now?*

He saw the Red Guard approaching his wounded men, who were pleading for help. He knew what was in store for them. He remembered the tent outside of the village of Plum.

He could hear the boy. *Can you protect us from the monsters?*

There was one way he could think to prevent it now. The words of Alton Whitney came to him again.

We should consider all possibilities.

LaNew walked among the wounded, carrying a large war hammer. He came across some wounded Amalgamates still alive on the battlefield. Approaching the first one, LaNew lifted the heavy hammer over his head and brought it down with a head crushing blow. Now, LaNew looked for more.

The rain had formed a pool of water tainted red with blood in a low-lying ravine of the pass. Two Amalgamates were in it, wounded but still alive. The first Amalgamate soldier was just a boy who had not yet shed his baby fat. He was bleeding from gashes to his shoulder and legs. Unable to walk, he cried out in pain, pleading to LaNew for help.

The second soldier sat waist-deep, in deeper water, bleeding from a wound on top of his head; blood streamed down his face.

LaNew splashed into the pool approaching the pair of soldiers in the water. His heavy war hammer rested on his shoulder. He smiled at the nearest young soldier.

"You're a real fat one, aren't you? I'll smash you like a pumpkin."

The soldier pleaded with LaNew from down in the bloody water, holding up his hands in defense. LaNew raised the hammer over his head.

"Please, no!" the boy cried as the hammer came crashing down, breaking the bones of his arms.

The boy screamed in pain, but the hammer strike did not kill him. LaNew raised it again, and dropped it hard on the soldiers' chest, breaking his ribs. Yet the boy was still alive.

"Stop it! Leave him alone! Can't you see he's going to die already!" The soldier said who was sitting in the center of the puddle.

"Eh? What's this?" LaNew asked, looking at the second soldier. Now, LaNew held the hammer waist high. "You dare order me? After this swing, I'll have something special for you, too."

LaNew raised his war hammer up and brought it down once again. This time, he recoiled breathlessly as blood spattered on his face. He wheezed for breath, the hammer still resting inside the soldier's skull. He let the handle fall and splash in the blood. Stepping over the dead boy, he splashed through the puddle toward the second soldier.

"I'm not a young man anymore," LaNew said breathing heavy to the second soldier, pulling out a long knife from his uniform. Wading deeper into the water, he grabbed the soldier by the hair, curly and red, and covered in blood. LaNew stood behind him pulling him up by his hair, stretching his neck. He placed his long knife to the boys' throat and readied himself to run his sharp blade across his neck.

"LaNew! Stop!"

Just then, Amtor rode up on his black horse.

LaNew startled.

"Leave that one alive," Amtor said. "I need him for intelligence. Gather your Red Guard and meet me back at the fortifications."

LaNew frowned at him. "Nothing intelligent about his one." But he released the boy anyway. "You want a little fun for yourself, eh Amtor?"

LaNew walked out of the water pool. The soldier fell upon his hands in the puddle.

Amtor dismounted and saw the hammer sticking out of the young soldier's head. The scene made him feel sick, but still he responded. "Well done, LaNew."

LaNew looked back at the soldier in the puddle, then whispered in Amtor's ear. "Make him scream."

He whistled to his Red Guard, who were also wading through the wounded, and motioned them back to the rally point. LaNew felt satisfied with what he, and his shock troops, had done.

Amtor carefully lifted the green-and-yellow soldier out of the water and helped him to his warhorse. He reached into a saddlebag and produced a bandage.

"Here, wrap this around your wound to stop the bleeding." He looked over the battlefield, where the fight still raged. He wanted to leave him in a place where he would be safe.

He carried the boy to the side of the pass where they both could take cover behind the relative safety of some rocks. When they reached the place, Amtor noticed that behind them led to the entrance of a cave. Amtor carefully lowered the boy to the ground and helped him with the bandages.

"My name is Amtor. This will help stop the bleeding, but if I were you, I would get out of that Amalgamate uniform before someone else from the Red Guard takes a special interest in you."

The boy, still dizzy from his head wound, asked Amtor, "Why are you helping me?"

"This war is over; we cannot be enemies any longer. A rebuilding of peace has to start. What's your name?"

The boy, still confused, was unable to give him one.

"You do have a name don't you?"

"Yes, of course." At last, it came to him. "My name is Kilmer."

"Well, Kilmer, there is a cave back here. Once you get out of those greens…!"

Amtor was interrupted as an arrow pierced his knee. He screamed in pain, and another arrow struck him deep in his left shoulder. Yet a third arrow flew by his face, narrowly missing him.

Archers from the Amalgamates hid amongst the rocks of the Blue Mountain. They had been trying to flank the army by following the goat trails through the mountains and around the pass. Here they saw Amtor and starting shooting.

Kilmer, in shock, watched the Amalgamate arrows strike the large man.

Amtor grimaced and scrambled backward, sliding deeper into the cave for cover. An arrow sank deep into the ground in front of him, and he backpedaled more. The cave entrance was too small for his giant body, and he remained an easy target. Needing to get lower, he looked behind him and saw the cave went further back. Unable to walk with the arrow deep in his knee, with a painful scream he slid himself deeper into the cave. With one last push, Amtor suddenly felt the rocks below him give way. The weight of his body rode the stones down that became dislodged, sending him over the edge, into a crevasse.

Amtor fell into darkness. He fell so long that his body rotated in the opposite direction before he landed violently on the rocks below. The arrows in his knee and shoulder broke off. The bones in his right leg and left wrist shattered upon impact. He felt the pain of ribs breaking. At the bottom of the dark hole, his body throbbed painfully in shadows. He fought against blacking out as if his life depended on it. Bleeding badly from several areas, he could not tell the extent of his injuries in the darkness.

His right arm was not broken and seemed to be the only part of him still functioning. Amtor carried a flint box in his pocket, and he frantically searched his uniform for it. Locating the flint box, he removed it from his uniform and spilled out its contents. Working as best he could, he got a piece of the tinder to spark, and with that tiny flame, he managed to light the candle in his flint box.

The candle illuminated his surroundings in a soft glow. He found himself in a circular cavern, about ten feet in diameter and thirty feet down from the top. Upon lowering the candle, he found that he was not alone here. He had landed on a decomposed body, lying face-up on the rocks now beside him, which had softened the impact. The dead body was clad in a black uniform, and upon its chest was a symbol of a silver circle emblazoned with a black crescent moon. Amtor had never seen a uniform like this and thought it looked like some kind of ancient priest. But by the look of the decomposition, the body had been there for years. The flesh had rotted away. The skull had a large opening on its side, no doubt from falling into this hold before Amtor had.

A glint of gold reflected beside it. Amtor held the candle as steady as he could, grimacing in pain as he stretched to reach it. Whatever it was, he pulled it over the corpse and closer to him. It was a dagger, and it looked like it was solid gold. A wave of pain shot through Amtor's body, and he dropped the golden blade in front of him.

"Help!" he said weakly, only just above a murmur. He cleared his throat and called out louder this time. "Help me!"

He did not expect his call for help to work. No one would come to help him. He tried to concentrate; he had to slow down his thoughts and think about how he could escape this situation. If he could not think of a way out on his own, he would die here. His life depended on it.

Just as that thought crossed his mind, a rope dropped from above and dangled in front of his eyes. Looking up at the top of the pit, a head appeared over the edge and peered down at him. At first, Amtor did not recognize him. Then the bandage unwrapped and fell off his head and floated down to into the hole. Amtor saw his curly red hair.

"Kilmer?" Amtor said as loud as he could. "Oh, thank the gods!"

"Grab the rope, Amtor! Can you loop it around your body?"

"Yes, yes. I think so. Give me a second." Amtor wrapped the rope around his chest. Kilmer had tied it in a loop so that Amtor only had to get it around his bad shoulder. It was a painful process, but he managed.

"Ready!" Amtor said and gave the rope a couple of quick tugs.

He felt the slack in the rope tighten, and his body started to slowly lift.

"Oh, wait!" Amtor said. He grabbed the golden dagger and stuffed it into his uniform. "Ready now!" He tugged back on the rope.

At the top, Kilmer pulled against the rope. He wrapped it around his shoulders and used one of the large rocks to give him some leverage. He pulled and wrapped, pulled and wrapped. Amtor was much heavier than Kilmer, but the boy was strong. Inch by agonizing inch, he lifted Amtor up to the rim. On the other end of the rope, Amtor was in blinding pain, but he could withstand it long enough to help get out. He took the pain. Anything was better than dying at the bottom of a hole with a rotted corpse. After much painful effort, Amtor reached the top lip. Kilmer continued to pull, then grabbed him by his uniform and helped him out of the hole.

Dragging Amtor away from the lip of the dark hole, Kilmer collapsed next to him.

"Oh, Kilmer! Thank you. Thank you, Kilmer." Amtor touched Kilmer's arm.

"You would do the same for me," Kilmer said.

"We are not enemies. We are safe now," they both said.

"We are safe."

"Don't turn your back!
Don't hold your breath!
Don't cross my path!
Or it's sudden death!"

Excerpt from *The Witch's Songbook*

KINGDOM OF ODESSA

The Mauveguard Pass in the Year 837 HRT

The white flag of peace unfurled at the bottom of the Mauveguard Pass from the Amalgamates' ranks. General Blaize Plum knew the army lay in ruins, with nothing to stop Leopold from exerting his will upon them and the Mid-Run Valley.

He thought that his best chances were to negotiate a peace, maybe get some favorable terms, perhaps even mercy, as improbable as that seemed from Leopold. The general had an even more noble thought: By surrendering, maybe Leopold would take his vengeance out upon him alone, and let the soldiers and villagers live. For himself, he expected no mercy.

General Blaize Plum sent a young liaison to parley with Leopold for the conditions of an Amalgamate surrender. The messenger carried the following note.

Your Majesty, King Leopold,

The battle of Mauveguard Pass determines that I must request a cease-fire between our armies to negotiate terms of the surren-

der of the resources at my disposal. We request terms of surrender that provides for the safety, welfare, and requisite compassion of our peoples to promote our land's future unity.

At your service.
From the hand of General Blaize Plum
Amalgamates, Commanding.

Under the white flag, the liaison rode his horse up the treacherous muddy hill, maneuvering around the casualties and through the wounded reaching out for help. General Blaize Plum watched him, lamenting giving the attack order that resulted in utter failure. The Amalgamates had never been defeated before; they thought they never could be. This overconfidence turned out to be just arrogance. Blaize Plum now saw the events of the last two years as Leopold's master strategy. Leopold had given the Amalgamates the illusion of victory, retreating, engaging, retreating again. All the while, Blaize Plum realized, Leopold had been building his trap here at Mauveguard Pass. The trap they were so eager to leap into. Despite being enemies, Blaize Plum knew he had been outsmarted, outmaneuvered, outgeneraled by Leopold's superior grand strategy.

Blaize Plum was through with this war. He could not go on anymore. Feeling the grip on his sword, he contemplated the one course of action still available for him: taking his own life.

I should, he thought. *But first, I must endure the humiliation of surrender, for the safety of the survivors.*

Leopold stood next to Lord Whitney. Through the spyglass, Leopold studied the situation at the bottom of Mauveguard Pass. He saw the white flags and the liaison prodding up the hill. That is when he knew he had won.

"Cease-fire, cease-fire!" Leopold shouted. "Let the white flag through."

The command echoed down the pass to all the units. The Amalgamates saw the white flag too, and those that still could dropped to their knees.

Leopold took stock. "Where is Amtor? Where is my Minister of War?"

"He was here, your Majesty, but now he is gone," Lord Whitney said. He did not notice where Amtor had gone either.

"Amtor is among the dead," LaNew announced as he came riding up.

"You saw him?" Lord Whitney asked. "Where?"

"Yes, he's dead, over there, around that pool of water," LaNew said with a chuckle. "A war hammer to the head. You'll find it sticking out of his face."

Leopold dropped his spyglass and gave a queer look to LaNew.

After a while, the liaison was received by the Red and Blue, and they escorted the unarmed man to Leopold. The liaison smartly saluted Leopold when he appeared in his presence.

"General Blaize Plum sends his compliments King Leopold. He told me to give you this."

Leopold read the letter without expression. At length, he asked for paper and quill to draft a response. These things were given to him promptly, and he scribbled a letter in a reply to the Amalgamate General. He folded it and had it sealed.

"Liaison, will you remain with me here and allow my Captain of the Red Guard to deliver my response?"

The liaison looked nervous seeing the infamous LaNew up close. "Of course, Your Majesty."

"LaNew!" Leopold said. "Please deliver this message to General Blaize Plum. And take care, LaNew, that no one gets hurt along the way."

"It would be my honor, Your Majesty," LaNew said. He gave a grin to the liaison, and a deep bow to the king. Then he rode down the pass with the letter.

After LaNew had gone, Leopold turned to Lord Whitney, and give a new order.

"Lord Whitney, please gather the Red and Blue and the Red Guard together. I have an announcement to make."

"Yes, Your Majesty," Lord Whitney said with a smile and excitedly turned to go.

"And be on the lookout for Amtor!" King Leopold called after him.

Lord Whitney sent word and gathered all the forces of Leopold's Red and Blue, and the Red Guard. They assembled around Leopold about the same time LaNew reached the Amalgamate line at the bottom of the pass.

Seeing LaNew's progress, Leopold turned and addressed his troops.

"The war is over! We are victorious!" he said to a rousing cheer heard all the way down the mountain. LaNew heard the cheer, and already had a list of which Amalgamates he would interrogate first. He would naturally start with General Blaize Plum. He could not wait to start on him. He rode the rest of the way anticipating it with a smile on his face.

General Blaize Plum allowed LaNew through his remaining defenses. LaNew rode through them all avoiding eye contact but feeling their stares fully upon him. They knew who he was, and what he represented, and they were frightened. It was the way LaNew wanted it. Soon, they would be even more frightened as he began looking back at them.

"Well, well, General Blaize Plum," LaNew said without formality. He produced the letter of the terms of surrender and extended it to him. "Your days are over, Blaize."

Reading the terms of surrender, the general's eyes suddenly widened. He looked at LaNew, then to his own captain. LaNew smirked.

In Leopold's camp at the top of the pass, he turned to face his troops. "Look there. Right now, as we watch, General Blaize Plum has just received my non-negotiable terms for the surrender of his forces. I have given LaNew of the Red Guard the honor of accepting the terms. He was handpicked to present the letter to the Amalgamates. Watch and remember this day!"

Once again, Leopold turned to watch General Blaize Plum through his spyglass accept the terms of surrender. The army of the Red and Blue and the Red Guard casually spoke among themselves, congratulating their efforts for the victory.

"This is a historic moment, watch it with pride," Leopold said.

At the bottom of the pass, General Blaize Plum read the letter twice over, just to be sure. Then, finally convinced, he folded and tucked it into his uniform.

"Captain!" the general called to his soldier nearby. The captain came riding up. General Blaize Plum prepared him for the surrender. "Please remove your sword."

Leopold dropped his spyglass again. Turning back to face his forces, he gave a new order. "Attention, Red Guard! I find you guilty of crimes against humanity and pronounce the sentence to all of you… of death."

The Red Guard gave him a questioning look and mumbled amongst each other.

"What did he say?"

"What does this mean?"

"Is this a joke?"

"Behold!" Leopold said, pointing down the pass.

At the bottom of the Mauveguard Pass, they soon received the astonishing answer to all their questions. As they watched the scene far below, they saw the Amalgamate Captain of the General's guard remove his sword. Then the captain made a swift swipe of it. Silently,

LaNew's head came off his body and landed on the ground. Shortly after that, his body rolled off his horse and landed on top of it.

A general gasp went up from all.

Leopold turned from the scene below to face the remaining Red Guard once again.

"Lord Whitney!" Leopold commanded. "Arrest the Red Guard and put them to death!"

The Red Guard, at first startled, tried to run. They tried to fight back. But Lord Whitney's forces greatly outnumbered them. The Red Guard ran against a gauntlet of violence. They were hacked by swords and pierced by spears to silence. Every one of them that wore the familiar red headband fell off their horse. On the ground they were surrounded by hacking swords. The Red Guard were silenced. Forever.

General Blaize Plum, looking up the slope of the Mauveguard Pass, saw every one of the red headbands struck down by Leopold's Red and Blue, until they were all dead.

General Blaize Kilmer could still not believe his eyes. He took out the terms of surrender again and read the words again. He unfolded the paper and read it out loud:

Dear General Blaize Plum,

The Amalgamates have fought with honor and distinction; you can be proud of them. Surrender your forces, and I will become the ruler and king of the Mid-Run Valley. As fellow countrymen, I deliver into your hands your tormentor, the villain LaNew, and I give you my first order as your king. If you accept these terms of surrender, have your captain remove the head of this evil man. When I see LaNew's head roll, I will respond in kind by executing the entire Red Guard. This will be your sign that the war is over.

From the hand of
King Leopold

Leopold walked up to Lord Whitney. “Well done. From this day on, the Red Guard is no longer needed.”

“So you made sure of it,” Lord Whitney said.

“No peace would be possible if the Red Guard and its leader LaNew survived.”

“You must have sensed at some point that it would only be a matter of time before LaNew would try to betray you.”

“He would try to assassinate me to increase his own power. For the rest of my life, I would have to look over my shoulder, waiting and watching for him. Until the day I die, I will never regret killing LaNew before he tried to kill me.”

“You may have made an ally of General Blaize Plum.”

“I hope that’s true,” King Leopold said. “I would rather have an honorable man like him as an alley than LaNew.”

As King Leopold and Lord Whitney stood speaking, horns began to blow loudly, bells started ringing in the valley, announcing that the war was over. All the forces in the pass and hiding in the rocks were rounded up or turned themselves in. Weapons from the Amalgamates were collected and stacked.

Healers came in wagons to assist the wounded. Carts began to collect the dead while priests busied themselves blessing their worldly remains. The healing had begun.

Kilmer helped Amtor to a soft place in the grass. He quickly ditched the Amalgamate green and yellow, disguising himself in the uniform of the Red and Blue. Kilmer and Amtor helped each other bind their wounds. Then they sat and waited.

A troop wagon eventually wobbled up to where they sat. The wagon was loaded with wounded troops from Leopold’s Red and Blue; most of them sat quietly, moaning in pain from their injuries.

The driver pulled up beside them. “Any wounded there?”

Kilmer nodded and asked for help with Amtor.

One troop in the wagon stood up, despite his wounds and bandages, and called out.

"Look! It is Amtor! Is he dead?"

"No, he's not dead," Kilmer assured them. "But he's badly wounded. He needs attention right away."

"The healers are here," the wagoner said, pointing down the hill. Several women dressed in red walked up to the wagon. A healer rushed to Amtor's side. She leaned over him, and blue energy crackled between them as she cast her healing spells. Amtor struggled to sit and found the strength to speak to the men in the wagon.

"This man saved my life." He pointed to Kilmer. "This man is a hero."

All the wounded soldiers in the wagon heard it. A cheer went up and they congratulated Kilmer.

"Do you know what you have done? You have saved the life of the most important person in the war except for King Leopold himself."

"He would've done the same for me," Kilmer said, turning around to look at Amtor again. Amtor lay back with a nod and a smile. He closed his eyes and laid his head down in the soft grass. There, the healer continued to heal him.

The estimated losses at Mauveguard Pass were massive: Over fifty thousand from both sides lay dead. Mauveguard Pass would go down in history as the largest battle the world would ever know.

After Mauveguard Pass, Castle Odessa became a magnificent castle. Lord Whitney finished building it with more skilled labor on the same aggressive schedule. It sat atop the Mauveguard Pass and became Leopold's seat of power to rule the Kingdom of Odessa.

King Leopold ruled all the known world, from the Mid-Run Valley, Port Harbor, the Gray Mountains to the east and the Blue Mountains in the west, to the Dragonbreath Mountain, the Fangs, and even the Temple of Chen-Li.

For King Leopold himself, he remained an aloof leader, spending more time with his dog, Babbit the Magnificent, than his advisors. His warring days were over, and now he entered a new chapter in his life. A change occurred in him; he became an empathic, benevolent ruler in peace. He established fair laws based on the people's needs, education, labor standards, commerce, and many other innovations to improve life in the Mid-Run Valley. During his war, Leopold developed the reputation that he would destroy anyone or anything that stood in his path. But now, with that power secured, the man who started as the little orphan boy was known as a generous administrator. Though one thing never changed: His need for privacy. He kept to himself, taking his own counsel.

He gave no reason to quarrel with Chen-Li. He respected the orphanages, needed now more than ever, as the war had created many more orphans than before. King Leopold would go on to support them with gracious financial assistance. As for Chen-Li, he took Leopold's words to heart, becoming the Defender of the Orphans, learning as much as he could about immoral behaviors, preventing any misconduct he found.

Amtor, Leopold's Minister of War, had his best years behind him. He never saw King Leopold again. For him, badly wounded, it took years to mend. He would develop a severe limp and would never walk normally again. Amtor fell in love with the healer that saved his life. He and Gilglad made their home in a small village named Homestead. Over the years, he became consumed with bitterness for King Leopold and the part he played in the unification of his kingdom and the Odessa empire.

Kilmer was hailed as a hero by both the people and the crown. For risking his own life to save Amtor, he became the youngest captain of Leopold's Red and Blue army and reported directly to Lord Whitney, who became Leopold's new Minister of War. Captain Kilmer would go on to do many great things for Leopold, but oddly his recruitment records into the Red and Blue were never recovered or found, blamed on lousy administration.

The Red Guard earned an infamous place in history, scourging, torturing, and murdering tens of thousands of innocent people, the full number of which will never be known for sure. LaNew was recognized as the villainous character he was. Legends grew to make him even more blood-thirsty. He would go down in history as the most hated person in the world, a title that no doubt would have pleased him.

The Mauveguard Pass became a serene and reflective place. Honors to the dead of both sides were erected in thoughtful ceremonies. It became the place memorialized by survivors and veterans with stone monuments dedicated to where fifty thousand humans met their death in glorious and selfless battle. Many remains were never recovered, and spirits of the dead roamed, unable to rest. Many clerics and priests performed blessings to ease the crossover for any restless spirits, confused about which realm they should exist in. Even King Leopold himself, accompanied by the Honorable General Blaize Plum, would together lay beautiful wreaths of flowers on these monuments in honor of the dead from each side. Despite these blessings and ceremonies, the Mauveguard Pass became a place where ghosts materialized under certain conditions. It was hard to argue with those who said they saw ghosts here. If ghosts haunted any place in the world, they would be found at Mauveguard Pass.

Thus, the War of the Mid-Run Valley ended and King Leopold's rule over the Mid-Run Valley as King of the Odessa Empire begun.

King Leopold would settle into peace and rebuilding.

"All the things you can't remember
Are the things they won't forget
The traveled road not taken,
in the end, it's just as dead."

Excerpt from *The Witch's Songbook*

A COLLECTION OF PERSPECTIVES

Castle Orlo in the Year 838 (HRT)

The Zorn sat on his throne in the silence of Castle Orlo. The castle, once a hub of activity of the Zornastic Order, had now long fallen into silence. His grandiose plans for the Zornastic Order, now slain by their own hand. His magical artifact, Soothsayer, now lost. The castle sat dark, cold, and lonely. But for the Zorn, he had become obsessed with the disease consuming his flesh. He spent most of his time searching his reflection in the mirror, watching the progress of his decaying yellowing skin, hollow eyes, gaunt face. He would obsess over it for several years, unable to stop it. Outside the castle walls, events were shaping the world, and he seemed to have no idea or concern about any of it. These were the battles between men, and they went on without his involvement.

He had his own problems. The castle itself conspired against him. In these halls and chambers, twenty thousand priests of the Zornastic Order had taken their own lives at his Grand Command. The stink of their bodies permeated the stone floors and walls of the castle. It was enough to make him sick. Yet there was something else roaming around the castle. The Zorn continued to find dead bodies. He would inevitably turn into a hallway or enter a room and there he would discover the corpse of a long-dead priest. He found them haphazardly scattered in places around Castle Orlo. They stained the stone with blood and bile, remaining frozen in silent screams, and staring out of hollow eye sockets. But the problem became more than just dead bodies and the stink that bothered him. The vengeful spirits of the dead roamed the hallways, trapped in the castle. Their wandering spirits haunted him night and day. As he walked down any hallway, entered any room, or even sat upon his throne, the energies of the vengeful spirits bombarded him, their loud terrifying screams replaying their most agonizing moments. The Zorn could absorb ordinary spiritual energy, but these vengeful spirits would not allow it and only existed to torment him.

Chen-Li is responsible for this! he would say to himself, over and over again.

Alone, he would pace the halls of the dark castle. He knew he could not defeat Chen-Li in a direct fight without the fear of being neutralized forever in a Great Negation on their own. He had lost Soothsayer, the one weapon that could tip the scales of the balance, and he had to find it.

Since he could not escape the stink, or the vengeful ghosts trapped in the castle, he often walked outside. Even when he walked in the trees of the Sanguine Forest, the spirits still tormented him, as their bones lay under his feet, in and out of the ground, in the world's largest graveyard.

As the battle of Mauveguard Pass was resolving between the Amalgamates and Leopold, Soothsayer was pulled from the depths of the hole that kept it from his vision. He knew that it was somewhere in the Mauveguard Pass, and suddenly, he could sense it.

But so many armed men were doing battle there. He could not go rushing off to collect it. He would have to wait until the time was more favorable.

In the meantime, he came to view Castle Orlo as the place where spirits were trapped, including his own, and as the place where Hazor died and the Skeletal King was created. The Zorn was just one more spirit trapped here. Until he could go collect Soothsayer, he would never be free from the spirits that haunted him both inside and outside Castle Orlo.

Consumed with so many thoughts, he could not concentrate on any single task. He could not sleep thinking about his vengeance on Chen-Li, the search for Soothsayer, the stink of the dead, his degrading flesh. He forgot what he had been thinking and changed his mind often. He had problems making decisions. All of these things twisted his mind in madness.

He had Langula to keep him company. She was neither disgusted by the blood or stink (she rather enjoyed the aroma), nor was she dismayed by the vengeful spirits. Where she came from, they were minor torments. She did worry about the Zorn, though. Someone with his power, in his position, should not have to worry so much about all these distractions that conflicted the thoughts of his mind.

"Zorn, my love, we need another plan."

"Don't bother me, now. I am thinking."

"But Zorn," Langula said, rubbing against him. "I need your help. I cannot do everything by myself. And you are in no condition to come with me. I need offspring, some sons. Someone to call my own."

After looking in the mirror, he seethed in bitter anger. He burst out in a tantrum, breaking every mirror, every window, every reflective surface in the castle. Langula rather enjoyed seeing this anger come from him. She fed off of negative emotions and thrilled with satisfaction at his outburst.

After his attack, the Zorn breathed heavily. Then he turned to face Langula and spoke.

"I know what I want you to do."

Langula remarked. "And just as quickly as that, he has an idea."

"The Witch created the Timmutes from a drop of her blood. Imagine what we could create if we manipulated reproductive material, instead of blood."

"Reproductive material," Langula gave him a confused look.

The Zorn said reassuringly. "It's what you do best, my dear."

"How delightful. What do you have in mind?"

"Along with your nightly collections of blood, I want you to add these new fruits to your collections as well."

Langula smiled. "What do you intend to do with it, Zorn?"

"Why, reproduce, of course. You said it yourself, we need to make you sons. Big powerful sons. If the Witch can do it in such small scale, so can we, in a much larger fashion. We will create new living beings of our own, one's like the world has never seen before."

"So delicious," Langula said, pulling her lips away from her fangs. Just then, the Zorn leaned to her and gave her a long, unexpected, intimate kiss. Langula looked wide-eyed at him. The Zorn's sudden show of affection made her look adoringly into his ghastly skeletal face and deep eye sockets.

"Magnificent," Langula told him. "Perfectly demonic."

In the Temple of Chen-Li

Elsewhere, Chen-Li found it hard to concentrate as well. He tried to take his mind off Soothsayer with rigorous training. But at the same time the Zorn felt Soothsayer lifted from the hole, he was feeling it too. Chen-Li took a towel and walked to the side of the training area. He wiped the sweat from his brow and tilted his head up, as if he were smelling the wind. In fact, he felt the pull of the Witch's blood, calling him like a distant voice. The call of Soothsayer blew in from the west, from the Blue Mountains. He could feel it around the Mauveguard Pass.

Chen-Li had his spies collecting intelligence, and they sent him reports regularly about the war of men. He was quite aware of the battle in the Mauveguard Pass. But his business was not in the realm of men. The war had no linkage with the Zorn, so he felt it was not his place to get involved. He already had to interfere once when Leopold razed Umbrick and the orphanage there to the ground. He had a battle with Leopold, at least spiritually, and it turned out to be a stalemate in their battle of wills. It still bothered Chen-Li how he been stymied by what should have been an ordinary man. Leopold had turned out to be a most willful human, one like Chen-Li had never encountered before. Leopold was wrong for destroying the orphanage in Umbrick, but there was something extraordinary about him.

For now, though, he did not have the time to think about Leopold. He had another problem.

"The blood of my mother is speaking to me," Chen-Li told Myra, his second wife.

"Is it Soothsayer you sense?" she asked.

"It has been revealed, lifted from whatever veil hid it. Now, it calls to me."

"That means it is calling to the Zorn as well. Maybe it will bring him out into the open."

"If so, Myra, he would be vulnerable. Our White Eminence could attack, and he would be weakened without his Zornastic Order."

"If this is Soothsayer calling, should we not retrieve it before he does?"

Chen-Li thought about it. He could not forget what his mother told him when he went to her in the Great Mapes Forest.

But when you see the signs in the sky, it will tell you that the Zorn, your brother, will be at his strongest. Use all your skills to create a weapon that will defeat his demon. Send this weapon out among the people. There, the weapon will find its champion. I will send more help, as best as I can, when the time is right.

"Soothsayer has tipped the scales of balance. I think as long as it stays out of my hands and the hands of Hazor, the realm of man is to decide its fate. Soothsayer has a part to play yet. But if the Zorn comes out his castle, we will defeat him. If he never comes out of his castle then he can never have Soothsayer. If he never leaves his castle, and never reclaims Soothsayer, then he is no threat."

"We will not go after Soothsayer?" Myra asked.

"My mother said it should stay in the realm of man. Amongst the people. It is best to have it stay where it is for now." Chen-Li thought about it some more. Then he continued, "But I will send out our spies to look for it anyway. It will be best to locate it, to watch over it. If it is supposed to remain with the people, we should make sure it stays that way."

Chen-Li and Myra walked back to the training floor. They practiced their warrior training. As they continued training, Chen-Li could not help but remember the Witch's last words.

"If the fates favor you, you will be victorious. If they do not, then Hazor will accomplish what he set out to do."

From his vantage point in the Temple of Chen-Li, he could see the Dragonbreath Mountain to the east. For several months now, a constant cloud had appeared, obscuring its summit. It hovered over the mountain like a veil, hiding something. He wondered if the appearance of the mysterious cloud coincided with his mother's disappearance. It was no matter. He had no desire, or the skill, to go to the top of the Dragonbreath to find out. Even if he could, he was not sure what would be waiting for him there. If his mother went there, then she wanted desperately to be alone. For now, he had enough to worry about. Until the mountain proved otherwise, the perpetual cloud was just a weather event, and posed no real threat. He would continue to prepare his warrior priests of the White Eminence for the battle yet to come. He would train, prepare, and keep watching for his brother's mischief.

Chen-Li and the Zorn would live to fight on.

In the Village of Homestead

In the northern lands, Amtor was recovering from his wounds. He would never be a soldier again, but he would survive. He would be forever grateful that he did not die in that pit at Mauveguard Pass.

Gilglad, the healer who found him, attended to his recovery. She was a beautiful woman with dark-brown hair and green eyes. Her power to draw upon the energy of love gave her a magical ability to heal wounds. With Amtor, she made such an empathic connection that it bonded them to each other in a deep love. His body responded to her magic and it healed his wounds.

Now he lay in bed recuperating. He reached under him and felt the cold metal. When he pulled out the dagger, the gold lit his face in a shimmering light from its blade. He marveled at the artistry, the inscriptions of vining oak leaves, the running deer across its flat surface, the jeweled hilt encrusted with rubies and emeralds on its guard. He knew it was a valuable treasure he found at the bottom of the pit. Taken from a dead priest of unknown origin, he would always remember the crescent moon wrapped in the silver circle. Maybe someday he would find out what the symbol represented. In the meantime, he knew this was no ordinary dagger; it vibrated with an energy of its own. It compelled him to want to use it. That is what frightened him about the dagger the most. It must contain powerful magic.

Gilglad came in to change his bandages and saw him holding the dagger.

"What a beautiful piece," she said.

"Yes, it is exquisite, but, there is something else about this dagger."

She asked if she could touch it. Gilglad had a special relationship with magic. She could use it, but more than that, she could sense it.

Amtor agreed and held out the dagger. "Be careful."

She nodded. Reaching out, she touched the side of the blade. Gilglad held her hand there for a moment and shut her eyes. Then, she startled, pulling her hand back quickly.

"I have never felt anything like this before, Amtor. It is more magic than I've ever known existed."

"I thought so," Amtor said. "We need to get rid of it."

"Get rid of it?"

"What I mean is, we can't have it lying around our home. Can you find me something to put it in, and I'll bury it outside."

"Something with a lock on it," Gilglad suggested.

Amtor nodded. Then he felt himself dozing. Gilglad placed her hand on his eyes. At Gilglad's touch, Amtor went right to sleep.

Upon awakening, he saw Gilglad had placed a metal box by his bedside. The box was open, and a lock hung loose around its latch. The golden dagger still lay in the bed with him. He placed it in the metal box. Gilglad came in to help him, locking it, and handing him the key. When he regained enough strength, he took the box and buried it around the back of their home.

"The best place for it," he said, wiping the dirt from his hands.

After a while, Gilglad had happier news for him.

"I am going to have your child, Amtor," she told him.

The little metal box, and the magical dagger inside, was soon all but forgotten.

ACT IV

The Long Way Home

"Sing me a song, one final song,
Sing me a Song for the Departed.
The things that I wanted are slipping through my hands
Oh, I'm all, all, almost gone."

Excerpt from *The Witch's Songbook*

THE LONG GOODBYE

THE DRAGONBREATH MOUNTAIN IN THE YEAR 1046 HRT

Almon and Aberfell stood together on top of the world. They walked out of the cabin, with the Timmutes swirling around them. They walked through the fog of the Dragonbreath cloud and stood at the base of the Praying Lady tree.

"So, this is where she stood for the last time?" Almon said.

"This is where the Witch spent her last moments in this world."

Almon turned to imagine the view through her eyes. He even looked up as if in prayer himself.

"It doesn't seem so bad once we are standing here," Almon said.

"Not too bad," Aberfell agreed. "A good way to go, I guess. It would be over quick."

"Aberfell." Almon turned to the Supreme Historian. "I have been up here for years now."

Aberfell shrugged. "But who's counting?"

"Well, it's been a long time, anyway. I wonder what the world is like down there now?"

"The world doesn't change much. Only people change."

"I've learned so much from you."

"I appreciated the company, and your friendship."

They turned to stare some more at the Praying Lady tree. It was a beautiful tree. So elegantly formed, mirroring the Witch's final pose.

"What will you do once I'm gone?" Almon asked.

"Oh, I suppose I'll go back to wrapping my head in linens and trying not to experience anything new. Like the way I did before you came. Maybe someday, someone else will come along and think I am dead too, like you did."

"Sounds horrible."

"Well, speak for yourself. What will you do down below? Do you think knowing what you know will help you fit in again?"

"I hope so. It is time to bring Almon Plum-Kilmer back from the grave."

"They are in for a big surprise."

Almon nodded. "But now I have the Provenance."

"If you are relaying the whole story, the Provenance is the best place to start before moving to the others."

They looked at the tree again before going back inside to shake off the cold.

"When will you go?" Aberfell asked his visitor as they strolled along.

"In a couple of months. In the springtime most likely. It is warmer then, you know."

"Yes, it would be too cold to come down off the mountain now. You know, you are welcome to stay with me as long as you like."

"Thank you, Aberfell." Almon flipped through the pages of the Provenance. "For that, and for all this."

"Oh well," Aberfell mumbled. "That is no problem, no problem at all. I hope it serves you well."

"We have talked about so many things," Almon said. "Gods, goddesses, demons. Jealousy, hatred. Love and lust. Witches and Timmutes."

Aberfell continued. "Orphans and spirits. Music and death. Forests and mountains. War and peace. Beautiful acts of kindness, and sadistic acts of senseless violence."

"What do you think it all means? What stands out the most to you?"

"How the smallest of things can change the world," Aberfell said. "And always try to be wise beyond your years, young Plum-Kilmer."

More days and months passed in a blur. Soon the weather started getting warm. Spring had arrived. The time had come for Almon to leave the mountain and bid farewell to Aberfell.

He collected his gear and packed up the manuscripts he wrote over the years. He collected some food, some water, and stored it in his backpack. Despite the warmer weather he dressed in layers of warmth. He would be starting the long walk home.

"It is time?" Aberfell asked.

"Yes, I think so. I don't know how to thank you, Aberfell."

"Oh, you'll think of something. By the way, I have a little gift for you. It's not much, but here." Aberfell reached into his pocket and pulled out a little wood carving he had been whittling for Almon, carved into the image of a dragon. Aberfell placed it in Almon's hand. Almon smiled.

"You have found your dragon," Aberfell told him with watery eyes.

Almon grasped the little dragon and closed his hand. He gave Aberfell a long, last hug. It took Aberfell by surprise. In all the years they had been together, a hug had never happened. Even he, the Supreme Historian, could not remember the last time he received a hug from anybody in this world. At first, Aberfell did not know what to do. But slowly, his arms came together, and he gave Almon an affectionate embrace back.

With tears in their eyes, they let each other go. Almon slipped on his backpack and adjusted the straps to distribute the weight. They headed to the door together.

"The Timmutes will help guide you down," Aberfell said. "But be careful anyway."

"It's a long way down. I appreciate your help, Timmutes. Thank you."

They walked outside together, back to the tree. Almon took a long, last look, then turned to face Aberfell again.

"Will I ever see you again?" Almon asked him.

"I hope so," Aberfell said with a smile. "I'll be around somewhere."

"After all the time we have spent together, Aberfell, I have no idea what you mean, yet I feel like I should."

"To a man my age, we haven't spent all that much time together."

"Goodbye, Aberfell."

"Until we meet again, my friend Almon Plum-Kilmer."

Almon carefully lowered himself over the edge and started the long climb down. At first, he held on to the tree, with thousands of Timmutes circling him. Soon, he had climbed down out of Aberfell's view.

He stood looking at the place where Almon departed for some time. Then, looking up at the tree, he took a deep breath and turned to go back to the cabin. He walked in slowly. It did not seem the same without Almon anymore. He slowly sat in his rocking chair and looked out at the constant fog outside his window. It was quiet again, just like all the decades before Almon showed up. He sat in the chair for hours. At length, he looked at the rolls of paper containing his writings.

"Bah." He took no interest in them now.

He let out a deep exhale. Then, reaching in his pocket, he pulled out a long strip of linen. As the sun went down, once again, Aberfell wrapped the linens around his head to dull his senses.

As the sky got darker, soft words filled the room; under the bandages, Aberfell sang an excerpt from *The Witch's Songbook.*

It may be dark, and I might lose my way.
So, float a soft light to me, I will send my love into the flame.
Close your eyes! Close your eyes! And wash the sorrow from your eyes.
And make a wish on angels' wings before they fly too high.
But you cannot see me since I have wished myself away.
While the world keeps turning in its own way.
Now I find myself laughing until I cry.
But I am not laughing anymore.
I am just a tear away.

The song faded away and silence returned to the cottage. The golden orbs of the Timmutes continued to float around the room, putting things into their proper place, making it seem as if they, too, floated in the air. They dutifully carried on, putting dishes away, folding the clothes, everything that Aberfell would need for the next day.

He sat comfortably in his chair, breathing slowly now. Shadows grew long as the room darkened. Not that Aberfell could have noticed any of this, having linens wrapped around his head, but after years of living on the mountain, he knew without seeing what time it was, and he instinctively knew the hour was getting late. Growing more comfortable and relaxed, his breathing became slower and steadier, and he fell asleep just as if it were any another night. Only this would be anything but any other night.

The sun went down, and the golden orbs were now the only light in the room. Suddenly, they all scattered.

A light started to shine through the window. It illuminated half of Aberfell's bandaged face in a soft, blue glow. His breathing became heavier, and the blue light grew brighter. The light coming from the window fell upon him in sparkles of stars. His body stirred as the light streamed into the room and encircled him.

As he gradually lifted from his chair, the energy of the light surrounding him carried him upward. While suspended, as if pulled by invisible strings, his right arm and leg stretched to the window toward the blue light.

Then, beginning at his fingertips, his hand crumbled into hundreds of blue particles. At almost the same time, his foot came next, breaking into fragmented pieces of the same blue energy. Working its way through his hand and foot, his flesh began disintegrating into thousands of little blue particles. His body was being erased from existence, vanishing into whirling sparkles. The decomposition of his body spread up his forearm and made its way toward his elbow. His body turned slowly, clockwise, and more of him turned into the tiny fragments. At last, his head rolled back, waking him.

"Who is there?" Aberfell said, finally waking as his body dissolved into pieces. "What is this?"

Reaching up with his still intact left arm, he quickly unwrapped the linens from his eyes. His immediately realized what was happening to him as light reflected the blue particles into his widening eyes, turning them an even more vivid blue. As more of the bandages unrolled, he started laughing uncontrollably.

"To one part goes the whole," Aberfell said between laughs. "We are all one and the same. Oh, glorious day!"

The fragmentation continued to sweep through him. He continued the breaking down of what was once parts of his body. Spreading to his left arm now, it disassembled into blue dust. He laughed more heartily now, as the remainder of his body twisted slightly, his hips and shoulders fell apart into miniscule pieces. His torso and head were the only part left of him now. Then they too started their slow disintegration. The blue particles gathered around him and streamed through the room. Into thousands of tiny flakes, he disassembled up to his neck now. All the time Aberfell laughed harder.

Swirling in a cloud of blue sparkles, only his face remained. With blue lips that were coming apart, he uttered his last solemn words.

"Please let me forget," he said.

Then he closed his blue eyes, and his face burst apart.

And Aberfell was gone.

The Timmutes, outside the cottage, turned from gold to blue to mimic the light that came from another world. Flashing through the entire Dragonbreath cloud, the Timmutes fell into immediate despair for the old man that they had dutifully served so many decades.

Inside the cottage, the particles that a moment ago made up Aberfell's physical body broke through the large window and streamed away, into the constellations as a blue comet. The force created a vacuum, causing dishes to break and sending papers hurling through the air.

The sparkling particles of Aberfell's body left this world the same way they arrived, riding a blue comet. What was once Aberfell blasted away through the night, leaving only the unrolled bandages lying in the rocking chair.

Once he was gone, little by little, parts of the cottage began disintegrating as well. Openings in the walls and the ceiling followed, undone by millions of Timmutes abandoning their posts. Soon, the entire cottage disassembled into a multitude of blue orbs. The cottage broke down to the very rock on top of the summit. The wind came sailing in. The bandages blew off the chair, as did his papers, dishes, chairs; everything inside either crumbled into blue Timmute orbs or fell down the heights of the Dragonbreath Mountain. Nothing was spared.

In the end, all that was left was the tree. The Praying Lady stood alone now at the summit, surrounded by millions of flashing blue and gold orbs.

There she would remain.

"Now, don't you worry,
About which road you're on.
'Cause it doesn't matter anymore,
Every road is leading you home."

Excerpt from *The Witch's Songbook*

THE LONG WAY HOME

THE MID-RUN VALLEY IN THE YEAR 1047 HRT

Assisted by golden orbs, Almon climbed down from the steep mountain summit, and the Timmutes followed. With only limited visibility, he descended through the thick fog. Reaching the bottom of the tree roots, he tapped them one last time before moving back to the rock. He was climbing on his own but felt the wind of the Timmutes around him, guiding him, holding him steady.

After a short while, he climbed out of the cloud of the Dragonbreath, dropping below the oxygen barrier for the first time in years. Suddenly, the air became too thin to breathe. Released from the protective oxygen cloud supplied by the Timmutes, he struggled to stay conscious. If not for the Timmutes pressing him against the rock, he would have fallen. In a haze of blurry consciousness, he lost long slices of time; parts of the descent he did not even remember. Yet he continued down safely.

Coming out of the cloud, moving lower, the visibility improved, and he could now see how high on the mountain he remained, and how far he had to go. He had forgotten after all these years just how far from home he really was.

The lower he climbed, the easier it became to breathe. He finally reached the base of the Dragonbreath by nightfall. For the first time in over six years, his feet stood on solid ground again.

Back up at the summit, the Timmutes had turned blue. Flashes of blue burst in the heart of the Dragonbreath cloud above.

A fitting tribute, Almon thought.

He looked up at the sheer vertical face of the mountain. Almon took off his glove and pressed his head to the rock, completing the journey he started so long ago.

Now, he just had to navigate through the Fangs. But this time, instead of getting progressively harder, they would get progressively easier. Each descent would bring him closer to home. Yet it took some time before they got any easier. The further west he traveled, the scarcer the Timmutes' presence became.

By the time he got to the last of the Fangs, the Timmutes had mostly abandoned him. Before climbing down the last of them, only a single golden orb floated around him. He reached out to it with his hand. He felt a strange bond now with the Timmutes. Almon hated to see them go, and the feeling seemed to be the same with this last Timmute who had followed him this far.

"My little friend," Almon said. He knew it understood, even if it said nothing in return. "I owe you a great debt. Thank you!"

The single orb circled his hand several times. Then the last Timmute departed, flying back to join the others. He watched it fly away. The Timmute got smaller and smaller until Almon could not see it anymore.

"So long, good friend. Give Aberfell my regards."

Turning back to face the last climb, he had to be extra careful now, as the Timmutes were no longer there to help him. He was fortunate that this final Fang was the smallest. It did not present any difficult technical challenges, so he rappelled down to the ground safely with no problem. His feet now touched level ground. He had navigated down the Dragonbreath and through the Fangs of the Gray Mountains. For the rest of the way, it was just a long walk. He was so glad that he did not have to climb any more mountains. For the rest of his life, Almon would climb nothing higher than the roof of his house. He'd had his fill of adventure.

The following day, he stood in the middle of the ruins of the Temple of Chen-Li. He found he could now pick up on the energy of past activity, and soon he saw ghosts materialize from the past, of the White Eminence in training. He could hear their shouts and see the ghost of Chen-Li flying and landing on the treetops. All of it, residual energy from years past.

Almon had not seen the ghost that brought him here years ago, and during his stay with Aberfell he had all but forgotten about his ghost. But now, returning to the world, he became aware of ghosts everywhere. He had become sensitive to the energies, able to see them clearly, not as they are, but as they were.

He entertained the nostalgic ghosts of the White Eminence for a while, then turned to leave the Temple of Chen-Li.

A little while later, he came to the Last Outpost of the East. He startled a group of sparrows, and they flew away when he opened the door. The Last Outpost was a dry, dusty and empty place now. Soon the ghosts of old energies materialized to him. He could see the ghosts of the old traders, the trappers, the old-timers sitting on the porch swapping stories. But then they too were gone, and the Last Outpost of the East turned back into what it really was, just a crumbling old building whose best days were gone.

Traveling down to Jorleston, he could see the harbor where his adventure started. He breathed in the thick salty air. Closing his eyes, he took the time to relish it. The Jorelston lighthouse towered over the Port where he last saw Captain Fortosa standing on the high railing of the *Forerunner*. It had been years; the captain might be dead by now. He could still hear his words as clearly as if he spoke to him today.

"It's bad luck to dwell on the dead." He'd tapped his temple. "Remember that."

Almon looked out over the ocean. He saw a single ship, its sails blowing in the wind, sailing on the horizon right into the setting sun. He saw no ghosts here, which did not mean anything as to whether Fortosa lived or not.

He considered booking passage back on the Endless Sea, to take him to Port Harbor the following day, but ultimately, he decided against it. He felt like walking. He knew it would take longer, but with a sense of renewal, he discovered a newfound freedom guided his steps. He felt as if he had all the time in the world.

He walked across the Mid-Run Valley for many days and nights, making his way back home to Haverhill and the House of Erland. But first, he took a slight detour.

Days later, he stood looking down at his father's grave. Tall grass and weeds grew over the stones he placed here years ago. He took off his backpack, and cleared the grave by hand, pulling the weeds away from the rocks. Memories came flooding back to him like ghosts. He had visions remembering his father, Erland Plum-Kilmer, and the special bond of love and laughter they shared. He could see Erland in better days, young and strong, laughing as he shot an arrow from the back of his horse.

But then something happened. In Almon's vision, Erland's stopped laughing, and his ghost turned to look directly at him. It was as if the ghost knew it was being observed. The laughter turned into the same silent scream from the ghost on the mountain. Only this time the ghost had something different to say.

Aberfell! It startled Almon. *Beware, Aberfell!*

Then the Mid-Run Valley came back to him. The ghost of his father was gone, the grave remained at his feet, and all returned to quiet. Unnerved from the vision, and its warning about Aberfell, Almon felt suddenly vulnerable. He now longed to get back home. Looking down at his father's grave, he gave it one last glance and picked up his backpack.

Before he left, he gave his father's grave a blessing. "Peace be with you, Erland Plum-Kilmer. May your ghost be at peace."

One more night out under the stars, and he would be home.

The next evening, as the shadows were getting long, he finally stood looking at the House of Erland. It needed paint, some boards had fallen over, the roof needed repair. But it had never looked better to him. Finally, he was home.

The inside of the house was full of dust and cobwebs, it was dark and cold. Dropping his backpack, he went to the fireplace and started some kindling blazing. He pulled wood from the pile, and spiders scrambled from their hiding places. After the fire warmed him, he roamed further into the old house. In his bedroom, his bed looked like a long-lost friend he had not seen it in years. He looked it over, how he left it unmade when he left in the middle of the night to catch the *Forerunner*. He flopped upon it in a puff of dust. Before he knew it, he was fast asleep.

The next day, he took a bath and put on some clean clothes. He had lost a lot of weight, and the belt had to stretch tight to make his pants fit. He spent the day cleaning the house and doing minor repairs. At one point, he leaned against his mop and considered the brewery where he used to brew the Red Curl. It smelled moldy and bitter after all these years.

Continuing through the house, he opened the metal door that led to the Plum-Kilmer crypt. Descending the stone steps, he used a torch to illuminate his way into the darkness as he went. He came to the portcullis and opened it. Down in the crypt of Johanna Plum-Kilmer, the years of cobwebs formed in the corners and stretched like silk across the bars of the portcullis. The crypt looked no different than Erland had left it long ago. Maybe it was his imagination, but the crypt seemed a little colder than before.

Almon lit the candle left on the podium. The last time this candle was lit, it was by his father's hand. There was so much Almon still did not understand.

You have to find that out on your own, his father had told him regarding when he would ever gain the ability to see the spirits of the dead. That seemed like such a long time ago. He still had so much to figure out. Now he understood why his father never spoke to him about it.

The candle cast shadows in the crypt that had not seen the light in years. Almon approached the stone likeness of his mother's face on the crypt. Then he looked around the tomb in its stillness. The candlelight flickered, shifting the shadows in the crypt. The longer he remained, he became frightened, and a feeling came over him that he was not alone.

Johanna emerged in the candlelight. She cast only a shadow of herself outlined in a blue tint. A robed gown floated around her as if underwater. Her face was as young as Almon remembered her from his childhood, hair black and full, listing through the air as if blown by gentle breezes. Erland now appeared too, standing behind her, holding her hand. He wore his hunting regalia, young and robust, with curly hair and beard. His eyes were pale, emitting a golden light.

They were finally joined together in the next life.

They did not communicate with Almon. They remained flickering in the flame light, fluttering between existence and the candle's shadows. Then Johanna lifted her hand, and with a sudden gust of wind blew the candle out. Only the torch on the wall illuminated his way out.

It was time for him to go. He made his way to the portcullis, then turning around one last time, he could still see them, but only partially now. Their faces had returned to the darkness, and they stood motionless in the depths of the crypt. He left them there, fading into the tomb's deeper shadows.

Soon, he heard them say, like a whisper on the wind.

"Soon," he repeated, and shut the iron gate behind him. His time in this world would be getting shorter with each day that passed. He took their meaning: Soon, his time would be over.

Leaving the dead behind him, he made the short walk over to the Haverhill Inn. He opened the door and walked inside without fanfare, as he had a hundred times before. Inside the inn, there were a few people sitting at tables, but most were empty. Jacko was there, cleaning the tables just like no time had passed at all; and there behind the bar was Mose, cleaning glasses with his back to the door. His hair was shorter and grayer now, a few extra pounds noticeable upon him. Without detection, Almon walked up and sat at a stool.

"I've seen better mugs on a pig's snout!" Almon said behind his back.

Mose stopped cleaning the glass. Then he turned suddenly to face Almon, and his bottom lip immediately quivered.

"Almon? Is that really you?" Mose said in shock. "I thought you were dead."

Mose embraced him and would not let him go. "I thought I sent you to your death. I thought the mountain got you! How long have you been gone? Hey, Jacko! Look who it is! It's Almon!"

"Almon?" Jacko startled and straightened. "I thought you were dead!"

"Look, he's alive!" Mose said, not letting him go. Jacko came over to embrace him as well.

"Where have you been?" asked Mose.

"Tell me you didn't go the Dragonbreath Mountain, did you, Almon?" asked Jacko.

How could he tell them all the things he had been through? They would not even believe it. "It's impossible. Stay away from that mountain."

"Almon, I so regretted giving you directions to that mountain. I wanted to go looking for you a hundred times. I am so glad you're safe. And alive!"

Almon shook his head. "I am glad you stayed right here where you belong, Mose."

Mose asked him questions while pouring beers all around.

"I found something," Almon told them. "That had been lost for a long time."

"What did you find?" asked Mose, setting a beer down in front of him.

Almon said. "Do you remember hearing about Aberfell?"

"I vaguely remember something," Mose said. "Wasn't he the boy who could not forget, or something like that?"

"Do you remember how he died?" Almon asked.

"No, I thought he was just a myth, so his death would've been a myth too."

"He was more than a myth, Mose. He's still alive, and I found him, alive, living on top of the summit of the Dragonbreath."

"Thought you said you didn't climb it?"

"I never said I didn't climb it. I simply said it was impossible to climb, and it is. Don't ever go there! Stay away from it. I didn't climb it; I was carried up to the summit with the help of the Timmutes."

"Timmutes?" Jacko asked.

Almon nodded. "The manuscripts I wrote were told to me by none other than Aberfell himself, and in no other place than the Dragonbreath Summit."

Mose took a bar towel out from behind the bar and started wiping. He shared a look with Jacko. "That's kind of hard to believe, Almon," Jacko said. "Sounds like a pretty tall tale to me. How do you know any of this was real?"

"It's for the reader to decide," Almon told him.

Suddenly, something very strange happened.

At that moment, both Mose and Jacko froze and did not move. It was as if time itself stopped. The lights dimmed.

Almon looked up from his beer. The ghost was standing in the corner of the bar, the same hooded ghost again, the same one that haunted him before he went to the mountains. The ghost said nothing, as before, and could only communicate with him in a vision. But this time, it was not the Dragonbreath Mountain. Instead, Almon could see spirits of the gods themselves.

Heironomus sailed floating over the lights of the inn, with burly red hair and beard, laughing gregariously. When Heironomus crossed over the bar, he vanished, only to be replaced by Hexor, his twin brother.

Hexor rose with his hands behind his back, complete with his hateful eye. He used it to look at Almon, then with a sneer, he too disappeared.

Hexor was replaced with an image of the Goddess of Beauty. Ehlona shined in golden brilliance, young and beautiful. She strummed her lyre by a bright waterfall, singing a song while watching the stars. Almon watched as the image changed again.

Ehlona's body transformed into the haggard Witch of the Great Mapes Forest. The Witch aged into an absolute horror and what she became in the end, extending her arms outward and looking up to the heavens. Then, she changed into a white oak tree, the Praying Lady, at the top of the world.

A swarm of thousands of golden orbs surrounded the Praying Lady, until finally, the tree tipped over and fell over the side of the mountain. A bright starburst then lit the world. The brightness of the star hurt Almon's eyes. Then in his vision, the star dimmed, and another vision came to him.

He saw the dazzling blue eyes of Aberfell laughing in his rocking chair holding a wooden dragon. The little dragon grew into Master Tree, then exploded like colorful fireworks.

Chen-Li appeared in the vision next, flying over the treetops. He touched down on the Temple of Chen-Li. His physical body crumpled away, and his Li soared colorless around the bar before coiling and leaping through the ceiling like a bolt of lightning. Then he was gone.

Almon thought it was the end of the vision.

But a new vision slithered along the floor like a shadow until it lifted its head to reveal the image of Langula. She came to rest in Hazor's lap. He was well-groomed, dressed in black properly buttoned up to his chin. With a flick of her forked tongue, Langula slithered away. Hazor turned a full circle, and he had changed into the Zorn, the scorned Skeletal King. With a turn of his cape, he morphed into a giant crow, flying away. Then the giant crow was gone.

One by one the ghost showed Almon a parade of dead priests of the Zornastic Order, marching and falling over like dominos.

After all the dominos fell, Leopold stood alone as the King of Odessa. He stood wearing a crown and a high-shouldered red cape.

Leopold burned in flame and turned into Amtor, who had now entered his vision. Amtor came into view rearing his black horse amidst the backdrop of the battle at Mauveguard Pass. Then they, too, faded away.

LaNew appeared walking out of a bloody tent drying his hands, followed by the banners of the Red Guard's masses. They were washed away in a river of blood.

Lord Whitney came into his vision looking through his spyglass, gallantly ready to defend the Mauveguard Pass with Castle Odessa behind him. Then he vanished from the vision.

An object appeared before him now. It was beautifully crafted Soothsayer, the golden dagger slowly spinning, gleaming in gold. Finally, it faded away too.

Throughout the vision, Mose and Jacko remained motionless, stuck, frozen in time, and dulled with no color.

There was a long pause in his vision, until slowly his father, Erland Plum-Kilmer, appeared in smoky waves of memory in the Mid-Run Valley. He gave his son a polite nod and a deep bow. Then he side-stepped out of the way to reveal the original ghost in the corner.

Standing alone, it was the image of the hooded man with the long gray beard. He filled Almon's mind with visions of the Dragonbreath Mountain one more time, but this time, it was more meaningful, more of a memory, just a recollection, than the driving impulse it had been before. It made Almon smile that he had completed his quest.

The ghost removed his hood. It was Aberfell.

I am sorry, the ghost said. *So sorry.*

"Aberfell?"

The ghost smiled.

As a tear welled up in Almon's eye, the ghost burst apart in blue particles. Almon knew he was gone. Not just in the vision, but for real this time. He had a feeling of certainty about it. Aberfell was gone for good, and he would never see him again.

The visions were gone too. Now, abruptly the Haverhill Inn started its normal movement and color again.

"Almon, are you all right?" Mose asked Almon

"Sorry, what?" Almon said.

"What about these manuscripts? What do they say?" Jacko repeated.

Almon regained his composure quickly.

"Oh! They are called the Provenance."

"The Provenance?" Jacko asked.

"It's the last words of Aberfell," he said sadly. "The history of the world, the origins of everything."

"You say this Aberfell gave you this Provenance?" Mose said.

"Aberfell, the Supreme Historian."

They both gave Almon blank stares.

"So, can we read it?" Mose asked.

Almon nodded, still in shock. "I'm turning the brewery into a printing press. I'm going to start printing copies of the Provenance and the other volumes."

"What about your brewery?" Mose and Jacko said at the same time.

"I'm getting out of that business," Almon told them.

"Aww! But we've missed the Red Curl," Jacko said, disappointed. "We've had nothing but stale piss water since you left."

Looking up at them now, Almon said. "Maybe you could brew it, Jacko. I can show you how."

Jacko shrugged. "Yeah, maybe."

"What will you do now, Almon?" Mose asked him.

"I'm going to tell the whole world about the Provenance, Mose. That's what I'm going to do. I'll start first thing tomorrow morning, but first, tonight, let's celebrate."

Then he took the little wooden dragon out of his pocket and set it down on the bar. "Because only a fool tempts the dragon."

"When my heart is sinking low,
In the torrents of my soul,
When I reach the end, I'll know
And I'll finally let you go."

Excerpt from *The Witch's Songbook*

A NASTY SORT OF BUSINESS

THE VILLAGE OF HAVERHILL IN THE YEAR 1047 (HRT)

It was a short walk to the House of Erland from the Haverhill Inn. On his walk home, he noticed the stars, how many there were sparkling tonight. It was one of those nights, dark and clear, where the fabric of the universe sparkled overhead. Almon left Mose and Jacko at the Haverhill Inn. He was satisfied to be making plans again. With Mose to help him print and Jacko to brew Red Curl, it felt like things were getting back to normal. It was good to be back from his adventure finally.

Unlocking the door to his house, he resolved to go to bed early and get ready for the next day, as he had planned to get moving on all the ideas he had in mind. He had a lot to do.

Almon washed, then hung the towel to dry. He went to his bedchamber, turned down the blankets, and climbed into his bed. He blew out the candles, and darkness descended upon him. Only a minimal amount of light from a quarter moon shined through his window. Soon, all was quiet, and he fell into a deep sleep.

He stayed asleep for hours, then around midnight, he awoke to feel something move his arm. He opened his eyes to see that the whole room had filled with blue light. The light had wrapped around him, causing his skin to sparkle. Next an emptiness, or lightness, permeated him, as his body lifted involuntarily from his bed. Rising from his bed, he turned slightly as the blue light increasingly surrounded him.

Is this a dream? he wondered.

Almon felt like it was a dream, but it was real. Whatever this was, it was really happening to him.

He felt a tug on his right hand and leg, pulling them toward the blue light. Then he saw his right hand dissolve into thousands of blue particles. His right foot, then his leg, disintegrated the same way, into many bits of blue color.

Almon screamed as his body fragmented into a cloud of blue mist and particles. He screamed, not from pain, but from shock. His body was decomposing in blue particles. The particles streamed up from his arms and legs, moving up to his hips, torso, shoulders, and neck. Finally, his screams were silenced by the bursting apart of his head and face.

Then Almon was gone.

Dropping from above, the two-hundred-year-old ring of the Plum-Kilmer family clan, worthy of all their family's considerable wealth, came spinning to rest upon his pillow.

Don't say I didn't warn you. Almon could hear Aberfell's words back in the cottage on top of the Dragonbreath Summit, before he told

him the forbidden information about the Cosmic Creation. *It's a nasty sort of business that could have unintended consequences.*

Almon Plum-Kilmer was gone from this world, but he was not gone altogether. He still had consciousness. He had changed, he had become a collective of blue particles, with no central point for this awareness to exist. Yet he sailed up and out of the world, into the deep reaches of the universe. Despite the destruction of his physical body, he felt limitless, swirling in mass from incredibly microscopically dense to infinitely large and translucent in some cosmic proportion devoid of form. This was unlike anything ever felt before, all obstacles of physical life removed, an ecstasy of emotions welled up inside him. Never had he felt this complete or satisfied in fulfillment. He had turned into pure spirit, without any of the senses he needed in life to survive.

Where am I going? he wondered. He was not sure his destination, but he got the sensation of moving impossibly fast. Wherever he was going, he was getting there in a hurry.

A voice entered his thoughts, but not in his ears, and a response came to him in his mind.

You are returning to the Cosmic Creation, the voice sounded in Almon's mind. The voice sounded familiar, like every voice he had ever heard, yet modulated into rushing water.

All things are about to be revealed, the voice continued.

Almon could feel his speed increasing. His mass became denser. The heat was building. Yellow and red plasma formed around his blue particles. His speed increased so much that Almon could no longer think about anything other than how fast he was going. He traveled a great distance where time held no meaning; he could have been speeding this way for centuries, or years or just merely seconds. He could not tell anymore.

Am I going to lose myself? he thought again, already forgetting his former self, his former life.

The voice spoke to him again. *You will be added to the cosmic pool. It has been arranged to keep you longer than those that have come before you. You are on a journey to the beginning and the ending of all things. Just as Aberfell revealed to you.*

Are you Aberfell?

I was Aberfell. I was Ehlona. I was Chen-Li. I was Hazor. We are all parts of the whole. I am everything, and I am no one.

His speed increased once again, and he violently vibrated and tumbled. The red and yellow plasma now dissipated, replaced by a ring-shaped rainbow around him; after another series of violent crashes, another rainbow formed outside the first one. Repeatedly he smashed his way through multiple barriers, too many to count. He was tearing at the fabric of reality. Each time his form crashed through a new barrier, it added another ring of rainbow light around him. Completely encircled in a multitude of rings and rainbows, he continued through space, encapsulated inside the shining light of the circling rainbows.

Finally, bursting through a final barrier, he splashed into something like water, that slowed him to a crawl, then brought him to a sudden stop.

Am I dead? he thought. *I don't feel dead. I don't feel anything.*

You are changed, the voice answered.

Obtaining some sense of vision, still in his particle form, he saw the old world, the Cosmic Creation the way it had been since the beginning of time. Overhead, the most prominent feature, a brown sphere tumbled in erratic movements. Inside the tumbling sphere, Heironomus and Hexor, the Twin Gods engaged in their War of Negation. As they punched, wrestled, hit, kicked, and smacked each other, the sphere turned with their movements. For all of eternity, trapped in the sphere, the Twin Gods fought overhead in the Cosmic Creation. Lightning peeled off the brown sphere at each strike the gods landed upon each other.

Almon marveled at Heironomus and Hexor. They looked exactly the way Aberfell described them. Barrel-chested Heironomus with his thick, muscular arms and legs, curly red hair, and long dark beard, hammered at Hexor with a fist to his chest while lightning spider-webbed through the gray sky. Hexor was dark, dressed in black, with his hateful eye; smaller but quicker, he viciously attacked his brother. Another bolt of white lightning struck the surface and lingered in a thick line of energy.

Except for the bright lightning cast from the sphere, no light shined here; there was no need for it, as there was no darkness either. The atmosphere glinted a shadowless thick color like rust. The surface of this world possessed no substance, but only became increasingly dense farther down, in the darker tones below. The density of the dark rust seemed to form a horizon to look like a surface, but he could see down through it. A core revealed itself far underneath.

In this world, there were no surface features, no mountains, no trees; all was smooth. But there were signs of life. A multitude of light blue orbs streamed up from the core below, rising from the horizon in the thousands. The rising blue orbs resembled rain, only going up in reverse.

These orbs rise to create new mortal lives. They come forth from the core of the Cosmic Creation, the voice told him. *They are new life. Born into the world for the first time. A new creation.*

An equal number of orbs, colored in gray, rained down from the sky, driving deep into the rusty matter, splashing through its surface, descending deeper into the darker core.

These orbs coming down are expired mortal lives, coming back from the world, going back into the Cosmic Creation for recycling and renewal. Every living thing in the world exists in both ways. Not dead, not alive, but merely changed.

Watching the transitions, he watched the blue orbs go. There was nothing good or evil here, just a pattern of change, perfect in its balance. Almon watched the outgoing orbs that would soon be a new infant, thrust into the world without malice. Each one an equal gamble, with unexpected challenges and opportunities, for wealth or poverty, health or sickness.

Then he turned to consider the in-coming gray orbs; each one represented an end. A pain released from the struggle of life. One orb could have been a sick older adult released from her physical pain or the life of a child. But whether young or old, all of them collected here inside the Cosmic Creation. Once again, he saw that they were equal.

Here, the gears have spun for centuries, the voice said.

Almon concentrated on his life force now. Assembling his blue particles into something of a form, he became not the Almon he knew, but just an idea of a living human being. Regardless, any living form was as much out of place here in the Cosmic Creation as the blue orbs were back in the other world.

The being that Almon had become drifted out of the smoky rust-color clouds and came to rest on the surface, or at least, something dense enough to stand on. His makeshift body started to sink; his feet went under, and the matter underneath slowed him as it got denser. Still, he dropped through the outer surface to just above his knees. Despite being knee-deep in the Cosmic Creation, he walked along with no problem; the rust matter was not dense enough to slow his steps.

He stood watching thousands of the blue orbs stream out from just below him, as thousands of orbs came pouring down like rain dropping into the core of the Cosmic Creation. Up and down the perpetual movement of life and death continued constantly under the sphere of the gods combating in Negation. All of this motion proved to Almon that the Cosmic Creation was alive and active.

Reaching down to the surface, he collected a handful of the rusty stuff. To him, the matter felt like a combination of water and gas. Weighing nothing, it stayed in his hand until he poured it back out to the surface.

Then, he caught a glimpse of a large face deep down within the core. The giant face was so large that he did not notice it until now.

Who is that? he thought.

You have seen the face of the Grand Creator. Now that you have seen Him, there are no more truths to tell you. You have been honored to see what you have seen, to know what you know. Now, it is your time. Are you ready to surrender your fabric back to the Cosmic Creation?

Will I be recycled into new life? he asked.

The particles that once made you will be reshuffled, to be reused with all the others. You will find communion, fellowship, and renewal with parts of the whole, and with all the others. Now, take a few more moments. Tell us when you are ready. There is no hurry.

What happened to Almon back in Haverhill?

He is no more.

What about the Plum-Kilmer clan? I was the last.

A new era begins as another ends.

Almon wandered through the Cosmic Creation, but everywhere he looked, it was all the same. Gray orbs went in and blue orbs went out under the tumbling sphere of the Twin Gods, who fought overhead. Occasionally lightning flashed.

Then, he suddenly realized. He could not remember what he was thinking. He thought he had a name once, but now could not remember it, or where he came from, or even what he was doing. He could only remember three words.

I am ready.

Good. The world is ready for a new Supreme Historian, the voice spoke to him for the last time.

The blue particles holding his generic form together burst apart, spreading out across the surface of the Cosmic Creation in gray particles, sinking deeper into the rusty mist until they were lost inside the cosmic shuffle with all the others.

So it was, that in the year 1047, Human Recorded Time, the life of Almon and the lineage of his family came to a convergence, and then, to an end. Almon Plum-Kilmer became the last device Aberfell used to fulfill his purpose.

The Provenance, the manuscript Almon transcribed from Aberfell, was left in possession of Mose and Jacko to share with a new generation. If they dared.

At the same time, the world would have to look to the heavens and wait for a new Supreme Historian. But then again, maybe the Cosmic Creation would have others plans. Nothing is certain, and just because you might hear the distant cry of a baby, take nothing as it seems. It may just be Langula enticing you to the bush.

So, maybe it is better for all of us if we do not speak any more of such things out loud. After all, they are still listening, and we have already been warned.

All that is left is the faint sound of a baby crying on the wind.

I love to fly under my own wings,
Consulting with the angels about heavenly things.
I like to hide where they can't find me,
Just to look at all the faces
Of those who said they would always love me.
But you can't see me since I've wished myself away
While the world keeps turning in its own way.
Now, I find myself laughing until I cry.
But I am not laughing anymore.
I'm just a tear,
Just a tear away.

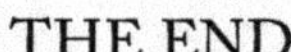

THE END

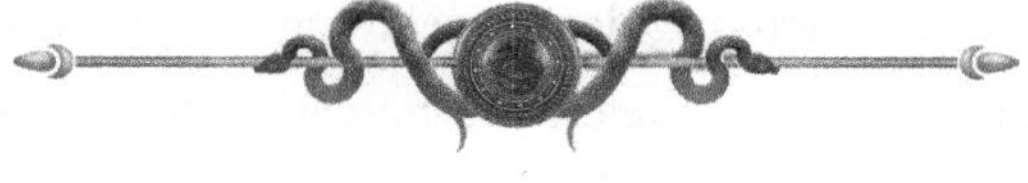

AFTERWARD

Death. Maybe it is morbid to think about. I have heard it said that "death is a part of life," but I never really understood the concept. It always seemed to me that death and life were mutually exclusive; to me it was like saying, black is a part of white, or wrong is a part of right. I found one little story, that hospice makes available for those who are losing, or lost, a loved one. The story goes something like this: consider death as a boat departing with your loved one away from a familiar home port. As they leave your presence, it is sad to see the boat depart, growing smaller, to finally disappear beyond the horizon. But imagine the gladness for the person on the boat, or the people on the farther shore, when it appears on their horizon, and what a joyful event it will be to those receiving them on the other side.

Maybe it is only a matter of perspective. In John Keel's *The Mothman Prophecies*, he writes: "the circumference of a circle can be measured starting at any point along the circle." Maybe when thinking about life and death as part of the same circle, then there might be a situation where life is death, and death is life; maybe they are not so mutually exclusive after all.

As I wrote the first book of the Astar's Blade series, *The Provenance*, I was fascinated by exploring this peculiar juxtaposition of life and death. I started by telling the legend of Heironomus, a merciful God of Light, the God of birth, a God that blesses long life to the grateful masses. But by doing so, would not this benevolent action violate the circumference of the life/death circle? By extending life, it would be denying death, delaying the process of renewal, and increasing the size of the circle, increasing its diameter. Would a watchful and concerned entity worshipped by humans be considered a violator, a trespasser, to the design for cosmic renewal? In other words, by extending existing life, would this same entity be delaying, maybe even denying, new birth? This entity would be so resistant to change that in a cosmic sense, not a human one, that this force would be held in contempt, even hated or feared, despite being loved by mankind?

Then, the God of Darkness, who would be a force of death, an entity feared and dreaded amongst humans, but one that provides the cosmic creation with recycling and renewal of life energy. Would not this force be considered to have a particular, if not peculiar, noble purpose as a worthy steward and dependable agent for cosmic renewal? His importance would keep the circle of life/death the same size, keeping the balance, and keeping the spiritual trains running on time. He would be considered the favored son, dependable, revered as keeping the faith of a higher purpose.

While we, human beings locked in this world, are forced into only one perception of time, we look at one God worthy of our praise, and one fills us with dread. The Cosmic Creation would see it completely opposite, where blessings of long mortal life would be thought of as an action more rogue, and the God of Death who kept a steady, dependable, and constant supply of renewable life energy would be held in high regard.

Perspective turns our truth to lies sometimes. Our views as human beings would fail to appreciate the mysteries of a much more complicated cosmic creation. My goal of writing this fictional book was to create a world of shifting the perspective away from our ordinary lives, and make the circle mean something else. Not evil, not good, but just in motion—a change. Albert Einstein once said, energy cannot be created or destroyed. Energy just changes.

But fear can develop from anywhere, anytime.

When I was very young, I saw a werewolf walking across a field in the middle of the day. It flashed by me very quickly from the safety of the backseat car window. No one else in the car seemed to notice the werewolf struggling to find his footing in the tall grass. When I turned to looked again, we had already moved past the grass field. The scene was gone, replaced by a blur of trees, light posts, and storefronts. I was never really sure if the werewolf was real or not.

Later, I remember sitting on the bending stairs of our house feeling bad. My mother saw me and sat a few stairs below. She was feeling bad too. She had been crying.

"What's wrong Mom?"

That is when she told me that my grandfather Joseph, my namesake, had died.

"Why did he have to die?" I asked thinking that death was a horrible accident.

He had died from a blood clot in his leg, she told me.

"But why did he have to die?" I asked again.

"We all have to die some time," she told me. That is when I received the biggest shock in the world. Someday, death would be coming for me too, and it was not just something bad that happened to people accidently. My life was a temporary condition. My Mom saw my panic.

She told me, "You have your whole life to live, and you will be ready when it's your time."

I could not imagine ever being ready for something like that. But now I believe, my only desire for myself, and for all of you dear readers, is to do the things that satisfies our hearts before that werewolf finds any of us.

– Joe Lyon

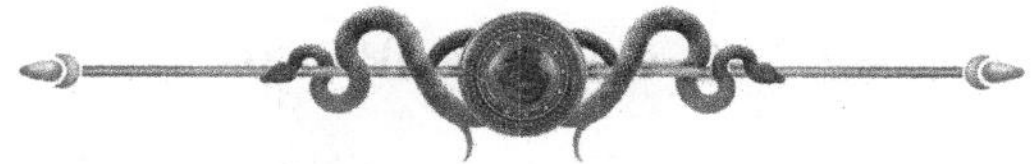

GLOSSARY

CHARACTER NAMES

Aberfell	*The man who remembers everything, the Supreme Historian*
Almon Plum-Kilmer	*Son of Erland*
Alton Whitney	*Head Council of Chase*
Amtor	*Bare-knuckle fighter turned Minister of War of the Empire of Odessa*
Blaize Plum	*Head Council of Haverhill*
Catosa, Sister	*Headmistress at the Orphanage in Husband, blessed with the Orphanage of the West*
Chavise, Sister	*One of the three sisters who left the Temple of Valor to find Ehlona in Husband, blessed with the Orphanage of the South*
Chen-Li	*Warrior name of Marus, son of Heironomus and Ehlona, meaning Body and Spirit*
Delbert Botta	*Fisherman of Clan Botta who would go on to establish the city of Port Harbor*
Dunhi, Sister	*One of the three sisters who left the Temple of Valor to find Ehlona in Husband, blessed with the Orphanage of the East*
Ehlona	*Goddess of Beauty*

Erland Plum-Kilmer	*Late head of the House of Erland*
Fortis Plum	*Trader, tracker, hunter and adventurer of Clan Plum*
Fortosa, Captain	*Captain of the Forerunner*
Gilglad	*Healer and Amtor's wife*
Hazor / The Zorn	*Son of Ehlona and Hexor, the Skeletal King of Orlo, the Master of Evil*
Heironomus	*God of Light*
Hexor	*God of Darkness*
Hobrick Jeter	*Blacksmith of Clan Jeter who would go on to establish the prosperous mining village of Hammerville*
Hoyt Whitney	*Member of the Amalgamate Council*
Jacko	*Partner of the Haverhill Inn*
Johanna Plum-Kilmer	*Late wife of Erland Plum-Kilmer*
Jule, Sister	*One of the three sisters who left the Temple of Valor to find Ehlona in Husband, blessed with the Orphanage of the North*
Justus Plum	*Head Council of Plum, cousin to Blaize Plum*
Kilmer	*Savior of Amtor's life during the Battle of Mauveguard Pass*
LaNew	*Amateur fighter turned soldier in Leopold's army*
Langula	*Half-woman, half-serpent demon summoned by Hazor, the First Lady of the Zornastic Order*
Leopold	*An orphan of the St. Ehlona's orphanage who became the first king of the Empire of Odessa*
Luna, Sister	*Daughter of Catosa, Headmistress, Umbrick*
Marus / Chen-Li	*Son of Ehlona and Heironomus*

Mose	*Partner of The Haverhill Inn, a dark-haired man with a handlebar mustache, about forty years old*
Myra	*One of the First Wives*
Nantz	*A boy used by the Zorn to parley with Chen-Li*
Nat Whitney	*Builder of Whitney Clan who would establish Haverhill, a wealthy village thanks to his building skills, also builder of the Church of the Illuminated*
Oskar Whitney / Lord Whitney	*Cousin of Jeter Whitney, an engineer in Bowling*
Tyla	*One of the First Wives*
Witch	*Creator of the Timmutes*

COUNTRIES

Kingdom of Odessa	*Leopold's growing empire*

CITIES, TOWNS & VILLAGES

Blaize	*Village*
Bowling	*Village*
Chase	*Village*
Darby	*Village*
Estes	*Village*
Hammerville	*Village*
Haverhill	*Seat of the House of Erland, village*
Homestead	*Village where Amtor and Gilglad make their home*
Jorleston	*Port and Lighthouse*
Olzen	*Village*

CITIES, TOWNS & VILLAGES

Plum	*Village*
Port Harbor	*Largest Port*
Umbrick	*Destroyed Village*

PLACES OF NOTE

Blue Mountains	*Western Mountains*
Castle Odessa	*Leopold's castle in the Mauveguard Pass*
Castle Orlo	*Hazor's castle*
Dragonbreath Mountain	*Highest summit peak*
Fangs	*Steep foothills of Gray Mountains*
Gray Mountains	*Eastern Mountains*
Great Mapes Forest	*Ancient forest*
Last Outpost of the East	*Final place of civilization before the Fangs*
Haverhill Inn	*Almon's local inn*
Jorleston Inn	*Where Almon stops on his way to Dragonbreath*
Mid-Run Valley	*Central Flatlands*
Sanguine Forest	*Haunted forest*
Temple of Chen-Li	*Marus / Chen-Li's temple and home*
Temple of Valor	*Ehlona's temple for her Acolytes*
Wilds	*Untamed lands where the ground dips dramatically to create enormous cliffs*

CREATURES

Demon

Ghosts

Gods

Grand Creator

Humans

Rock Larva

Supreme Historian

Timmutes

Living Things of the Forest

ORGANIZATIONS & GROUPS

Acolytes of the Temple of Valor

Army of the Amalgamates

Church of the Illuminated

Council of the Amalgamated Villages

Cult of Horror

Death Wardens

Red and Blue (Leopold's army)

Red Guard

Star Prophets

Village Council(s)

White Eminence

ORGANIZATIONS & GROUPS

Zornastic Order

TIMELINE

511 HRT	*World-at-Large, Heironomus, Hazor, and Ehlona introduced*
800 HRT	*Wedding of Ehlona and Heironomus*
800–801 HRT	*Ehlona flees to Husband and founds St. Ehlona's Orphanage*
801–810 HRT	*Ehlona / the Witch lives in the Great Mapes Forest*
810 HRT	*Hazor binds Langula to him*
810 – 818 HRT	*The Witch creates the Timmutes and learns to control them*
818 HRT	*Marus / Chen-Li visits the Witch*
819 HRT	*Construction of the Temple of Chen-Li*
820 HRT	*Leopold is found as an infant at the St. Ehlona's orphanage in Umbrick*
825 HRT	*Hazor / the Zorn lives with Langula at Castle Orlo*
826 HRT	*Hazor attacks his mother in the forest (catalyst for her leaving Great Mapes Forest)*
827 HRT	*The parley at the Temple of Chen-Li*
828 HRT	*The Zorn orders the execution of his twenty thousand priests in Castle Orlo, birth of the Sanguine Forest*
829 HRT	*Chen-Li searches for his mother*
832 HRT	*Leopold defeats Amtor in a wrestling match in the village of Hammerville*
833 HRT	*The massacre at Umbrick, ordered by Leopold; LaNew's Red Guard is formed*

TIMELINE

834 HRT	*The forming of the Army of the Amalgamates*
837 HRT	*The Battle of Mauveguard Pass and the founding of the Kingdom of Odessa*
1040 HRT	*Haverhill, the ghost appears to Almon Plum-Kilmer*
1040–1041 HRT	*Almon travels to Dragonbreath Mountain*
1041 HRT	*Almond reaches Dragonbreath Summit*
1046 HRT	*Almon leaves Aberfell's house on Dragbonbreath Mountain, Aberfell is returned to the Cosmic Creation*
1047 HRT	*Almon returns home, announces he's going to turn the brewery into a printing press to publish the story of the Provenance; before he can do this, he is made into the new Supreme Historian.*

MY PERSONAL PARANORMAL EXPERIENCES

(Age 5)	*I saw the werewolf.*
(Age 10)	*I woke in the middle of the night terrified, then had my bed sheets completely pulled off me, exposing me to the cold night.*
(Age 17)	*I got suddenly and mysteriously sick for no reason (throwing up) after my uncle (my father's brother) died.*
(Age 19)	*I heard mysterious tapping on the glass of a picture frame three days after my grandmother (my father's mother) died. This happened at dusk, when alone, while I was thinking of her. The picture frame was a gift from my grandmother to us before I was born. I never knew that it came from her.*

MY PERSONAL PARANORMAL EXPERIENCES

(Age 25) *In the US Army / Basic Training I shot the only perfect score (20/20) at the M16 qualifying range out of 222 others, after building a small religious shrine out of rocks on the range.*

(Age 40) *Some supervisors were fired shortly after I prayed to God to turn my enemies into my foot stool.*

(Age 45) *I saw a bright-eyed creature standing beside the road, that I can only explain as a humanoid (bigfoot, skunk ape, etc.). It looked like a tower of dirt and leaves, but then it opened its eyes—the eyes were blue—and stared right at me. But being in heavy traffic I could not stop, and so I drove past it and never saw it again.*

(Age 50) *I heard mysterious breathing on my cell phone in the room my father spent his last dying days in. No call was ever like that before or after my father's death.*

(Age 51) *I felt touched twice by a ghostly hand at the Bird Cage, Tombstone AZ*

(Age 52) *I felt a ghostly hand grab my foot at Devils Den, Gettysburg PA*

(Age 52) *I captured the "Harmon particle," a mysterious orb of light at the Harmon murder house, Gettysburg, PA.*

(Age 54) *A 'penny from heaven' appeared out of nowhere and dropped on the floor at the Bell Witch Gift Shop and Cave, Adams, TN.*

(Age 54) *I recorded disembodied screams at the Bell Witch, Adams, TN, with an associated EMF spike.*

(Age 55) *My bed started to shake repeatedly, like someone was gently pressing both hands on the mattress. This happened at my mother's house on the first visit in six months after my sister died in the house. The bed shaking lasted for about three minutes and never happened before or since. This took place at around 5 a.m., just when the sky was coming out of its darkest phase.*

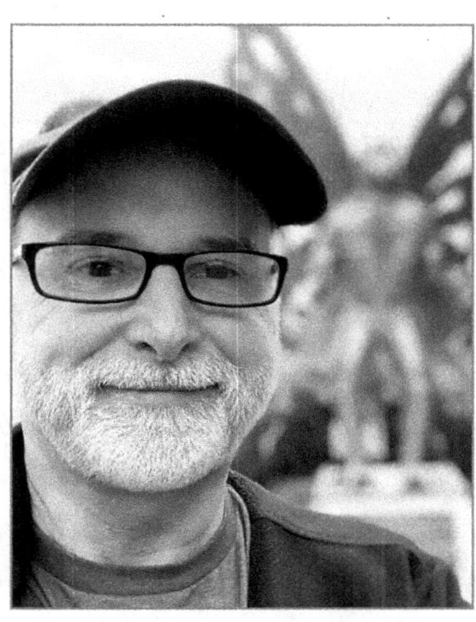

Joe Lyon was born in Springfield, Ohio, on May 13, 1965. He grew up creating monsters and characters and home-grown comic books. In his first epic fantasy series, *Astar's Blade*, Joe creates a world some have called "wonderfully epic with great texturing and grand scope worldbuilding." Joe has a master's degree in business administration, is a former Military Intelligence School graduate, and is a U.S. Army veteran. As a musician and prolific songwriter, he has written over 100 songs and a book of poetry entitled *Poetry is Cool.* Joe currently lives in Aiken, SC, with his family.

I hope you have enjoyed *The Provenance.* Thank you for the time we spent together.

Check out more stuff by Joe Lyon:

WWW.ASTARSBLADE.COM

OTHER BOOKS BY JOE LYON

Kilmer's Ghost (Book Two of Astar's Blade)

The legends say the Sanguine Forest is haunted by evil magic. Those that dare go in, never come out alive. But those are just tall tales, aren't they? Ever since he was a young boy, a ghost had been appearing to Kilmer in an unlikely supernatural friendship, making Kilmer the perfect choice to go into the Sanguine searching for the king's missing archer. Guided by his ghost and bent on revenge, he is doomed to bear witness to the cataclysm around him. Helpless to prevent the birth of a brand-new evil, his life comes down to whether he can be saved by Kilmer's Ghost.

Temple of Valor (Book Three of Astar's Blade)

It had been a year since the Star of Ehlona shined, leaving the world to wonder if the soul of the Goddess of Beauty had returned. But while a weary world looked to the heavens for answers, a new terror was being unleashed from below. Deep in the steamy darkness hatches a plot bent on vengeance. When powerful forces collide, there is no safe place. Will any survive in the final battle over Astar's Blade?